The Rebirth of

ISBN: 1-4196-9922-9

ISBN-13: 9781419699221

Visit www.booksurge.com to order additional copies.

The Rebirth of

Julian Traas

I dedicate this book to my family:
To my father, for financing my ambition.
To my mother, for constantly editing my work with me—
even though I'm not the best at taking criticism.
And to my brother Cory, for helping me to flesh out certain
plot elements, and for his amazing cover illustration!

Chapter 1
Born of the Storm

A small village, set in a wooded glen, buzzed with the activity of its inhabitants. But beyond the surrounding trees, and the illusion of peace, lurked monsters, curved horns behind their backs and rusted scimitars at their sides. Their yawning mouths revealed fangs the size of kitchen cleavers.

Lynca village was so tranquil, oblivious to its nearing destruction. Hungry eyes took in the sights, the eager stare present in each pair. The smell of baking and cloves hung thick in the still air. Cheerful greetings interwove with the clamor of the smithy.

The signal was given. The cover of the trees was forsaken. Heavy mud silenced the monsters' approach. Saliva dribbled down their chins as weapons were readied.

A keen-eyed farmhand gave a shout, calling for help. Impressive was the speed at which the peasants had their pitchforks in hand, but it would not matter. The fastest of the hairy, gray armored beasts crashed into a little, stout man. Steel pierced flesh. On to the next. Men, women and children were hacked indiscriminately. The only act that delayed more slaughter was when one of them would stoop to taste the blood of the latest trophy.

Her hands cupping her dead grandson, an elderly woman cried out just as a dagger kissed her neck.

Brekk admired the work, pleased with his warriors. All his life he had been the strongest and cruelest. Thus, the burden of leadership rested in his corrupt hands. A high lord of great importance had demanded the death of one man in particular, but Brekk enjoyed the sensations of battle and nothing made him happier than to open the belly of some peace-loving commoner. The more that got in his way, the better.

"We have come for your head, Rhin," Brekk roared.

Brekk brought an iron-toe boot down on a child's skull, scanning the bodies. Could he already be dead? Brekk hop ed not. Surely one of his fighters would have told him. After all, this Rhin was difficult to miss with his red hair and green eyes. No one had red hair.

"Here, little piglet. How's about a game?" Brekk sniggered as he grabbed a torch from one of his subordinates.

Brekk held it up to the nearest thatched roof. The dry hay burned bright.

Two dozen houses were scattered sporadically throughout the glen. Brekk had the same amount of warriors at his disposal. He commanded them to take torch in hand and follow his lead. Soon Lynca village, in its entirety, ignited.

Columns of smoke spiraled into the sky. Still, their quarry did not appear. Brekk had the surviving villagers line up. He took his battle-axe in both hands, grinning.

"Maybe you don't like the fire game? I have a new one," he grabbed a blood-spattered girl by the shirt collar. "Where's Rhin? For your sake, I hope he turns up."

This produced the desired result. A young man, his hair red as sunset, stepped into view from behind one of the roasting houses.

By then the loud screams had died down to hushed murmurs.

"I am Rhin."

Brekk grimaced, flashing his rotting teeth, and tossed the girl away.

"You're very brave, boy, to show your face."

"I'm the one you want. Let them go," Rhin said.

"Oh, thinks he can bargain, does he? No deal. They'll die right after you."

Rhin held a sword with two hands, but that didn't stop him from shaking. Sweat beaded on his skin, his eyes full of fear.

The fear was replaced by anger as he said, "You won't harm them."

"Kill him, Brekk," said one of them.

Brekk seemed amused. He gestured for Rhin to come, casting a silencing glare at his brothers-in-arms as they began to protest. Rhin took a couple of slow steps, as if he were treading on broken glass. Brekk lost his patience. He leapt forward like a starving mutt, lashing out with the axe. The blow never landed, blocked by Rhin's blade. Brekk wheeled around, aiming a strike at Rhin's head. He sidestepped, the evasion looking almost accidental as he tried to maintain his balance. The large brute laughed. The plate mail Brekk wore clanked with his every motion. He saw an opening on Rhin's side and took it. Gravel crunched underfoot as Rhin parried the blow. Brekk growled. Rhin grew more confident, and when the head strike came a second time, he was ready. He jumped away from the slow attack and then moved in. Rhin's blade caught the beast in his ribs, stunning him.

Brekk was so shocked by the sudden riposte that he didn't move in time to counter the following thrust. Rhin's sword tore into Brekk's stomach. A frown of disbelief crossed the monster's face before he toppled over, taking the sword with him.

The warriors under Brekk's command howled in rage. They wanted to charge immediately but, leaderless as they were, confusion took hold of them.

Rhin planted his foot on the corpse and with that leverage yanked his blade out. He wiped the sweat off his brow, counting them. Well over a dozen. He held perfectly still, trying hard to seem invincible.

"If you want to die then, please, come closer," he taunted.

"Let's kill the brat," one of the fighters shouted.

Forsaking tactics and discipline, the beasts broke ranks and rushed at him.

Most of those that had been standing in line scattered. Some of the men, however, took up any weapons they could find among the bodies and rushed to Rhin's side.

With every step there came a squelch of blood. The flames spread and burned fiercer than ever. Consuming everything in its path, the fire even claimed the corpses that littered the ground, creating a vile, festering stink that gagged beast and man alike.

Rhin whirled his weapon around and struck two demons in the chest, then ducked and swiped upwards, cutting the throat of another. He then punctured the stomach of the last.

For a moment he was stunned. In his twenty-two years, he had never killed before, but what really caught him by surprise was his sudden skill with the blade. Rhin took the scabbard of his late father's sword and strapped it to his waist. Still holding the weapon, he contemplated the dead around him. Nearly all his friends, everyone he had ever known, were dead. How had it come to this?

Rhin deflected a slash at his chest and thrust, puncturing the flesh of yet another enemy. He felt nauseous. He was almost wading through blood.

His eyes darted to the left, where he beheld the bodies of the women and children that had tried to flee. Then he heard one final, terrible scream coming from behind. Before he turned around, he knew that the last of the townsfolk of Lynca village had been slain. Only he remained. As for those responsible, there were only two that still breathed.

Rhin took a good look at them. He wanted to make sure he knew their faces perfectly before he stabbed them. Those parts of them not covered in heavy armor were hairy and black, their eyes were but yellow slits. He even took special notice of their stench of burning feathers and rusting metal and guts. Rhin wanted to forever remember those demons that had ruined his home and his life.

The larger of the two came bounding at him, fangs bared. Rhin dodged one swipe and blocked the next. He then kicked the beast in the kneecap and heard the satisfying crunch of cartilage. But before Rhin could bring his sword down upon the wounded monster's skull to finish him, the other one was on him.

Rhin noticed how much faster this beast was than the rest, and its armor was lighter. He waited for an opening in its defenses. The chance for attack came when it raised an arm for a head-strike. The undersides of the arms were unarmored and vulnerable. Rhin feigned to the right and the beast swung too far in anticipation. Rhin lashed out at the exposed flesh, and the beast screeched as the steel cut in. Rhin then dislodged the sword and swung it back, this time the blow struck the beast's neck. The agonized cries were put to an abrupt end.

Meanwhile, the foe Rhin had almost killed moments before was crawling away from him in panic. Rhin walked over, taking his time. He kicked the monster in the ribs and then ducked down to turn it over so he could see its face.

Rhin held his sword over the weakened monster and said, "For Lynca."

He lowered the blade.

Rhin searched everywhere for signs of life but found none. It was growing dark, clouds covering the skies. The fires had burned out a while ago. Ash floated in the soft breeze. Then it began to rain, a cold, quiet rain. Steam rose from the corpses and the bloody ground sloshed with each of Rhin's steps.

He found the scorched remains of his family's house. No matter how long he rummaged through the rubble he found no trace of his parents. They had been caught in the house when the fires started, he knew. They never even made it out the door before they died. He fell to his knees and pounded his fist on the burned wood until he bled. He screamed wordless screams of rage and injustice.

"You fight well, for a forest boy," said a voice.

Rhin squinted and looked around, but couldn't find the source.

"I see you are the only one who survived this dreadful mess. Well done."

"Who are you?" Rhin spat.

The rain fell harder then, making it even more difficult to see.

"My name is not important. But I was the one who ordered this... test."

Rhin felt his blood grow hotter.

"You may be wondering," the voice continued, sounding almost bored, "why I would do this. You shan't have the answer from me."

"How will I kill you, without your name or your reasons?" Rhin shouted.

"The truth behind all this lies in Kremmä. You'll find the city to the west. Make your way there, little forest boy, and you may yet have your chance at vengeance."

"Whoever you are, I'll find you! And when that time comes you'll wish you'd never heard the name 'Rhin'!"

"Whatever you say," the voice replied with a chuckle.

The silence spoke for itself. Rhin was once again alone. He vowed then and there to go to Kremmä and discover the truth behind these devastating events.

First, he kneeled before his house, his parents' final resting place, and prayed. He prayed for their souls, for retribution, for vengeance. He prayed longest of all for forgiveness.

Rhin found the village storehouse mostly untouched by the devastation. For this he was thankful. He salvaged what food and clothing he could and made his way for the road leading out of the forest.

Rhin turned, glanced once more at the mangled villagers and beasts, the rain-soaked ash and piles of charred wood, and walked away.

Even though he walked under the canopy, rain drops gushed from between the leaves. It felt more like hail than anything else. Rhin enclosed himself within his coat, pulling at the hood in frustration. Depression weighed him down, the bleak sky and frigid winds adding to the gloom.

He saw no moon that night, nor did he find a single star. But the rain never stopped. The pattering orchestration pressed on, playing out every note in its bitter, damp music.

When the hour of midnight had long since passed, Rhin surrendered to weariness. He found a patch of soft, plush grass sprouting beneath a dying sapling and unrolled the dirty cloak that he used as a mattress.

As soon as he rested his head on his forearm, he slipped into a fretful slumber. The dream he had was powerful and seemed so real to him.

A strong wind picked up from the west. With every passing moment the storm grew in intensity. Trees swayed and thin branches splintered, spinning into the overgrowth. The clouds sped across the northern skies, the moon stealing fleeting peeks at the hamlet below.

A single house stood out above the rest in the village. Little more than a small shack, still it brimmed with an inexplicable importance. Its metal roof trembled with each of the wind's breaths.

Inside, a newlywed couple hid under a table in fear. Never had a storm this powerful passed through the village. Amid the wheezes of the winds a heartbreaking wail was heard.

Rhin's subconscious tried to make sense of what he was seeing. He had a strong feeling that these were his parents, years earlier, in their home in Lynca. They looked so much younger, their facial features being different then how he remembered, but Rhin knew the truth of it in his heart.

"What could that possibly be? What makes that horrible noise?" said the wife, pulling a rug over her as if it would protect her.

"Dearest, I don't know," the husband said as he reached over and patted her hand. His touch was like ice on the water in winter.

"Could we go and see?"

"No," the husband commanded. "It's far too dangerous now."

The wailing grew louder.

I haven't been born yet, Rhin reflected. *This storm took place at least two decades ago. Is this even real? If so, how am I seeing it all?*

Rhin's attention turned back to the lady—his mother?—as she cast a frightened look around the room.

"I'm going to see." said the woman, climbing out from under the table. "And there's not a thing you can do about it. No soul should suffer as the creature making that noise must be suffering."

The man knew that there could be no arguing, not when she got that mad gleam in her eyes. No amount of logic or common sense would sway her judgment. He resolved to accompany her.

Upon opening the door and scanning the horizon, his wife cried out within a spectrum of diverse emotions, "Look, a baby! Look."

An infant, perhaps two weeks old, wrapped in a frayed brown blanket, dangled from a branch in their modest backyard. When the couple moved closer, they beheld the babe in all its innocence.

Strange as it was, the husband said only, "So it is."

The woman screeched, waving her arms at the child, "Get it in. It'll catch disease and die if we don't. Get it in the house."

After he had lumbered over to the tree, the man stood on the tips of his toes and, reaching as far as he could, carefully lifted the child out from amidst the branches and held it in his arms.

The man stared at the pale-skinned babe, and deep, soulful green eyes stared right back. A lock of hair tumbled between those eyes, like a finger of flame.

"It's a boy," said the wife who was now peering over his shoulder at the squalling baby.

They tilted their heads slightly and their minds shut themselves down. A fog covered their thoughts.

The husband uttered words not of his own volition. "You were born of the storm, lad. We'll call you Rhin."

Me? I wasn't plucked from a branch like a fruit. What is this? the sleeping Rhin thought.

As the name was spoken, the storm appeased itself as if by some magical force. The rain calmed and the thunder clattered only far off in the distance.

Rhin understood. His name was consequential. Maybe he had some larger role to play in the coming weeks. Whatever the reasons, he knew the dream was a warning.

Without delay, the dream changed. A lean, red-haired man moved silently through sapphire halls.

White light flickered and five symbols of different colors appeared before his eyes. It was strange... as soon as Rhin's mind attempted to process the symbols, with their intricate shapes and jewels, he found himself unable to even think straight. He took time to come to grips with the red-haired man. The man turned his head and stared back at him. The eyes, green as a pasture, gave it all away. Rhin was looking at himself.

The symbols became more accessible to him. The veil that must have covered the images before had been removed. These symbols, ranging from simple triangular shapes to spiraling circles within circles, were set in plates that were in turn placed in five separate slots above a massive archway. The archway was sealed and gave the impression of never having been opened. The plates rotated smoothly around and around.

The first plate was made of white gold and covered with onyx stones. The second was plain jade with no other visible adornments. The third was of steel and lined with sapphires. The fourth was pure, solid gold and in its center was planted one, large diamond. The fifth, and last, was made of black iron and bathed in rubies the color of sunset.

A light touched the red-haired man, Rhin, as the sleeping Rhin watched the scene unfold.

The plates stopped spinning. A voice from behind the door announced, "The Legend of the Fallen Angel has begun."

And the dream ended.

Rhin awoke, drenched in his own sweat. He remembered nothing of the sequence of dreams from the night before, but he was overcome by a nameless feeling of anticipation. Every muscle in his body tingled with an excitement he could not explain.

After he had composed himself a little he ate a piece of dry bread and hummed to himself, mostly to keep unwanted thoughts from his mind.

Rhin's first journey outside of his village would take him to the city of Kremmä, known for its legendary criminals and large population, the only place he had ever heard of in the world beyond.

People of all races lived there, and its history traced back to the earliest years of the Four Isles.

It was founded near the western part of the North Isle. The Kimians, descendants of the Kenkros and an ancient race of the west, built its beginnings.

Rhin had left his village to find the creatures that slew his parents. At least that's what he told himself. But at some level he felt like he was going home, not leaving it.

Chapter 2
Murals, Paintings, and Prophecies

Rhin had already traveled far and he felt wearier by the moment. He had crossed fields and plains and forests on his journey. Often he would spot riders on the horizon, galloping between the settlements. Rarely did the clouds part and when there was a break in the vast gray mass it was brief and chased by a thunderstorm.

Along the way, Rhin had stumbled upon a village much like Lynca, calm and pristine. This one remained unspoiled by demons. He wasn't proud of it, but he poached clothing and food—as much as he could carry. Even the leather tunic and padded bearskin armor that he wore were stolen from a daydreaming armor smith.

The concept of thieving had never occurred to him before, but it had been so easy to hide, perfectly still, among the shadows in between a couple of identical homes. He watched, waiting for the smith to step inside his workshop, feeling the thrill. And when the time came, Rhin didn't hesitate. Of course, when he heard the man yelling at him from behind, the guilt set in.

Borrowing, he told himself, *I'm only borrowing it. When all this is done I'll return it to the smith.*

Along the lines of trees and broken, forgotten roads, Rhin followed the signs that pointed to Kremmä. On the drier days he could smell fires and cooking meat somewhere nearby, but didn't ever bother to take a look. He knew no one would share their food with some forest boy, so he ignored the nagging of his stomach and tried to think of better things.

His mind's eye dwelled on his parents, their deaths haunting him even more than before. How sudden the end must have come for them. How cruel a fate for such humble and benevolent souls.

In life Meela, Rhin's mother, had been a kind, comely woman. She would call him 'bony boy'. Whenever the night mists swaddled Lynca she would walk through the woods, uncaring and content. Meela was proud and loving of her family and life.

Rhin's father, Lincian, was a quiet man who experimented with sarcastic quips that his son had always found funny, albeit a bad joke or not. His most valued treasure had been his grandfather's sword, which he kept safely stowed away in a worn box in the tool shed. It was Rhin who now carried the weapon. It was Rhin who had avenged Lincian's demise with his ancestral blade.

Lincian had told Rhin, years before, that he was 'born of the storm'. His father's meaning behind this riddle, Rhin could never decipher.

They had both been wonderful, happy people. And now they were gone.

A jaw-tearing yawn reminded him that he had barely slept in days. He accepted sleep's embrace, welcoming the chance to escape the waking world.

As his eyes unfocused, Rhin saw Brekk and wished he could kill him again.

Rhin had entered Kremmä at dusk and the light was fading, slowing his progress. The air was fresh and cool, making him feel rather cold. Rhin wondered where he was as he rubbed his hands together in an attempt to stay warm. He had no money for lodgings, so he had to find a sheltered area to spend the night. He ended up on a street in a dilapidated area. It was a strange and twisted sort of place, frequented only by the scummy inhabitants of the city. Notably: thieves, bounty hunters, and other sorts of bizarre folk. Rhin tried his best to stay out of the way.

A tall, gangly group with short-cropped hair and green-striped clothing passed him by, each of them giving him a forlorn stare. One man had half a black beard, thick and tangled on one side of his chin and on the other clean-shaven. Another came up to Rhin pressing a bowl of what seemed to be pickled eyes in his face. Rhin refused as politely as he could, putting distance between the pickled-eyes person and himself.

From every alley emanated a different scent, some only half-sickening, but the predominant smell was that of vomit.

Threads of gossip caught Rhin's attention, as shadowed speakers dangled in and out of earshot. None of the tidings that passed his ears comforted him. The thieves had spread rumors of a warlock in their midst—a powerful magic wielder and an enemy to be feared. This made the slums even less welcoming.

Boards and slabs of stone barricaded most of the doors and windows. Iron fences sealed the slums off from the rest of the city. This did not stop the more agile criminals, however. Most of the richer folk had abandoned trying to 'tidy up' the area. Those who still attempted the vain, self-glorifying quest died within hours. It was not a comforting place to be for a young man, all alone, as the sun set.

It appeared as though Rhin's only option was to sleep in the street. This did not improve his mood as he had no wish to discover what kind of horrors came out at night in the slums. There was no choice in the matter though. So he would have to be strong and keep a ready hand on the hilt of his sword.

Moving shadows stirred Rhin from his thoughts.

"You're in the dark parts of Kremmä," said a voice.

"Who said that?" Rhin cried, a slight quiver to his voice.

"A lad like you shouldn't be here."

Rhin spotted a stranger sitting in the middle of the street. "Who are you to make that claim?" said Rhin.

Despite himself, he could not stop from twitching. His nerve threatened to break.

"I'm afraid you're trespassing," he replied darkly. "Now I am going to do to you what I do to all trespassers."

From its brown, tattered robe the stranger revealed a thick-veined hand, blue and covered in prickled, white hairs. Light spun in green webs between the cloaked stranger's fingertips and down its wrist.

"You're the sorcerer!"

The spindly flares of emerald magic rocketed over its flesh. The stranger ignored the question. "I shall feast on your soul,"

Rhin drew his sword from its scabbard. He ran up to the stranger and jammed the blade into its belly. It had merely passed through the cloak, tearing the cloth.

"It didn't even scratch you! What are you?" Rhin exclaimed.

"Merely a bad dream compared to the nightmares you'll soon face," replied the stranger.

The cloaked figure fired a bolt of sparkling, green energy from its icy blue hands. The streets filled with light as the already crumbling buildings shattered and fell. The cackling of the warlock was Rhin's lullaby as he slipped into unconsciousness.

When Rhin awoke, the stranger was gone.

Rhin was moving. He looked down and saw that little blue creatures were carrying him through the air. They covered his back—he could feel their tiny little palms pressing him up, their miniscule wings propelling him constantly forward. They appeared to be quite small, ranging from the size of a thumb to that of a hand.

Rhin felt too weak to move. As they flew toward a large building looming in the darkness, he felt sick. They stopped and touched down in front of a structure resembling a huge temple. Ten well-armed soldiers guarded the entrance.

"Your business?" the Decuri, a squad leader, asked.

"We have come to deliver the boy to Joabom," the biggest of the blue creatures stated.

"Very well," the soldier said, eyeing Rhin.

The soldiers gave the order to open the doors. With a surprising amount of force, the creatures flung Rhin into the hallway and the doors closed behind him with a clang.

Left with no other choice, he followed the treacherous twisting paths that winded before him Paintings of great battles between the Gods covered the wide walls. The archways were an intense red and gigantic, leaving Rhin with the feeling that they could swallow him at any minute.

Passing into a more rounded chamber, he noticed a book on a pedestal. It was laid open and its pages clearly shown. Light poured down upon it from a stained glass window depicting a stern figure clad in gray with dark red eyes. There was something special about this person and this book, and some grand, important message must have been concealed within this room.

Rhin moved toward the way out. A steel wall immediately crashed in place, locking him inside that room. He tapped his fingers on the metal and then pummeled it until his fists bruised. Defeated, he slumped to the floor, leaning against the impenetrable blockade.

Rhin had no clue who wanted him to stay in there, or why. Perhaps whoever it was just wanted him to die. But some inner logic told him that was too simple a ploy.

No, he thought to himself, scratching his head, *someone wants me to learn something.*

"What is it?" he asked aloud, to the stone walls.

Rhin's eyes wandered to the pedestal and the book.

Could that be all that was required of him? How stupid.

He scanned the room, trying to find a way to escape somehow. He found none. His will dissolving in the face of this enigmatic situation, he made up his mind to read the book.

Stepping up to the pedestal he brushed his fingers over the left page and read:

'The three champions of Lord Jiaïro stood upon the cliffs of the island examining their foe. They did not believe they had a chance of being undone by a Mortal. The giant they faced proved a worthy foe: he annihilated all three champions and tossed their heads into the ocean where they formed the surrounding isles of Nen, Savt and Ghu—after the names of the fallen.

Lord Jiaïro Himself—having descended from the heavens—scolded the giant, Monos-Khar, calling him a liar, a thief and a merciless killer. Monos-Khar rallied with strong words, though he was but a feeble man.

"You are only a pretender. The only Gods worthy of worship lie there."

And with those words he regarded the skies and a storm brewed from the northern most reaches of the world.

This angered the God greatly and upon the sacred isle of Naa-Teria a battle of such ferocity ensued that the seas around the isle shook from their very depths. With each clash of the mighty weapons the sound and energy of the storm was matched.

The most unlikely outcome occurred: Monos-Khar defeated the God, embarrassing him profoundly. Lord Jiaïro retreated for the time being but He warned the giant of His return and when at last He did touch mortal ground once again it would not be Monos-Khar He would claim, but his descendant. This descendant would suffer a fate tenfold worse than death, the God promised.

Monos-Khar simply answered, "Return from whence you came, False God. I do not fear you and neither shall my descendant. He will drive you back as I have done this day."

Upon that cliff did Monos-Khar summon forth his comrades and construct a temple of worship for the "True Gods" as he called them. Lord Jiaïro vowed to destroy this temple one day, yet only when He could destroy all hope of man and giant alike at once.

It was recorded that Monos-Khar sired the eventual Denzak race of giants who chose the South Isle, Kenner Karg, as their homeland. A shrine was built in Monos-Khar's honor. His bloodline has been lost to the passing of the River Time, however.'

An interesting story, Rhin thought, *I wonder how much of it is credible, though.*

Little time had passed, since he had finished reading the words before him, when the metal barricade was pulled up and out of his way.

Well, that's great. I can't believe this, Rhin crossed his arms in thought. I should find a way out of this place before I'm locked in here again.

The next obstacle encountered was a dead-end corridor, a closed book rested on a plain shelf at its extremity. Rhin noticed two steel walls, one on either side of the shelf.

This is familiar enough, he thought. *Turn back? No. There's nothing to be found where I came from. I should play this game, at least a little longer.*

The book was more a collection of theses and papers. The information provided within was fragmented and full of the writer's own personal opinions. Rhin read it anyway, his fingers tense and agitated as he leafed through the weathered pages:

From the Book of the Craft

'In the beginning, before anything had been created, there were two beings who proclaimed themselves enlightened. Their names were Cryöd and Rymæco. They were the dawn of a higher conscience.

Experiencing loneliness, the older of the brothers, Cryöd, decided to make new life, for He had the power to do so.

Though it is not known what manner of things Cryöd first caused to be, it is assumed that they were good and pleasing to Him. The wives He fashioned for Himself gave Him many sons who continued their Father's great work, spawning all sorts of beautiful, ethereal creatures.

Rymæco, after seeing His brother's crafts, created His own descendents out of jealousy. They were clever and adept at sowing discord. And they were, as it happened, too numerous to count.

As Cryöd's progeny grew, Rymæco became angry and hostile. He took the actions of His divine sibling as an insult. He thought that Cryöd did not wish to live with Him and His brood. Rymæco saw arrogance and condescension in everything Cryöd made or did.

Eventually, and inevitably, war broke out between them. Rymæco became known as Evil. As for Cryöd, He was regarded as the savior, or 'Good'. Though, let it be known that the original meanings of these words were far different than the ones we employ in this age...

The brothers and their descendants became known as Gods, for they possessed more strength than any other beings in existence. And the battles they fought among the stars created the boiling, writhing foundations upon which our world was founded.

To Cryöd, a son was born named Jiaïro. Even at an early age, Lord Jiaïro felt nothing but disdain for His family and the stalemate within which they found themselves. He refused to join either side. He was eventually cast out by Cryöd and called a renegade.

But through our Lord's hardships we find salvation.

Because of this betrayal, Lord Jiaïro fashioned Iora, building a wonderful, neutral kingdom of His own.

And, one dark night, He looked at both sides and despaired, for they were all set in useless conflict. Together they could have had ultimate power!

Ages passed and Lord Jiaïro had ten sons.

Sons of the Greatest King, kind and strong like their Father in heaven.

Lord Jiaïro kept out of His Father's affairs, while He brewed in His mind a secret plot. If the war somehow *escalated* so many would fall to their doom. Entire galaxies would shatter like glass... Worlds would erupt, spiraling out of control... The Gods would bleed... and He, Jiaïro, would be there to collect the fragile remainders of a cancerous universe. This was not greed, it was justice.

Through brief turmoil the world will be cleansed.

Lord Jiaïro remembered His Father and Uncle—how foolish they were.

Why should those corrupt imbeciles be allowed to control all life? I would be the better master, He brooded.

The Evil nature within took hold of His mind and He became increasingly calculating. The word 'Evil' is used only because it is the name given to a certain faction. Those who are called thusly see the fairness in their actions. Very few men are truly malignant at birth. And it should be said one thousand times that our Lord Jiaïro is not cruel. Those who claim that He is are heretics.

May they burn for their transgressions!

He is the instrument of our salvation, the hammer that strikes the nail of freedom. It is bizarre, but all those who are labeled so blindly as 'Evil' are the *true* believers. They are scions of a better breed. They will lead us all, one day, to a brighter future.

They will make Cryöd pay for His crime.

Beware the aged traitor! Cantankerous nonbeliever!

Each time Lord Jiaïro reviewed His plans He admired their brilliance and genius, and rightly so. With but a twist of His hand the world would belong solely to Him. He prepares His mighty army even now, forming the grandest force in existence. Lord Jiaïro is truly magnificent and cunning.

May He light the darkness of our minds with His wisdom!

The majestic God even learned of a way to gaze into the streams of time and thus gleaned knowledge of what cruelties lay in store for His beloved people, we Iorians. Long before the ripples in the River Time stirred the powerful current, He knew of His predestined end.

It was predicted that Jiaïro's last son, a boy completely unlike Him, would ascend from the ashes of forgotten history and take our sweet Lord before he could finish His works. And, in the grandest of ironies, Lord Jiaïro would be the one to set these events in motion.

But He feared not the falsities of Fate. All He had to do was move the pieces into place. His son would come for Him and one of them— God or Fallen Angel—would have to die.

Lord, cast off the chains that bind Thee and destroy the prodigal son, messiah of the wicked!

May Akvius—soulless, creedless—be disemboweled by the Hound, Nahjician! May all that he stands for crumble and topple about him. False, treacherous, fanatical...

Crush the anarchist, Lord, for he oppresses us!

When the day of Akvius' death comes, all the world shall rejoice. Lord Jiaïro's toils will be at an end and His authority absolute.

Good and Evil, He mused. *How inaccurate and vague. Such concepts are only words that define the two eternally competing forces. Strange that neither can exist without the other. Some day all will be revealed. When that time comes, I shall laugh at those fools from the heavens as they fester and rot! Then, when I am proclaimed savior of the Sacred Balance, they will know of what I am capable.*

The dogmatic, squabbling wretches could never outdo our God.

O, Lord Jiaïro, douse the flames that burn us!'

Rolling his eyes, Rhin skipped ahead and found an ancient legend concerning Jiaïro from an alleged alien race's point of view.

'The planet Baraïk's elders told stories and legends. The most famous one was "The Legend of Jiaïro, the Tyrant". In this tale, a broken man regains his legacy and uses the Sword of Purity to save the world.

The historians of Baraïk confirmed that Jiaïro created Iora, Baraïk's sister planet. Lord Jiaïro fashioned a world in which He would be the supreme ruler. What He did not foresee was the birth of free will. Those who began to oppose His dictatorial reign were quickly slaughtered according to the tales passed down by the priests loyal to Him.

He was the Dark Creator, His followers were most loyal to their Lord. The priests chose death over dishonoring Him. They would even self-sacrifice to further glorify His image.

The priests told of how Jiaïro had made everything perfect and in balance. To those who were called the Blinded this was the worst lie they had ever heard pass another's lips. There were two major points that were not so: the sense of injustice that penetrated the souls of the people who were not corrupted by Him, and the violence that would cause history's most tempestuous and bloody wars to repeat themselves over and over again.'

Baraïk? Another world? Rhin placed a hand on his head, struggling with the revelation.

He walked up to one of those blasted steel walls and kicked it, shouting, "What do you want?"

In response to his outburst, another metal curtain dropped down, this one blocking the way back. Whoever his unseen observer was, he or she might be watching from anywhere—the halls held many shadows and the murals had many eyes.

Rhin inhaled long breaths, trying to stay calm. He was effectively trapped. He glanced over to the book again and resigned himself to the will of those who imprisoned him.

The next passage was as follows:

'A boy was born unto this Father in the darkest corner of the world. To his parents he was a curse, a horrible fate that would haunt them if not dealt with.

Unto this boy the name Rhin was given. The word Rhin held great power within it but had lost its meaning millennia beforehand. This great name was not given out of love, but was meant to be a curse—a curse that would cause the child to dwindle away and leave this world as a dead tree decays over time.

The father had looked into the child's destiny. If the waters of fate were to run swift and true, this boy would be the end of him. He could not have this.

Let it be known, Lord Jiaïro dictates that none of this blasphemy should be heeded. The narrow-viewed Baraïkian stories are not based on truth. They are mentioned only to discredit their inadequacies. Jiaïro is the ultimate form of purity and wisdom.

All hail the One God! May those who doubt His divine conscience be stricken with leprosy and boils!"

"The One God?" Rhin whispered with a frown.

Without warning, the steel barrages were removed, redrawn into the ceiling, and the way lay unobstructed once more.

Is it finally over? Will there be more biased babblings on Gods and Angels? Rhin snorted.

He continued along the narrow passages and finding no more unexpected diversions, he stepped into what was apparently the main hall of the structure. The arched room was colossal. The stained glass windows showed battlefields and a being that he recognized as the God Jiaïro from the texts of before.

In the center of the dull brown walls was a tapestry woven of red threads. It rested half a foot higher then the floor, upon a set of small steps. Standing calmly before the tapestry was a dark figure with glowing ominous eyes who slouched slightly to one side. He had a golden goblet that he held aloft with his right hand. He was grinning, showing his decaying, yellowed teeth. His eyes were so small that they seemed all red. Rhin made all these observations on the assumption that this thing was indeed male.

"I have been waiting for you, Rhin of Lynca," the figure said, resting his weight on his right side.

"Were you the one who taunted me in the forest? Were you the one who directed me here?" Rhin said, his sword hand giving a slight twitch.

"What is the meaning of all this? No, I have no idea who told you to come here. I want you dead. Or at the least very, very far away. Since the latter is no longer an option, that leaves me little choice," he slurped some wine, dirtying his lips and chin. He then said, "You may not know, but you must perish by order of Jiaïro himself. I trust you have read the books on your way here? It took you quite some time."

"I read them. I couldn't continue until I did."

"Ah, good. As for me, I am Joabom, *first* of the Lord's marshals," he said, twisting his mouth into a broad, vain smile. "I command one tenth of his armies, my brothers control the other legions. My reach covers all of the city of Kremmä and the regions immediately surrounding it. Thus, you needn't run, for I will find you… always."

"I'm no threat to a God," said Rhin.

"Hah. You really do know nothing, then? Our Lord's magic is powerful. You are a grave threat to us. You must die, mortal."

"I don't understand," Rhin shouted.

"Good. Then you will die the ignorant swine I always knew you to be. This conversation has outlasted my interest, I'm afraid." The marshal turned to face a particularly active shadow and commanded, "Daish-rog, destroy him."

The agitated shade finally emerged from the darkness, a curved blade readied.

It turned out to be a man, a sturdy looking middle-aged man, who had been observing the entire discussion. Rhin noticed that he was bald except for a black sprig of greasy hair, braided and dangling from the back of his head. His eyes were a pale yellow and his armor was the same as all common soldiers of Jiaïro. He assumed this because whenever Jiaïro waged war in the murals he was accompanied by footpads in black and red.

His movements were dull and lifeless. By the way he advanced, this man gave the impression that he was no longer amongst the living.

"Entertain me," roared Joabom. "I'll make you a deal, boy. If you kill Daish-rog, your death will be a parcel less painful. Fair enough?" The marshal then turned and walked to the northern extremity of the hall and sat upon a throne of metal. "I have been waiting to see what all the fuss is about. Apparently you're some great warrior." He laughed at the idea.

Daish-rog slashed his sword out at Rhin who responded with quick, twitchy defensive moves. He had never been a warrior, up until the slaughter at his village, but now he felt as though he were rediscovering his power with each blow. Daish-rog's face changed during the battle from frustration to an unidentifiable expression, perhaps shards of a broken grin. He continued to fight until a smile spread across his face. Bashing his sword against his opponent's, Rhin then struck the weapon from Daish-rog's hands. The stricken dropped to his knees.

It was as if the warrior had been released from a spell. His eyes were no longer dull but full of vigor. They shone a light green as opposed to a pale, ugly slime-yellow. His smile grew to encompass most of his face. He pushed himself up slowly until he stood eye to eye with Rhin, the boy who had stirred him from sleep.

"What are you waiting for? Destroy him," said the first marshal.

"No," Daish-rog gasped and as he spoke he panted as a new form of life pumped through his veins, "his fighting skills are superior to my own." He looked around the room and then at Joabom. "What am I doing here?"

"End it now!"

"Why am I here?" He paused a moment. "What have you done to me?"

"Weakling! You were always lamentable and always will be. I regret ever attempting to salvage your sorry soul," Joabom bellowed.

"I have no memories of being alive. You had nearly robbed me of my existence. I will ask you once more: Why?" Daish-rog spread his arms as he said this.

"You sniveling jackal. You will never understand. I should have killed you when I had the chance. I should have accepted Jiaïro's orders."

"Jiaïro? He ordered this?" Daish-rog seemed to ponder this information for a moment until reaching a decision. He said, "Then I will destroy you and when this task is done, I shall come calling for your master."

"You would not dare. His powers range beyond anything you could imagine."

"Then why be afraid of a simple boy?"

Doubt passed through Joabom's mind but it soon left him. Daish-rog raised his sword to the level of the marshal's neck.

"You will never even reach my Lord. Your quest begins and ends here. I will save Jiaïro the task of destroying you and the little worm," Joabom's voice rang through the room.

Joabom launched himself with ease to the other side of the hall and took hold of a long sword that had been resting in its sheath nailed on the wall. He then pounced at his adversary and seconds afterward they clashed swords sending sparks throughout the area.

Rhin decided he would be better off escaping than witnessing this battle.

He chose the nearest window and started to run.

"Where do you think you're going?" the marshal shouted at Rhin as he fended Daish-rog off. "We've only just begun." Then to Daish-rog, "Die, you runt!"

Just then three guards entered, garbed in black plate mail. Their faces hid behind full helms with only narrow slits for eyes and mouth.

They must be Joabom's personal protectors with all those rubies on their armor, thought Rhin, unsheathing his sword.

"We will teach this whelp a lesson," one shouted.

The bodyguards stood legs apart, arms crossed, broadswords dangling from their belts. One whistled without tune, adjusting his glove.

"I propose an alliance for the time being," Daish-rog called out to Rhin.

"Doesn't look like we have a choice," he answered.

Sharing the load, the duo focused on their defense. The two were back to back, parrying blow after blow. Rhin thought of how the demons he had battled before were much larger and more threatening. This gave him courage enough to fight. Rhin punched the jaw in of one of the soldiers then turned and took out another two. He then kicked another in the stomach and brought his blade down upon the warrior's skull.

At the same time, Joabom was kneeling in front of Daish-rog, panting.

"This is not over, you dogs," Joabom raged, raining blood and spittle as he spoke. "I shall return."

The marshal was cut all over and losing substantial amounts of blood.

"Yes, you shall return," Daish-rog said in a tone of finality. "When that time comes, you will fall to my blade. Oh, how I'll revel when I tear that forked tongue from your horrid trap."

"By the way, *soldier...* perhaps you should inform the boy of his fate," Joabom's last words were coupled with a weak laugh.

Then he was gone.

After pausing, Rhin asked, "What did he mean by that?"

Daish-rog sighed and sat down, cross-legged on the floor.

He said, "You are believed to be the long lost son of Jiaïro, the eleventh marshal, had your father not denied you that birthright."

"Tell me everything you know," said Rhin.

Daish-rog's eyes flicked up and to the right, as if noticing an object only he could see, before he responded, "This is the story as far as I can remember it. You see, when you were born, Jiaïro placed you with a mortal family by means of a magical gale or storm of some kind. It was on the wings of the wind that you were brought to your home. He made this family think you were their own by casting a spell which cleansed their minds of the truth. He fears you for some unknown reason. However, that night forces other than Evil were at work. It does not make sense, I know, but if the legends are true, you have certain abilities that could prove to be quite a nuisance to Jiaïro," Daish-rog explained.

"What of the other ten marshals?"

"These other marshals are also your brethren and they say there is one lost son, besides you, one that has not been seen for a long time—though I personally would discredit any such claim. One thing is for certain: you are the youngest of the offspring." Daish-rog paused. "I'm sorry, I don't think I introduced myself properly. My name is Daish-rog. Proper etiquette is very important where I come from."

No one cared for that kind of formality in my village... but now my village is gone, Rhin contemplated.

"I'm Rhin. But hold on, this is a little hard to understand. You're trying to tell me my whole life—everything I've ever thought to be true to me—is a lie?"

Daish-rog hesitated, but finally he said, "No."

"Then what part isn't?" Rhin demanded, leaning over the other man.

"You are not really a God anymore, even though everyone thinks you are. You are only a Half-God. So that would only be half a lie," Daish-rog's smile was painful, sympathy was new to him. "You see, your powers disintegrated long ago, according to legend."

"Oh, that clears everything up," he retorted sarcastically.

All those memories of his father and mother and the time they had together, it was all just a lie. He even carried a sword that was not his property. His mind was a boggled mess that he alone would have to deal with. No help would be offered to him. And this Daish-rog—could he be trusted?

His words caused Daish-rog to laugh. "That's the spirit. It looks as though we share an enemy. Might I join you on your journeys?"

"I'll need all the allies I can get if I'm about to take on a God in single combat."

"Come then, Rhin, there is work afoot," Daish-rog patted him on the shoulder.

At the word 'Rhin' the whole room shook, tremors and quakes rocking the hall. The archways crumbled one by one. The paintings on the walls fell, canvas tearing on the hard stone. Dirt showered from high in the beams near the roof.

"This place will destroy itself now that the Evil within has departed. We must leave at once," Daish-rog said, shoving Rhin in front of him. "Move."

"Where to?" Rhin asked.

"The Turndäo Inn."

Rhin felt he had no choice but to trust Daish-rog. The two ran out of the gate just in time to turn and see the walls collapse as fire tore through the area. The sun had not risen as of yet when a gold and gray cloud engulfed the temple of Joabom. A frail yellow light shone through and allowed them to see the struggling forces at work. As soon as the turrets and stained glass windows fell to the soil the cloud vanished, as if inhaled by the sky itself.

"Ashes to ashes…" murmured Daish-rog.

"That's the end of that place. I'm glad at least that part's over with," said Rhin.

Daish-rog contemplated the idea, "Over with? Hmm, no, I would say it has scarcely begun."

"That's encouraging." Rhin put a hand over his eyes.

"Come. Let us go now." Noticing Rhin's hesitation he said, "It is best not to dwell on the past. Your future lies not here, but elsewhere. All one can do is follow the thin thread of Destiny."

It was going to be a long enough walk to the small village ahead. And if the forces of a God were searching for him he would not be able to escape—at least not easily.

"Never will I live to speak of this," he murmured.

Daish-rog overheard and commented, "That is not certain. Nothing is ever certain, but that is something no one can teach you. You must know it through experience. You will find the light to your path, one day, most likely sooner than later. Have no fear, be stout of heart and good will always prevail."

"Wise words," Rhin said aloud, but his thoughts were far darker and conflicted.

As he continued to think, the next thing that came to him was that he had nothing to live for, so if he could fulfill his purpose and kill Jiaïro, he could let go of life altogether. It all seemed meaningless to him anyway.

Daish-rog was his only guide now, and the only person he lived for at the moment. This quest he had embarked on was not to kill Jiaïro, not then anyway. It was to find meaning in life again. To find his purpose.

Chapter 3
Night at the Inn

*R*hin and his newfound companion had set off for a small village near Kremmä. The air was humid, making their shirts cling to their skin. In this thick stillness it was difficult to breathe. The wind only made occasional lazy attempts to rustle the reeds and stir the quiet.

The area around their destination was covered with swamps and the like. Filthy, festering marshlands laid claim to the land, conquering more of the calm grasslands with each passing season.

The village to which Daish-rog and Rhin made their way served Kremmä city as a supplier of fish. This was because it was bordered by a lake, and the Jagged River connected that lake to the sea in the east. The town was quaint and had no palisades or barricades of any kind, nor any militia or soldiers to speak of.

A pacifist village, Rhin noted.

Rhin and Daish-rog had come across highly elevated terrain—the sharp cliffs that ranged from the eastern shoreline all the way to the northern corners of the Isle. It had not been a long walk however, only an hour or so—far less of a trial then the boy had expected. The cliffs and hills proved somewhat of a challenge to the battle-weary men, for they had suffered light wounds.

Mostly bruises, Rhin told himself.

He then stepped on a loose rock and winced as he twisted his ankle. Daish-rog moved to help but Rhin kept him away with a glare.

"It's nothing," he said.

It was late at night when the two looked down from the top of a hill at lights below. The clustered pines seemed like black pools in the darkness. The wind was more active then, on the cliff. Rhin thought he could hear a mad howling, a voice in the gusts of wind.

Daish-rog placed a hand on his shoulder and said, "We have arrived. Come, we must reach the inn. We can rest safely there, for a time."

"Then will you tell me about my past?" Rhin asked.

No answer. Rhin hadn't expected one.

They could both feel the air getting hotter again, as they descended from the cliff. Rhin hoped that maybe they would have to leave the town. He didn't like it there, something did not sit right with him.

The two men arrived at the village after having trudged through damp dirt roads. It was a quiet town, even by day, known for not meddling in the affairs of others. A thick smell of olives came from a market nearby. It was a custom for this village to have night markets. The merchants would come out after midnight and put their goods and works on display.

Rhin saw a disgusting pork rib cage, overrun by black swamp-flies. *Anyone who would buy their meat here is insane*, he thought as his nose wrinkled.

He caught a glimpse of a pile of what looked like melted wax which turned out to be apples. The fruit-merchant, a fat man with a big nose and yellow beard, came up to the stack of apples and took one in his hand. He spat on the rot-blackened fruit and rubbed it, and then he set it on the top of the pile. Averting his eyes, Rhin pleaded that his stomach not let out on him now.

The sights and smells of the food market were appalling, but they soon came to the inn. It was a most welcome sight.

The door of the inn was ajar with a shaft of light pouring out. They opened it and were greeted by the innkeeper.

"Good evening, fine sirs. Would ye like a drink?"

"Yes, thank you," Daish-rog answered for both of them.

"Sit down at the bar and I'll be with ye in a moment," the keeper said.

They ordered two uïrol juices, the common drink of Iorians in that part of the world, and began to make idle chit-chat. Rhin secretly hoped to leave trivial matters behind and have Daish-rog reveal to him his destiny, for he grew weary of mysteries.

The bartender brought them their drinks as the smell of meat and pastries wafted through the room. People all around them danced, happy and drunk, telling jokes punctuated with loud guffaws. Some spoke of the thrills of adventure, and losing oneself in the wild, while others sang with a mug of juice in their hands, despite the late hour. One man toppled off his stool at the bar and two burly lads carried him out into the dark streets. Rhin did not feel secure here. It was almost too joyful and innocent a place.

"Where do you come from, originally?" Rhin said sliding his mug from one hand to the other.

A fine line spread across Daish-rog's face. He frowned.

This did not deter the boy's resolve, "Where did you live before you joined those soldiers?"

The frown instantly turned into a grimace. "I did not join them. I don't even remember ever speaking to any of them before you smote me. How could they have done this to me?" Daish-rog stared at Rhin a while, then gave him an apologetic look. "Only vague images appear in my head. When I was within that cursed structure it felt as though I had strayed into a dream, a somber and clouded sleep from which I could never wake. How long did they keep me there? I can't even remember how old I am."

"I have no personal reason to hate Jiaïro yet, but I find myself increasingly aware of his cruelty. What his marshal did to you is horrible, anyone would agree. What will you do now?" Rhin raised his eyebrows.

"My life has been whisked away from me. I must find purpose in this world. That shall be my quest. It seems as though you are the reason I have been restored. I do not know how—or even why—you were brought to that temple but you saved me. I must repay the debt."

"How?"

"Traditionally, I suppose I'd have traveled with you through thick and thin until I had saved your life."

"Traditionally?"

"Tradition never harmed anyone. At least, no incidents come to mind."

They chuckled.

"Well, let me ask you this: how will you find purpose with me if I have none myself?" the boy asked.

"Perhaps in helping each other we can find purpose together," said Daish-rog.

"I have no idea where I'm heading. I don't have a map or anything."

"I know these parts well. And as for finding a map, that can be arranged."

Rhin had come to the conclusion that Daish-rog was a very surreal man. The way he moved about and spoke hinted at nobility, but the tattered rags he wore contradicted that theory. His black ponytail seemed a bizarre choice of hair style but Rhin thought it could just be customary where Daish-rog came from. Rhin found himself frustrated with how little he knew of the world, and Daish-rog became aware of this through his increased frowns and glum words.

"So who was that figure in the cloak that attacked me? Do you know anything about the blue-handed demon with the ability to wield magic?" asked Rhin.

"Evok, second Marshal of Jiaïro. All of Jiaïro's soldiers know about you now. They will all hunt you. Rhin, you must believe that they will not stop until you are either dead, or worse: in front of the God himself."

"So what did Joabom mean when we were inside the temple?" asked Rhin.

"Innkeeper," Daish-rog called.

The keeper hurried over, "Yes, gentlemen?"

"Might we have two rooms, one for my companion and one for myself?"

"Why of course, kind sires. Let me just go and fetch the keys for ye."

"Thank you."

Rhin's gaze rested on Daish-rog. Daish-rog stared back, a vague expression clouding his face.

"You didn't answer my question," Rhin said his legs squirming.

"Oh, I'm sorry. What was it you were saying?" said he.

"About Joabom, and how he said I was doomed?" Rhin waved his hand in concentric circles for effect.

Daish-rog did not answer. Rhin counted to ten twice. It felt as though his blood was turning to steam.

The innkeeper then came over and handed each of them a key.

"It's getting late. Let us locate our rooms," said Daish-rog, ignoring Rhin's angered expression.

Rhin, who had been far from done questioning Daish-rog, followed his comrade to their rooms, screaming in silence at his friend's utter refusal to answer him. He did not even imagine, for one moment, that Daish-rog might not know any more than he had already told. Fuming, Rhin stayed well behind. He had developed an irritating itch on his right hand, he noticed. He felt like his eyes were going to pop out of his head.

"Room two," Rhin said, "better be off to bed."

"Room one, this is the place," Daish-rog said.

The inn did not have many rooms to offer weary travelers. The bar within was its real source of revenue. Most people who came to the inn were residents of the village wanting spirit to warm them on cold nights. There were not many voyagers in these parts, either. Thus, the lodgings were close and a bit cramped.

The two did not find the rooms to be unbearable, however. They were warm and had drapes to shut out unwanted morning light. Little bundles of candles could be found, some lit, some not. The bedding and sheets were soft. In short, a nice place to spend a night.

"Sleep well," Daish-rog called from his room, the sound traveling through the thin wall.

Rhin did not answer. He took a deep breath and slept, dreaming of a white sunrise and a stretch of beach lined with black candles. The tide was waxing in his dream. It was all peaceful and sad, a fading portrait of tranquility. He basked in the calm, until he was suddenly engulfed by a wave. The water crushed his body, tearing at his limbs. There was nothing after that, only rest.

A far off noise, maybe a fallen tree crashing into the dirt, disturbed Rhin from his slumber.

It was a gloom filled, rainy day. Stretched out all across the sky was a single, seemingly swarming, gray cloud. The light was weak and gave Rhin a headache.

Upon awaking, he stared out the window. He couldn't remember what he had dreamt.

"Room service," a knock accompanied the polite voice.

Rhin felt like he had been very close to unlocking a tightly sealed door in his mind. But the knock came again, pulling him by force back to reality.

"Come in," Rhin sat up and shouted, throwing his pillow across the room in irritation.

Upon entering, a concierge—the cocky smile never leaving his face—hurled a butcher's knife aimed at Rhin's heart. Even as unpredictable as the attack was, Rhin caught it and slung it back. It struck him between the eyes. The assailant stared in disbelief for half a second before crumpling like a dropped sack of rocks.

Daish-rog burst into the room, dagger in hand. Looking at Rhin with less surprise than was due, he raised his eyebrows.

"You know, you could have come to me first if you were having problems with the staff," said the weary older man, sheathing the dagger at his belt.

Although he was shocked at the precision in which he caught and then threw that knife, he managed to answer in a blasé manner, "I just had a few complaints about the service. And if that doesn't get the message through, nothing will. We should get out of here, I think."

"Do you? Do you really?" Daish-rog replied, already out the door.

The pair raced out of the room, into the hall and down the stairway. Daish-rog was around the corner on the road when he, on second thought, doubled back to the inn. Inside Daish-rog tossed a few coins at the innkeeper and then chased after Rhin.

The keeper stood flabbergasted as he watched them fly out into the grasslands. He stammered, giving his wife a tired sidelong glance, "Everyone's in a hurry nowadays. Always running, never takin' the time to live."

Daish-rog caught up to Rhin and gestured to have the boy follow him. He ran at a man walking through the street and tore the paper from his hands.

"Thank you, sir," he called.

The man simply stood and stared, dumbfounded, as the pair raced off.

Still running, Rhin said, "What's wrong with you? You stole something."

"Not just any old thing... a map, my boy. I know this is going to sound bizarre, but *we* are in need and he is not. He will never leave the village, therefore he will never find any use for this thing."

This is wrong. Rhin told himself, but Daish-rog's logic was taking its effects, well, maybe... if he doesn't need the map.

"Listen," Daish-rog started, "if it means that much to you, you can return this old piece of paper at the end of your travels."

Rhin knew, of course, that his friend was not serious. But, after all, had he not robbed a smith earlier? Had he not used the same excuse?

I am many things, but certainly no hypocrite, he thought, pushing himself to keep up with Daish-rog.

Rhin and Daish-rog journeyed for two days with few breaks. They would have to make good time and stay hidden, as Jiaïro's forces often patrolled these regions. And now that every bounty hunter and mercenary in the land was after them it made it next to impossible to travel unnoticed.

The area was made up of an entire landmass of hills protruding from the grass. Scattered pines showed themselves often to the weary eye of a traveler. They had bought some provisions from the shops near the inn, hoping these would last them until they reached the next town.

The whole time, the sky had been gray, as gray as metal. Not a single bird graced the sky.

"We must tread softly, and make no sounds. Jiaïro's men could lurk behind any given bush or tree in this cursed land," Daish-rog said, shading his eyes.

"What does Jiaïro want with this world?" Rhin sighed.

Daish-rog's response was flat and matter-of-fact, "Dominion.".

Eventually, they arrived at an outpost guarded by five of Jiaïro's soldiers. It stood on an otherwise abandoned hilltop where the grass had been burned and because the sky was gray, everything took on that hue. The outpost consisted of a single tower with soldiers stationed in it. Daish-rog and Rhin crouched behind a few bushes that grew between the trees.

"What do you suggest we do now?" Daish-rog asked Rhin.

A great bell tolled, shaking the foundations of the outpost itself. Rhin understood what it meant. A summons. The soldiers and patrols of the region were being called to arms, and Rhin had a nasty suspicion that these heightened measures of security were meant for him.

Three of Jiaïro's finest horsemen rode up to the tower from behind the hill—actually they were half–demon, half–horse*.

"I've never seen anything so revolting," Rhin whispered.

"They seem to be elite warriors," said Daish-rog. "We'd best avoid conflict here. I propose we use the nearby overgrowth to pass by these beasts unnoticed."

"Can't we just make a wide loop around this place? That way we could make sure they don't notice us."

"Normally, yes, that would be the best option. It would, however, take us days to trek around the thickets, woods and bogs in this area. This road we have been following is the fastest way to where we are heading. You may decide the best course of action," Daish-rog explained.

---

* These twisted abominations thirsted for blood day and night, preying helplessly on their enemies. Their origin was unknown. Yet one thing was certain: their race joined Jiaïro not for his cause, but for the chance to mercilessly slaughter as many people as they could.

They were dark, reptilian creatures with shining red eyes. They made for vicious as attack dogs. Known as 'Seekers', they fought with spears. Perhaps the common name of their evil race was related to how they searched desperately for sources of blood. Some referred to them as vampires but others knew that they enjoyed the taste of fresh blood, but did not require it to survive.

To the more ancient and learned folk on Iora their true name was far more terrible than their common one: 'Bludsuräii' - 'fallen from grace'.

Rhin thought about it. Even though he would have preferred to stay far away from that eerie outpost he also wanted to leave these dreary lands behind.

"We'll risk it," Rhin decided.

The two approached the structure as much as they dared on foot and then dropped to the ground. They pulled themselves along the grass and into the bushes.

As they crawled, they heard a soft squeaking. Fleeting, white shades darted back and forth before them.

Mice, Rhin realized, his pulse thundering in his ears.

Daish-rog put a finger to his lips, Rhin nodded and they carefully crept around it. But, as quiet as the two companions were, the mice became distraught and scurried out of the bushes and up the hill, squealing. At the high pitched sounds being emitted from below the soldiers reared their ugly heads.

"See what all the trouble is," said one, maybe an officer.

"Probably a fox or a wildcat. There's never anything dangerous that comes through this way," another soldier complained.

"Dare you defy an order?" said the first voice.

"No, sir," stated the second.

Muttering to himself all the way down the hill, the soldier made his way toward the bushes.

"What do we do?" Rhin hissed, lying still as a stick.

"Put our blades to use," Daish-rog replied.

The two jumped to their feet, swords drawn, and stared at their enemies.

"There will be more of them coming now," said Daish-rog. "Ready yourself."

The Seekers commenced the onslaught and Rhin swung his sword at them, daring them to approach. Five other soldiers started to attack, too, but it did not take long for them to flee fearing for their puny little lives. The three Seekers remained, fighting violently with the two.

"Surrender," growled one of the Seekers.

Rhin was kneeling on the ground, still parrying the attacks, but it was obvious he and Daish-rog were being defeated. Then something happened to Rhin. Blue light surrounded him. His eyes started to burn and he clutched his face in an attempt to fight the feeling of pain. He gasped and unleashed a small, blue, circular wave of energy.

"Stay back," Rhin threatened, in a tongue he did not know, with a voice that was not his.

The Seekers heard him and glanced at each other in a nervous fit. They backed away. Daish-rog felt his stomach jolt.

"What's wrong, Rhin?" asked Daish-rog.

At that precise moment, the circle grew and surrounded the Seekers and they were lifted up. Briefly, they hovered in the air and then smashed face down against the ground, paralyzed. Their mouths were full of dirt and burnt grass, which they were forced to swallow as they gasped for oxygen to fill their black lungs.

Fitting that they should eat the very land they poisoned, Rhin observed.

"What happened?" Daish-rog gaped at the sprawled, twitching husks.

"I can't believe it. How did I do that?" Rhin blurted.

"You tell me. What the blazes did you do to them?"

"I think I stunned them."

"Well, there's no time for this discussion. The rest of the patrols are most likely already aware of our position. We must seek shelter in the caves near here," said Daish-rog, and he led the way, his black pony-tail flapping.

Rhin stole one last glance at the foes he had defeated and then, stumbling, he trailed after Daish-rog.

Chapter 4
Cave of Spaetuus

The two runners needed only go a short distance before they came upon a cliff wall spanning at least a mile. Whereas behind there were but endless fields. Black dots marked the entrances to the dozens of caves, the refuge to where Daish-rog had been leading Rhin.

Just as he dared hope that they had eluded their pursuers, he turned around and saw, to his horror, squads of Jiaïro's elite soldiers winding among the hills.

Daish-rog pulled Rhin into the darkness of the stone mouth.

"I've let them chase us to a wall," said Daish-rog.

He flung the sack he had carried off him crushing the knee-high blades of grass. He stared at it, scowling.

He said to Rhin, "I am sorry. I did not mean for this to happen. It is my doing that we die together this day."

"I'm as much to blame as you are, friend," said Rhin with a soft smile.

He stretched out his hand and Daish-rog shook it. They sat, backs pressed against a pair of boulders, facing the emptiness. They unsheathed their weapons, the pale, clouded, outside light that reflected off the steel blinding them in the gloom. Once their eyes had adjusted to the dark expanse, they spotted a corpse pressed against a rock, its skull fractured.

Without, orders were shouted from the Decuri. Growls and threats poured about Rhin, thick in the air, becoming a threatening symphony, the final note of which would be his screams as he died. The clamor of hoof beats foretold the arrival of horsemen.

They then heard a roar, the strangest and deepest sound that had ever passed their ears.

"What was that?" Rhin breathed.

"Not a clue," Daish-rog whispered back.

The spine chilling guessing game was cut short when a huge black lion jumped out and rushed past Rhin and Daish-rog. Rhin shot upright, watching in both awe and dread as it pounced on a soldier, tearing him apart as he screamed for help. The lion soon overwhelmed the field, taking victim after victim by surprise, slaver and gore flying

"That thing..." he stuttered.

The army scattered and fled in all conceivable directions. But the two companions froze there, unwilling to move, lest it break their amazing luck. That horrible beast had passed them by without noticing them.

It couldn't have chosen not to attack us on purpose, could it? Rhin wondered.

An obnoxious snicker came from within the cave. Rhin's heart almost stopped.

"Remember me?" said a familiar but unanticipated voice.

"Joabom! I knew I smelled scum in this cave. I should have been more vigilant," said Daish-rog, compensating for being caught off guard.

"This time we will finish you," Rhin shouted, his threat resounding throughout the cave.

Rhin and Daish-rog charged. Outside, the lion was tearing at a defeated soldier's flesh and devouring a well-deserved dessert. The few that still lived—the warriors who had limped off during the onslaught—continued their desperate flights.

Rhin lunged at Joabom and Daish-rog spun round to strike from behind.

"You obviously have no clue what you are doing, *brother*. If you fight, you will destroy us all," said Joabom.

"What? What are you babbling on about?"

"So you haven't told him everything, Daish-rog," Joabom said with a shake of laughter in his voice.

"Told me what?" Rhin said.

"You are dangerous. Dangerous beyond what you can imagine," Joabom said.

"Dangerous to whom? Evil dwarves like you?"

"Hold your tongue, monster," Daish-rog shouted.

"With a wave of your hand you have destroyed everything, Daish-rog. If it were not for you, our world would not come to an end. If only you had just killed him, you blasphemous fool."

"Be quiet. Your vision of the world is perverted!" Rhin yelled. "I don't understand your plots yet, but I will find an explanation. On my own if I must."

Then the great beast burst forth into the cave and leapt at the marshal, swiping at his nose. Joabom slashed at the monstrosity, shredding tough flesh with his steel. The beast howled and retaliated with a bite, jaw clenched, fangs digging into Joabom's arm. Blood spurted, cascading like rain.

The struggle was brief. The marshal lay on the cave floor, his eyes blank. The great beast's teeth were stained red and its eyes glowed green in the gloom.

"Leave," Rhin mouthed to the other, as icy sweat moistened his brow.

"There is no need for you to go," was the answer as Rhin and Daish-rog backed away toward the mouth of the cave.

"Who is there?" Daish-rog asked, his eyes darting around, searching the darkness.

"My name is Spætuus. Long have I kept safe this sanctuary in anticipation of my lord's rebirth. My creator and master, Rhin, the Lord of Light has returned, and thus my assignment is complete."

The source of the voice seemed to be the *lion*. It did not move, however.

"Speak, Spætuus," Rhin said using the very same voice that had passed his lips on the hill an hour or two earlier.

"You must stay here for the night. This region is secure. I have hunted down and chased away all the soldiers that were following you. It will take days for any reinforcements to arrive and the locals fear me. By then," the lion yawned, a massive fang-filled stretch, "you will be gone. So if you please, my home is your home."

Since Rhin held no suspicions of Spætuus, Daish-rog decided to brood enough for both of them. Still, this seemed the only safe place for them to spend the night. They accepted Spætuus' offer. Rhin had questions for the lion.

Quite late, after the moon had arisen and Daish-rog had dozed off, Spætuus urgently turned to Rhin.

"The time has come for you to find your own way, Rhin. You must leave Daish-rog and head for the forest to find your answers. A messenger from the Gods will await you there. You must leave tonight before your companion awakens."

"Why leave Daish-rog? He has proven himself loyal and courageous."

"You must separate for a time. You two must stride different paths."

"What proof do you have that you are not leading me into a trap set by Jiaïro?"

But Rhin knew the lion spoke the truth. He could sense this. He had known the answer before he ever asked.

"I have waited my whole existence for this moment. When you created me I was entrusted with this most sacred of tasks, helping the destroyer of Jiaïro the Tyrant," Spætuus explained.

"I created you? I don't recall doing so. I'm finding this very hard to believe. I don't know who to trust."

"Trust in me. I have waited centuries for you. I am loyal to you. You must believe me. The answers you seek lie in the forest."

"I must search for purpose," he said to the night and the black lion. "I will go."

So without even a minute's sleep, he got to his feet and ran into the night without even sparing a backward glance.

"Go with my blessings. May the Gods be with you," said the lion.

Days passed and Rhin's condition worsened. The sky was dark and gloomy as it had been since he and Daish-rog had set out from the inn. But now Rhin was alone. He regretted abandoning Daish-rog, but as his thoughts churned he began to feel only rage. After all, was it not Daish-rog who had changed his life? Was it not Daish-rog who had directed him, leading him astray in the wilderness? These dark thoughts subsided after awhile. For he knew in his heart that Daish-rog had been indebted to him. Daish-rog would never have betrayed Rhin the way Rhin had done to him.

I must find answers, he repeated as he walked.

It was hard going, the path he tread alone. The wood was unforgiving and merciless, testing him at every turn. In the dark it was treacherous. With no light to guide him, he stumbled and fell.

Delirium set in after the first two days of chewing on moldy blackberries and rough seeds. He became convinced the trees hated him and the animals, invisible and taunting, wanted him bloodied and dead.

On the third morning he ate a brown apple and couldn't keep it down. He tripped and felt the dumb thump of his skull hitting the dirt. When he tried to move again, defeated and famished, his sight left him.

Within the realm of non-sleep in which he found himself, he had a vision, a terrible vision. One of pain, destruction, and death.

Rhin heard a voice scream, "No. Leave me!"

The second voice he heard was sinister and destructive, but the words were unclear. The voice was accompanied by a whirling of shadows. The dark thing advanced toward the cowering figure on the ground.

"No, don't," pleaded the first voice.

"Pitiful. Death is a mercy for your kind," growled the second voice.

Everything was blurred. Rhin heard only the tormented screams of the defenseless person. The cowering lump howled once more as the dark shadow loomed above it. Rhin called out in dismay but awoke moments thereafter, as the vision faded.

And a new sensation of pain washed over him. He was lying down by a great tree. A fire crackled to his right. A figure sat close to the flames humming a soft and sweet tune. Rhin sat up with effort, as stinging pains shot through his ribs.

"So, my friend, you are awake."

"Who are you?" Rhin asked, feeling too vulnerable for comfort.

"No one of consequence."

Rhin examined the figure by the fire. He was carving a small piece of wood with a short blade. Dressed in a blue tunic striped horizontally in a slightly darker shade, he wore a bandana on his head of baby-blue silk. A dot was painted on his forehead to match the color of his hazel green eyes. His ears were long and of a peculiar shape, sort of like pocketknives with arrowheads at the tips.

"I can't feel my legs," said Rhin.

He tried to stand but he stumbled and tripped, ending his weak dance on the dewy grass.

"Rest. You are far too weak to be able to do anything. Right away, that is to say."

"What's wrong with my chest? I don't remember."

"Who's to know? When I found you, you were lying face down in the dirt. Maybe a wild animal is to blame. But I swear to you that I took no part in your wounds," the man put down the figurine he had been whittling to give Rhin a plain look.

"I believe you," said Rhin. And he did.

"Aroukana is my name. I am a Vevlea and, may I add, proud to be one."

"I thought the Vevleï people were make-believe… a bedtime story," Rhin said.

"I know that is what you think. That is also what Jiaïro would have you believe, but we Vevleï are far from 'make-believe'," Aroukana explained. "Jiaïro slaughtered us mercilessly, but we weren't all killed. Nevertheless, our old way of life is gone," he gave a pained sighed. "A long time ago, Jiaïro's men attacked our cities and *thousands* of us were slain in the battles that ensued. You see, we Vevleï do not give up easily. Cryöd, rest the souls of my deceased brothers and sisters... But there are still many of us left. And somewhere out there is the Vevlehen Resistance Army."

"But why did Jiaïro attack you?" Rhin asked.

"We were a kind, generous, prosperous people. Too well off in Jiaïro's eyes, one supposes. But I believe it was because, of all the races in this world, we were the most likely to abolish his atrocious rule. He fought and destroyed us after he was turned away from the Forces of Balance."

"The Forces of Balance," Rhin repeated, his brow furrowed. "I've heard mentioning of the *Sacred* Balance once before. Are they the same thing?"

"You will come to know of them in time Rhin. Even if I were able to aptly explain, I fear it is not my place to tell you."

"How did you know my name?" Rhin looked at him suspiciously, inching away from the strange man.

"Ah, there are many ways of acquiring that sort of knowledge."

Rhin made up his mind to stay. He felt no hostility emanating from this Aroukana person. He kept his guard up for a time, to be safe.

Though Aroukana did not reveal any hints as to how he came by Rhin's identity, he seemed all too eager to give a detailed summary of his own kin's history:

"The inhabitants of Baraïk are far more advanced than those of Iora, being an older civilization. Their planet is an intellectually driven, mechanically refined world with many massive cities on its surface and ore mines in the lower chasms. The population takes to the mines for wealth and respite, for the surface world is torn and ravaged by ages of war. Much of Baraïk remains unknown to us.

"As the story goes, a strange form of life was brought to Iora the very hour it was created, by the Baraïkian spacecraft. As a gift, or tribute, it was claimed. They evolved over many generations, until they eventually became known as the Vevlehen race.

"Understandably, many Iorians do not believe in space travel. I haven't seen this technology for myself, so I would not know.

"Of the beginnings of the Vevleï much remains a mystery, even to us. Even our records cannot discern fact from fiction concerning our origin, as our race is one of the eldest in existence."

By the time Aroukana's long-winded, elaborate account was over with, Rhin was yawning. The Vevlea laughed and wished him goodnight, telling him it was wise to get as much sleep as possible.

Rhin drifted off under the warm, woolen blankets.

Chapter 5
An Unsurpassable Power

Aroukana and Rhin cut across the bleak country. It was strange how they came to like each other in a profound way over so brief a time.

Aroukana was tall and his face hard. He had few lines in his skin to show he was aged but his glittering eyes revealed wisdom only obtainable through centuries of living. His pronounced cheekbones and pointed chin made him a handsome man.

Though he had lived a great many years he was still in awesome physical condition. In fact, it seemed as though he had more stamina than Rhin. When they had passed through the hills and grasslands Rhin had been exhausted, but the Vevlea did not even break a sweat.

"How do you do it?" said Rhin, wheezing as he spoke.

The two were on a rounded, sheltered hilltop with a few large pine trees creating a wooden barricade from the rest of the world.

Aroukana stood atop a rock, his back to Rhin, looking out through the trees into the fields beyond.

Twirling a twig around in his hand in an absentminded way, he said, "Do what?"

"Just how old are you?" Rhin walked up to the rock.

Aroukana grinned, pointed the stick he was holding at the fields and, waving it about slowly, said, "As old as these fields, older than these trees. I have lived to see the fall of peace and the rise of chaos. I have seen hope and death and fear. I have seen much," his voice trailed off and Rhin saw the elder's eyes soften somewhat.

The winds whispered, as they did most often in these parts, in subtlety. Here the wind did not howl. There were no fierce tempests or gales. Here the wind was calm and wary. Perhaps this land had already seen horrors and grand deeds. Perhaps the wind did not howl because it grew weary of the noise it made. Perhaps it did not want to stir the dead.

Aroukana looked back over his shoulder at Rhin and stated, "A battle took place here, ages past."

Though the fields of the North had been the arena for the clashes of civilizations for thousands of years, one could count on the weather to remain unchanged with its gray skies and cold rain. Yet, sometimes, on the rarest of days, you could see the sun struggling through the overcast skies.

"I don't like this place," said Rhin, scratching his head.

The Vevlea nodded. He did not ask why.

"It is a dry land, though it may rain a lot," Aroukana said. Upon seeing Rhin's puzzled expression he added, "Dry in the sense that its vitality has been breathed out as an old candle's flame, having struck its final spark."

The cold rain slowed their progress but did not dampen their resolve. Aroukana noticed smoke columns rising in the distance. A glade of trees postponed any attempts to discover the cause. Rhin and Aroukana approached with caution, keeping as low as they could, and stayed well within the darkness of the trees. They discovered that the smoke had been rising from a bonfire, a dark shape resting in the bed of flames. It appeared to be a funeral.

The banners that courted the breeze were familiar to Rhin. It did not take him long to recall where he had seen those flags before.

The temple in Kremmä, he thought and cringed. *This is Joabom's funeral.*

A crowd of soldiers had assembled. Two hundred or so in total, Rhin deemed. These were the remains of Joabom's Legion, the warriors who had fought, in his name, for the glory of their God.

These men had gathered to honor their deceased leader. His ashes would become one with the earth once more and his spirit, no longer tethered to the flesh, would depart for a rewarding afterlife.

A strange fright clouded Rhin's mind. This land was critical to him in a way he could not place.

A pale white mist rose from the soil, causing the earth beneath their soles to appear gray as ash. When Rhin voiced this complaint to Aroukana, the Vevlea whispered, "It is no wicked illusion. The grass in this land was cast alight many moons ago as a sign, a prelude, to Jiaïro's war. And at this very instant, he prepares for his finishing blow... one that will secure his throne and stamp out any hopes of freedom for this world."

A chapel lay behind the army and flags of red and black cloth were erected all around the stone building.

A testament to the glory of Jiaïro, Rhin scoffed.

The world was dead around him. The air was insubstantial and though he tried his best to breathe he could not. He felt that something was about to happen, and he knew he would not be prepared for whatever it was.

From afar, shrouded in the shadows of the oaks and pines, Rhin and Aroukana could hear the minister eulogize.

The minister, or whoever, spoke in a calm, rehearsed voice, "Men, we are gathered here to bid farewell to our master and friend Joabom. He was a righteous and powerful leader. We shall all mourn the loss forever. Yet, despair not, my brothers, for a servant to the great God will be rewarded from above. His domain in the other world will cover leagues and leagues of fine earth and his harvests will be ever bountiful."

Rhin blocked out the rest of the service.

So that's what a servant of Jiaïro gets for his slavery? Eternal glory in the after life. Disgusting, he thought. Then he wondered aloud, "Daish-rog... What happened to Daish-rog?"

Aroukana was silent. He cast a wretched glare at the soldiers from the safety of the trees.

"So many enemies," he said.

A pair of soldiers broke off from the rear of the gathering, joking and snorting in laughter. They sat down barely four feet from Aroukana and Rhin. The Vevlea remained inanimate, though Rhin could sense his tension.

Rhin stifled a gasp, as they stunk of foul ale and moldy cheese.

"How many arrows can a drunk Vevlea loose a minute?" said the first soldier, as he stumbled a bit.

"Tell," replied the second.

"None, 'cause he would've died drinking!"

The listener crowed, bending over to slap his knee.

From the corner of his eye, Rhin spotted Aroukana's fingertips brushing against the hilt of his dagger. Rhin touched his companion's shoulder and, when he had the Vevlea's attention, shook his head.

"That Joabom hadn't never done nothin' for me," said the first soldier.

"Aye. That there," the second soldier pointed toward the minister, "it's a waste of my time."

"Too true. Jiaïro is the only one worth salutin'," replied the first, and gave a salute to the heavens to demonstrate.

Rhin scowled at this. *Jiaïro is being worshipped by his men? Now that is a waste of time.*

"How 'bout getting ourselves a pint later? What say you?"

"Sure thing. At any rate, after this damned show is over."

"Hey what're you two doin' there?" a Decuri shouted at them. "Too good to honor yer commanding officer's departure? Ye'll be moppin' the chapel floors for six months, uou lazy slackers!"

"Now wait just a minute, sir," said the first soldier, audibly tipsy. "What can you say? You haven't ever done a good day's work yer whole life."

"At least we didn't get a nice safe desk job by means of our father's bribery, now did we?" said the second.

"Why you little…"

The Decuri pounced on the soldier and the struggle led them right into Rhin and Aroukana's hiding spot.

"Hey, who the hell are you?" the inebriated soldier barked.

"That hair… Make no mistake, it's Rhin!" the Decuri screamed.

"Come on, men! Jiaïro will be pleased with the death of this scoundrel."

"Sublime timing, as always," said Aroukana. He then planted his dagger into the drunken soldier's eye.

The units of the late Joabom's legion rushed at them at full speed to avenge their fallen marshal, pushing and shoving one another out of the way, fighting over who got to make the promotion-worthy kill. Rhin waved his sword in front of him for protection, threatening any foe who dared approach. These few frantic moments were punctuated, of course, by the piercing screams of the blinded warrior.

The dispute came to an abrupt end when head-splitting, mechanical clanking noises were heard. The earth itself seemed to growl at them. The forceful quaking knocked most of the soldiers off their feet. Then, out of nowhere, a pack of massive steel monsters appeared.

The shocking creatures stood on two legs, but in place of arms were huge cannons thrice the size of a man. Fumes of black and blue steam spouted from triangular joints. In place of heads they had circular glass compartments, with little men inside.

The minister screeched like a bleeding hog, while some soldiers murmured, "Monolï."

Rhin looked to Aroukana. The Vevlea choked on the words even as he said them, "War machines from another world."

When Aroukana had told him of Baraïkian spacecraft and the like Rhin had been skeptical, but in light of the present circumstances...

A creature inside one of the machines proclaimed, "I speak for Uli Ariaö Jasé, captain of the ancient army."

The voice had sounded scrambled and patchy. The fear these 'machines' instilled in the hearts of the warriors beneath them was palpable.

"And who are you?" asked one of the troopers.

"I am Rofa Chirmo," said the creature.

Blue skin, thought Rhin, *they all have blue skin, white beards, and black beady eyes. Where did these things come from?*

"Who gives you the right to barge in and interrupt us?" said another.

"Hold your tongue, private, lest you lose it," the commanding officer snapped.

"I am a general from Baraïk, I have my rights," the creature bellowed, enraged at the disruption.

The mourning army, in its entirety, bowed. The troops buried their foreheads in the dirt.

"Forgive us, my lord. We humbly beg for your mercy. Is there anything you wish of us? We are yours to command."

"Yes, there is something I require from you all," the Baraïkian laughed.

"What are the orders from Baraïk?" the officer asked.

"Your immediate and unconditional death. Kill them," Rofa Chirmo commanded with a sickening grin.

The battle began. On one side were the machine-mounted ancients and on the other the frantic and desperate soldiers of Jiaïro. The organized Monolï warriors fired in unison at the massed groups of Jiaïro's troopers. Fires spread, covering the fields and forests. Dismay and chaos bathed the soil in blood.

Aroukana grabbed Rhin by his cloak and threw him into the woods.

He shouted, "Out the other side of the trees! It's the only way."

As they cut through the woods an explosion burst not ten feet away from them. A trail of blue flames licked the low branches and soon the entire patch of oak and pine burned like kindling. Rhin and Aroukana went on, using their cloaks as shields against the fires.

"I see an opening! Hurry," the Vevlea told him.

Rhin saw it too. For a few heartbeats he thought it was over.

"Any second now, the flame will take us," he yelled, choking on smoke and fear.

But just as he was making peace with death, he and Aroukana emerged in the open. Clear air filled their lungs. Aroukana tore off his cloak and stamped out the few remaining vines of flame.

Rhin took note that they stood upon a hill, overlooking a vast, dried out lake bed. Squinting, he saw that at the bottom was a single grave.

"Where are-"

Before he could finish his query, however, the screams filled his head again. Rhin's eyes darted from side to side. Soldiers fled in all directions, the Monolï close at hand.

"We aren't safe yet. We must run, or die," said Aroukana, searching for a place where they could hide or an escape of any kind.

Rhin opened his mouth to speak, but only a drop of blood came out. He shut his eyes and dropped to his knees, a great pain welling in his chest. He lay there, on the ground, twitching, when a pair of hands grabbed his shoulders and shook him. He could feel hot froth pouring from his throat.

"Rhin awaken," a clear voice sounded in the deep emptiness of that forsaken land.

It could have been Aroukana who had spoken, but Rhin wasn't so sure. It felt like he had received a blow to the heart.

When he opened his eyes and felt he could talk, he said, "It's all so very wrong."

He stood and a weight seemed to drop onto his shoulders, pinning him in place.

He fell back down and retched. His entire body, every muscle, ached with a tremendous burning. Growling in agony, his legs and arms expanded to twice their original size. His hair became as white and bright as the lightning that strikes the earth, and his eyes burned as the blue fires had burned him earlier.

After he had arisen he reached a hand to his forehead. His fingers stroked a newly spawned gem, cold to the touch. There he stood, seven feet tall.

Even his memories changed. He suddenly knew he had lived for thousands of years. He knew it as well as he knew his own name. The sensation even went as far as making him feel that he had lived since the beginning of time itself. Then, in all his glory, he remembered his duty.

"Ryul, recall your servants," Rhin shouted, the echoes carried into the lake bed beyond.

And, as if on cue, all the plains around him quaked in cataclysm.

Aroukana was aghast but managed to ask, "Who are you addressing, Rhin?"

Rhin silenced him with a wave of his hand and suddenly time stood still, caught in place like a fly in the web of his will. All the soldiers and Monolï faded. The sky darkened dramatically as all matter, with the exception of the earth and sky, faded away, too. All that remained material were the silent figures of Rhin and Aroukana.

But, then there was a third figure.

"Rhin, it has been a long time since I heard from you," Ryul said as he stood on the adjacent hilltop, a cloak wrapped tightly about his thin body.

"What are your lackeys, the Baraïkians, doing here?" Rhin continued in the same passionate, echoing tone.

"I see you have regained your memory. It is only temporary," Ryul said, arms crossed as if he were in complete control of the situation, yet Rhin could sense the twinge of fear that rattled his mind.

All that was visible from the confines of his cloak was his straight, blood-red hair and his glowing, dark eyes. His stance was straight like a tower, highlighted by the blackening sky.

"I knew of your plot. That is why you orchestrated my death," Rhin pointed at Ryul in accusation. Then he chuckled, "Or did you plead for help? I may be overestimating your influence. After all, though you claim to have control over most of Jiaïro's legions, you seem to have little strength in the real world."

"I don't have the slightest care concerning what you think," Ryul riposted, a slight quiver to his voice.

"You lying rat! I should have destroyed you at the battle of Jurya. The war we fought so long ago, right here. It seems you have broken the Law—the Sacred Law—and you have corrupted the Balance of the world in the process,"

"You should have killed me, Rhin. But you lacked either the chance or the skill necessary. My mercenaries await eagerly for the command I am to give them," Ryul regained his confidence. "That command will spell your demise."

"Send me your finest mercenary, or twenty, and we can do our little dance… it makes no difference to me," Rhin said with his right hand raised. He then turned it into a tight fist, as if crushing a bug.

Rhin's words attacked Ryul's mind as spears would pierce a wild boar.

"Singrot, Ero, Résaan... Kill him! And when this deed is done, bring his blasphemous tongue on a silver platter," Ryul spat with hatred.

"Three?" Rhin mocked, drawing his sword.

Suddenly, Rhin had angel wings. They had not sprouted, or grown, they were just there. None of those present, not even Rhin himself, could have told you how this was possible.

Feeling invincible, faster and stronger than he had ever been, he was able to defeat Ryul's minions with ease. Résaan ran up to Rhin and struck at him with all his strength, but Rhin dodged and answered with an uppercut to the jaw, rendering the fiend helpless. Ero attacked swiftly from behind, but received a brutal blow in the stomach, as Rhin spun around and sliced downwards. Singrot attempted to run from this demi-God having witnessed his strength. Rhin simply gave chase and grabbed the demon's neck, tossing him across the field. His enemies were forced to crawl back to their master—defeated. Rhin bore no marks, no cleaved wounds, nothing.

"I see the ages have weakened your men, Ryul. A pity I cannot kill you instead," Rhin gave a fake sigh of resignation.

"And why is that? Am I too threatening to you?" Ryul stretched his arms wide, taking Rhin's mockery for true reluctance.

"No. It is because you will most likely flee before I get halfway up that mound you're standing on. It's what you usually do."

Ryul growled, "This is not over, Rhin. Don't you even dare think that this is over! Whatever you may be concocting in your puny mind, you cannot stop the inevitable."

And he was gone.

Rhin's wings disappeared in a flurry of white feathers and he returned to his normal size. Then he sat down with his eyes closed, exhausted.

And Aroukana was just kneeling where he had been during the entire skirmish. Only once before, in his centuries of existence, had he seen such power and mastery of the sword.

But that was long ago. The Vevlea looked around.

The world as they knew it returned and the corpses of Jiaïro's men littered the ground.

Rhin raised himself up and stared at the heaps of bodies. The legion had been massacred. But there was one perturbing question that outshone all other details in Rhin's thoughts: Why did these beings destroy their own servants? Internal strife? No answer that Rhin could think up pleased him.

I am beginning to hate this God as much as Aroukana hates him, Rhin told himself as he wiped the thick, gelatinous globs of blood from his sword.

Daish-rog was in a forest—cold, hungry and lost. No light graced his path. More than once he had noticed widespread spider webs, trailing from branch to branch, spanning more than a few trees. He took extreme care to make wide loops around these ghastly impediments, and he preferred not to imagine the size of the spiders that spun those abominations.

Daish-rog rubbed his shriveled belly, longing for a warm bowl of fish.

All he could think was, *The last warm meal I partook of... has it already been four days? Here I starve in this forsaken, festering brush and where is Rhin? What ran through his foolish head to make him act so brash?*

Of this he wondered as he fought through his private purgatory. He knew, though, that he had to find Rhin. There was some part of the boy that betrayed a supreme importance.

The world needed him. Daish-rog had come to understand this days ago. He could not see the sky for hours at a time, as he delved into the woods. A faint aroma of raw meat filled his nostrils, reminding him of his hunger and driving him mad. It was impossible to judge from whence this tantalizing scent came, but he was soon disappointed when he no longer smelled it.

Another hour passed and he crossed a sign that hung from chains off a branch. The wood was soggy and draped with veins of mold but the writing was legible enough. It read:

"Gogsïg route nine-twenty."

Daish-rog wanted to scream, "What sort of help does that offer a traveler," but his throat was parched and cracked. He had a slight idea which stretch of forest he found himself in, but knew not his exact location and the signs were of no use. Events were not transpiring the way he hoped.

He had lost the map and compass to a vicious creature upon entering the forest. It had growled at him and foam flowed from its throat. It seemed to be a cross between a horse and a reptile, with brown scales and a bushy, coarse gold mane. It was tenacious, and when the chase was over it had Daish-rog cornered. His back to a tree with no escape visible, he knew his doom had come. But before the bells of inevitability could toll, an even larger animal of the same species crashed through the tangled growth into the aggressor and tore it to shreds. Daish-rog's brain needed not send the command before his legs took him as far away from the morbid scene as they could.

As he ran he could see clustered hovels of eggs, steaming in the humidity. The eggs were the size of his fist and gave off the foulest smell, as if a dog had been gutted nearby.

A *breeding ground*, Daish-rog thought as he swallowed bile that had gushed forth during his narrow escape, small wonder the animals acted that way.

Minutes of sprinting later, he beheld the large tear his food sack now sported and was thankful it had been the tattered leather and not his own skin. He dared not return to retrieve his belongings out of fear of the horrible beasts that roosted there.

He reached another sign. This one had written upon it:

"Ye be warned."

"That could've been helpful a half hour ago, or three days ago. What unmentionable terrors wait beyond that they should merit a warning while the others did not?" he rasped in the dim light.

He heard a lot of high-pitched squeaky voices cackling nearby.

Mischievous laughter filled his ears.

"Who is there?" Daish-rog groaned, straining his voice. "Could somebody help me? I have no food."

From the surrounding saplings sprung four tiny children. Their blue hair resembled strands from a weeping willow and framed their cute green faces. The children were garbed in beautiful white tunics with golden medallions hanging from their twiggy wrists.

"Well, well, well. Seems we have a visitor, Agail," squeaked one.

"Seems you are right, oh Aseil, my brother…" another replied in a sing-song way.

"Should we help it?" yet another said.

"Or should we eat it?" said the smallest one, hopping into a perfect handstand.

With those words, fear struck Daish-rog like a lead weight being dropped on his foot.

They are not children, he thought, frozen in place.

He knew now that they were Forest Wisps: beings about half the size of the average man, their diminutive stature masking their carnivorous nature.

"Catch him, Catch him. He will make a fine meal," the Wisps hollered.

Before Daish-rog could react he was already beaten into submission and fastened to a log. The wisps carried him away to the Camps. Horrible things happened to prisoners in the Camps. The Wisps did not devour their guests straight away.

Daish-rog lost count of the hours and days that rolled by during his captivity. Every once and a while a young group of wisps came to tease him and gnaw at his fingers and toes. He would have liked to kick them in their deceptive, cruel faces but he was bound tight to a jagged tree. What family the tree belonged to he didn't know, and didn't care, but the bark rubbed his back raw.

Daish-rog did not sleep for the pain he experienced was intense. On the first day he had dozed off. The rude awakening by one of his hosts was reminder enough not to try again. He could still feel the throbbing on his forehead where the branch had whipped him.

All he could see around him were the fleeting forms of the jade-skinned wisps and the delighted glances they shot his way as they passed him by.

Not much longer, he promised himself. Soon they will kill you. How much more pleasure can they derive from this torment?

Another day, as he slumped in silent resignation, praying for death, he was paid an unexpected visit.

"It's time you met the queen," the Wisp named Aseil said, poking him over and over in the ribs.

At last Daish-rog understood why the Wisps had kept him alive. The time had come for the Wispian Feast. All the twisted fairytales he had heard as a child rang true in his mind.

Never would he have thought to be caught in a fairytale, but he recalled his old grandmother's story of the Wisp custom of royal dinner.

There were other Wisps standing around his tree then, pointing and whispering to one another.

"Wispian Feast," he murmured.

"My, you are a clever one. It'll almost be a shame when we roast you alive," Aseil giggled with the others at the joke.

Grandmother had said, 'Once a year the Wisps would dine on the flesh of giants, a much anticipated delicacy.'

"Very well, just hurry and be done with it," Daish-rog gave the little Wisp a dark stare.

"Now, now," Aseil chided, "let's not be so hasty. You may not die... today."

Four Wisps were required to carry Daish-rog from his post to the palace. They took no care in transporting him, and he bounced roughly about for it. Once in motion, they blindfolded him.

An unnecessary precaution, he contemplated, *what's the point in blinding me?*

They arrived and Daish-rog heard the soft creaking of door and floorboards. He could hear the buzzing of hushed voices and the chink of Wisp swords.

Then the Wisps that held him came to a sudden halt and dropped him on the floor. On instinct he flattened his back. This way, most of the impact was spread, but still it hurt like nothing else. He groaned. A warm hand touched his nose and then lifted the blindfold from his eyes.

Chapter 6
Trials

*D*aish-rog found himself at the center of a large room. On the highest chair sat a small female wisp with a crown of berries on her head, the color of fresh blood. Daish-rog needed no introduction. This slender Wisp was the queen.

The sizable court of the Wisps lay at the heart of their domain, within the darkest reaches of the forest. Built right into the ground, it was made of gorn wood, as was everything else in their kingdom, for it was their chief resource. Wreaths of fresh berries decorated the walls and moss covered with leaves served as cushions for the attendants and guests of the court. With such jovial surroundings and amiable appearances Daish-rog found it hard to understand how the Wisps could be so malevolent at heart.

The Wispian Royal Guards had already escorted the queen to her dais, the seat from which she would spell Daish-rog's demise.

Gracefully positioned on her luxurious throne, she spoke, "You are guilty of trespassing in our forest. How do you plead?"

Queen Ameila made no attempts to hide her ravenous hunger.

"All I am guilty of is trying to find my friend," said Daish-rog, knowing full well that he would need nothing less than divine intervention to escape this mess.

"May the record show that the defendant is lying," said the queen.

"I speak the truth. I lost my friend several weeks before and now I am lost as well," said Daish-rog, pointing an angry finger.

"Lies, lies, nothing but lies," said the queen. Then she turned and told Daish-rog in a very matter of fact tone, "Look, we want to have our Feast. It's nothing personal, dear, but we need to get this trial over with as quickly as possible. And it needs to look official, you know."

"Doesn't seem to be a fair and just judicial system then, O honorable queen," Daish-rog snapped.

After that he was silent. He knew he was on enemy grounds, for in the past Daish-rog's people had had wars with their enemies and the Wispian Forest was their arena. This greatly upset the Wisps, for the battles had destroyed their homes and killed many of their relatives and friends caught in the crossfire. Thus, if Daish-rog revealed his identity, he would surely be slaughtered even though he did not compete in the battles. Old grudges are not easily forgotten.

"What is this? Your tongue stays fast. Finish pleading—finish!" the queen commanded.

Her glance pierced him and for half an hour she was relentless in her questioning. In turn, he never answered more than he needed. This angered all the Wisps present. There were impatient protests from many of the spectators. As they were about to cut the trial short due to plain irritation, a great growl broke out, like a gong being struck, deep in the woods.

"Groägs!* The Groägs are coming," yelled one of the guards, covered in blood. "The rest of my squad—they're all dead. I'm all that's left from the North Gate!"

"Impossible. We sealed it with a fierce magic," exclaimed the queen, fear in her eyes.

"They have a mage with them," the guard whimpered.

"No," the queen hissed.

But it was too late.

---

* Iora's historians claimed that Groägs were helpless with magic and little more than ruthless monsters. The Béros, people of the North, were another beast race. But they were kind, generous and a prosperous.

A pack of enormous wolves raced into the courtroom as the Wispian guardians unsheathed their knives. These were no ordinary lupines for they moved on their hind legs as men and fought with sophisticated three-pronged spears and double-bladed scythes.

No sooner had the conflict begun, than Daish-rog had leapt off and made for the door. Adrenaline fueled him during his desperate dash, as the Wisps were hacked to gory bits. Some of the wolf-men carried torches instead of spears, all the better to sear the flesh of their prey.

Daish-rog crouched as a throwing-scythe whistled overhead. At last, he was out the double doors of the palace and in the open.

Concealing himself in the nearby shrubs he recalled an incident in his youth when he had come face to face with one of these vile, wolf-like creatures. The Groägs were cruel, cunning and violent. It had only been through luck that he had managed to slay the beast. Now, decades later, he was not so confident.

A horn sounded in the night. The skirmish was short and one-sided. It did not take long before the Wispian warriors were either dead or bound in chains. Those that lived wept for their fellows, drenched in the blood of the dead.

The entire hall was steeped in blood. Bodies were heaped near the dais.

"Why do you do this, Groägs?" the queen cowered in her dread.

"Do not think we are fools, Wisp," the chief started to say. "We know very well that the Nature Crystal is in this forest somewhere. We claim its essence for the Lord Jiaïro. Do not oppose us any longer."

"You must be mistaken. The Crystal is nowhere near here," the queen's voice was a shrill quiver.

"A curse on you, Wisp," the Groäg spat in her face, "Where is the Crystal we seek? I advise you not to lie."

"Even if I had the slightest idea of its location, I would not, under any circumstances, tell you," the queen said, throwing herself at the wolf-man in a flurry of limbs.

The broad-shouldered lupine gave the queen a gloved slap, knocking her down.

Then a score of Seekers leapt in from the main entrance of the courtroom and surrounded the Groägs. They surveyed the beast-like warriors, their spear-tips between them and the wolf-men. At the slightest sign of movement on the part of the beasts they would strike, swift and to the point, skewering their necks.

A tall man was framed in the doorway, looming behind one of the dark soldiers. He strode with confidence, weaving between his Seekers, stopping just short of the dais.

"I am Reng, a marshal of Jiaïro. I speak for the Lord."

"Why are your men holding us at spear point?" the Groäg said, worry written all over his face.

"You have done well, Rocaa, Groäg chieftain. But enlighten me, how did you escape the Keep of the Béros?" Reng said, massaging his forehead.

"I am master of escaping, Lord Reng, even be it from the Keep of the Béros. No material lock or bolt can hold me."

"Very well, indeed. In the years we have been friends we have never had troubles, would you not agree?"

"Yes, lord," Rocaa answered, frowning with uncertainty.

"That's what makes what I'm about to do so very difficult," Reng turned his back on Rocaa, smirking. "I am under strict orders from Jiaïro himself. You know I cannot hope to disobey him."

"Of course…"

Reng faced the chieftain once more and stated, "His orders dictate that you and your group are to be terminated immediately."

Rocaa did not answer. Instead he kicked the Seeker behind him in the chest and snatched the shaken warrior's spear.

"Kill them all," Reng waved his hand to indicate the Groäg band.

The Seekers acted on the order. The battle took its course outside the hall, in the shadows of the trees, forcing Daish-rog farther into the shadows. At first he feared the warriors would discover him, but the fight did not last long.

The Groägs put on a great show, leaping from tree to tree, fighting with utter fearlessness and expert agility. Rocaa even killed a Seeker or two. But, outnumbered three to one, soon they were all dead. The trees were splashed with their life's blood. The dripping could still be heard minutes later, as audible as rain.

"Bring me the head of their leader," said Reng.

After a few moments of searching the battlefield, they found the body. One deft slice and the head snapped free with a sickening, wet sound.

"Here it is master," said the Seeker who had recovered the trophy.

All Seekers present grinned maliciously. All this murdering was a treat for them.

"This will make a lovely gift for Lord Jiaïro," Reng said with a chuckle as he walked back into the wooden court.

"What do we do with the Wisps?" asked a soldier, marching beside him.

"Wait until dawn, then bring them out into the open and kill them. I heard once that Wisps do not do well when exposed to direct sunlight," Reng said, giving the queen a little wave.

Daish-rog had stayed crouched, stalk-still, behind a patch of growth. He had heard what had happened and had even seen parts of the battle. He felt sympathy for the Wisps, despite their recent plans for him.

He knew he had to do something.

"Daish-rog," a voice plunged into the depths of his mind. "Help the Wisps. They are not wicked. They act in accordance with their nature. You must save them. You are sitting at the roots, Daish-rog, of a tree that bears golden apples. It is the key to finding the Shrine of Nature where the Nature Crystal resides, the source of living things in the Four Isles. Find the large knot on the tree. Hurry!"

Daish-rog found a knob on the tree and stared at it, puzzled for a moment. He tried pulling and then pushing. Then he attempted to turn it—this did the trick—and slid into a hole that opened up in the ground. The next thing he knew, he was at the entrance of the Temple and the voice was instructing him once again to make haste.

The structure had much in common with a greenhouse. It was made entirely of glass and white marble and had vines spiraling up the pillars. The architecture was ancient and different than any he had ever seen. How this place had survived the ages and remained undiscovered Daish-rog would never know.

Upon entering he heard the bodiless voice again, "Welcome Daish-rog, Son of Nature, holy protector of Iora's flora and fauna."

"Who are you?"

"I am none other than the voice of Nature itself."

After Daish-rog had surveyed his surroundings, he asked, "Why did you call me 'Son of Nature'?"

"I would gladly explain it to you but we are short on time. The Seekers are coming. I shall return your age old powers to you," the voice said. Then in a ceremonious tone, "By the power of Tora, Bull of the Great Fields, by the power of Planïk, Mighty Tree of the Northern Forest, by the power of Aqa, the Silver River, I return the strength of Daish-rog, Lord of Nature," and as it sang the last three words, lightning flashed, the voice echoed throughout the Temple and the Seekers destroyed the door and entered the Shrine. Daish-rog's body brimmed with energy.

"Demons of the dark, seekers of blood, leave this sacred place or suffer the vengeance of the forces of Nature," Daish-rog thundered.

"Hah. Who is this man who speaks as if the world is his own?" asked the captain of the Seekers.

"I am Daish-rog, son of Chor and the Lord of Nature."

"We challenge you, oh mighty sovereign," bellowed the captain, raising his spear.

Then vines started to grow all throughout the temple and bright, yellow flowers burst into bloom upon them, revealing a white rod in each.

"Pretty little flowers are supposed to frighten us?"

The Seekers burst into tears of laughter. But one should never judge appearances for just then, the flowers shot out their poisonous darts and brought unto Jiaïro's minions instantaneous death.

Pretty flowers that contain a high amount of poisonous pollen, Daish-rog thought. *Now onward to save the Wisps!*

Because of his new inner enlightenment, Daish-rog transformed into a gray wolf and sped across the forest headed for the Camps, with only two hours left before sunrise. The golden apple tree had dropped him down a chute to the opposite side of the forest, thus he could not return that way. He would have to go on foot. He quickened his pace.

Upon his arrival, he returned to his natural form with only moments to spare.

He noticed the leader of the battalion, Reng, who was yet another of Jiaïro's marshals and darted toward him, but several Seekers shot in front of him, blocking his target from view. Then, after being ordered to do so, they stepped aside so that Reng was completely visible. He stood, unemotional and unafraid, before Daish-rog.

"I command you to release them, monster-"

Reng cut him off, "What will you do to stop me? Make little flowers grow as you did with my men?" his laughter a testament to his power. Then he stopped and his eyes darkened. "Yes, fool, of course I knew you were the chosen one, the Lord of Nature. We came here searching for the Crystal in order to stop you from gaining power."

"You hog faced jackal," Daish-rog spat.

It's my fault all these lives were lost, Daish-rog realized.

"Kill him," Reng ordered.

Daish-rog saw his chance and started speaking a language that the blood-lusting fiends could not understand. Confusion spread among the ranks.

At first there came a harsh squawk, but then louder fowl responded. The deadly song of these birds resounded through the forest and into the morning air. The ash trees filled with large brown hawks.

The birds answered Daish-rog's distress call by attacking the Seekers. A flurry of talons and pecking showered down upon all.

"What sorcery is this?" screamed Reng, ducking to dodge several swooping woodland eagles.

"Not sorcery. The birds have a score to settle with your men. For centuries you have burnt down their homes, all in the name of Jiaïro and his abhorrence of trees."

But the struggle was not won. A ball of fire illuminated the sky as it blasted upwards and the birds sped away, fleeing from the lick of the flames.

A transformation was taking place. The century old Reng was abandoning his body to make way for a new one. His vile, putrid form exploded as two muscular arms burst from his back. They clawed and pushed their way out of Reng's broken shell and at the end of those long, groping arms was a hideous body covered in slime. If Daish-rog had not been furious he would have cowered at the sight of this demon.

A head looked up at the newly fledged Lord of Nature, its red eyes darting about. Brownish sludge dripped down its face. The monstrous leviathan arose, tearing out from Reng's battered, ripped flesh. It grabbed a tree, yanking it by the roots and snapping it in half as if it were a twig. He then shot a wall of flame into the sky, sending the remaining birds cowering for safety.

"Rixaï," the queen of the Wisps screeched, hurling a jagged rock at the demon.

"You," Daish-rog screamed, sweat streaming down his nose.

He remembered Rixaï and all he had done. He recalled the horrible memories of when he was a boy, some forty years ago. He began to weep and moan uncontrollably. He fell to his knees and stared at the beast before him.

"Yes it is I, Rixaï. The 'Destroyer of Wisps', 'Eater of Vevleï'. I seem to have crushed another one of your precious trees. What are you going to do now, little Daish-rog, send more flying rats to do the work for you?" he said in a deep, dark voice.

Every creature present could hear his breathing. The terrible, resonant panting.

"May hell take you when I am through," Daish-rog screamed.

He spoke in the same tongue that Rhin had used. It was the ancient, forgotten tongue of the Gods. The Eldest Speech.

"You are that confident? I wonder why. Do you not remember how I butchered your whole family?"

Upon beholding Daish-rog's torn face, split between fury and heartbreak, Rixaï roared in sinister laughter.

Daish-rog charged at the monster leaving his heart behind. Pure, unfiltered hatred took control of him. A black energy surrounded him. He screamed his foulest curse as he hurled himself into the giant of darkness.

"Is Nature boy going to cry?"

Daish-rog's blade struck Rixaï. The demon absorbed no damage.

"Fool. You are consumed by the power of hatred, which happens to be the very element that birthed me. Strike me now and you will only give me strength." Rixaï laughed again, making his red eyes bulge. "I grow weary of this. Men, I require your powers."

He then killed his men with one swift spell and absorbed their vital energy. The wails of the Seekers echoed their pain and sense of betrayal.

This act had given him the power to summon a unique weapon.

"Let the Sword of Darkness come to my aid."

The sword was said to have belonged to the great general of the legions of Rayïm when he led his forces to do battle with the Gods of Light and could only be called by a being of true demonic origin.

Rixaï took the Sword of Darkness, which had appeared in a burst of black lightening, and cut right through Daish-rog's sword. The steel spun in mid air and, when it touched the dirt, dissolved. The dark blade gave off an intense aura.

In the next instance, he stabbed Daish-rog straight through the heart. Daish-rog gasped as blood trickled from his eyes and mouth. He fell to his knees. And there was silence. He slumped onto his back, his fingers twitching.

Daish-rog's body disintegrated. He was dead, and all that survived of his corpse was an energy crystal.

When a being was destroyed, his or her energy crystal was left behind. It was also known as an Orb which the enemy could drain, claiming the powers dormant within.

"Thank you, Nature brat. I think I will add your strength to my own," said Rixaï, satisfied with the day's work.

Yet, as he reached down, Rhin appeared, hurled himself between Rixaï and Daish-rog's Orb and dug a small knife into Rixaï's pulse. Thick droplets of blood surged upward, keeping time with the beat of his foul heart. Rhin then spun round and away from Rixaï.

"Leave the Wisps alone or suffer another wound. And next time it will be fatal," Rhin said, enraged.

Rixaï applied pressure to his wound and telekinetically stopped the blood flow. He vaulted at Rhin but was blocked by an invisible barrier.

Rixaï howled, "You interfering rat. I want his powers. Give them to me! If you do my bidding perhaps I will let you live."

"Tell me, demon, was it Jiaïro who sent you?" said Rhin, trying to keep a level tone.

"It was the arch-devil who sent the puppet I inhabit. I am my own master, runtling!" Rixaï growled.

Rhin then made for the sunny fields with Daish-rog's Orb clasped firmly in his hand, Rixaï's howling still audible as Rhin put more and more distance between them.

"We will meet again, mongrel. Mark my words, this is not the end," Rixaï spoke, infuriated.

A few days later, Rhin and Aroukana were sitting around a campfire pondering what to do next. The twilight spilled through into the glade, the nippy wind promising a cold night.

"We have to do something about Daish-rog. There must be a way to bring him back." Rhin held out his hand, the Orb rolling in his palm.

"I have been wondering… how did you know where to find him in the first place?" Aroukana asked.

"You could call it a sixth sense, I guess. It's been happening more often lately."

Rhin looked at the energy crystal. It shone with a hazy, green light, a gem glinting inside of it in a brighter shade. He fingered it, his eyes got ensnared in the depths of its richness. Aroukana saw its reflection in his companion's eyes.

"Rhin?"

Rhin freed himself from its snare with difficulty. He decided it was best to not touch or behold the Orb again, not before he knew how to deal with it. He stowed the energy crystal away in his trusty sack that he had carried with him since he departed from the desecrated village he had once called home.

Aroukana's thoughts then drifted to a terrible vision. Agony and pain washed upon him like a wave crashing on a rock at sea. Thousands of citizens were being slaughtered, dozens at a time, at the hands of a new foe. Houses burnt, wives lay crying as their husbands were beheaded. Aroukana could not bear it. The Vevlea whipped his head around, facing south, to look at the sky. He stood as if he were paralyzed. Rhin walked up to his side and beheld the same dreadful sight. Columns of smoke were rising into the sky.

"Kremmä lies in that direction," Aroukana stated urgently.

The senses of Vevleï were more attuned than most other beings and they possessed heightened senses. The stories of their race boasted that they were aware of every murder that was committed within a dozen square miles.

"An attack?" Rhin asked.

The Vevlea nodded. The frown on his face made him look a hundred years older.

"We've got to move fast, Aroukana," Rhin shouted.

Rhin grabbed his sack and slung it over his shoulder. Aroukana followed, his own pouch belted around his waist.

And thus they raced several miles, under cover of nightfall, crossing the Great Aqa* until they found Kremmä. The fiery ruins confirmed their fears.

"No, it didn't happen. It's not true," Rhin covered his ears.

A continuous wail of dismay spread across the burning ruin. The streets were filled with heads jabbed on pikes and mangled bodies of all ages and sizes littered the ground. The horrid, skeletal warriors with pale green skin were hacking away at the doors of buildings, seeking any who still lived.

"Lithinians! They burned the city," said Aroukana. He bellowed the foulest curse he knew, "Ariaé nuun!"

Aroukana's cry had been heard, for a few moments later a group of Lithinian swordsmen raced toward the two of them. But before they could reach them, a sea of arrows struck Rhin and Aroukana down.

Rhin awoke in a jail cell lying next to Aroukana. He examined their wounds with care. Rhin had been hit in the leg and Aroukana in the hand, the wounds covered in a craggy crust. Rhin cringed as he stood, the confining walls taunting him. He shook the iron bars.

"Let us out, now," said Rhin.

"Be quiet. Tomorrow is your execution, so enjoy the time that is given to you."

In the corner, caressing his ravaged hand, Aroukana murmured, "Execution."

---

* A giant river that ran through all of Nénamburra.

"This one's a Vevlea, ain't he? And you're his friend, right? Those are crimes to us Lithinians," the jail keeper explained.

"You destroyed a city, that's a crime to me," Rhin spat, rattling the bars in a frenzy.

"You can keep yelling," the jail keeper said, "won't make much of a difference."

Rhin, out of control, continued to shake the bars with all his might. Aroukana sat in silent acceptance. The guard cackled and dozed off.

Chapter 7
A Face from the Past

The Vevlea managed to keep calm and quiet, but Rhin was being driven out of his mind. Both of them had lost track of time as it passed at a snail's pace. They were parched and starving. They had not received one meal from the Lithinians, which made sense since their execution was imminent.

Rhin looked at the Vevlea, his hand resting on his head, his eyes half-closed.

He asked, "Why did they burn it?"

"Kremmä's history is so deeply entwined with that of the Lithinian people that even I know of only half the stories. The Monraïkians would know more."

But before Rhin could ask who these 'Monraïkians' were the cell door opened with the horrible sound of stone scraping over stone.

"It's time," the keeper said, ready for some excitement.

The keeper gave Rhin a severe kick in the back, sending him crashing through several doorways and down a flight of stairs.

"I hope that hurt," the keeper called down to the slumped pile of flesh that was Rhin.

Aroukana ran at the jail keeper but was stopped by a group of spear points.

"Do not try anything foolish," one of the Lithinians grunted.

"The least you lowly scum could do is die with dignity," said another.

"There is no dignity involved when Lith filth is about the place," Aroukana retorted through gritted teeth. This earned him a crack to the jaw.

"Shut it. Take him away."

Their accents were heavy and their voices deep. Their leathery skin was vomit-colored and made Aroukana sick.

Several hundred Lithinians stood in the courtyard, awaiting the execution with eagerness. The favorite saying of these beings was, "Pinch 'em and lynch 'em."

"Farewell, my young friend," Aroukana said, his voice steady and his head held high.

"Death is but a rest after a long journey," Rhin answered in the old Vevlehen language.

Drums rolled, resounding through the stone fortress. Rhin swallowed, picturing his gruesome fate.

"Bring me the torches," a Lithinian dressed all in brown shouted. "Bring the torches."

After a few moments, the commander found the Lithinian, who was supposed to carry down the flames to ignite Rhin and Aroukana, dead. A guard fell from a tower and another followed. With bloodcurdling screams, they crashed through the wooden roof of a small building. Rhin heard loud splattering sounds and detected the heavy scent of smoke. Several Lithinian guards went to investigate. An arrow soared through the skies and hit the jail keeper in the neck.

The Lithinians growled in futile anger.

A repeated crashing, a harsh thumping on the gate, told them a battering ram was set against the stone walls.

The Lithinian warriors formed up with the commander at their head. They made use of their most trusted military tactic, the 'Sweeper'. This was a highly defensive formation where the enemy charged forward and the defense in the first rank unleashed one uppercut per unit. Then the soldiers from the second rank replaced the first. The whole sequence was repeated three times and, when lucky, it caused all hell to break loose, stomping out enemy morale, and ending with the Lithinians abandoning strategy for brute force. A lamely named, yet effective, strategy.

But before they could gather in the proper formation a flurry of arrows came careening down at the dismayed soldiers. The gate of the Lithinian fortress swung open, revealing scores of Monraïkian* warriors through the opening.

"You won't escape us forever, Föga," shouted the captain of the Monraïkians as he decapitated one of the enemies in his path.

An arrow shot by Rhin's face, and his heart lurched.

Two Monraïkian foot soldiers saw the sticky situation Aroukana and Rhin were in and hurried over to free them as the battle raged on. The two companions took shelter in a trench behind a small stone structure.

From the hiding place, Rhin witnessed the atrocities of war once more. A fleeing Lithinian bounded toward the trench and paused in mid stride. With a disoriented gaze at the heavens, the Lithinian slumped, twin plumed shafts buried in his nodular skin.

It seemed for a while as though the Lithinians were winning, for their archers had climbed the towers of the fortress and were loosing fiery arrows at the Monraïkians below. But the leader of the Monraïkian army had commanded his Knife Bearers, the elite stealth units of Monra, up to the towers. The archers fell down from their posts before they could react to the swift, concentrated assault of the Knife Bearers.

The last remaining Lithinians used their grappling hooks to hastily ascend the walls and then descend to the other side and flee across the fields for their lives. The swordsmen cut several of the ropes, dropping many of them to their deaths.

In the end, two dozen of the Evil soldiers had escaped the castle, one of them being the chief, Föga the Vile.

---

* Warriors of justice. They dressed themselves in dyed, violet armor and wore green jewels. Their kingdom was in the southern part of the isle. Its capital was the great city of Monra, where the Counsel of Ten judged the fate of the world and acted when they found it necessary.

"Vara*," the warriors cheered, clapping and tapping their swords onto their shields in rhythm.

A soldier marched over to the trench where Rhin and Aroukana were lying.

"You can come with us now, my friends. The battle is over," the Monraïkian warrior said as he noticed how bony and frail they were. "Do not worry, you will be looked after and fed. There shall be a feast tonight. You will ride with us to our city."

The Monraïkians sang,

"Prevailed we have in battle
Our enemies do fly
Far, far and farther still
All their plans awry

No longer will they torment those
Who cannot stand their ground
Now they know that Monra rides
And when his horn resounds
They'll tremble at the sound

Tonight we'll feast and drink
As we did in olden days
Toasting our Lord Monra
And his upholding of olden ways"

The leader of the Monraïkian army came before Rhin. His voice was muffled, as he spoke with a helmet covering his face, "My salutations, Rhin. How long has it been?"

He then removed the helm.

"Pélénor?" Rhin forgot about his hunger altogether.

Pélénor used to be Rhin's only friend in Lynca village. He left when Rhin was quite young and had never returned. The boy never had known why. But he knew now was not the time to hold a grudge.

---

* The victory cry of the Monraïkian troops.

"Ha, you look great! A little skinny though… no matter, we will give you our special remedy for famine. And there shall be a great feast tonight back home!" Pélénor said with a lighthearted smile.

"Where is home?" Rhin asked.

"Monra, the capital of our country Monasta. Where else?" Pélénor said, a twinkle in his eyes.

Rhin felt a sudden jolt of pain in his legs but hid it well when he said, "You are a Monraïkian now? How did you join?"

"Well, after I left the village I wandered for a while, until I stumbled upon the expanding border of Monasta. A battalion was marching that day and the general took pity on me. He fed and clothed me. In return for his aid he asked only one thing, that I become a Monraïkian soldier. He always said I was a great fighter. Soon I was promoted to the status of sergeant after I—along with my friends and most trusted brothers-in-arms—raided a small Lithinian camp. After a few other successful raids I became a lieutenant. But the vast majority of the credit goes to my men."

A soldier walked up and saluted.

"That's not entirely true, sir, with all due respect. You are the greatest strategist the Kingdom has had for a decade. It's thanks to you that we killed all these fiends. And you forgot to tell him the story of how you became a captain, sir."

"Yes. Thank you, private. After we raided the first major city of the Lithinian Empire, we killed the last of Föga's descendants. This gave me the title 'Captain of the Monraïkian Army'. Today we successfully destroyed their largest fortress in the area. Their so called Empire has been reduced to a small splinter on the map. But there are still many Lithinians left in the world and I won't stop until they're all lying in pieces. The last of the Royal Lithinian Bloodline is none other than Föga himself and he will fall to my blade," Pélénor flicked his blade with his fingers, the twang punctuating his words.

"Cut off the head and the body will die," said Aroukana.

"Right."

After Rhin and Aroukana were given food and water and horses to carry them, they rode for a few hours across a dull, grassy wasteland that had been stripped of its former beauty by the Lithinian Conquering Wars. Pélénor taught them a bit of history along the way.

"It is said that the order of Monraïk was founded centuries ago in response to repeated crimes against the people in this region by a rising power. This power soon grew and became an Empire. The Lithinians ruled through use of fear and pillaged the towns on the outskirts of Kremmä. They were unopposed for several years until a rabble of villagers fought them in an ancient valley. No one recalls exactly where this battle took place, however.

"The townsfolk were unskilled warriors and though they had a lot of heart they were promptly slaughtered. The uproar caused by this massacre spawned a movement of such tremendous determination that the resistance quickly formed its own army. The Monraïkians were born. After the Lithinians had been pushed out of the city they were booted from the outskirts as well. Quickly they lost every camp within a thirty league radius of the city and as soon as a Lithinian crossed the border into Kremmä he was met by a sea of arrows. The government of Kremmä saw the skirmishers as vigilantes, unfortunately. All the followers of Monra were exiled.

"The Monraïkians were sick and tired of the politics and sought to form their own country through strong wills, the clashing of iron, the whisper of arrows and the rage of war. Ever since every man, woman, and strong child in our country has been devoted to the annihilation of Lithinia. That, my friends, is the tale—as I know it—of our people."

Then, they passed the gates of Monra.

The marketplace in town was always busy, day and night, with cheerful people bargaining for hours on end. The common people were well fed and everyone greeted everyone else in the street as they passed by. Tapestries of brightly colored silk, portraying scenes of battles from centuries ago, hung on all of the larger buildings, another custom of Monra.

A Referect, a senate of common people, was formed to serve the citizens and the armies. It ruled the Monraïkian capital. The Council of Ten sat at the top of the Referect. They controlled the military campaigns and trade routes. Even common business, like determining marketing prices, was dealt with by the Referect. Pélénor explained this to Rhin and Aroukana as they walked through the city, having left their horses at the military stables near the outer wall of the town.

The hustle and bustle of people diminished as they neared the heart of the capital where they saw a huge building with purple and green drapes hanging from its sides.

Once inside, Rhin noticed that there were no doors or windows, but only a large wall right in front of them with a green crystal placed exactly at its center.

"What now?" he asked.

"You'll see. Gontoöma," said Pélénor. Then he added to Aroukana, "The name of the first elected ruler of Monasta, our realm."

The wall opened. They entered the new-formed doorway and saw a massive table decked with hundreds of shades of colored cloth with an unbelievable variety of foods so tempting to the eye that Rhin's mouth watered.

When everyone was seated, Pélénor proclaimed, "Begin the festivities. We have beaten the Lithinians back for a time."

"Vara, Pélénor," the assembled guests cheered.

Rhin found himself unable to remember the last time food had tasted that good. There were potatoes with sour cream, pork ribs, apples, grapes, dates, steamed cabbage soaked in sweet sauce, and even olives. Rhin soon became addicted to the olives.

They ate and ate and ate, savoring every mouthful, until questions started to stir in Rhin's mind.

Pélénor took a swig of ale and said, "Tales of your deeds have spread through the world like a plague. A good plague. The Lithinians, who have sided with Jiaïro, are quite cross with you. That is why you were about to be executed. That and the fact that you're traveling with a Vevlea."

Pélénor was an abnormal sort of fellow with a pitch-black scarf around his neck and a turban of the same color on his head. He had brown skin and long, dark brown hair hanging in a ponytail off the back of his neck.

Rhin stared at the turban and said, "What is under there that needs to be hidden?"

Pélénor looked at Rhin with a smile and then unwound the cloth. Rhin could not believe it—he had the Mark of Jiaïro on his forehead. Rhin's throat tightened, the words would not come. He spat out his food and choked.

"Yes?"

"That mark," Rhin said and slammed his hands on the table. "Do you work for him? Answer me, Pélénor."

"Oh, you mean this?" said Pélénor, calm as ever. "I was taken captive in a Lithinian camp once. They branded me with this mark to disgrace me in front of my fellows. Fortunately, it did not give the effect they would have liked. The prison in which you were held was the same one that I had found myself trapped within."

Rhin sat down, "I'm sorry I acted that way, Pélénor. I didn't know."

Pélénor clapped Rhin's shoulder, shaking his head, "You are forgiven."

"How long ago did this incident take place?" asked Aroukana.

"Several months ago. I had been planning the attack that you just happened to witness today ever since I escaped."

Pélénor's eyes trailed over to Aroukana's bags and he said, "My men checked your luggage and nothing appears to have been disturbed. Though, I don't know what you had in there in the first place."

Dread washed over Rhin. In panic he thought, *What if they stole the energy crystal?*

He was relieved when he found Daish-rog's crystal undisturbed.

"This Orb... it belonged to a friend of yours?" Pélénor asked before he bit at a scrap of bread.

"Yes," Rhin said.

"How did he die?" Pélénor asked.

"That is bad news. You know Reng, right?" Rhin asked.

"Yes, he's Jiaïro's marshal."

"Well, turns out his true identity is Rixaï, a ancient demon. This freak murdered my friend, Daish-rog," Rhin answered, sipping from his water goblet.

Pélénor was shocked.

He set down his cup and murmured, "Rixaï, the enigmatic demon that feeds off its host like a parasite. Bad news, true enough. I do not think that Reng is Rixaï though. I think Rixaï had simply been using the marshal as a vessel and has chosen this time to crush his spirit and take full control of the host's body, rather then being a mere symbiote."

"That would have been my assumption," Aroukana acknowledged. "I could sense great distress from Daish-rog as he was dying. I felt immense suffering inside his soul. The demon had wronged him many years ago. Vengeance was his primary motive, therefore an unpleasant experience awaits him Beyond."

"You mean purgatory?" Rhin asked.

"I am afraid so. I do not enjoy suggesting it, but that would be my guess," Aroukana said. "He's in the hands of the Lord of Kaïle, now."

"Evil place, that is," Pélénor stated.

"I don't care if I have to spit in the Arch-Demon's face! If there's a way to save his soul I'll do it," said Rhin.

Pélénor stared at the Orb for a long time and then said, "I have the solution to your problem."

"Really?" Rhin's face brightened.

"But you will have to trust me," Pélénor said. "The old Temple of Resurrection on the East Isle is where he can be restored, brought back to life."

"Yes, go on," Aroukana raised an eyebrow.

"But…" Pélénor stopped.

"What's wrong?" Rhin asked.

"It's already a fair distance to Rosh City, the nearest harbor," Pélénor said. "The Temple lies within the Orronor Mountain range. It is said that ancient sorcerers live there. It will be an arduous task to find."

"That doesn't matter. In the morning I shall depart for Rosh City," Rhin paused and looked at Aroukana.

"I have been through fire and rain, war and famine with you. You think I will stay behind now?" Aroukana gave a dramatic shrug.

"Then I shall lead you to your rooms, and begin preparations for your departure. I shall suggest, however, that you two take a full day's rest here. You are both exhausted, I can tell, and you are more then welcome to stay a while longer," Pélénor offered.

"We shall graciously accept your offer, captain," said the Vevlea.

"Oh, once again, I am sorry Pélénor for yelling at you before," Rhin muttered.

"Say no more, Rhin," they traversed the winding hallways, and then, "Ah, here we are. Here are your rooms. Sleep well."

"Thanks, Pélénor. You're a true friend," the boy said.

Rhin and Aroukana crashed face-first onto their beds as soon as the door closed and fell asleep.

Rhin awoke to the sight of silvery moonlight and the fresh smell of grass after a rain storm. That moist, clean smell had always brought back his favorite memories. The air felt new and full of life after a lot of rain and thunder.

Without remembering how, most likely being half-asleep at the time, Rhin found himself in a garden. Violet blossoms of the finest hues swayed with the wind's gentle touch. Water gushed from fountains decorated with carven fish-men. And there, admiring the flowers, stood Pélénor.

"Ah, you're awake. Did my men disturb you?" he asked.

Rhin had the uncanny feeling that even though Pélénor had asked the question, he knew the answer.

It took Rhin a moment to respond. "Oh, no. Not at all. I couldn't sleep."

"Strange, isn't it?"

"What is?"

"How life has brought us to the same crossing. Do you know what I think, Rhin?"

Rhin was silent, so Pélénor continued, "I think that there's a reason. Life is full of magic," He picked a blossom and inhaled its fragrance.

"You knew I would come out here didn't you?" said Rhin. "I don't know how but you knew I wouldn't be able to sleep. You were waiting."

"Magical, isn't it? I'm here, you're here. We're here to become master and pupil. I shall teach you some magic I've learned over the years."

"You know spell-casting and incantations?"

Pélénor kept on speaking as if there had been no interruption, "My magic is of the sword, of war and death. My magic is made and honed to kill or stun without making too much of a mess of things. It is depressing that it should be used to such ends, but my people need learn these skills to counter our growing number of enemies."

Rhin felt himself rouse from his sleepy state. "Teach me. Show me what you have learned."

"The pupil is ready. Very well," he paused. "You'll need a weapon."

The boy looked about his person instinctively but there were no swords to be found.

"No, my friend."

The Monraïkian man threw him a stick. "Not all weapons have to be blades. Now, come with me."

The two walked into a grove under the stars where they would duel, using twigs and magic, with the moon as their only witness.

At noon, with bags packed and two healthy horses given to them by the Monraïkian stable boys, a group set off. They had decided to cross through the forest that had never been named, rather than risk passing through the lands of Borckéa. Pélénor had informed them that barbarians with gray skin and black hair had recently overrun that realm.

To the north lay Orno village whose popularity and wealth came from the mountain next to it. The mountain was the stage for the great battle between the Béros Elite and Jiaïro's army. The Béros had won the battle and pushed back their enemies, forcing them off the cliffs. Yet the great leader of the Béros army, Séolnas, died in the fighting and was buried in a shrine on the highest peak. Her sword was put to rest by her tomb. On the blade, the captain of the guard engraved her last message to the world:

"Though my blood is undone, and my strength has failed, suffer not the tyrant."

Thus, the mountain claimed its fame and the site of Séolnas' death became a holy retreat where no Evil could ever come, for it was guarded ferociously by the Monraïkian troops.

Pélénor and the rest of the Monraïkian warriors wished the Vevlea and Rhin farewell as they parted ways for a time.

They traveled for several hours across flat grounds—common terrain in the areas around Monra. Although it was without elevation, it had its beauty nonetheless. The realm of Monasta was simple yet elegant, its vast plains of high grass and wildflowers nourished by near constant sunlight.

The horses were tireless and seemed eager to leave Monra behind. They were war mounts, Rhin had been told, and had seen much carnage over the years.

A quiet, country ride will do them some good, Rhin thought as he inhaled the still, brisk air.

Aroukana spied a road block ahead and tugged at Rhin's shoulder.

"Many powers struggle to conquer Monasta," said the Vevlea, "we must take care."

He must have very keen eyesight, Rhin noted as he squinted down the road.

Rhin kept on riding, unconcerned. He even whistled an easy tune he learned from the Monraïkians the day before. At last, after most of a half hour had passed, Rhin could make out a squadron of Rixaï's men standing firm on the road with spears and lances prepared.

"Halt," the Decuri of the squad thrust a gloved hand forward.

Rhin and Aroukana unsheathed their swords. While Aroukana pointed out that there were about twenty of them in a voice that was barely audible, Rhin swung his sword in a circle, creating a large blue hoop that smashed away three of them.

"A little magic trick I learned from Pélénor last night. Monraïkian magic," Rhin said.

The squadron forgot about Aroukana and enraged, they all charged Rhin. Electric blue sparks exploded off of Rhin's fingertips and all of the soldiers bodies were hurled into the sky and landed somewhere far away, in a clearing, where a few farmers had settled.

In a state of befuddlement, standing right in the middle of the soldier's trajectory, a boy nearby said, "Now that's somethin' ya-dohn see evereeday. Mai, commoutchere an' see thisinere thing."

Although the battle was over, in his mind Aroukana was still there, pondering a troubling concern.

Aroukana cupped his chin in his hand and asked, "How could you use your God-like strength just now, if you could not when you faced the Lithinians?"

"I don't know," Rhin replied, shaking his head. "Let's not worry about that now. We've got to hurry if we want to reach the forest by nightfall."

So they remounted their horses and continued the long ride from Monra to Rosh City.

On the way to the port city they noticed huge maple trees sprouting from bumpy, dwarfed hills. Here and there a cabin or two could be seen, clotheslines traipsing from branch to roof.

These sights meant that Rhin and Aroukana had put the fields of Monra behind and neared the shore where the terrain was still wild and untamed.

They reached the forest at sunset, set up their tents and tied their horses to a sturdy oak.

As the sun drifted off behind the distant mountains, Aroukana taught Rhin the song of Ranlun and Ilyra, the Vengeful Lovers.

Rhin lay by the fire, drifting serenely toward sleep, noting that Aroukana's passions for history and lore were insatiable.

"You see," said the Vevlea, "Ranlun and Ilyra were made together but they drifted apart. It was from this sorrow that love became such a tumultuous guessing game. Before the first Vevlehen city and the first man, love did not exist. The years were easier, but emptier as well. Ranlun and Ilyra fell for one another but were both too stubborn and powerful to admit their feelings. Thus, Iora's first battle was for love."

"That's kind of stupid," Rhin commented, lifting his head.

"It is understandable that you would think this. However, much of the story is a mystery to me. I know what I know, but I suspect that there are far wiser scholars who could give you a much more detailed version."

"Maybe someday," Rhin yawned as he spoke.

They slept under the stars near the edge of the forest.

The next morning, the two friends felt well rested. There was not a cloud to be seen as they continued their trek. For once it was a sunny morning and Rhin would have preferred to be in the open rather than face the darkness of the forest, which seemed to warn them against coming closer. Rhin felt uneasy entering it. Yet it was easier then traveling on the outskirts of the forest, which would have cost an extra two days to cross the wild terrain of Noreach.

The sun gleamed around the trees and beyond on the fields but the luminous qualities of the astral body was lost in the shadows of the large wood as Rhin and Aroukana pressed on.

Trees seemed to wall them out. The path was overgrown and small, ugly creatures hopped and scurried past them as they carefully marched forward.

"I've put a lot of thought into it and the best word to describe this forest is 'dreadful'," Rhin said.

Aroukana laughed, "Yes, I agree. But that is all the more reason to pass through here as quickly as we can."

"The sooner the better," Rhin shivered, "once we arrive at Rosh we can hitch a ride to the East Isle."

"And resuscitate your friend."

"How long will it take until we finally can say goodbye to this place?" asked Rhin.

"Only several hours, lad. It won't be too long."

There was a pause, then Rhin said, "You are very wise, Aroukana."

"Thank you."

"How did you gain so much knowledge of so many things?"

"Bits and pieces here and there. I devoted much of my life to the study of languages, both dead and those still in use."

"Which ones?"

"Without meaning to brag, I have learned many. I speak Vevlehen, of course, and I am fluent in many dialects of Common Speech. I have also learned of the more robust tongues of the barbarian tribes."

"Barbarians? What is the name of their language then?"

Rhin had always been interested in the history of languages. He had never really been able to study them, however, because his parents did not have the means.

"Coturr, mostly. It is a very rough speech but complex in its origins. They say the dialects sprouted from the original Cotoar which is supposed to have been used by the civilization that came before the Ancients—the Ancients are the beings who first employed the use of Ancient Iorian, from which your Common Speech is derived—that civilization was a nomadic one and many ruins can still be found across Iora."

"And the name of this civilization?" Rhin asked, completely enthralled.

"Arcotr, I assume. The scripts that I have read became very vague when mentioning their true name. Something about the 'Great Ones', those who were 'Spawned by Magic'. And there was one very simple reference to their people which read – if I remember correctly – 'Arcotr, named. Famed for ruins, war, and deep thoughts. Tresori Lechendé'."

"Tressore Legendee?"

"Tresori Lechendé," Aroukana corrected, "I translated it and it means: 'Treasurers of Legend'."

"Ah," Rhin did not know what else to say.

There the conversation ended and they went on in silence.

A short while later they came across a gargantuan gorn tree blocking their path, which already was scarcely wide enough for them to pass in single file. The thickets around them were impenetrable. With this gorn impeding their progress, they would be forced to turn back and travel another, more indirect route through the forest. But neither of them enjoyed the idea of surrendering to a tree. The two contemplated things for a while.

Suddenly, Aroukana's bag opened up, acting on its own, and Daish-rog's Orb shot out. A shadowed figure hanging high in the branches of the gorn caught the energy crystal. With eyes narrowed it dropped down right in front of Rhin.

"He is of Vevlehen blood," said Aroukana.

"Where did you get this?" the Vevlea asked, a threat obscured in his words.

"What is it to you?" said Aroukana.

Rhin examined the newcomer's pointed ears and green eyes. A red fabric, tied around his face, masked his nose and mouth. His clothes were torn and dirty. His build was similar to that of Aroukana. He had the ears of Vevlea and was even bald. He had the air of one who had seen dark days. Rhin could tell that for a long time, this person had struggled to survive. The only contradictory item was a necklace of amethyst that this stranger bore.

"Answer the question," the Vevlea scowled, clasping Daish-rog's Orb between index and thumb.

"Our friend Daish-rog is dead. We are going to the East Isle to revive him," said Rhin.

"How do you know my brother?" the Vevlea questioned.

"Brother?"

What a convenient accident that we should find him here, thought Rhin. He did not know what to believe. He did not know what to say, so he said nothing.

"It seems this one is hiding something," Aroukana told Rhin.

The Vevlea turned to Aroukana and said, "You do not trust me, friend? Tell me, though, why should I trust you?"

"We come from Monra under Captain Pélénor's guidance," Aroukana answered. "This lad has traveled far. His home, Lynca, was destroyed not two months ago. You would do well to be more polite," he glared at the other and added, "friend."

The Vevlea relaxed and said, "Your words ring clear. It would do me good to remember the old courtesies. I am Chainæïa of Adwren."

"I am Aroukana of Alkari, the Sundered Prince."

Rhin wanted to know what Aroukana meant by this, but held his tongue.

"Are you the boy?" asked Chainæïa.

"What boy?" said Rhin.

"You remind me of a three year old child I encountered long ago. If you really are the boy I am referring to, then you will have a blue and yellow mark on your left arm."

Chainæïa walked up to Rhin and saying, "If I may," pulled the sleeve of his shirt up, and gasped.

"I knew it. I remember that mark as if I had seen it but a day ago. I took particular interest in you when I visited your village all those years before. The ancient texts describe a young man who will give the Vevleï, my people, another chance at life. A chance for retribution against the forces that overwhelmed us centuries past," his voice trailed off, perhaps because he was reliving old memories, or he was noticing mental scars that had begun to sting again.

"I recall those tales as well. I live by them. I was even warned by a man, one that bore significant resemblance to this boy here, to keep a watchful eye for the day when my calling would come. I would need to aid the one chosen to right the wrongs of time," Aroukana turned to the other Vevlea and asked, "You too believe that Rhin is the one."

"His name alone is legend, sir."

"This name was given to me," from the sound of his voice Rhin seemed to be offended. "I don't know my real name."

"Few know their true names. It would be prodigious if you knew yours at such an early age," Chainæïa said.

"What are you saying? No more riddles," Rhin said, his voice unsteady.

Aroukana paced over and regarded the mark on Rhin's arm and he too became a believer.

"This mark is identical to the image in the scripts, Rhin. There can be no more doubts."

Aroukana recited a verse that had been passed down for centuries among the Vevlehen people:

"Our lord has come my brothers
The day of glory is near
Weapons we shall gather
Sword, bow and spear
Our lord has come my brothers
Down, down, our enemies shall fall
Claim our land back we shall
We shall claim it all"

"Aroukana, can you please tell me what is going on?" Rhin clapped his hands, cutting through the song.

"You are the chosen being. You were said to have counseled Akra himself, the leader of the Vevlehen rebels. You are the reincarnated form of Rhin Akvius, the God of Light. I am sure of it.

"You see, when I was but a young Vevlea of approximately a hundred years of age, Jiaïro's armies besieged Alkari and slaughtered many of our people. But it was prophesied that a being—the same man that fought with us—would come and wage one final battle at our side. The last war, the one to defeat the dark God. The man would be Half-Blood and chosen by the Gods themselves," said Aroukana, waving his hands in excitement.

"And I am that being?" Rhin asked, choking on a sarcastic laugh. "Daish-rog conveniently omitted that part of my destiny."

"Yes, you are the one," the two Vevleï reverberated off one another.

"Alright, stop that. You two are making me uncomfortable," Rhin shouted.

Chainæïa seemed taken aback. Aroukana whispered in the other Vevlea's ear. They both bowed their heads and were silent.

In the unnatural stillness that followed, a high-pitched shriek sounded through the dank forest. It chilled Rhin to the bone.

Rhin's ears almost popped from the pressure, he was convinced he heard the words, "Leave this place," formed within the shriek. It was as if two voices were fused.

"What was that?" Rhin asked, feeling cold and alone all of a sudden.

"No idea, Master Rhin," Chainæïa said.

Normally Rhin would have made a remark about the 'Master Rhin' title, but at this particular moment, he was too frightened to say much of anything.

"We should leave this place, Master," Chainæïa said.

"We're not turning back," Rhin stated, unyielding as solid rock.

"There has to be a way around this obstacle, Chainæïa. Though, we cannot climb as you do."

"I shall go with you, Aroukana and Master Rhin. I wish to fight at your side. I will even die on the battlefield, if I must," said Chainæïa, handing Rhin the Orb. "I wish to aid in the resurrection of my long, lost brother if, of course, that really is the embodiment of his soul you hold. So whether you like it or not, I am coming with you."

The shriek from before started up again.

"Let's leave," Aroukana said, pulling Rhin by the arm.

"But how do we get past the gorn?" Rhin asked.

Chainæïa tapped on the third root from the right.

"Vevleï magic—natural and efficient," Aroukana mumbled.

The tree pulled its roots out from the dirt. It then hobbled to the side of the road with wooded clumsiness and became immobile once more.

"Irritated you didn't figure it out for yourself?" Rhin said as he nudged Aroukana.

"A little," he admitted, rolling his eyes.

"I never knew trees could walk," said Rhin.

"The Vevleï spawned a great number of thaumaturgic trees. But now, I feel, is not the time for a history lesson in the ways of my people."

They rocketed down the road, cutting their way through the overblown thickets and dodging the immense trees that split the gravel.

Aroukana would occasionally pause and his ears would prick up. Chainæïa was also worried, Rhin could tell, but he never stopped.

Maybe he knows what's out there, thought Rhin.

"I warned you. I told you to leave. I gave you fair warning. I did not deceive," the shrieker was heard again, except the words resounded much clearer this time.

"What are you?" Rhin asked.

"I am a penumbra. I am invisible in the dark, but what am I? Think I am vile and evil if you wish, it matters not to me. You shall not complete your destiny, Rhin Akvius, for I am Foro-Caratosa," the shrieker answered.

"Spare us your riddles. What manner of creature are you?" Aroukana demanded.

"My God," Chainæïa whispered.

"Shadow Born," Aroukana realized, answering his own question.

They heard the Shadow Born's long, drawn-out laughter. Then it jumped out in the shape of a black, spiky figure with a bestial, shark-like head. Rhin could only see the shadow for a split second before it was gone, entwined with the shades of the forest. That was the nature of the Shadow Born, or Shadavia, creature of Kaïle.

"Where is he?" Rhin called.

The Shadavia shrieked and laughed with wild enthusiasm as it circled them, unleashing its fury, narrowly missing their heads each time.

"How can we defeat an enemy we cannot see?" Aroukana yelled.

"Use your ears," Chainæïa answered and cringed.

All three of them looked around and listened until their ears pulsed from the strain. Every now and then the Shadow Born would bite at their noses and gnaw at their fingers.

"It's toying with us," Rhin growled, swatting thin air.

The shrieks grew louder still until Aroukana fell unconscious, followed by Chainæïa. Rhin, alone, stood to face this thing that threatened their lives. The Shadavia demon hurled its husky body at him, grabbing Rhin by the throat.

The demon's hand felt coarse and rough on Rhin's frail neck. The Shadow's eyes flashed red. It spoke, its voice a deep rumble, "You still believe you could destroy us, do you?"

Rhin desperately attempted to break free, but eventually weakened. He felt as though his head were about to burst.

"What do you want?" he gasped.

"Only your souls."

"You won't have them."

The Shadow snickered, "Naïve, aren't we? You have no idea what I could do to your fragile body. You will die, don't fret."

Rhin could feel the blood pulsing in his ears. His entire body ached with pain as the world around him grew darker and darker. All of Rhin's senses dimmed as he, too, succumbed to the will of the Shadavia.

Rhin awoke alone in the middle of a field. The sun was shining and the birds were chirping, but that did not cheer his mood. He had lost his friends. He got up and, darting forward, hit his skull. He groaned and his eyes focused ahead and from side to side, but nothing was to be seen. Feeling around with his hands, his fingers touched invisible walls.

A drop of sweat ran along his nose and rested on his upper lip. The walls began to close in, lightly pushing at his outstretched arms. At first the boy thought it might have been his own agitated mind tricking him. However, he soon realized that there really was less and less space between him and the walls. Claustrophobia can only do so much, this was real.

Rhin pushed all his weight against the magical force, which threatened to crush him at any moment. It wouldn't be much longer.

Then Daish-rog's Orb began to shine a dark green color and two glowing arms sprouted from it and started pushing on the invisible walls. It was not enough, and Rhin's body tensed from the effort. Daish-rog's energy crystal flashed.

Fight, he willed, *keep fighting. You have to go on, Rhin.*

Hope filled him, and at last he broke free with an explosion of lights. The shards of the barriers were now visible, steaming and melting away. The energy crystal hovered for a few seconds and then dropped into the pouch of Rhin's sack. There it resumed its dormant state.

Rhin could hear cries for help. He followed the voices until he found the source: two pentagonal shapes, stark and brown in contrast with the greens. Rhin knew that the Vevleï were trapped within.

As Rhin stared, helpless and distraught, at the devices the pentagons shrunk. Not knowing what else to do, he took up his sword and slashed at the walls.

It was a great deal less difficult to destroy the barriers from the outside. For every one of his strikes, a large gash opened. Rhin could see Aroukana lying on the ground, almost completely crushed, but it was only another heartbeat before he was freed.

As soon as Aroukana was out, Rhin assaulted Chainæïa's prison—with the same result.

They left in haste but as they sprinted they heard, "No. I should have killed you when I had the chance. The agony of ages is too good for you, Rhin!"

The Shadavia demon formed itself into a hand and sprung forth, closing the distance. The hand and arm together were twice the size of Rhin's whole body and its nails were filthy and sharp, like century-old metal shafts. The gigantic arm stretched like a rubber band, reaching. Then Chainæïa caught glimpse of a glint in the tall grass and scooped the object up without hesitation.

"Master," Chainæïa panted as he tossed the sword to Rhin, "use it."

The blade whirled through the air and, the second Rhin caught it, light shone down from the heavens.

Then the sword spoke, "Show me the Evil one."

Rhin did as ordered and pointed it toward the Shadavia. The hand dissolved, as if it had never been.

Rhin pointed the weapon at the sun. The rays of light seemed to catch and absorb into the blade. And then, three beams of sunlight touched each of the companions and transported them away.

Years, days, or minutes passed. Rhin patted himself, checking for wounds. They had been returned, safe and unharmed, to where the shrieking had first begun by the gorn.

"What the blazes happened?" Aroukana asked him.

"You tell me. It was like the sword was controlling my movements," Rhin said.

Then whatever magic controlled the sword spoke again. The voice seemed ancient and learned. It wavered and spoke in a tone that reminded Rhin of a warm fire crackling in a hearth during cold winter days.

"Lord Rhin of the ancients, I am the Sword of Purity. It is I whom you created two thousand years ago. I am yours, and yours only, to wield in combat."

"Why can't I remember any of this?" Rhin asked the golden weapon.

"Two thousand years ago, Evil created a sword which would have destroyed the world—no, the universe—if you did not seal it up in a sacred temple. Its name I cannot speak, for it is dangerous to do so."

"Why?" Rhin asked.

"I am too weak to defend myself from it, but I can speak of the past. After the One Evil had created its sword, you challenged him to fight on mortal grounds. This intrigued him, for the divinities, Good and Evil, have rules. The first and most important rule is that Immortal blood of old and Mortal blood of new cannot blend. If thou wish to test thy Mortal power, thou must become Mortal thyself. Thus, Evil sent its disciple to Iora to test his might against you. You were victorious and drove away Evil into the Shadow Realm of Kaïle. Now, he has returned and grown stronger than before."

"I did that?" Rhin asked.

"Yes. And your recent deeds prove that this world has not forgotten you. You must now reclaim your ancient strength and destroy Jiaïro, the dark God of Iora."

"This is all really interesting, but I have a question for you, ghost. Why could I transform and use my powers before, when I saw Ryul and... well, why can't I now?" Rhin asked.

"Your last fraction of power was exhausted when you fought Ryul's minions. In order to gain back your divine powers you must visit the five sacred Temples that Lukor had built for the Gods."

"Talking to a sword is something I never would have dreamed that I'd do, but I'll ask anyway. What is the purpose of these structures?" said Aroukana.

"Spread out across the world are several Temples. Each of them contains Divine Gifts."

"Divine Gifts?" Rhin repeated.

He knew he had heard of this before, long ago.

"Divine Gifts granted the True Gods power at the dawn of Time. You must visit them to regain yours. Once your friend is resurrected you must head for the West Isle."

"What is the West Isle named?"

"Tümraark. Bevrorenk is its capital city. Remember the name well, Lord Rhin. Your true journey begins this day."

"And this is my purpose? To save the world?"

"It is," the sword answered.

"Then it is ours as well," the Vevleï told Rhin.

With the words of the sword still in their minds, the three emerged from the forest. The sun still shone brightly as it set, bathing the open clover fields in orange light. Beyond, the roar of the sea could be heard, its tumultuous breaths crashing upon the rocky beaches of the southern shore.

At last, they had arrived at Rosh City. Rosh, as one would expect from a port town, clung with love to the shoreline. Some of the city was even built on the water, upon wooden platforms that shifted with the tides. The city had but one wall to speak of, on its northeastern flank, for the salty waters provided a natural barrier to enemies. Rosh had not been besieged in centuries, however, for it was a merchant town and no longer partook in wars. Rosh City's claim to fame was its crawfish, the likes of which no other harbor town could match.

Rhin practically fell over with disappointment when he saw the gate was sealed. Before he did anything rash, he walked up to the gatehouse wall and called a greeting.

A minute or two thereafter a soldier peered over the edge, a crossbow in his hands. Rhin could see the man had a short, black beard and tired eyes, as the wall was only fifteen feet high.

This city wasn't built to withstand a siege, Rhin contemplated. *Something has happened here to make the citizens fearful.*

"Sir, might we gain entry to the city? We wish to take to the ports," said Aroukana to the guard, cupping his mouth with his hands.

"Sorry lads, my orders are to let no one in."

"Pray tell, why?" Chainæïa asked.

"Not four days past, a Lofa came into our town and burned the harbor with barely a spark. A Kaïle worshipper, for sure," the guard coughed. "So no one gets in or out of the town, without the Mayor's prior consent."

"What are we supposed to do then?" Rhin asked, his temper flaring.

"Any ideas, Aroukana?" the younger Vevlea asked.

"Lofa, jargon for the race of Lowrfrazir. They are dangerous and adept magic users. Long have the Frozen Gates lain shut, why should they open now?" Aroukana muttered, more to himself than the others. He raised his voice a little and said, "Let us camp here for the night. Sleep may bring answers."

In the middle of the night, when no light but the moon shone in the sky, Rhin awoke with a fright. He lay unmoving, blaming the merciless wind for the disturbance. And yet, he could not close his eyes. He thought he had heard the pounding of heavy hooves, many of them, and the thrumming of marching lines. He got up and peered out of the tent. In the distance, armed men were advancing toward the town. He shook his friends from their dreams and they, too, saw the advancing host of heavily armed Seekers. Each demonic warrior carried a torch, scattering a trail of ash behind him, defiling the earth with every step.

Their gleaming eyes pierced the fog, exposing all to their gaze. Rhin could taste the foul air that came before them, and smell death on the warriors' lances.

As they drew nearer Chainæïa gagged, then said, "The blood of peasants and farmers decorates their armor."

"Arm yourselves," Aroukana murmured, blade in hand.

The tent was of brown-boar hide, nigh invisible at night. Chainæïa had seen to that. This fact had given the three of them a few more precious seconds to prepare.

The warriors of the enemy scouted the perimeter of the town, quickly locating and surrounding the small encampment. Rixaï himself came marching up to see what they had found.

"You have led us a marvelous chase through the fields and forests, you scum," he called, "but no more. Come out and play, children. Let us show you our toys."

The spirit that animated the sword gave Rhin the best advice it could, "Fight with honor, and you will prevail."

Rhin nodded and reached for the sword's jewel-covered hilt. With a quick glance he saw it in all its glory. The blade itself was made of pure gold and bedecked with silver and blue jewels as well as diamonds. The hilt seemed to be made of light as Rhin slipped out of the tent.

He could say with honesty that he was no longer afraid. After all, he had almost died several times over the past few weeks. Rhin had made his peace with death, and he would rather face it with a blade in his hand then cower in a corner.

"Ah yes," Rixaï said, "Rhin, the savior. Come forth, anarchist."

"If you want to die, then by all means come and face me," Rhin taunted.

"I see you wield the forgotten sword. As much as you want to believe it, that dull, aged edge will not save you," Rixaï drew a clawed thumb over his neck, hissing. Then he laughed, saying, "Are you alone? Where are the others? If it is just you, then I needn't have brought so many soldiers."

"He's not alone," said Chainæïa, as he and Aroukana stepped forth from the tent and stood by Rhin. Their silvery curved scimitars dazzling in the moonlight, the Vevleï waited.

"Rhin's little friends come to help. How touching, but enough," Rixaï growled, "Give me the Orb and your death will be swift."

"As it was when you tore Daish-rog's heart from his body?" Rhin shouted.

"No, the nature boy was not worthy of the honor."

"Neither are you," said Aroukana.

"You may yet claim the Orb once you turn me to a rotting, shredded corpse… that is, if you can manage it," said Chainæïa and he winked at Rhin as he and Aroukana charged the line of Seekers.

Rhin waved the sword. It was more for intimidation than anything else, but the clouds split and were whisked away, revealing the stars.

"What are you doing, boy?" said Rixaï. "I grow aggravated of all these cheats."

A powerful wind began to blow. The grass grew higher and higher until it was up to Rhin's chest.

"Daish-rog," Rhin looked up and the Orb circled around his head, a fierce jade light blazing within. The crystal was aiding him again.

"Give me the Orb or die," Rixaï screamed with fury.

"Never," Rhin leapt at his enemy, his chest thrust forward in defiance, his sword held high above his head.

Then all he could see was a black veil, one that would not lift from his eyes. The familiar vision returned, although it was altered. The voices were clearer, the sky darker, and the figures visible at last.

He was standing at the entrance of a temple. A foul demon was chasing a girl.

The demon grunted, "Pitiful. You make me sick to my stomach."

"Leave me alone, please," the girl wailed.

Rhin ran at the fiend, bending all his will toward killing. But when he stung it with his sword nothing happened. The beast did not even turn his bulk around to face the new opponent. But Rhin was not truly there. He could play no part in these events. He was only a witness.

"Death is a mercy."

The demon thrust out his sword and black fire spewed forth, scorching the very clouds in the heavens. The barrage collided with the girl, consuming her entire form. She did not drop, for there was nothing left of her to fall.

Rhin awoke and looked around. He lay under cover in the tall grass. It was still night and his eyes had to readjust to the darkness. A peek outside revealed that there were soldiers patrolling, searching. And he noticed that there were two square cages in Rixaï's encampment.

The Vevleï. Rhin cursed.

Then he watched, awaiting a gap in the patrol routes. When his chance came he did not hesitate. He ran up to the cages, staying as low as he could without doubling over.

"A shadow took you," Aroukana whispered.

"It is a miracle that you were not found by Rixaï," Chainæïa added.

"What are we going to do?" Rhin asked.

"Go for help," said Chainæïa.

"Where?" Rhin asked, feeling nauseous.

"Anywhere. Go, hurry!"

Rhin left his friends and made for the top of the hill that brushed the right side of town. Dawn came. The sky was a brilliant blue and red as Rhin caught Rixaï's scream. They had spotted him.

"Blast you lazy fools! To the hill! Rhin eludes us," he howled until there was no breath left in his lungs.

It must have been quite a sight for the soldiers and their commander. There stood Rhin on top of a mass of stone and dirt, touching the sky as the sun embraced him. That hill seemed strange, as strange as a hill could.

He faced Rixaï and shouted, "I dare you to come and get me."

Then the mountainous mass of grass and moss quaked under his feet. It split all along its edges. It cracked as it resculpted itself, heading skyward. Rhin saw a shape emerging from it all, though what it was he could not tell. The hill unrolled, stood up and Rhin rolled downward. He landed with a hard thump on his backside.

His eyes moved up along the mass before him. Another splitting quake formed a round head-shaped boulder on the top of a standing figure. From the folds in the rock Rhin could see a nose, mouth... even eyes. A puzzled look cracked across its 'face'.

"Who awakens me?" the hill bellowed.

The crevice that was its mouth showed massive granite teeth that were as large as Rhin's body.

Every syllable was punctuated and loud, "Ah, more soldiers. I know just what to do with you."

It bent over and raked up the Seekers. Then the hill threw them in its mouth and all that was heard thereafter was a disgusting crunch.

"Tasty. Could have used a bit of sea salt, though."

The hill grabbed a handful of the remaining soldiers and hurled them into the sky.

Rixaï scowled and vanished along with what was left of his force.

The hill then lightly tapped the two cages that held the Vevleï, or at least tapped as lightly as a gargantuan hill-man made of rock could. The bars bent and the hinges swiveled. Following a final metallic groan, the Vevleï were able to push their way out. They stretched and breathed deep, grinning all the while.

Chapter 8
A Helping Hand

The hill turned to Rhin and said, "So you are the rumored 'forest boy'. You have become somewhat of a myth, little lad."

It smiled, breaking chunks of rock from its mouth which caused tremors upon landing. Suddenly, the idea of standing near the behemoth became less appealing. Rhin cautiously took a few steps back.

"Tidings have passed my way about a boy of great skills and promise," the hill rocked with a 'little' chuckle.

"My name is Momagé," the hill said, "I am of the race of Namka. I fear I am but one of three that remain. For hundreds of years I have rested here, watching the ages go by, and have heard many tales. The most peculiar one was yours, Rhin. And that is saying something. Ever since news of you reached me, I have waited for you."

"What is so peculiar about me?" Rhin asked.

He wasn't sure whether he should take any of it as a compliment.

"I can't hear what you're saying. Speak up boy."

"I said, what makes me so interesting?" Rhin shouted as loud as he could, but to Momagé it must have been a mere whisper.

"The wind carries information now and again. And when it tells tales of you and your travels I pay particular interest to its tidings. The

Namka are a wise race, if I do proclaim so myself. My kin know many secrets of this world. I know you are a kind soul and if you would allow it I could aid you in crossing the sea," Momagé thundered.

"That would be very kind of you," said Aroukana.

"Then I shall swim you across."

Rhin was knocked off his feet by the vibrations of that last bellow. Just as Rhin lay questioning Aroukana's wisdom, Momagé set all three of them on his right hand and walked slowly into the sea that separated the North Isle from the East.

Rhin couldn't understand why an ancient hill would help him. This lead to a deeper question. He asked himself, why, out of all the fine warriors in the world, was he the one who was destined to fight Jiaïro? The world was a bizarre and twisted place at times. It was always the weakest needing to be strong and the strongest that took advantage of the weak. He was, after all, still half a boy. He knew, however, that all he could do was trust the two Vevleï and this strange being made of stone. Ironically, his ability to trust was all he could rely on. Although he had made friends, he still was alone. He always had been. And that day, he felt he always would be.

He set his sights on the ocean ahead.

From what few stories Rhin's father had told him back home, he knew a little about the East Isle. The island was vaster than the northern one. The king of Kranfaraas, who resided in his fortress city, owned much of the land. It was boasted that all the king saw from his tower was his garden, and all the earth that the men and women could walk across in a week fell under the king's rule. Thousands of years before Rhin's day, the eastern king's ancestors had waged many wars against many enemies. They won virtually every battle. It was a glorious age for the Kranfaraasar.

"Best hold on tightly, now," Momagé warned.

He swam for several hours, sometimes dipping his head under water to see if there was any ground to step on. He was not a gifted swimmer, being composed of stone. It was lucky that he could stand in most of the deepest areas of the northeastern sea.

Rhin's mother had once told him "The sea floor is inhabited by thousands of different life-forms, each stranger than the one before."

She told him that the creatures beneath were entirely separate from the 'earth dwellers'. She warned him that many a sailor had attempted to capture a few specimens to study them. Only a few returned alive. "The sea is a treacherous maid," his mother would say. "There are few species known to man and those that are have been documented in an academy of sorts not far from the East Isle, a place which devotes all its resources to the study of aquatic life."

Thunderclouds were brewing. Momagé hummed and trembled, betraying his nervousness.

What can we expect from the deep? Rhin wondered.

A bad feeling intensified when he glimpsed an electric blue shape, slick in the water. He said nothing. Again it happened and again he did not bring it to his companions' attention. Then lightning struck the mainland and a wave of black water brought forth a gigantic mass dark as night. The titan covered the skies, vanquishing the light.

Rhin wanted to scream, but his voice caught in his throat at the sight of this colossal being that had exploded from the depths of some watery hell.

"Apocalids*!" cried Momagé

"We're doomed," said Chainæïa.

"You forget who we are traveling with, young Chainæïa," Aroukana gave his companion's shoulder a squeeze. "Keep your faith, as I will mine."

They expect me to protect them? Rhin thought. *What am I supposed to do? Single-handedly create a miracle and save their lives? That's insane!*

He, too, succumbed to lamenting his fate while Momagé utilized all of his remaining strength to break free. They watched the monstrous forms mingle in the waters, camouflaged. The hill man was a perfect target. Momagé looked around nervously, his rock eyes popping, pieces crumbling down and splashing into the water.

"Rhin, listen. If I do not survive, you must know—go to Tümraark. You must do this!"

Rhin nodded even though he was skeptical about his chances.

---

* Huge blue-black creatures with seaborgium—an ever mutating chemical—in their genetic make up. These sea-dwelling beasts could rearrange their shape and size infinitely.

If you are pulled under, what am I supposed to do? Rhin wanted to say.

"Over there," Chainæïa shouted at the top of his lungs.

He was pointing toward a dot on the horizon. Whatever it was, it seemed their only chance. If only they could get there.

A wave rocked the hill man, the spray washing over Rhin. The salt stung his eyes, and for a moment he could not see.

He blinked and rubbed his eyes with his fingers, until he heard Momagé scream as he was forcefully drawn into the depths of the ocean.

"Momagé!" Rhin called.

They managed to break free from the current that was pulling the great mass of rock down and were left floating helplessly while the enormous blue-black abomination splashed toward them.

"Swim to the island," said Rhin, the freezing waters tugging at his body.

He had never enjoyed swimming, even in the small valley lakes that appeared after the seasonal rains near Lynca. Now he was under the pressure of having to swim for his life, and the Apocalid was gaining on him. He swam and swam with raging adrenalin pushing his strained legs. The sky was as bleak as the black water. The Apocalid was nearly invisible, a hidden but ever-looming threat.

"Faster. You must go faster. Come on, man!" Aroukana cried.

Chainæïa screamed as a tentacle latched onto his legs and pulled him under.

"Chainæïa," Rhin panicked while the Vevlea sunk ever downward.

"Go on without me," Chainæïa gurgled, as he bobbed up briefly.

"No! We will not leave you," said Aroukana.

Rhin, acting on impulse, took firm hold of the sword of Purity and swam toward the Apocalid. He stabbed deep into its membranous flesh. A concentrated ray of light flashed from out of the water as the Apocalid sputtered and jerked in agony. Rhin heard a horrible squeal. He feared the worst, but seconds later Chainæïa resurfaced. The Apocalid shaped itself into a giant drill and charged toward Rhin, bending the sea as it made for him.

"Chainæïa is unconscious," Rhin yelled, exhausted. "What do we do?"

"Pray, Rhin. Pray," Aroukana answered.

The Apocalid rose up, out of the seas, revealing its full bulk. The width of it seemed to stretch from horizon to horizon. It reared and began to descend upon Rhin and the Vevleï when, out of nowhere, a bolt of lightning pierced it. The creature roared and screeched, at last retreating to the deep. A wave shaped from the crashing of the Apocalid into the waters. The three men were shoved toward the island. Rhin held his breath. For one awful moment he thought he was going to die. Then he collided with wet sand.

It started to rain.

Rhin's front had hit the beach, earning him sand in his nose and eyes. He tried to look around for his friends, but the pangs of pain he felt in his neck paralyzed him. Taking it slow, he dragged himself over the coarse grains. Both Aroukana and Chainæïa were lying on their backs nearby.

He checked to see if Chainæïa was breathing, which he was. He gasped for air himself, trying to recover from the impact with the shore. He could see the Sword of Purity glinting just ahead. He crawled slowly away from the water, pulling himself with painstaking effort toward the golden light. Everything around him was one massive blur of colors, the dominant one being black. His efforts proved for naught. He had barely moved at all before his mind collapsed and all turned to darkness. His last thought was a hope, a hope that this was a hospitable enough island and that they might find some other means of getting to the East Isle.

Most of all, he hoped he would not die that night.

Chapter 9
The Deserted Isle

*R*hin came to on the beach, stirring to the sounds of moving water and the crash of waves and spray. After he spat out a mouthful of sand he saw a wasted land. This isle seemed to have been destroyed by an unnatural catalyst, a ghastly curse whose aftereffects still drifted low like dense mist.

The dry land seemed devoid of life, not even the tiniest of creatures could be seen. The air was dusty and stale, dirt delicately weaving in the intense, shining sun.

Rhin began to search for Aroukana and Chainæïa. The absolute stillness was unnerving. He tried to recall the events of the night before, but it was all dark and blurry to him. He remembered the stink of saltwater and burning flesh.

Rhin neither heard nor saw any birds. Even the insects were gone. How this could have come to pass he did not wish to know, all his will bent to finding a way to leave.

He found those he had been searching for lying nearby, their tranquil breaths mingling with the smooth sweeping of the low tide.

They're still alive, Rhin sighed with relief. He roused them with a few nudges.

Chainæïa was quick to awaken, but Aroukana only groaned and frowned. The night before, he had been propelled into several small boulders giving him many bruises and even more cuts. Rhin removed a pouch from his sack, and poured a few drops on Aroukana's forehead.

The last of his water, Rhin reflected. *No doubt it will be a challenge to find a lake or river nearby. Wake up, friend. Don't leave me here alone.*

Aroukana stirred and muttered in the Vevlehen tongue. He opened his eyes. Rhin could see how weary he was.

The sun was setting. The sky was a tapestry of magnificent blues, purples, oranges and reds, the threads of light interwoven with the lemon yellow sun. But Rhin imagined that even the sun was abandoning that wasted isle. He was consumed by a feeling of dread, but chose not to put it to words.

At last, Aroukana managed to utter, "Where are we?"

"We landed on the island we were trying to reach last night," Rhin answered. "Lucky."

"I do not feel so fortunate," Aroukana rubbed his elbow. He noticed the setting sun and asked, "Have I truly lain here a whole day? Or has it been more than that?"

"I don't know," Rhin said as he looked out to sea.

"Do either of you know what became of Momagé?" asked Chainæïa.

"He did not survive," Rhin said, staving off the tears.

That one, last excruciating cry echoed in Rhin's mind.

Then he took out his sword and picked up a piece of driftwood he had found on the beach. He carved a small rough figurine of Momagé and put it in the water. The statuette floated off, bouncing from wave to calm wave.

"To Momagé."

Chainæïa sang a verse in his honor.

> "Though we did not know you
> We regret your loss all the same
> You died for us, we who
> Barely knew your name

But we are most grateful, for through
Your courage and will
We overcame"

The lyrics were accompanied by a melancholy tune, but their beliefs (at least those of the Vevleï) told them that Momagé had departed for a better world, a world of beauty and serenity. This comforted them.

Rhin hadn't known Momagé long at all, but he still felt as though the death of the hill-man came as a terrible loss to Iora.

Aroukana traced a spiral in the sand with his finger. At the center of the spiral he drew the sign of an eye. When the picture was complete he sat on his knees and, facing west—to the setting sun—he prayed for the safe passage of Momagé's soul.

"Rest well in heaven," said Rhin.

"He was most likely very ancient," Aroukana said, not looking up.

"As old as the sands we stand upon this day," Chainæïa agreed.

Aroukana chanted soft syllables and Chainæïa hummed along, sitting on his knees.

When the two Vevleï had finished their rites Rhin asked, "What were you doing?"

Chainæïa was the one to answer, "It is a ceremony where we ask the life-giving sun to give rest to the souls of the departed."

"But why the spiral?"

This time it was Aroukana who explained, "My people strongly believe in resurrection—that the world constantly revolves in a spiraling form. Thus one life never truly ends. The soul is simply transferred into another corporeal manifestation."

"And the eye?" Rhin inquired.

"The eye is the divine vision that is granted to us when we reach Ragamandæ—heaven—and it stays with us until we are born again. Then it waits for us in the heavens once more. You see, when someone dies we believe that the Gods grant that person divine wisdom but if he is not receptive to it than it evaporates as soon as he is reborn."

"That makes little sense to me," Rhin admitted.

"Someday, perhaps it will," said Chainæïa.

The three sat together for a while deciding on the best course of action. They opted to explore the island.

"What else are we to do?" said Chainæïa. "With the port in Rosh closed to all seafarers, we have no chance of being found."

A smallish, crusted, gray stone lying on the deserted beach caught their attention. Upon it, carved into the rock, was a glyph. The glyph was that of a white sphere within a black one, the center was assaulted at a forty-five degree angle by two parallel lines.

"What is that?" Chainæïa asked.

"I haven't a clue," said Rhin.

He was on the verge of remembering something, a memory long forgotten. This symbol was so familiar to him. It held great importance, he knew, but all the memories and forgotten clues remained lost as Aroukana interrupted his thoughts.

"Rhin," Aroukana shook his shoulders, "I sense someone is surveying us."

The wind began to whistle loudly. The dust and sand traveling with the breeze seemed to thicken. The air dragged a scent with it, something that had not been there before. Rhin could almost...

He could almost see the hoods, eyes and teeth. Waiting. Watching.

How they could stay hidden while being so close was beyond Rhin. They even made the wind blow through them so as to not be caught by it. But the one thing they could not prevent the wind from carrying was their scent. Every hair on Rhin's neck, down to the tiniest sprout, stood on end. Something primal within him responded to the call. He spun round and slashed an arc with his sword. The blade tore through black fabric.

On the edge of hearing was a faint noise like a cat purring. Everything seemed perfectly normal until the very earth and air around them blackened.

The figures were hooded. No, they *were* the hoods. They seemed to be *made* from the black fabric that entwined them. They were one with the air, writhing in the wind. They did not lurch, for 'to lurch' implies locomotion. They just seemed to sway with the breeze, drifting from side to side. And the worst part of it all was the silence. The absolute silence was horrible and frightened the three companions. The cloaks seemed to absorb sound when they moved, transmuting noise to stillness.

The wind died and the air grew thicker still. It was so dense that Rhin was almost certain he could cut it should he have chosen to do so. With every inhalation, he felt like he would choke. He slashed at the advancing shroud, trying to keep whatever these things were from touching him. He could see then that they were part of the air, the veil that clouded the environment.

Then there was laughter. At first it was faint but it soon grew in volume and intensity until the three had to cover their ears. The sadistic laughter became Rhin's world.

He felt he should say something, anything. He just had to stop the laughter. Just as he thought he was about to die it ceased and was replaced by a voice, *"Ich nich varniq qich Raqich."*

The sound was so abhorrent and disturbing that it could only be described as inward—a bad sound effect or a broken sentence. None of the three could understand a word of the horrible dialect, but as their minds ached the words reformed into the Common Speech.

"We are shadows of Rayïm," said a voice.

"Suush chach nich nich. We are warriors sent to destroy the disturber of Fate," said a similar but separate voice.

There's more than one, Rhin told himself, his eyes widening.

At the beginning of each word there was a horrible clicking as the tongue they spoke morphed into understandable language. The voices were low and aged beyond time.

"Drach tach ix nich ix-ix. Death to those who upset the Evil," said the second voice.

"What are you?" Rhin gasped.

"Narrx ix qich arx nix nich. We have many names but they are beyond your words. In your plane we are known as Cloaked."

Aroukana thrust without hesitation, penetrating his target's upper body. After the attack a third one of these twisted beings revealed itself. The three Cloaked responded with diabolical laughter.

"Surchix nix chix kinch ich ix-ix. Your weapons cannot hurt the Cloaked."

"Chich ix vach erx nix qich. Cease your useless rebellion."

"*Varnich ich-ich nich qix-chach.* Prepare yourselves for ultimate judgment. Kill."

"*Ich suurr nax nich, Karaäk.*"

Rhin knew it would not be facile to surmount three invulnerable enemies. He guessed that the last word of that freakish speech, Karaäk, was a name—the name of the third Cloaked.

Rhin slashed at Karaäk, but to no avail. The Cloaked seemed to curl around the blade as they were struck. It was as easy to stab the hooded things as it was to hold water in one's palm.

The Vevleï were soon exhausted, and all the while the Cloaked took no damage to their bodies—if you could call their main mass a 'body'.

When Karaäk responded to Rhin's onslaught it was with two abrupt slashes. Rhin knew nothing of the strikes' coming until he felt splitting pains in both shoulders. And as he looked down he saw his clothes drenched in blood. Their swords were substantial enough.

The Cloaked fought in total silence. None of the Iorians could tell, but the black figures were actually amused. The specters from Rayïm had no muscles and thus moved with a queer and unpredictable grace.

Rhin clenched his teeth and set his eyes on the leader. Rain clouds formed again making Rhin's flaming eyes all the more vivid. He looked around, muttering in the ancient tongue. The three warriors looked at him and continued their merciless laughter.

"You don't know me, do you?" asked Rhin with sudden clarity.

"*Nich ix.* We only serve. We do not know. We do not care."

"Return to your makers then," Rhin replied.

The Sword of Purity glowed fluorescent blue. Rhin felt all of his rage building up for one strike. The thick air around him seemed to thin, absorbed by the sword. He unleashed his wrath with the blade, his instrument of valiance. He struck down Karaäk.

There was a scream of agony accompanied by an orchestra composed of cymbals of thunder and drums of rain.

The remaining Cloaked were wroth but stayed their ethereal weapons.

"Return to the Pits, scum," Rhin said, the fire still raging in his eyes.

"*Selich idxe nuich...* You cannot prevent your death, you can merely postpone it," one said.

"*Urch ix ich ix xi ix...* The Judge will hear of this. Beware, Rhin-boy, for none can escape him," finished the other and they vanished.

Vanished however, is not the right term. Evaporated would be more apt. They appeared to blow away with the wind. Even the echoing of their voices had trailed off as the air pushed them away.

The skies seemed to brighten and the sun returned to its full radiance.

"Who were they? What did you do to it?" Chainæïa asked Rhin, giving him a bewildered look.

He eyed the spot where the Cloaked had been slain.

There was no corpse. Only a shred of black cloak flapped with futility, caught beneath a pebble. But as Rhin leaned closer the fabric disintegrated, leaving only stone to stare at.

"Chainæïa, have you ever seen anything of that sort?" Aroukana asked.

"No. And I hope I never have the misfortune again."

Rhin's eyes widened. He made wild hand gestures and then said, "I remember... I remember! Aroukana, Chainæïa listen. That was an ancient technique used by the Half-Gods."

"What ever do you mean by 'Half-Gods'?" Aroukana frowned.

"Thousands of years ago, when the world was divided among feuding factions, the five shrines were created.

"The first one guarded the Spirit of the Holy Eye
The second one defended the Hawk's Claws
The third protected the Angel Wings
The fourth watched over the Golden Fists
The last brought Completion to its finder

"I learned that long ago, but it only came to me just now," Rhin explained.

"Go on with the story," Chainæïa said, leaning forward.

"Rhin's followers, the Light army, created these shrines to protect the Gods' powers. They used the same technique as he did to defeat Evil creatures. It concentrates all the power of the air around you into a single blow, fatal and efficient."

Rhin spoke in third person, unwilling to accept that he was referring to himself, "The leader of that army, Laoko, disciple of Lord Rhin, fought against the ever rising Evil. He fought Jiaïro. He tried to defeat him."

"He tried and failed?" Chainæïa asked.

"He tried and died," Rhin said with a solemn expression.

"I think I have heard this story before," said Aroukana. "It was said that when the entire world was sinking into the darkness, a flickering light appeared and gave the people hope. Laoko failed, did he? I do not remember reading of that particular tragedy."

"Why could you not remember this earlier?" Chainæïa broke the silence that overtook them.

"I tried, but there was always a block right when I was close to recalling something," Rhin told them.

They were quiet again. The swirling dusts had settled as the night began to take control. The sickle-moon rose high and the first constellation to appear that night was Mirin, the Light Tower.

Aroukana gazed at the heavens, stood and said, "Our fates may not be any luckier than that of Laoko if we stay here, I think."

"I agree. It is better to die with hope and pride than shrivel away and accept ones fate," Chainæïa said.

"Shall we explore this deserted place further, then?" Aroukana suggested, holding his hand out for Rhin.

"Definitely," said Rhin and took the Vevlea's hand.

While they explored the island they found many signs that proved it had once been inhabited. White ruined domes, a well, and a crumbled stone wall told them a illustrious city had once been there. Atop the crown of a hill they found a field of Orbs. The energy crystals emitted weird, alien sound patterns. These beings had been very different from any Rhin had seen.

"Who do you think used to live here?" Rhin asked, holding a rusty ax.

"I do not have the slightest clue," Aroukana replied, staring at one of the hundreds of Orbs.

Rhin moved to pick up one of the energy crystals but Aroukana caught him, "Don't touch, lad," the Vevlea shook his head, "Let us not disturb the dead. I have an ever-growing suspicion that a great evil dwelled—or dwells—here."

Rhin looked Aroukana in the eye and nodded.

"Excuse me for interrupting," Chainæïa started to say, "but look at this."

He was holding what looked like a skull. It was shaped like a turtle with a bird's beak and gigantic eyeholes. At least, that was the closest analogy that any of the three could come up with.

"Strange," Aroukana said, examining it. "Chainæïa, best you put it down. Now."

Chainæïa put the skull down as if it were a bomb.

The search for life followed its course until the sun brightened the eastern sky. Dawn had come. They had not rested all night long, devoting all their efforts to the fruitless quest. But now fatigue overcame them.

Rhin and the Vevleï slept a while in one of the desolate shelters. It had rained all night, but at dawn the clouds seemed to vanish. They were famished, but this only made them more determined.

The only pretense of food they found was a pair of maggot-ridden cows that had had every scrap of meat stripped off the bone. It seemed the only live inhabitants of this land were the flies buzzing over the corpses.

When Rhin felt himself ready to drop, they came to an area that was completely flattened. It was no natural force that demolished this island. They were sure of that much at this point.

Then, in the distance, a shape loomed into view. A crouching figure.

Could it be a survivor? Rhin wondered.

He could hear the thing as he approached, repeating the word, "Onoät. Onoät. Onoät."

"Let's go to him," said Rhin.

This creature was the only living being left on the island that they had found, besides the scavenging flies, so the meeting made Rhin anxious.

Up-close, Rhin realized that the figure was praying. He observed the thing and assumed it was male.

His large, oval-shaped head sat atop a thin neck and spindly shoulders. He had a stone-colored beak that brought a facet of sharpness to his otherwise rounded features. A rough shell covered his backside from neck to lower spine. On his brown and white cowhide shorts he had strapped two sheaths complete with golden daggers. A material Rhin would have described as moss (or possibly a kind of fungus) grew on the underside of his legs and arms, and his fingers and toes were webbed and clawed. He smelled of seawater and wild mushrooms.

"I have heard of these beings before," Chainæïa whispered. "They live completely in tune with nature, surviving primarily on fish and vegetables grown on their island. The cows they breed provide for much of their clothing."

"What an unjust end to such a civilization," Aroukana said with a sad sigh.

Rhin worked up the nerve to break this thing's concentration. "Excuse me. Who are you—what are you?"

The creature stood and turned round. He wasn't very tall, a bit beneath six feet. But his lanky physique gave him the illusion of towering height.

He placed his right hand over Rhin's head, took a deep breath, and said, "Ah. Rhin, emissary of the Light, I have been waiting for you, praying to the Gods that they bring you here."

Rhin asked, "What is your name?"

"Cononsareth Onoät."

His eyes, though red, weren't evil looking at all. They shone like rubies, expansive and deep.

"Why have you been waiting for me?"

Cononsareth ignored the question, "It is you, for I cannot mistake such a soul for another," he spread his arms wide and said, "This was my home. I am a Conkatokæ, one of the many former denizens of this isle. I am the last alive, I fear."

"So, how did you come by my name?" said Rhin.

The turtle-like creature tapped his chin. "Perhaps it was a god or an angel who told me. I cannot be certain. But the name was revealed and here you are."

"Cononsareth, what happened to your kin, if you don't mind me asking, sir?" said Chainæïa.

"Ah," Cononsareth's face became grim and it seemed a shadow had grown around them, "I was swimming off the coast of Tümraark—fishing—and I was about to come back when-"

Cononsareth stopped talking, his beak rose in alert. He stared at nothing in particular. A sudden cold breeze swept across the deserted isle and it felt as if it were passing through them. His webbed hands brushed the hilts of the golden daggers at his belt. He looked Aroukana in the eye.

"I sense it also," Chainæïa said.

"The dark one you slew, Rhin... *they* have come to avenge the Cloaked," said Aroukana.

"By the pits of Rayïm, could we maybe go a few days without having to defy death?"

The sky turned black as a shower of arrows pricked the earth a few feet short of Rhin. An invisible enemy was taunting them. The three companions unsheathed their swords. The Conkatokæ, Cononsareth, unclasped his two golden knives from his belt. They stood firm, back to back, awaiting the inevitable.

A demon marched forth, speaking in the tongue of the Cloaked. With a hairy hand it produced a war horn. The demon sneered and put the horn to its lips, trumpeting two blasts.

Chainæïa tried to say something but all he could manage was, "Kaïle. Our souls!"

A cloud approached and then a green portal split open across the black sky, as a sword would slash a body from one side to the other. Scores of black creatures burst through the opening like a mob of angry rioters and unsheathed a range of different weapons. Each demon was tall and muscular and sharp strands of dark mane hung loose from their temples. Some wore heinous masks, while others had pierced their flesh with jagged ornamentations.

Rhin recognized them as mythical Daïmaan warriors from ancient scrolls. In the old tales, the Daïmaans formed the standing army of Kaïle, a hellish realm where damned souls reside for all eternity. The word 'Daïmaan' meant 'Child of Death'.

"How can this be? Devils from another realm come to assail us?" said Chainæïa.

"Indeed. It would appear so. I recall these things from an era long past. My blade will have its vengeance," Aroukana growled.

"As will mine," said Cononsareth, after which he shouted to the Daïmaans, "So you've returned! For what exactly? Do you all seek death by my hand?"

"Stay close together. Don't let them separate us. Ready?" said Rhin.

He beheld the others' unyielding strength and loyalty, and he felt proud to fight by their side.

Then the tide was upon them.

Rhin danced between the blades as the Daïmaans came at him. After a missed strike, he would swerve around his foe's guard and cut into them. What was perhaps most disturbing was that the Daïmaans did not scream when they died. Nor did they acknowledge it in any true way. They only fell and the green fire in their eyes sputtered out.

Aroukana and Chainæïa never strayed from each other's side. The Vevleï had become as brothers in the short time they had known one another. They fought in perfect, mirrored unison, circling around in a graceful sweeping arc. Their curved blades sang as the steel scraped with other weapons.

The Conkatokæ was an animal. Sometimes Rhin would risk a glance at Cononsareth. He twirled, leaping over heads and standing on shoulders, having his adversaries do the work for him. Spurts of blood splashed his webbed feet during his prance. When there were fewer footholds he would stand on all fours. Switching his daggers from feet to hands, he would wriggle between and slice at ankle, belly and spine. He was limber as well as agile, striking with every limb.

The green gap in the sky expanded to push more demons into the world. The Daïmaans cascaded from the portal to overwhelm the four.

Rhin caught sight of an ax whirling at him and if he had not ducked, he would have been a head too short to live. Chainæïa received two gashes, one in each leg. He screamed as Aroukana removed the axe from his left shin. As he dragged Chainæïa away from the skirmish, Aroukana got slashed across the stomach and clutched the wound. He would keep the scar for the rest of his life. Cononsareth remained unscathed, but the look he gave the Daïmaans could have melted rock.

The flow of demons never ceased. The hellish-creatures cursed and spat and licked their daggers. Their green, flickering eyes slanted in relish.

"There are too many of them," Rhin shouted and slumped.

And then the black warriors formed a semi-circle around them, and then froze in place. They hummed a deadly hymn. The Daïmaans watched the sky and the hole from which they entered the mortal plane.

"What is happening?" Chainæïa asked, as his voice cracked.

Rhin heard himself screaming, as he mind was a great distance from his body. The gap between worlds split further across the inky sky. A great gray skull tore through the world as if it were tissue paper. Its glowing, yellow, bloodshot eyes popping open as it ripped sea and heaven alike.

The black warriors exalted and tossed their weapons high, roaring as they did. Rhin, Cononsareth and the Vevleï stood motionless with the horror that was looking straight into their very souls. Rhin gasped in torment as the eyes pierced his fragile shell and pawed his naked mind. The giant mass of gray bone reared its ugly head and became noticeable from the other side of the dimensional gap. It opened its mouth and more Daïmaans rushed from it like a swarm of horse-flies.

They touched earth, standing before Rhin, and one among them squalled, "The Judgment of Fate awaits."

Chapter 10
The Incarnation of Fate

*S*oon, the entire horde of demons barked like feral dogs. Their voices seemed to combine into one. The wind fused the syllables until the phrase was barely audible. It carried the sonic waves along with it until the cry had become a whisper in the dark.

The warriors around them guffawed. The sky shone green as the portal between worlds grew larger still. The skull tore through the gap as the portal reached its climax. Rhin lost feeling in his legs. Chainæïa doubled over backwards in response to the gigantic, popping eyes.

The Daïmaans kept reiterating the same two words, "The Servant."

The abhorrence had by then fully crossed the ethereal portal. It stopped moving and to Rhin's absolute terror it began to speak—if speak is the right description of the sounds it uttered. The language it spoke was less of words and more like the yawning of a mountain or a thunderous tempest.

A sinister cheer erupted from the horde. As the skull spoke it made a thick, chinking noise. Rhin knew that toothy grimace brought fear into the hearts of every living creature it had ever encountered. It was a sort of permanently frozen expression—if a skull is capable of expressing emotion.

As with the Cloaked, the evil tongue twisted and altered itself to become the Common Speech.

"I am the Incarnation of Fate. I am that which causes the River Time to bend. My name is not important, I am only the Servant."

"This is a bad omen, Rhin. This is the Guardian of Fate, the first in command of the Judge of Rayïm and Kaïle," said Aroukana, shaking his head.

The skull hovered high. It screened the skies with its impressive presence. As gargantuan as a mountain, its dome was craggy and pock marked. The way it delved into Rhin's soul with its gazing, twitchy, yellowed eyes was disheartening.

"Ah... so Rhin, thou art having fun?"

"Is this your idea of fun?" Rhin retorted, pointing at the creature with the tip of his sword.

"I thought it amusing enough for thee. A shame," the Servant laughed.

All else was silent.

"Verily, such tidings would have done pain to mine ears. Thankfully, I have no ears. I would have hoped that thou wert more comfortable, for thy life span grows shorter still. Thou hast murdered mine finest pawn, Karaäk, mine most loyal minion."

Rhin's face froze. This did not bode well.

"He is known to you as Cloaked. I am distraught over his sudden demise. But now, 'tis thy turn. Thy death is inevitable Rhin. Thine life ends here, Fate has decided thus. The flicker that is the Fire of Life can be breathed away in a fraction of an instant."

"But a spark can create a fire. And you forget one important fact," declaimed Rhin.

"What is this thing that I hath forgotten? Thou shalt find me relentless when in pursuit of knowledge and perfection."

"I don't believe in fate."

At that blasphemy, the Daïmaan warriors shrieked and howled.

The Servant emitted a wicked chuckle and continued, "Thou doth not believe in Fate? Truly thou art joking. Fate is the ultimate cycle of Life," the Servant continued in a more forceful tone, "from which none can escape."

"Back to the pit from whence you came. We fear none in this world or the next. Be gone! Back from whence you came," Cononsareth called, his voice rising above the howling wind and the screeching Daïmaan horde.

"I assumed my armies had thoroughly dealt with thy race, Conkatokæ. Thou art the last, yes? Then consider this following act a mercy from me. Rejoin thine forsaken kin!"

"I do not fear death," Aroukana stated.

"Nor do I," rallied Chainæïa.

"Do your worst," said the elder Vevlea, achieving greater balance by lowering his stance.

"Such nobility… shameful and wasted, but it is nobility nonetheless. Prepare for thy doom."

Lightning from the storm clouds above flashed and sparked as the mass of bone distended its jaw. It stretched and stretched until the opening looked wide enough to swallow the land itself. A blinding green light flickered into existence, its energy gushing forth. Then the demonic light turned to fire, and precipitated upon the island.

Rhin shielded himself with his arms. The last sensation he could register was lying on the ground, contorted in spasms of anguish. Immeasurable hurt raced through his body. But soon the pain was replaced with emptiness, and he slept. He felt peaceful as he slipped away.

"Rhin. Rhin wake up."

A sweet voice was calling him back, back from the white-flower fields through which he ran. The sun set on the empty land.

The voice was warm and pleasant and musical to the ear. Rhin opened his eyes and saw a girl leaning over him.

She had stormy blue eyes and her hair was bright violet. She was cloaked in green and her skin was a light pink shade. She was an Eramkéras, commonly called a 'dog-ear' by other races. This primitive word was considered an insult to the race, though. The only difference in her appearance from that of Rhin's were her ears that flopped down like those of a hound.

"You're awake," said she in the same musical tones.

Her voice reminded him of spring in Lynca village when the birds took wing and the dark of night never troubled the light of day.

Yes, Rhin remembered what spring felt like. He had almost forgotten everything, but this girl had called him back.

"Who are you?" Rhin asked.

"I am Luu-ka."

Rhin posted himself up on his elbows and asked, "How did you know my name?"

"Your friends told me, how else?"

"What is this place?"

"The Institute for the Study of the Aquatic Life-forms of Iora. ISALI for short."

She answered in a calm, kind way. Rhin liked that.

He looked around the light blue room. There were shelves upon shelves with fish tanks on them. Because of his recent experience with the creatures, when he noticed paintings that showed the Apocalids and the destruction of great ships in bitter seas he felt a weight drop on his chest. He would not let it show in Luu-ka's company. He felt a need to impress her. Why, he did not know.

"Do you want some breakfast?" Luu-ka asked.

"Yes, if it's no trouble," Rhin felt his stomach growl. Then remembering what had happened the night before he asked, "How did I get here, Miss Luu-ka?"

She laughed for a brief moment—a calming, beautiful laugh which was as vibrant and full of life as her speaking voice—and then said, "Call me Luu-ka. There is no need to be so formal," she paused. Her smile disappeared, "I was taking a pleasure cruise on a small boat near the coasts of the island and I saw a flash. Last time I saw a flash like that one was when my home was destroyed. I thought nothing could survive that blast… then I found you and your friends."

"I don't remember anything," he said, feeling various welts on his head.

"You're lucky to be alive, Sir Rhin."

"Just Rhin," he said with a goofy smile.

"Come eat your breakfast… Rhin. I trust you like honey?"

With that she turned her back to him.

Rhin watched her leave, grinning like a fool. He did like honey.

Rhin walked into a spectacular room decorated by ornate stained glass windows. The sunlight shone so bright there that he had to squint. The place was open and airy, the warm breeze coming in from the left through arches that overlooked magnificent rainbow-tulip gardens. Along the walls there were rows of red clay bowls. Each bowl was filled with crystalline water and pink water lilies sprouted from beneath the surface. At the heart of it all was a grand rectangular table, complete with fifty chairs. Each of them was carved out of gorn wood with silvery jewels running along the sides. The chairs seemed so delicate Rhin was afraid to sit on them.

He saw his friends with so many plates of food in front of them that it was impossible to count them all before his mouth watered. They all had smiles on their faces. Rhin was glad, until he noticed their heavy bandages.

Rhin sat down at the head of the table, near his friends, and took a piece of bread coated with honey. He had to confess he was starving.

Luu-ka entered the room and asked, "I trust you're all enjoying your breakfast?"

"Yes. What a fine selection you have set out for us," Aroukana said with a smile.

Chainæïa added, "You are most gracious."

Luu-ka left them at that and the group talked amongst themselves.

"This place is truly remarkable, wouldn't you agree Chainæïa?" said Aroukana.

"Yes, it certainly is. What a wondrous island."

"We owe our lives to Luu-ka," Cononsareth said, wearing a neutral expression.

"She is very-" Rhin began but stopped short, aware of their stares.

The others exchanged glances, suppressing laughter.

After they were done eating, they took a short walk in the vast gardens of the college. To Rhin, it felt like being home again as he walked between the sunflowers. Cononsareth was more interested with the aquatic flora, and would move up close and sniff at them.

When they had finished their tour of the establishment a rounded, little woman led them to the bathhouse where they found four small tubs. The bathhouse was in a secluded wing of the establishment, but it too had a breathtaking view of the flower garden.

"It must stay warm all year round here," said Rhin.

"Yes, it never gets too cold here. You can probably tell that we really like our garden." When the woman was through giggling she said, "I trust you want to take a bath?"

Rhin gave Aroukana a sidelong glance and muttered, "We must smell like horse dung."

Aroukana snorted and said, "Speak for yourself, I had a bath recently."

Aroukana wandered around the corridors of the college with a purpose. He was searching for the library. The Vevlea thirsted for the knowledge this school could provide him.

He did not find the library, but instead made another interesting discovery.

Chainæïa stood there, not ten feet from him, a collection of nervous twitches, standing he stood on his toes.

"Greetings. What are you doing?" Aroukana asked.

"Oh, me? Nothing really. Just standing, you know."

His whole body was shaking and his voice quivered.

And Aroukana also noticed the other Vevlea's forehead was drenched in sweat. Chainæïa also seemed to be holding something behind his back.

"What have you got there?"

Aroukana became concerned at his friend's bizarre behavior.

"No really, there's nothing going on here." Then, with a blundering attempt at tact, he changed the subject of discussion, "What were you searching for, Aroukana?"

"Me? Just the library. You, however, are not getting out of disclosing what is behind your back so easily. Chainæïa, you might as well tell me now for I am not leaving until you do."

"Alright, I submit to your will. It is a rose."

"A rose? Whatever would you need a-" it dawned on him. "Chainæïa meet a pretty girl, did he?"

"Stop that. Leave me be."

"A nice maid that needs grooming, perhaps?" he said with a sly smile.

"No. It's nothing like that."

"A handsome lady needs courting, does she?"

"You can be very childish at times, Aroukana," Chainæïa said, his gaze boring into the marble floor.

"Very well. I shall leave you now to pursue the evasive library." And, after reflecting, he added, "Have fun."

Cononsareth was enjoying himself. On the school grounds there was a large lake that he had been privy to visiting. He found that he would rather stay there. The water was crystal clear and he felt wonderful bathing in it. And it had lilies. Often he brushed up against the moss carpeted lakebed. It was soothing to be in the water once more. He had spent days on land, waiting for Rhin to arrive, refusing to drink or swim until the Gods had sent their angel. Pious as he was, he did as he vowed. But now he had found Rhin and the sacrifice need not go on.

Marvelous. What a wondrous place. I would be content spending eternity here.

One thing he found rather amusing was that the children—residents to the college—took a profound interest in his appearance.

Well, can I truly put the blame on them? After all, to those who have been sheltered here all their lives I suppose I am unorthodox, he reflected.

One little girl went so far as to approach him as he paddled through the cool water at the lake's periphery.

"Um, mister turtle?"

"Yes, young one?"

"How long can you hold your breath?"

Cononsareth winked, "We shall see."

Such innocence. Charming.

The Conkatokæ plunged downward. Picking at the sleek rocks with his toes, he stayed under for a long time. The children were beginning to wonder if he was still alive. He raised a leathery hand above the pool to reassure them after three minutes. Finally, Cononsareth resurfaced and beheld their fascinated faces.

A boy wheezed, "We thought you were dead!"

"Where I come from I am one of the least gifted swimmers, and I cannot hold my breath long at all. My eldest brother could stay under the surface for an hour at a time on a good day," said Cononsareth.

It was an ideal environment in which to raise children to be kind, warm and gentle people. He knew because *his* island had been much the same.

Aroukana and Cononsareth lounged on a balcony overlooking the fields, the beach and beyond them, the ocean. The orange sunset added to the spectacular wonder of the college.

"Tell me of your world, Aroukana," said the Conkatokæ.

"If you so desire," the Vevlea's face frowned, "It was six hundred years ago when my city was destroyed and my people fell from grace. We have lived in hiding ever since. My people are scattered and broken, hungry and wilting like a withered rose," he looked at Cononsareth, who was staring into his eyes, "I remember white walls and grand libraries. I recall the magnificent Vevleï Hunters with their brightly colored feathers and armor. I visited the Elder often as well, for he was wise beyond his years—though they were many and well spent—and he always had a new lesson for me.

"It was from him that I first heard the legend."

Cononsareth nodded and said, "The prophesied return of Rhin Akvius."

"Yes. I truly believe. I have never believed in anything more than this. And now I know the legend is unfolding. This boy we travel with is the Savior, the angel mentioned in all the Vevlehen books."

"Yes. He is the one. I know it to be true. I can sense this. He has a certain air about him—a strong will and a lack of arrogance. His kindness will prevail. My race also knew the prophecies held unprecedented truth."

Aroukana leaned forward, "Soon the Vevleï will rise again. Jiaïro will learn that we live on and are still just as willing to fight, and die, for the glory that once was ours."

"But what of the Monraïkians? Do they fit into this equation?"

"It has been many years since we had dealings with the realms of Monra, but I do not think they will forsake us in our time of need. They have intense feelings of hatred for the God. They would see him fall."

"I hope you are correct in your assumption. A premonition tells me that we shall need all the help available to us."

"Yes. But we will be victorious."

"I know," said Cononsareth.

Rhin had been walking around dazed all day. When he ate, things seemed a little more 'tasteless' than they should and he mused that his vision was getting blurry.

His one reoccurring thought was of Luu-ka. She was stunningly beautiful and he could not stop thinking of the sound of her voice or the way she walked. Her image had taken control of his mind. The very idea of her made it a trial for him to draw breath.

He made his way to the dining room for he had received word from a handmaid that supper would soon be served.

At dinnertime, the travelers were clean, well fed and happy. Compared to what they had been through those past weeks, this was paradise. But there was always some little voice inside Rhin's head telling him that this was not where he belonged. He could not stay here much longer, however much it pained him to leave. He was not used to such hospitable treatment.

Rhin wondered if Aroukana and the others would even want to come with him. Most of his friends during his life had abandoned him. He could not blame them for wishing to stay here.

He found all the diners waiting, fifty male scholars of varying beard lengths. Luu-ka was the only woman attending that night, perhaps the only female scholar, for all Rhin knew.

He, the Vevleï and Cononsareth sat down at the dinner table and a dozen gold-collared chefs entered, bearing many exquisite platters. Among them were cooked oysters, shrimp in a buttery sauce, stir-fried green peppers, mangoes, pineapples, salted bread, and white fish cooked with lemon. To wash it all down, Rhin was given a glass of honey-sweetened coconut milk.

Luu-ka sat down between Rhin and Aroukana.

"Now I have some questions for you," she said to Rhin, resting her palm on his forearm. "Why were you on that ruined island?"

Rhin looked at his friends, who were laughing and eating without care, and said, "We're on a journey."

"What sort of journey?"

"I don't know if I should tell you," he said, glancing at his companions again.

Chainæïa wolfed down a chunk of salted bread and told a joke with his mouth still full. When he laughed at his own punch line, he spat crumbs at Aroukana. The elder Vevlea, after he had finished scolding Chainæïa and declaring him a barbarian, returned to a hushed talk with Cononsareth. The Conkatokæ bowed his head and slurped at the delicate fish. When his eyes met Rhin's, he gave a little wave.

Rhin looked at Luu-ka, gazing deep into those blue eyes. She had him. He was enchanted, prey to her charms. He could not lie to this girl.

"Come on," she giggled, "you can trust me."

I know, Rhin thought and then he said, "We're on a journey to stop Jiaïro."

Rhin had expected her to dismiss him with a mocking laugh, but she believed him.

"Jiaïro, the God? You and your friends are very courageous to take on a God. Finally someone is standing up to him," it was her turn to stare into his eyes. "There is something else I want to ask you. This is going to sound weird. Is that the Sword of Purity?"

Rhin was amazed. Luu-ka smiled.

His expression must have answered the question.

He was sitting next to a person who knew of a sword that had remained hidden for two thousand years. No one had seen it except Aroukana and Chainæïa and of course, the Conkatokæ.

"I had a dream a few days ago that I was being chased by ghosts and I fell. A man holding a golden blade—the Sword of Purity—appeared and vanquished the evil haunting me. That's how I came by the sword's name, in case you were wondering."

Rhin was at a loss for words but he suddenly understood something that had been nagging him for weeks. The vision of the murderous demon and its victim was of her, Luu-ka. He felt nauseous. But that meant that she would die. His stomach jolted.

Beads of cold sweat cascaded down his neck.

"What's wrong?" asked Luu-ka.

"Oh, nothing… better be off to bed," he said with weak desperation, trying to cover up his feelings.

"Good night, Luu-ka. Thanks for all your hospitality."

"Alright, sleep well," she said, frowning just a bit.

Rhin could feel her eyes on him. He tripped as he reached the doors and cursed his clumsiness. Feeling embarrassed he hurried up the steps and into the room he had been given. He slumped onto the bed and shut his eyes.

He had left his meal unfinished. His appetite lost. He did not feel tired at all.

In the middle of the night Rhin gave up trying to sleep. He flopped out of bed and landed on the ground with a loud, but muffled, thud. He hurriedly hopped up to sit on his knees and listened a minute. Luckily no one seemed to have heard his clumsy drop.

Twice in several hours. You're outdoing yourself, he told himself, grinding his teeth.

He stood and, creeping toward the door, stretched out his hand to open it. He touched the cold, brass knob. A little static shock greeted his fingers. Turning the knob, he waited for the door to open the right amount—just enough for him to slip through—and pushed himself into the hallway.

This thing you do, waking up in the middle of the night, is beginning to become an annoying habit, Rhin, he told himself.

There were no drapes covering the windows in this hall, so he had to wait for his eyes to adjust to the dense moonlight pouring in from the outside world.

He paced through the college until he arrived at a large double-door bordered by stained glass windows. Rhin opened the door and stepped outside. A cool breeze soothed his nerves, but several hundredths of a second later he tensed up again.

Sitting a few feet away from him, on a bench by the edge of the marble balcony, was Luu-ka.

She must have heard the doors open because she turned around.

"Couldn't sleep?" she asked when she saw him, combing her hair behind her ears.

The wind sang a moment.

"No."

"Oh, I'm sorry," she said, "Is there anything I can do to remedy that? Should I replace the bed or-"

"No. No, it's fine. The bed is fine. I just couldn't sleep," Rhin reassured her.

She smiled.

Rhin broke the awkward silence by saying, "Well, I should probably leave you. You want to be alone, so I-"

He moved toward the door. Luu-ka stopped him in his tracks, "No, it's alright. Stay with me a while."

Rhin turned, "You sure?"

"Yes, definitely. I'm glad you're here now."

Her eyes glanced at the vacant area of the bench on which she was resting. Rhin sat down, as far away from her as possible without it being obvious that he was trying to do so. Relaxing a little, he heard birds singing.

Luu-ka caught his grin and explained, "These birds chirp at night instead of during the day. It's a mystery why they do so, for they are very shy creatures and you barely ever catch a glimpse of them. I'm one of the few that have seen their green feathers and distinct orange beaks. Maybe one day we will know more."

"You really love animals, don't you?" Rhin asked.

"Oh," she frowned, "I'm boring you."

"No," he said, "Not at all."

The girl smiled again. Rhin liked her beautiful smile. He thought then that his greatest gift and talent was his ability to make Luu-ka laugh and, most importantly, make her happy—if only for a moment.

The two of them sat on the bench for a while, admiring the stars and the moon.

Rhin returned to his room, where he at last got a few hours of rest.

The next morning, exhausted, he got up, knowing what he must do. In order not to endanger the girl's life he must leave at once.

"Good morning Rhin," everyone said as he entered the same open room with the stained glass windows and garden view.

"Good morning," he answered, warping the words with a yawn.

They ate in much the same fashion as the day before. Only that morning, to everyone's delight, there were fresh strawberries and pears to accompany the honey-bread.

Rhin was dreading the moment he would have to break this heaven for them.

After they had all finished eating, he said with a heavy heart, "I'm sorry everybody, but I have to leave. You're all free to stay, though. No oath binds you to me."

"As my master, and friend, I follow you faithfully," said Chainæïa. "And I think the rest of us feel the same."

A chorus of agreement.

"My service is at your disposal, Rhin," said Cononsareth, extending one of his daggers hilt-first.

They showed such sincere loyalty. Rhin would have shed a tear knowing that he at last had found true friends, but he could not. Not then.

"But your wounds haven't even healed yet," Luu-ka said.

Aroukana and Chainæïa exchanged looks.

Rhin knew that if they stayed they would jeopardize the school's very existence, not to mention Luu-ka's life.

Rhin's destiny was no longer hidden. He and his loyal friends would engage Jiaïro in the greatest battle they would ever know.

Luu-ka walked up to them with a determined look on her face and said, "I'm coming with you."

For a moment there was silence. Then the companions answered in turn.

"Absolutely not."

"We cannot let you do that."

"Too dangerous."

"Please," she pleaded. "I can help you."

"Why do you want to come with us?" Rhin asked.

"Because," she paused, "because a great Evil destroyed my home and killed my family. If I go with you I have more of a chance of finding it than if I stay here. I hunger for retribution."

Aroukana whispered in Rhin's ear, "We both know what she feels. Her people were put to the sword, the same as mine and yours."

"And even if you don't let me go, than I'll follow you," said Luu-ka.

Rhin sighed, "Fine. You can come with us."

The only reason he accepted the idea was that he felt as though he knew her and would not have been able to stop her anyway. And perhaps, if she came with him, he could protect her.

Later, Rhin realized that he had been selfish in his thinking. He didn't let her come along to protect her—though he did want to, that was not his first concern—he agreed to her joining him because he wanted her by his side.

She looked at each of them again and they nodded in agreement as her gaze fell upon them. Rhin tried to keep his look serious but then she gave him a disarming smile.

Luu-ka told them that there was a boat at the harbor, a few miles from the college, which would take them to the East Isle. The time they spent walking down the gentle slope to the small town was peaceful. The trees were scarce on the island, but the prairies plentiful. The flowers were mostly violet and blue. Luu-ka explained that they were native to the island and were called Alasi, named after a fair Vevlea maiden who had lived there many years before.

By noon, they arrived at the town. The sun was high in the light blue sky, troubled on occasion by puffy white clouds. They were met by two guards who saluted them and bade them a safe journey.

"Their job is more ceremonial," Luu-ka explained, waving at a child running through the streets.

On their way to the harbor Rhin saw all sorts of creatures, mostly aquatic. The animals were kept in glass aquariums that lined the streets. He even saw a little fish that looked like a mix between a squid and a turtle. Some households were decorated with small lily ponds, others with sapling birch trees.

"What do you call that fish?" Chainæïa asked, pointing at one of the turtle-squids.

"It's called the Orion Twik," she answered, smiling at him.

The majority of the houses were made of pale—almost white—brick, and square. The streets were composed of cobblestones and had many drainage gutters.

When you have a lot of fish, you need a lot of liquid. So, then you also need a lot of sewers, Rhin observed.

"Well, I should say this place is spectacular," said Cononsareth, scrutinizing a tank containing a cross between a shark and a salmon.

"We're almost there," Luu-ka told them and pointed at a giant building that was bedecked with weeds and sea urchins.

"The people in this town adore all forms of sea animals. They serve many of their needs. Insulation, clothing, food and jewelry—things like that."

Rhin knew she spoke the truth because he had seen the black-haired, black-eyed men in their rainbow-scale outfits, glittering with every step. And the women wore crab claw earrings and shark-tooth necklaces.

Luu-ka turned to Rhin whispering so that only he could hear, "Can I ask you something? Why are you going to the East Isle?"

"I had a friend who died at the hands of Rixaï. We are going to resurrect him."

"I'm sorry for your loss... wait. Not Rixaï? He killed many people! You actually faced him?"

"Only for a minute. I just grabbed Daish-rog's Orb and ran off. There is nothing heroic about that," he answered, harsher than he intended.

She did not seem to notice.

"Well, even stealing something Rixaï wants and running away from him takes a lot of courage. I think you're very brave."

Rhin blushed. Then he raised his hand.

"Look," he pointed at the docks, "we're here."

There was a pause. Suddenly a fork of lightning burst in the sky, followed by the thrumming of thunder. A cataclysm of energy stirred the air. The luminescent shine that spread through the town was the most fluorescent shade of green Rhin had seen. It blinded the citizens, striking panic in their hearts.

"The foul one has returned," said Cononsareth, trying to compete with the clamor.

The sky splintered to reveal that dreaded green light. As soon as the portal had opened dozens of Daïmaan drones pulled themselves through.

The daunting Daïmaans, insectoid limbs clutching all manner of gruesome weaponry, rushed at the buildings. Some held torches of almost fluorescent flame. Luu-ka froze in horror as the Servant chewed its way through the world itself.

The five companions stood back to back, waving their swords at the advancing shadows. The town militia, the ceremonial guards, fought the main army of Daïmaans, but as the black creatures fell to the blades of the valiant guardsmen more and more poured out like thick mud from the gap between the dimensions. Most of the guardsmen had never engaged in actual combat. Within moments they were overwhelmed.

Rhin and Cononsareth dashed straight for the skull. The Servant growled and launched a flickering, electric missile at Rhin. He dodged the blast, taking cover behind one of the brick houses. He sheathed his blade, threw up his arms, and began to climb. He crammed his fingers in the sharp slits between the bricks. Once he reached the roof, thin trickles of blood oozing from his fingertips, his eyes darted about, searching. To the left, he saw the slanting roof of a saw mill. Without thinking, he sprinted and jumped. He landed where he had intended and proceeded to run up the slope. The shingles clacked as he went but Rhin saw the Servant hovering not ten feet from the blades of the mill. This made him quicken his pace. At the peak of the structure, he looked down at the slow revolving blades and the massive demonic skull floating just beyond. Rhin ousted his sword from its scabbard, swallowed his fear and vaulted.

Soaring over the conflict below, Rhin knew he was going to make the jump. Until, that is, a drooling, hooting Daïmaan collided with him in mid course. Tumbling, he and the beast wrestled. They crashed right through a bright red and yellow drape that had hung from the mill to a large hall across the street. Then there was nothing between them but the paved roads. The Daïmaan took the fall, and Rhin's landing was softened by the other's bulk. But when he noticed the demon still had some life in him, Rhin pierced its heart with his sword tip.

Then, his entire body tensed, every muscle flexed. All his joints locked themselves in place.

"I can't move," Rhin said, his teeth clenched.

His efforts were futile but he noticed up ahead that the Daïmaans too were rooted in place. As were the inhabitants of the island. It was as if time itself had stood still.

None but the Servant was able to move.

"Ah Rhin, once again we meet. I see thou and thine companions hath survived mine assault," the Servant said, accompanied by the usual chinking noises. Then, staring at Rhin's wounds, it said, "But not wholly unscathed."

Rhin felt shooting pains in his chest. It was as if someone was ripping him open from the inside out. He felt his heart being plucked at from inside his rib cage. He shrieked in pain.

"Feel the agony, Rhin. None can escape Fate."

"Leave him alone," a lonely voice articulated.

It was Luu-ka. Although small and frail, she showed no fear.

"Who is this miniscule creature? Verily, thou disappointith me. I much desire a worthy opponent."

"Leave him alone," she repeated.

The Servant laughed, its whole mass twitching, "What art thou to do about it? Dost thou have a clever plot to unveil that requires no movement, perhaps?"

"You sack of filth," she spoke in the tongue of her people, the Eramkéras.

"Ah yes, thou art the girl whose village I destroyed ten years past. I find thee at last."

Then all the Incarnation of Fate did was look at her and she, too, felt the agonizing torture. With the torture came a heightened awareness. Rhin felt everything in tune with Luu-ka and he was aware of her doing the same. The shared agony had bound their minds.

Just as Rhin understood the implications of this, he felt his flesh tear. He whimpered in between screams as the sensation overwhelmed him.

"What sorcery is this?" said Aroukana, finally breaking from his deep meditation.

The Vevleï had joined in a furious attempt to regain control of their bodies. Cononsareth, who had been petrified during a spinning strike, grunted with helpless frustration.

Rhin's back split at his shoulder blades and light radiated from the fissures, forming one beam that blasted skyward.

Rhin, Luu-ka and the Servant roared in anguish, light flashed for miles, and then all were released from the fixing snare as if Time had never stood still.

"The pain!" Rhin yelled at the top of his lungs.

A thousand white feathers twirled and weaved, falling from above, covering him in a blanket of ivory. He emerged from the mountain of white, changed. Wings spread behind him, now part of him. Bedecked in golden aura, he was released from the pain, the horrible suffering that triggered his evolution. He fell, naked and unconscious.

A beam of energy discharged from Rhin's sleeping form, puncturing the mass of bone. And it was no more. The Servant left behind a pitch-black Orb, the size of a fist. All of the Daïmaans were struck down by consecutive beams and they, too, were gone as sudden as they had come. Their legacy was a rain of black energy crystals that pattered and bounced as they hit the cobblestones.

The ground on which Rhin lay became sacred some years thereafter. In song he was remembered on that island only as the Slayer God, the angel from Ragamandæ who graced their town with his enlightened presence. This event was recorded as 'The Vanquishing', a chapter dedicated to Rhin's exploits in the Book of Baraïk.

But as the town reveled in the Half-God's triumph, the dark remains of the Servant and its Daïmaan slaves reformed from the ashes of their defeat. The skull hovered a few feet above the ground, fully regenerated.

"As I have said, none can escape Fate. Thou hast merely prolonged thine existence for a while. Good bye, little God."

And it was gone, along with the Orbs of its demon soldiers.

The Vevleï uttered their worst curses as Luu-ka ran to Rhin, followed by Cononsareth.

Chapter 11
Ferry to the East

Rhin woke up in a cabin, the slow rocking making him queasy. He was lying on feathers. He tried to shove them off the bed but as he did, he felt an ache in his back. With a jolt, he stood up and found that the feathers were attached to him.

"What's this?"

Luu-ka entered the room and gave him a wide smile.

"You're awake," she said. "How are you feeling?"

"What's wrong with my back?"

Rhin was aghast.

"I don't know... They just sprouted out."

"Just sprouted out?" Rhin half shouted. When he regained his composure he asked, "Where are we?"

"We're on the ferry, making our way to the East Isle," said she. "Want to come and see the ocean?"

"Maybe later," said Rhin.

He was done with water.

"I won't hear it. Come on, you don't know what you're missing."

She led him out of the cabin. On deck they saw fisherman everywhere. The shipmates were hard at work, doing whatever it was they were supposed to do. Rhin did not know precisely what that was since he had never been on a ship before. Luu-ka told him that the crew was the finest in town and personal friends of hers.

"This ship is named the Isali, after the college," she informed him. She then bobbed her head, indicating a stern, short man, and said, "That's Captain Latvar. A weird name for a good man. He keeps the crew in check, but he's kind when you get to know him."

Latvar would shout orders or give them the right to rest— although the latter did not often occur. The sailors would answer with a sharp 'Cap'n,' to each of his demands, and spring to action. They respected him, despite his harshness.

"I'd like to thank you for letting me and my friends aboard," Rhin said.

"Always room for a few more, lad. Just as long as you don't get in the way," Latvar said as he folded his arms behind his back.

"Yes sir. Thank you." Rhin then asked Luu-ka, "Where are the others?"

"They're asleep, it's still early," she answered.

It was a pale, misty morning with not one ray of sunlight cutting through the wall of clouds. A light, soft sprinkling of warm rain added to the bleary conditions.

Rhin and Luu-ka leaned on the railing, overlooking the gentle churning of the currents.

"The ocean," said Rhin. "This is only the second time I've seen it. The first time, someone died."

Luu-ka said nothing. He hadn't expected an answer.

A tear rolled down Rhin's cheek. He wiped it from his mouth with his sleeve.

There was something about the sea that made Rhin nostalgic, as if an old friend resided in its depths. Rhin sang a verse in honor of the deep and dark water:

"The sea, the sea, of yonder days
With pikes of steel and shields of gold
All the warriors drowned today
None now shall grow old

Ships have sunk
Cities have been immersed
For seas and storms of mighty rank
Claimed them in eternal thirst

The knowledge that now lies submerged
Beckons many to a watery grave
Yet the sea will crush this wicked urge
Teaching Man he must behave

Pikes, spears and potted gold fade deep within
And all the songs are washed away
With certainty, I can say
Only to again begin"

"That was beautiful Rhin," said Luu-ka. "So sad, but beautiful."

"I learned that verse when I was younger. I always wanted to see the ocean," Rhin said, observing two birds flying side by side. He blushed, "I'm actually a little embarrassed now."

"Don't be, it was really lovely."

"Miss Luu-ka," a man dressed in white and blue rags yelled from across deck, "breakfast."

"Breakfast?" Rhin asked, confused.

"Yes. You slept an entire day."

At that she looked straight into Rhin's eyes and it was as if she was released from a spell. She laughed as they headed downstairs to the dining cabin.

The room was filled with the smell of raw fish. There were fishermen and cooks and all were occupied. One cook came up to them and scowled, pointed out their allotted seats, and shoved a platter of raw squid at them.

Then he said, while sniffling, "Eat 'em up or I'll see that you'll be thrown off the ship. It ain't gettin' any better 'en this, so no nose liftin', ya hear?"

The man yanked a gray kerchief from his pocket and blew his nose. The noise was loud and wet. He left as he had come, scoffing.

"People are real friendly here," Rhin said, eyeing the squid on the platter.

It still had ink pouring out of it and parasites clinging to its wet hide. Rhin looked away in disgust. He turned to Luu-ka, who carried the same expression and looked as if she wanted to hurl it into the sea. Their eyes met and they understood each other.

"A little stuffy in here, don't you think, Rhin?" she said, grinning.

"Yes, it is a bit cramped."

"Shall we get some fresh morning air, then?"

"Certainly."

They climbed back on deck with squid in hand and returned it to its' home. Two faint splashes. Rhin thought he heard a 'Thank you' coming from the water. He said nothing, not wanting to sound ludicrous. Then he recalled all the strange events of recent weeks and noted that a dead, talking squid almost seemed sane by comparison.

For the rest of the day he and Luu-ka just talked, swapping tales and legends. And they ate their own food. Rhin convinced himself that it was the best day of his life.

Eventually Aroukana, Chainæïa and Cononsareth woke up and had the same experience. They slipped out of the dining cabin and tossed their meals into the sea, too. And they also heard the distinct 'Thank you', but the Vevleï and Cononsareth could communicate with many life-forms so it was not unusual for them.

That night, Rhin awoke to a distressed call of, "Man overboard!"

Rhin shot up, threw on some clothes, and rushed to the deck. Sailors with torches lined the railing all about him, speaking in nervous tones. The rain was coming down hard by then, strong and blatant.

Rhin thought of his wings. They seemed powerful enough to carry him. Then he felt his own eagerness to fly overrule caution. He climbed up the mast to the crows nest and spotted the drowning sailor. Even from that distance, Rhin knew it was the fisherman who had given them the squid the day before.

He flapped his wings and flew down to rescue the man who, in the meantime, was losing the struggle with the great waters. Rhin plunged headfirst into the freezing liquid.

Those who watched held their breath.

Rhin resurfaced a moment later, his soaked, feathered wings shielding him from sight, and flew back on deck with the man hanging limp over his right shoulder. He then set him on the boards.

"Is he-" Chainæïa started.

The man stirred.

Rhin looked at the fisherman, who coughed, and asked, "Are you all right?"

"Yeah, I'm fine," the fisherman replied, then sneezed.

A cabin boy fetched a towel and a blanket for each of them. While he was walked away wrapped in his blanket, the fisherman turned his head to Rhin and thanked him without words.

"That was brave of you, Rhin," Aroukana said, patting him on the shoulder.

"Well, what was I going to do? Let him drown?"

"Let ye respect all beings, and thy path to righteousness thus be completed," said Cononsareth.

"A verse?" Luu-ka asked.

"It is an old code once used by the armies of Light," Cononsareth replied. "But I cannot remember what comes thereafter."

Rhin then recited,

"All things must be at peace
Let it be as if it were forever so, as if it never changed
Erase the evil in thine hearts and rejoice in the wilderness
However you must stay wary
For in some parts
Still does stir the darkness
Light and Dark
Battle they shall
Forever missing their mark
Neither can be eternally disintegrated
For they shall be imminently reintegrated
Unto this world
Thus is the will of Gods and the Sacred Balance
And we serve this will eternally"

A flash of memory illuminated his mind. He added,

> "Laoko, son of wolf, beast and Light
> Show thine courage and might
> For the time has come
> Evil is rising
> Take thine spear
> And surrender not
> This battle must be forever fought"

"There is your proof. You are Rhin Akvius*," Aroukana exclaimed.

"Akvius...? Why does that prove anything?"

"It is impossible that you would have known that verse without being Akvius. Only the Vevleï who survived the battle six hundred years ago would have known that verse. I was there, at the last stand of the Vevleï before they fell," Aroukana frowned. "Rhin told us this verse before the battle, giving us hope. I remember it well. He rose up into the sky, the sun shining in his silver hair, and he spoke to us of how no deed goes unnoticed and even if we all fell that day, that the war would continue and our race would prevail. After the battle he had spoken to the Béros people and he had given their leader, Laoko, his final order."

"I know it because Rhin once visited our island, long before my birth, and my people wrote scriptures of his words and deeds," Cononsareth added.

"And I believe that the repeat of that battle is at hand. Rhin Akvius is among us once again. This time we shall not fail," Aroukana told them.

"But let us not forget," Cononsareth said in a grave tone, "that he is not powerful enough to face Jiaïro yet."

"Wait a minute," Luu-ka interrupted, "you're a *God?*"

"Half-God, actually, if what these two say is true," Rhin answered, his eyes avoiding hers.

Luu-ka stayed silent after that.

---

* A derivative of 'Akviät' from a tongue even older than the so-called Eldest Speech. It meant 'Lord of Swords'.

"Rhin, you must try to remember who you are," said Chainæïa. "You are the keystone to all of this."

Rhin traced his thoughts back hundreds of years.

The memory returned of the One Evil and its sword and how he had vanquished it. But just as soon as he tried to recall it, it was gone. It was replaced by another memory of his two disciples, Akra, King of the Vevleï and Laoko, Lord of the Béros.

He saw a black sword with its blood stained edges and heard the screams of thousands, the blood curdling roars of despair. Then he witnessed another image. A dark shadow used the sword to split the earth. From the fissure an unspeakable force bubbled forth.

Suddenly, he found himself on a mountain, watching the scene replay from several miles away. As the sword was shoved into the dirt and rock, he saw red waves of energy. When the energy had dissipated he found only desolation, near-complete annihilation—with the exceptions being the One Evil in the middle of it all, and the sword. The architect of this calamity was but a vague outline, yet Rhin then saw a Béros fly into the scene and swipe the sword from the black figure and hurl it into the sky. The Béros was promptly hacked down for this grave defiance. Death seemed to set the tone for most of Rhin's dreams of late.

"Rhin," a voice from afar called out to him. "Rhin wake up."

Chapter 12
Freeland

Rhin opened his eyes and returned to the real world, roused from his memories.

"Rhin, we're here," said Luu-ka.

Rhin jumped out of bed and rushed up onto the deck alongside Luu-ka. The sky was covered with puffy gray clouds with a blue-gray horizon.

"Land! Forest path ahead, mates," the outlook bellowed from the crows nest.

Rhin gazed across the grassy plains. Beyond, as far as he could see, there were great morsh* trees. From this distance, he could just make out the thousands upon thousands of fruits that ornamented the twisted branches. At the limit of Rhin's sight, bathed in fog, the forest ended with a mountain.

The anchor plummeted into the water with a wet *klonk* and the ship came to an abrupt stop. The slow currents pulled at the chain a little, rocking sidelong, but the anchor held firm.

The docks were not part of a town, as Rhin had assumed. This was no city, nor even a village. The docks here were just a collection of weaving, wooden platforms that brushed the waves. There were ships

---

* From the East. Similar to orange trees.

all along the coast, ranging from west to east as far as the land itself, it seemed. And everywhere, there were sailors at work.

On the East Isle peace was common in most villages, the inhabitants enjoyed quiet contemplation of life. There were not many cities and there were no major ones, except for the King's city. But it had not always been so.

The mass of land in the great sea of the Fardan was home to many strange and fantastic beasts and wild flowers. The realm was gorgeous and overwhelming in its calmness, if one avoided the High Grass farthings, that is. In those parts, travelers had fallen prey to unknown and undocumented dangers. Rhin hoped he and his friends need not go there.

Rhin's eyes caught the mountain once more, its rock surface cleaving the clouds, for the peak rose even above the highest white cauliflower-shaped puff.

"What do you call that peak?" he asked Luu-ka, who was standing beside him.

"Orronor Mountain, after the huge gray creatures that live there. Their backs are covered with rock and they carry great stone clubs as weapons. They live in the caves of the mountain and are supposed to have a taste for anything with skin and bones," she said.

"Best stay out of their way," Aroukana said as he walked passed them, hefting his pack.

"If the information that Pélénor gave us is accurate then we will have to find a way into those cliffs," Rhin told them.

"Those creatures you spoke of, are they real?" Chainæïa inquired.

"The people here call them Ogres and fear them every day. No one has approached the mountain in centuries."

"Are we going to cross through that forest?" Rhin asked, eyeing the cliff ledges.

"We have two options. Take the Ofern forest road, or else skirt the coastline, which could take weeks. By the way, the Orronor stay in their caves during the day. The sun burns their flesh, they say. As long as we stay hidden at night we should live through this," Luu-ka laughed.

Rhin raised an eyebrow, "That's encouraging." Then he became serious, "Tell me, how do you know all this?"

"I used to live here."

Rhin knew not to press her further. Instead, he changed gears.

"We'd better disembark now," he said.

She agreed and followed, glued to his side, with the Vevleï and Cononsareth behind.

The fisherman whom Rhin had saved came up to them. He was garbed in his ragged white and blue outfit again, yesterday's troubles forgotten.

"Here boy," the man said handing Rhin a bundle of filthy cloth. "It's my grandpa's dagger."

Rhin unfolded the cloth, the action appearing more ceremonious than he would have liked. The dagger had a carp carved on its wooden sheath. The blade had one blue jewel near the hilt and four tiny trout circling it, touching fin to snout.

"Let it be your guide when the time comes," the fisherman muttered in Rhin's ear.

Having given Rhin a satisfied smile, he turned on his heels and walked away.

The sun had conquered the skies and sat upon its high throne before the five companions reached the periphery of the woods.

Bushes on either side of the road were covered with rich-flavored, blue-pulp berries. The oaks and morsh grew broad and some leaned. Where the branches met natural arches formed, within which one found golden halls. The path had nary a turn, thus they needed not change direction. There were a few crossroads, appearing every mile or so, where cheerful signs pointed to villages within the wood or quick ways out.

Luu-ka told them to the pay the signs no heed, their destination lay straight ahead. Rhin trusted her judgment.

Sometimes, Rhin would see a little creature dash by—perhaps a rabbit, but it seemed faster.

"What are they?" asked Chainæïa while he watched one eat a berry and then scurry into the overgrowth.

"Irlorn. They live in burrows underground. Their natural enemy is the oryox, a cunning beast with orange fur and a long, black tail," Cononsareth answered, his voice sounding frail as he watched another irlorn scurry into an opening beneath an ancient morsh tree. "I used to come here with my brothers."

A slight, cool breeze tickled the backs of their necks. Stringy, jade mushrooms hung from rigid, bland bark. Rhin found the contrast of colors spectacular. He often heard the sounds of rushing water, as if a gulley were just beyond the wall of oaks.

They had no need for the food they had brought along with them just then, for the Ofern Forest provided for all their nutritional needs.

The fruit of the Isle was like no other. Every bit was plump and juicy, and stayed so even during what was considered a bad crop or growth year. Some of the bright hues included orange, banana yellow, kiwi brown, violet and rose. And some were beyond the standard color palette. They filled a man's stomach and gave him a boost of stamina. The taste was known to soothe pain and cure indigestion. Sorcerers and Thaumaturges* would often walk through the glens and valleys in search of powerful herbs. All manner of wondrous things grew in those woods.

The road stretched out beyond eyesight. Rhin soaked up the beauty of this majestic world.

They set up camp in a small clearing. There they were nicely shaded from the sun and could lie down in the soft grass.

Eventually the sun slipped away and the moon took its place. The azure scythe lit the serene landscape. After an hour the stars appeared— a glittering awning that spanned the heavens.

Aroukana and Chainæïa were fast asleep. Cononsareth was meditating. Rhin was caught off guard when he saw the Conkatokæ levitate a foot from the leaf-strewn ground. Cononsareth was one weird creature, but he possessed many evident talents. Rhin thought he might ask the Conkatokæ just how he pulled it off sometime.

The sight made Rhin ponder the concept of impossibility.

---

* A man or woman who accepted the Balance of all things and worshiped it, and in some cases, died fighting to maintain it. Their skills ranged from the knowledge and use of healing herbs to powerful spells. A Sorcerer was a man/woman who worshiped the more advanced powers of magic, such as the spells that allowed the caster to fly or inflict instant death.

After his inner consideration, he concluded anything could happen in this world. Maybe he could even beat Jiaïro. What was impossible?

He wandered, setting his thoughts in order, as Luu-ka surveyed the moonlit night through an opening in the canopy. His legs worked of their own accord toward a pool. There he stood and watched a toad hop into the silver liquid. As the ripples expanded, the Sword of Purity was aroused.

"You are being tracked. You must leave now," it said.

"What do you mean? How could we be tracked? Jiaïro doesn't know we're here," said Rhin.

"Evil has more eyes than you could fathom, Rhin. And Jiaïro has many sons. If you do not leave now, you will die. Then Evil shall assert its dominion and all things shall wither and die with you—it is already too late, the servants of Evil have come."

Rhin raced back to their campsite. If what the sword said was true, then he knew who was involved.

Jiaïro, he thought, grimacing.

He found the camp deserted. The fire had been put out and their single tent had been punctured many times. His friends were gone.

"Aroukana, Chainæïa, Luu-ka, Cononsareth, answer me!" he cried.

But no answer came. The sword slipped from his fingers, landing with a muffled thump on the grass.

"I have failed you, my friends," he said, cupping his face in his hands.

Then he felt an immense and untried power rising within. Stooping, he reclaimed the Sword of Purity and sprinted into the darkness. The rage coursing through his veins bestowed unto him more strength than he had ever known.

The Sword of Purity's golden aura turned pitch black. Rhin cut his tongue on fangs that should have been teeth. He felt a tingling sensation as blood pounded in his ears. Even the dark held no secrets from him then, for he could see every insect, every minute movement in the shadows. He smiled, though he did not know why.

When he spotted a Daïmaan ahead, he lost his true purpose. His desire to kill was uncontrollable. He grabbed the demon by the shoulder and impaled it, a horrific screech untangling from its lips. Anxious shouts gushed into the dim woods in response to the call of distress. From above, a half dozen Daïmaans glided downward, their demonic wings spread wide.

Rhin stood still as the Sword of Purity transformed into a sharp, curved saber. Upon the blade was written in Kaïlanian runes, "No will but mine."

Rhin bowed his head. When he looked up, the corners of his mouth twisted into a menacing grin that frightened even the Children of Death. Rhin could feel his energy surge.

He vaulted, slashing in mid stride, decapitating a pair of Daïmaans. His wild, flailing frenzy of fierce attacks resulted in many others tasting his steel. Chaos ensued. The Daïmaan warriors struck at any movement in the shadows. Rhin was amused.

They fear me, he thought with delight.

The survivors fled. He gave chase. Before long, they were all dead and he was on the move again.

The moon had vanished and the sky was covered with black clouds. Not a single star shone. Maybe it was his hate that consumed the forest.

He scoured the woods until dawn. It was another bright day, as the one before had been, and all around him the forest was busy with life. This time, instead of gladdening his heart, it made him ill. Along the path there was a breach in the trees and so, because of the absence of the leafy roof, the sun shone through. As he passed through the small clearing, rather than warm his body, the sun scalded him. He growled in pain as he felt his flesh sear and bubble.

Rhin carefully walked along the outskirts of the sunny spots and began the chase again. The sun's treachery had a lasting effect on him. He could not control the malignance that had taken root in him anymore. He began to think like an escaped beast. He howled and clambered up the oaks as if he had done so for a thousand years. It did not take him long to adapt to these novel conditions.

He found an extinguished campfire and sniffed at the ashes.

It smells of steel and blood, Rhin thought.

Rhin knew the stench of Jiaïro's men sure enough.

He marveled at his improved sense of smell. Sharp and attuned, he could now find his friends without issue. All he had to do was track the fresh scent.

Rhin's longing for blood was insatiable. Laughing, he forged ahead. The hunt was on.

Within the confines of the abandoned camp, Luu-ka was mulling over the facts.

I took a walk last night. I got a little lost. I finally found my way back only to discover that everyone has disappeared. What is going on here?

She followed the trail to a clearing where the sunlight was fierce. Not two feet in front of her lay a shred of tissue off a cloak.

Luu-ka recognized the material. Fabric from Rhin's clothes.

But when she bent to pick it up it sizzled like wet wood on a fire.

This isn't right, she told herself.

She followed the path, near tears.

Rhin's search had lasted hours. No luck as of yet, and his impatience grew with every whiff of his prey. They covered their tracks well, and traveled in several small groups to confuse any pursuers. Rhin, with his newfound skills, was too clever for this tactic, though. He had already dispatched a pair of soldiers who had backtracked to erase footprints.

Rhin climbed a morsh and he saw them, Jiaïro's soldiers. He noted a prison pavilion beyond, watched by no less than six men.

He told himself, *Friends there, must save them. But where is the girl?*

Something within urged him to forget her. A voice inside his head told him to focus on the task at hand. Rhin's thoughts were sluggish. The more he used his animal side the less remained of his other half. It scared him, yet at the same time fueled his new power.

"Fifty, easy prey," Rhin muttered to himself.

He was certain that his abducted companions were being held in the prison pavilion. All he had to do was slaughter the guards.

Though it irked him, he awaited nightfall before his attack. Since sunlight harmed him and there was little shade in the camp's environs, he thought it best.

This plan also gave him a lot of time to watch the patrol routes and the guard's shift changes. Rhin grinned, threads of saliva dangling from his canine teeth. With the amount of noise the soldiers made and how slow they marched, he may as well have been given a private invitation.

The sun had set at last. He leapt from his tree and padded toward one of the guards, slit him open and dragged his body behind a fern. He repeated the process many times, creating a nice hole in the camp's defenses. When the way was clear, and near a dozen warriors lay oozing in the shrubs, he approached the pavilion and sniffed.

Rhin stuck his head in and saw the Vevleï and Conkatokæ bound to pikes. Their fear was obvious, even to him.

"What is that thing?" Chainæïa asked, horrified.

Then Cononsareth, answered him, "Do you not recognize him? It is Rhin."

"That cannot be," said Chainæïa as he gaped at Rhin.

Rhin's stomach writhed as he thought, *Am I ugly?*

"Alarm! Demon," a soldier screamed.

A bell tolled from somewhere in the camp. The troops were alerted.

"Dead! The brush is filled with corpses," another man called from the outer ring of the camp.

Rhin brandished his blade and attacked his foes before they could rally. The dance of gore and shadows caused the nearby wildlife to flee.

The commander emerged from his tent in full armor, a deadly long axe in hand. Rhin recognized him. Evok, one of Jiaïro's many marshals and the warlock that had stalked Rhin on his first night in Kremmä.

"I am amazed, Rhin. My own brother, who was always standing up for everything stupid—I mean 'good', of course. Now look at you. Your power has tripled. Do you not see how profitable the sweet touch of Evil can be?" Evok said, watching Rhin engage in the slaughter.

Rhin turned around and remembered the night Evok attacked him. It seemed to him that Evok had grown since the last time they met.

"Your soldiers—weak. You lost training skill," Rhin barked, his voice harsh and choppy.

"Why do you say that?" Evok asked in the same way one might ask someone to pass the butter.

"Fight like mice. Worst fighters I've seen," Rhin answered, severing a foe's lower leg.

"I advise you to keep your forked tongue inside your trap," this time Evok's tone held anger.

"I do what I want. You won't stop me."

"I am warning you, brother. My strength spans mountains above your own. Besides, if you cannot speak properly then you should not speak at all."

"Warn me, eh? I laugh."

"I would have you join us, Rhin, but if you keep this conversation going I may be forced to destroy you."

"Never join you. Even if Rayïm was only other choice. Never."

Evok's eyes brightened and a green light started to glow about his figure. Rhin remembered the hands. The cold, hairy hands.

"I am most disappointed. Lord Jiaïro, however, won't give a damn. Very well. Die now," Evok answered as his eyes became clear as glass, refracting the moonlight.

Soldiers and Daïmaans alike crawled from the tents. From all directions, they encircled Rhin.

"I'll kill you and your brothers," Rhin called.

"They're your brothers as well. If this is what you want, to die so uselessly, then so be it, anarchist."

Rhin growled as he dug his jagged saber into a neck. He did not care whether it be demon or soldier, they were all his enemies. He lopped a head clean off a pair of shoulders and shivered, reveling in the bloodbath.

He recognized at once that the Daïmaans possessed superior skill when compared to the soldiers. The only possible conclusion Rhin came up with when he asked himself why they worked together was that Jiaïro had the power to manipulate Kaïle. He did not enjoy that thought.

As he tore through an enemy's armor, he wondered, *How far is Jiaïro's reach?*

The tide turned against him. The soldiers jammed their spears into Rhin's cloak, pinning him to the ground.

"Rhin," said Evok, "your friends shall die a most painful death. Take that knowledge with you as you perish."

Whatever virtue was left in Rhin resurfaced upon hearing the word 'friends'. He mustered all his strength and leapt to his feet. The cloak ripped. The soldiers that had pinned him down were launched into the air and overgrowth.

"Leave them alone or I'll rip your ribs out," Rhin said, overcome with rage.

Evok ordered his troops from the field, "This one is mine."

Rhin lunged at Evok, but the marshal was too strong. Before Rhin could retaliate, Evok grabbed him by the neck and lifted him from the earth. The marshal held his sword aloft for all to see. He prepared to deliver the coup de grace, but just as all seemed lost for Rhin, a clear voice chimed.

"Rhin, what has happened?"

It was Luu-ka.

Rhin remembered the Sword of Purity's warning at the pond. Then he remembered arriving at the meager campsite. Finally he remembered that she had not been there.

"Luu-ka," he murmured.

Evok hurled Rhin to the soil. Luu-ka ran up to him and stared at the creature that he had become.

She turned to Evok and shouted, "What have you done to Rhin, you monster?"

She unsheathed her sword and took a swing at Evok, who jumped back but was still caught across the cheek. The cut bled black blood.

Evok started to laugh but his face betrayed his fury.

"Fool," he said, "you cannot save him. He has embraced the powers of Evil."

"You tricked him into doing so," Luu-ka answered.

She slashed at the marshal, who sidestepped. The point of the blade caught his forehead nonetheless.

"Why you little-"

Evok punched her and she toppled.

Rhin screamed and sprung. The black aura around his sword ceased to exist. Instead, there was a golden light. The Sword of Purity had returned to its original state and Rhin with it. He had turned back to the light. In the blink of an eye he was himself again.

To Evok he said, "Now you will die."

He removed Evok's sword-hand, knocking the marshal off balance and then stabbed him through heart. There was a sickening squelch as the flesh was caught in a steely embrace. To finish him for good, Rhin removed Evok's head.

The soldiers scattered. Where Evok's hand had fallen there was something new. A sparkling, solid gold ornament had taken the place of Evok's ghastly manus. In the shape of a human hand, etched upon the artifact was a series of indecipherable runes.

Though he could never be sure of it, Rhin could have sworn he heard a soft, echoing voice say, "To the West, Rhin."

He scooped up the hand and put it in his sack. It did not weigh much at all, to Rhin's surprise.

He felt proud with his rejection of the Evil within his own body and soul.

He knew that he and his companions must not remain in that clearing.

Rhin scooped Luu-ka up with one arm, cut his friends' chains and said to them, "Follow me. Don't worry, I'll fly low."

With those words he carried Luu-ka into the sky.

Rhin tended to her all night long, never leaving her side. Aroukana told him many a time that he was overreacting, that the girl had received but a tiny bruising. Rhin did not heed him. He rested on his knees in the grass beside her. When Chainæïa came by to check up (more for his sake then for Luu-ka, Rhin suspected) he knelt by the girl.

"A pleasant surprise is in order when she awakes," he said.

"Good, thank you," Rhin breathed. On impulse, he said, "Chainæïa, I'm sorry."

"For what?"

"For being a lousy savior."

"Rhin, it is only through fright that we become brave. And it is only through war that we achieve lasting peace. Thus, it is only through darkness that we may find the true light. Do not dwell on these nightmares of yours. Sleep well, young friend."

Chainæïa walked off.

"Twice you saved me," Rhin whispered in Luu-ka's ear, "and for that I'll watch over you forever."

In the morning Luu-ka woke up to the grandest display of fruits she had ever seen. There were blueberries, blackberries, strawberries, oranges, mangoes, and more. The sunlight glinted, golden dew droplets glittering in its radiance. The world seemed brighter that morning, and the millions of deep green leaves and shrubs whistled with life. Squirrels, irlorn and other woodland critters were but darting specks and hushed footfalls, excited and bursting with vitality.

Around her were her friends, the two kind-hearted Vevleï, the mysterious but sweet turtle-man, and Rhin. They stood over her, eyes aglow with happiness. After all, they were still alive, and a new day had begun.

She smiled and tossed a blackberry in her mouth. And when her eyes met Rhin's, she understood everything that had happened. They had remained linked telepathically ever since the Servant's attack.

Rhin stood with his arms crossed, resting his back against a tree. He gave her a sheepish grin, and she grinned right back.

Chapter 13
Out of the Forest

The five companions trudged along the forest path while Rhin told them all that had transpired the day before. When the sun reached its highest point, they came to the end of the wood. Before them, stretching across the land, was the massive mountain range of Orronor. Its tip dusted with snow, the mountain was so tall that, once they got close enough, the peaks blocked the sunlight and shaded the group. A modest wood bordered its left edge and a pond graced its right, gullies funneling the water back to sea. The stone giant seemed to beckon them ever forward.

"What's our next destination, Luu-ka? You know this land better than we do," said Cononsareth.

"The village of Tandar is where we'll rest. We can buy enough supplies there to circle the mountain twice," she told them.

"Luu-ka," Rhin said with a shrug, "we don't have any money."

"Don't worry, Rhin," she held up a small bag of Vilts, the currency of the Four Isles. "I've enough."

"Can you believe it? Miss is quite the planner," Cononsareth stood there, astonished.

"How did you get all of that?" Rhin asked.

Its size was deceptive for the bag contained enough Vilts to buy a small house.

"I told you she would be of use to us," said Chainæïa.

"Ah. Actually, I believe I heard otherwise," Aroukana replied, rubbing his chin.

"But I did, I did," Chainæïa riposted as he stood.

The others laughed. The two Vevleï had become great friends since they had met. The quarrel was only for comedic distraction.

They treat each other as equals in spite of their noticeable age difference, Rhin noted.

Tandar was a humble village at the very foot of Orronor Mountain. They lived mainly off fish from the lake in the center of the town. Colonies came through once a month and the villagers were able to trade their fur and fish for spices and meats. The soil was rich enough for farming, in part because of the mountain spring that supplied the lake. The townsfolk cultivated grains, such as rice, most of the time. When the corn they planted every fifth year grew tall they feasted on the rare delicacy.

There were many small settlements, whose folk lived much the same as in Tandar—these communities stayed out of each other's business. This did not mean they were inhospitable people. To the contrary, the general population was very welcoming. When distant family members arrived, there would be a show and a celebration in their honor.

Halfway across the world, a man watched Rhin through his Crystal of Sight. The Crystal, a tall, faceted object the size of an average man, sparkled. Though the light irritated him, all light did, the man needed it to travel great distances in a matter of seconds. Whenever he wished, he would recite some Evil words, specify the destination loudly, step inside the Crystal and disappear. It was a rare artifact and there were only a dozen souls in all Iora to be fortunate, or devious, enough to possess one.

The room around him was dim, lit only by candlelight, and decorated with skulls of all sizes. Hundreds and hundreds of books lay scattered across a sizable, sturdy table and the room in general.

The man read the passages in his spell books again, shuffling through the pages in irritation.

He stopped and laughed. Hunched over, he squinted at the runes in triumph, a little glob of drool spilling onto the parchment.

"Yeshh, yeshh that'shh it," he said to himself.

He was a Sorcerer, and one of the most cunning of the brood. He and his kind were an age-old abomination that the world had cast away long ago.

Sorcerers had become a part of myth or legend. This particular soul did not mind. He was not interested in the so called prophecy of the 'Restoration of Order'—a story told by many proclaiming that one day Sorcery would return and claim its place as the Order to which all beings would be compelled. He would call such nonsense a 'waste of time and effort'.

He was only interested in his own restoration to power. He had planned for many centuries to achieve his goal.

His voice was his strangest aspect. Even his brothers had not known the truth of how it had been impaired. There had been much speculation, though, but at long last the true story surfaced.

Ages ago, he had participated in magical skirmishes with other Sorcerers. On one such encounter, the last one of which he partook, he had been vanquished and the opposing Sorcerer, irritated by having been challenged by such an unworthy adversary, numbed his tongue. Ever after he 'slished' his words.

But his time had come. He was eyeing a spell of pure Evil. One of the oldest ever fashioned.

"Foolshh. I'll teach them," he coughed and stumbled through the arcane language. "Take me to Tandar."

Tandar slept. A whisper came with the wind and passed into Luu-ka's ear. It told her to rise and go to the kitchens. At first, she was reluctant, but soon she could no more disobey than awaken.

The whisper clouded her mind like a dense brume. Luu-ka stood up and opened her eyes. She was about to vomit when her body embraced the wooden floor and all was gone, her life as well as her mind.

Her soul was trapped in another world while an alien wickedness spread throughout her body. Her possessed form floundered toward the edge of the stairs and began to descend. Down, down, down into the kitchens she went. There she found a butcher's knife.

She was lead into Cononsareth's room across the hall. The slumbering Conkatokæ breathed rhythmically. Holding the knife aloft, she screamed and struck for Cononsareth's heart. He woke with a start and somersaulted out of bed.

The Conkatokæ got a good look at the girl. Her eyes resembled writhing worms, her teeth were sharp and stained yellow. Her skin was greasy and sallow. Luu-ka screamed again. She ran at Cononsareth with the knife and attempted another attack. She bore down with the weapon but, before she could strike, Cononsareth shone through the darkness with a luminescent aura.

"Be gone, Evil spirit. Leave this girl and return from whence you came. The light of my race compels you. Be gone!" he bellowed.

Luu-ka collapsed, sobbing—all the vile energy of the phantasm that had resided within her was dispelled. What was left was her frigid body on the floor.

Rhin entered, and froze in the doorway. Bewildered, he asked, "What happened to her? Are you both alright?"

"She was possessed by evil spirits," Cononsareth answered, cracking his knuckles. "After a night of rest she should be fine."

Rhin looked at Luu-ka on the ground. She was pale and shivering from the cold, rotten taste of evil. Together, they carried her back to her room and tucked her in bed.

The Sorcerer howled in fury.

"I washh shho closhhe."

He took out his spell book and stared at the Crystal of Sight. He flipped through a few pages and another spell caught his mad eye.

"Firshht shhome shhleep. In the morning I shhall commenchhe with the preparationshh for my greateshht shhpell yet."

He had been alone for so long that he engaged in philosophical but schizophrenic conversations with himself. On rare occasions he spoke to his spell books, asking them to help his magic take more potent effect.

He lumbered into a small room with a bed at its center. The bed, instead of the usual comforts of a pillow and covers, had spikes protruding from its hard metal surface. He lay to rest on the spikes and dozed off. Soon the room was filled by a profound snoring.

In the morning Luu-ka awoke feeling woozy. She walked down to the first floor of the inn and got a piece of toast with honey, the common breakfast at most inns and her personal favorite. But then she found she was not hungry. All she felt was weakness and illness.

Rhin came in the room and, seeing Luu-ka's expression, asked, "What's wrong?"

"I don't feel too well."

"Do you remember what happened last night?"

"I was asleep. Nothing unusual about that, eh?"

"You don't remember anything?"

"No. What are you talking about?"

Rhin recounted what had occurred as she sat there with a dry, open mouth.

"Why can't I remember?" she asked him.

"I don't know. Cononsareth said you will stop feeling sick soon. He said, 'the taste of Evil will wear off quickly in a heart as pure as her own.'"

She blushed. And after a moment of awkward silence Rhin helped her prepare her baggage.

Soon they were off to Orronor Mountain, the final obstacle between them and Daish-rog's resurrection.

Aroukana had seen to purchasing mounts at the stables. The creatures were nothing like northern horses, however. They had beaks like a bird, the legs of a reptile and scaly heads with glowing green eyes. Two oversized spikes protruded from their heads. Some of them were cracked and broken from charging at a foe or tearing up the ground. Their tails and hind legs were speckled with feathers. Their front legs sprouted bird wings. These served no purpose, for it was said that none had flown for hundreds of years. Some claimed the ability had been lost, while others, who had more intimate knowledge, supposed the magnificent animals awaited a day when their gift would be needed.

Chainæïa was not too fond of the beasts but Luu-ka and Rhin in particular seemed to enjoy the ride.

"Uderraad, the peasants call them," Aroukana informed, giving his mount a fond pat.

"Long live the Uderraad," said Rhin, smiling.

He rubbed his steed under its chin. It sneezed in response.

"Indeed," Chainæïa said.

Then Chainæïa's mount bucked, dislodging him from the saddle. It was lucky for him that he was holding on tight enough to regain balance. The Uderraad gave a loud snort, as if amused.

"Lovely," Chainæïa said, turning as green as the grass.

"I think they are adorable," Luu-ka said kissing her Uderraad on the head.

"Do they have names, Aroukana?" Rhin asked.

"Yes, the stable boy told me their names. He seemed to care greatly for them. Yours is called Valerraad. Chainæïa's and Luu-ka's are Perraad and Vorraad. Mine is Adorraad and Cononsareth's is Herraad."

"Is it customary for their given names to end in such a way?" Cononsareth asked.

"Yes, I was told that it is," said the Vevlea.

"I think I'll go ahead and scout. My wings need exercise," Rhin said.

With that he lifted off, increasing in speed with every stroke of his powerful new limbs. He flew over Ogre Mountain in the East, the wind blowing through his hair. The more he took to the skies, the more he enjoyed the sensation. He followed the shoreline until he found the docks where he and the others had first arrived on the Isle.

There he witnessed a terrifying sight. The familiar green gap split open in the sky and the black shadows flew out, dozens at a time. Thunderclouds formed as he hastened back to his friends.

"The Servant returns, its shadow brews near the northern shore," he warned his friends.

"Why has it taken such an interest in us?" asked Chainæïa.

"The Servant thirsts not for our blood, but for his," said Cononsareth, indicating Rhin with his scaly, webbed hand.

They left in silence, making their way southeast toward Ogre Mountain. The threat that was the Servant and its host of immortal demons loomed over them as much as the storm clouds.

At Ogre Mountain the sky was pink and blue with patches of rich purple. It had rained for hours before, and thunder had clapped to the south and west. But now the weather was peaceful, and the tenebrous forces of the storm spent. Now, there was only the mountain towering before them, the behemoth a testament to the undeniable powers that shaped the world.

They came to a cave, one of the few breaches in the outer wall of the mountain, and saw the passage that led to the beginnings of the trail they must follow. They decided to spend the night there, for to enter Orronor at night was to invite death to one's door.

It was pitch black and soundless inside the mouth of the cave. It did not take long for Rhin to fall asleep from pure fatigue after the effort spent to reach the foot of the mountain a day ahead of schedule.

In the middle of the night, Rhin woke up to the sound of water dripping off the stalactites. When he thought all was well and tried to sleep again, he heard a deep, rumbling boom and then another.

He stood up and looked ahead, squinting. In the distance, there was an orange-red wave of fire. It bloomed like a brightly colored lotus, ever expanding. Then he heard the noise again, this time louder and closer. *Boom. Boom.*

The last tremble shook the earth and he lost his balance, biting his lip and cutting his wrist on a jagged rock. He ripped a strip of fabric from his shirt sleeve and tied a tight knot over the wound. This did not stop the swelling or the discoloration.

He looked up again and saw a catapult hurling spheres of fire into the forest. The Daïmaans were burning it down. It seemed that the pain from his wrist had improved his vision.

Because of Rhin's love for nature, he was infuriated by this folly. He did not care who stood in his way, he would sabotage the catapult.

The cool night breeze soothed his wound throughout his flight, but a little voice in his head kept repeating, *This is insane, Rhin, and you know it.*

It was his voice of reason, but Rhin could not remember the last time he had listened to it.

From far off he could see who was responsible for the burning.

Daïmaan scum, Rhin thought.

When he arrived what he saw was unexpected. Monraïk warriors were attacking the Daïmaans. This would aid Rhin in destroying the catapult. A useful distraction.

He soared down, hovering slightly above the ground, right next to the catapult. There were several of the beasts hauling the ammunition into place and then launching it. He crept up behind one of them and tapped his shoulder, catching him off guard.

"Hey," he said.

The Daïmaan guard growled. Rhin realized the beast was calling for help. Soon, there were three more, those that had been operating the siege weapon, who stood before Rhin. They eyed him cautiously. None dared approach him just yet. Rhin, however, made their choice for them when he turned and dashed off. It was easier to pursue a fleeing and broken enemy than stand against a bold one.

Rhin ran into the forest. The Daïmaans followed. They were a few yards behind him and were moving very fast. Twisted, jagged scimitars slashed at the branches as the demons gave chase. Their cruel and perfect eyes remained locked on their prey, like pale green spotlights.

These creatures were bred for war, Rhin thought.

It was difficult to keep ahead of them, but he managed. These Daïmaan creatures were nearly flawless and did not go wanting for agility, and yet, while Rhin could not help but marvel at their impressive speed and strength, he found that in wit they were lacking. He kicked a stone up and caught it, in mid stride, and tossed it into the bushes to his right. He then rolled into the overgrowth and the Daïmaans chased the rock, not him.

They trust their ears more than their eyes, Rhin observed.

Before the Daïmaans knew of their mistake, Rhin had returned to where the catapult was stationed.

With deft flicks of his sword hand, he sliced a wooden brace clean in half. Then he carved at one of the wheels, just enough to make it unstable and capable of buckling under the weight it carried. Then he cut a rope or two.

In self-gratification, he took a step back to admire his work. Arms crossed, a crooked grin on his face, he took to the sky.

After the demons returned from the chase, screaming at one another, they resumed operation of the catapult. Rhin watched from his unique vantage point, still grinning. All he had to do was to wait.

The Daïmaan loaded a fireball into the sack at the end of the arm and positioned the catapult.

Rhin clenched his fists when he saw that the demons weren't even targeting their enemies, the Monraïkian soldiers—they were aiming for the trees on purpose.

"Scum," he hissed, his pulse pounding in his ears.

But the sabotage worked. The wheel rolled away, tilting the siege weapon to an awkward angle, and the catapult fired by accident hitting the reinforcements of the dark warriors and giving the Monraïkian warriors a powerful advantage over their enemies. Then the ropes came loose and the catapult fell into pieces, crushing a few more Daïmaans.

The Daïmaan captain, who Pélénor recognized as the sadist Söero, was furious and started screaming at his men. Rhin understood what he was saying.

"You idiots! You did not tie it tightly enough, useless fools."

He lopped off a few heads and told his army, what was left of it, to go to the sea and make their last stand there.

"Let the black waters take these filthy 'warriors'. We shall see them all in hell," the Daïmaan captain spat, stomping his hoof-like feet.

Rhin saw the captain of the Monraïkian army urging his men on, asking them for one last charge. Rhin looked closer to see Pélénor at the head of the army, commanding them into a formation. Rhin gasped.

"I know you're all battle-weary and exhausted, but hear me now. Give me one more drive—one more push at these faithless husks—and let's end this."

A group of soldiers in the frontlines beat at their shields with the flats of their blades, the rhythm resounding clean and clear in the night. Others followed along, growing more eager with every clash. Flickering flames danced on shiny plate, light and dark engaging in a skirmish of their own.

"Archers," Pélénor directed, holding his hand up high. "Loose."

He slashed the air with his arm, reaching for the stars. Every one of the Monraïkian bowmen was well trained and experts in accuracy. Each arrow pierced flesh or chain mail, leather padding or muscle. And once the shaft had tagged its mark, the archer would already have another nocked and readied.

"Hold your fire," Pélénor ordered. "Infantry, move in. Take them out."

He raised a flag, a gold sword on a green field.

The infantry advanced, moving ever faster toward the demons.

"Cavalry, ride with me," Pélénor called, mounting his horse.

"Here, who'll be hewn first?" Söero screamed.

The Daïmaans charged, their blood stained swords and spears held in front. For a moment there was almost silence, with only shallow breathing to be heard. Then, the battalions were as one—a torrent of death and confusion, swallowed whole into the chaotic mass.

The first rank of the Daïmaans was quick to fall. The sounds of demon skulls crushed underfoot added themselves to the cacophony.

The second line of beasts proved more determined, but just as it seemed they would break the Monraïkian infantry, the Elite horsemen threw their pikes and hit the middle row, piercing Söero himself.

The Daïmaans retaliated with a scattered and weak volley, striking a half-dozen of their enemies. But the Monraïk cavalry was far too strong, outnumbered as they were on the field of battle. Söero arose from a pool of his brothers' blood and took a pike from one of the fallen soldiers. Pélénor charged toward the Daïmaan captain, but Söero was prepared. He took the spear and hurled it at the horse, killing it. The animal whinnied for the last time, falling to the grime-and guts soaked dirt.

"Die, Monraïk," Söero exclaimed, relieving one of his few living soldiers of his sword. The nameless warrior, defenseless, received an axe-blow to the neck, the blood spattering over Söero's face. The demon captain rubbed his clawed hand over his soiled skin, and then licked it. A crazed sneer revealed his snake-like fangs. He gestured for Pélénor to come at him.

Pélénor picked up a stray arrow from one of his fallen comrades, launching himself at Söero. Dodging two of the Daïmaan's blows, he stabbed the demon in the chest.

"You won't burn any more forests, you slimy wretch," said Pélénor, jerking and twisting the shaft.

Söero was the last to fall in the battle. The cheers erupted from the Monraïkian warriors and they punched the air.

"Vara, Pélénor!"

The soldiers shook their brothers-in-arms' hands and saluted their captain.

The army then searched the battlefield for any survivors and prayed for the souls of their fallen comrades.

Rhin had watched everything, glad the destruction of the woods had ended.

"Touching moment... Do you not think so, Rhin?" an icy voice said from behind him.

His head pivoted round and he saw Ryul.

Ryul took a knife out of his boot and lunged at Rhin. Rhin used his wings to push himself to the side and punched Ryul in the face. Ryul licked the blood off his mouth and flew higher. Rhin followed. The chase continued into clouds that formed circular patterns, the two of them focusing only on each other.

"I should have known you were behind this, Ryul."

Rhin's ancient strength was slowly returning to him.

"And I should have known you would be here to stop me."

"Your army has lost, Ryul. Jiaïro will fall."

"Ah yes. I nearly forgot you were the last son. You will never stop him. You are weak with compassion and love," Ryul's eyes flickered with a sudden boost in confidence. "Yes... I know there is one whom you care about above the others."

By now Ryul's revolting rictus could have caused his face to explode. He crossed his arms, his face a mask of wicked elation.

"What are you talking about?"

"Compassion and love, Rhin. Compassion for all of them, love for one of them," Ryul laughed, exposing yet another facet of his sadism. "I know your greatest fear, Rhin. I know about that dream you had right before you met the Vevlea rat. I know because I gave it to you."

"So it is not a prediction of the future."

"Are you so sure, Rhin? Are you so sure? Do you know where you are when the vision takes place?"

"The Temple of Resurrection," Rhin made the words sound almost like an insult and he shot a grimace at Ryul.

Undaunted, Ryul continued, "Yes, your quest shall be her undoing."

"I won't believe it."

Rhin charged at Ryul, flailing at him. Ryul barely even took notice and then punched into Rhin's stomach holding his fist there. The stench of his breath blackened Rhin's lungs.

The last thing Ryul said before letting him go was, "Rebel angels always die. I give you permission to fall from grace and rot."

Rhin fell and fell, the air knocked violently out of his lungs. He had no strength left in him. His joints froze up. His eyes were wide open and all of his energy was diverted into the effort of catching his breath. Images flashed in his mind. All of them were centered on Luu-ka.

He hit an object with a loud thud. But before he could think he fainted.

He was in a white room. It was completely empty. He could not tell if he was seeing clearly because there was nothing to see.

"Am I dead?" he whispered, his voice sounding hollow to his ears.

"No," another whisper told him.

The voice that answered him was identical to his. He could not tell if he was talking to himself or not.

"Where am I?" said Rhin.

"You are in your own mind," was the answer.

"Why is it blank?"

"Because you are not thinking of anything. Except for me."

Rhin tried to look around but could not find his own body. Instead he saw bright light emanating from where he thought he was lying on the floor.

"Who are you?"

"I am you and I am your worst enemy. Paradoxically, I am your creator and destroyer. I am an individualization of your subconscious."

"I don't understand."

"The worst enemy anyone could ever have is one's self."

"So I am you?"

"Yes and no. I am you and I am your opposite. I am the cause of your life and death. I am what you are and yet I am completely different."

"How do I leave?"

"You shouldn't."

"But my friends-"

"Are no longer your concern."

"But I must-"

"Let Fate direct you along the road you must take."

"I don't believe in Fate."

"Fate has decided that your role has run its course. Your curtain call has come."

"Have I dissolved into an Orb?"

"No."

"Then why am I trapped here?"

"You are not trapped, far from it. You are unconscious and are dying slowly. I have kept you here to save you from the suffering of your corporeal self."

"I will save them."

"Are they worth it?"

"Worth dying for."

"If that is your choice, then Gods' speed, Rhin Akvius."

Rhin woke up to find himself in a critical state. He was shaking and bleeding. The only thing that kept him alive was a sort of defiance. Rhin would not lie down and die. He stumbled and tripped several times and his wings were being dragged through the dirt. He kept thinking how he must persevere. That thought was all that he had for the moment. He walked on and on, hauling himself in no apparent direction. When he could go no further he collapsed upon himself, falling to his knees.

With a final effort he gasped and whispered, "Failed."

After the fall he landed, face first in the mud, as the rain tinkled on his body.

Luu-ka was pacing back and forth around the campsite. She would have been out looking for Rhin but Chainæïa had restrained her. Aroukana said it would be a better idea to just wait. He said that Rhin could pop up any minute now.

That was four hours ago.

Luu-ka was clenching her left fist. She had had enough of this waiting. Then she felt a pain in her ribs and an image came to her of Rhin falling and hitting the ground, hard.

"Rhin!" she cried.

"What is it?" Chainæïa asked, jumping to his feet.

"He's hurt, I know it. I'm going to look for him!"

"No-"

But before he could finish, she had mounted one of the Uderraad and was off. After several minutes she was a tiny speck on the horizon.

She searched for a long time not finding one lead. Then she came to a hill and looked out at the forest and she saw the remnants of last night's battle... the broken catapult and the heaped corpses of the fallen Daïmaans. She went toward the exact spot where Rhin fell from the sky. She saw the crack where he had hit the ground.

"Rhin," she called. "Rhin," she repeated, "come back."

Rhin was in the blank room again. This time he was not as disoriented - he knew where he was.

"I told you there is no escape from death."

"I can still save them, even if I am an inch from death."

"You are an inch from death."

"Then I can still save them."

"How?"

Rhin was silent.

"See, you don't even have a clue."

"Let me out."

"Why?"

"I want to try again."

"What is the point, Rhin? Death comes for everyone."

"That may be true, but it is not at my door yet."

"But it shall be soon."

"You don't understand."

"You have no idea how much I understand."

"Show yourself."

A boy no older than twelve came forth. The red hair, the bright green eyes... it was obvious to him then that this was no joke. He was caught inside the web of his own thoughts.

"You... I-" Rhin started.

"I told you that I am you. I come to you as a child because children are innocent and pure, and not yet corrupted by Evil."

"If you are as pure as you say, then let me out, please."

Rhin shouted the words but soon they lost meaning. He was angry, and his anger shook the white emptiness around him. With his every breath, the tranquility of that void was upset.

Out of fear of losing control of the situation the boy said, "If this is how you want to die then I will let you do as you wish. But know this, you cannot survive. It is impossible. Go."

Luu-ka heard rustling nearby. She dismounted the Uderraad and rushed toward the sounds. And there he was, Rhin, leaning against a rock. He smiled and toppled over backward. His head hit the ground, and he was gone again. Luu-ka kneeled by his side, sobbing.

It was pitch-black but Rhin could sense light and began to turn around until he saw a speck of it. At least he assumed it was light.

"Rhin come. Rhin your time is now. Come with me."

It was a mighty echoing voice that was beckoning him.

Rhin felt warmth inside. He was floating around but he was trying to disobey the voice.

"Rhin come," it said again.

Rhin shook his head.

"I am not dead," he said.

"Yes you are."

"And who are you?"

"I am the Infinite. Come."

"Why?"

"Defy me, will you?"

The voice twisted and did not seem righteous anymore. In that instant, Rhin saw through the masquerade.

"I know who you are now. You are the King of Daïmaans. You're trying to take me to Kaïle and the Pits of Rayïm."

"Clever, aren't we?"

'Try as you might, you will never claim me."

"Rhin, Rhin please," said another voice.

It came from elsewhere. It was the voice of Luu-ka.

"You think you can escape?" the Infinite echoed with fury.

"I have already eluded death's grasp twice. What makes you think I can't do it a third time?"

And with his words still resounding in the vast destitution, Rhin unsheathed the Sword of Purity and tore a hole in the world. A blinding, glaring light beamed from the new gap, and this attack seemed to have cut the source of the Infinite itself. There was a terrible scream, like the high wailing of a thousand demons.

Rhin soared into the emptiness of his imagination and came out of the darkness. He chased after the kind voice and awoke to see Luu-ka, sitting on her knees, holding his hand. Tears had moistened her cheeks, but she was as beautiful as ever.

"Rhin," she shouted with joy.

He almost fainted a fourth time from the rough hug she gave him. Noticing his weakness, she restrained herself.

"Can you move?"

"Yes."

He somehow managed, with Luu-ka's help, to slide onto the Uderraad's saddle. And they rode away together as the sun set behind Orronor Mountain.

Ryul was watching from high in the clouds.

"How many times must I kill you, Rhin?" he growled.

He soared away toward one of his other base objectives.

The most diabolical voice he knew spoke to him. The telepathy drilled into his mind, unwelcome but overpowering, "Do not fail me again, Ryul."

The voice chilled him to his black core. Even more disturbing, however, was the knowledge that his mentor had been angered.

The beating of his veined, bat-like wings became his uncomfortable companion. The joints of his bones ached under the constant strain. He had to push himself, though, for many tasks still required his attention. The dark designs could not wait. The master would not wait.

He flew on.

Chapter 14
Orronor Mountain

Rhin lay atop Valerraad, the sun in his face. When he tried to shift his weight he felt ropes binding him in place. He squinted. Luu-ka and Cononsareth were riding beside him on their own steeds. They had not noticed that he was awake and he could not tell them for he was too weak to speak. A trickle of blood rolled down his nose. He was inclined to move his right arm but the rope held fast.

The caked coating of pollen draped the brown grass. Little yellow clusters of the stuff fluttered around him as Valerraad trotted onward. Every now and then an irlorn would scamper into view only to hide in the bushes. The furry animals watching the procession of strangers pass by with large, curious eyes.

Rhin had just enough energy to move his eyes. He looked up and there it was in front of them, the central cliff of Orronor, also known as Ogre Mountain. Within this very cluster of rock the Temple of Resurrection lay hidden. The place he and Aroukana had set out for, from the city of Monra, three months ago. The sanctuary where they would restore Daish-rog's soul to his body would be hard to find and Rhin knew this. But he also knew that if it was his will, it was good enough for them.

It was from this point that Rhin had seen the fire in the forest two days ago. Rhin groaned and closed his eyes again.

From one of the many caves of Ogre Mountain, a figure was watching, gritting its teeth. His yellow eyes were glowing from inside a cave. He looked down on his unsuspecting prey and grumbled. Three more of them appeared from the depths of the blackness.

"We feast'en well 'night," one growled.

"Good'en feast, plenty blood for drink'en'," agreed another.

"Yep, yep. We have'en big, big food'en," a third one grunted.

The other was silent. He was sharper than the rest and he was the one that would trap the 'fools'. The rest of them knew it as well as he did.

The Orronor tribe paid homage to the slyest of their pack. In return, he would hunt and supply for them. The Ogres had a lot of trouble pronouncing the words of the common speech. But since they had no language of their own they had to attempt it. Their large lead tongues could not make the proper sounds half the time, and even when they did manage it, they would put an 'en' sound after most words.

"Why'en you no bein'en happy, Groaer?"

The silent Orronor, Groaer replied, "These be'en big smart'en men. This be'en hard."

"No, you be'en more smart'en than all small'en men together."

"We will'en see'en about that."

"Keep in the sun," said Cononsareth, "If we do not, the Ogres will come for us."

Rhin was sleeping.

"Let's rest here. I worry for Rhin," said Luu-ka.

"He must have taken one nasty fall if your explanation is true, Luu-ka," Chainæïa added.

"It is," she answered harshly. She sighed and said, "I'm sorry."

"Think nothing of it," said Chainæïa. "These last few days have been grueling."

"We all worry for Rhin, Luu-ka. Yet I can think of nothing to do except hope. Hope that there is somebody who resides in the Temple who can help him," said Aroukana.

"Yes. But don't you think he should at least be awake by now?" Luu-ka answered, looking at Rhin's pallid face.

Rhin bled from an invisible wound. Luu-ka took a cloth and dabbed his forehead.

Cononsareth was scraping at his tortoise shell.

"What are you doing?" asked Aroukana.

"A Conkatokæ's passage into adulthood is heralded by the growing of certain lichen on his shell. This lichen has great healing properties," Cononsareth answered, rubbing the mossy stands between his fingers.

"Why did you not reveal this before?" Chainæïa demanded.

"The stuff just started to grow this morning."

"Then that means-" Luu-ka started to say, but Cononsareth cut her off.

"Your guess is adequate. I have only just become an adult this morning, two hours ago."

"How old are you?" asked Chainæïa.

"Ninety nine, in your terms. The Conkatokæ race is—was—one of the eldest. My people were able to live up to several centuries old. The Vevleï, however, live a great deal longer than my race," Cononsareth explained.

"Yes. But in standard Iorian terms you are aged, my friend," Aroukana said, smiling.

"It would seem so," Cononsareth stared at Luu-ka's gaping mouth.

"Quite," said Aroukana.

The two laughed.

"They'en be'en smart'enen like you say'en Groaer," an Orronor said while spying upon the travelers. "They'en stays in sun."

"Yep, we'en switch'en plans."

The Ogres struggled with the complex words, but thanks to Groaer's teachings they were becoming more adept—their large, leaden tongues ever more capable of forming the syllables.

They smashed their large stone clubs against the ground in anticipation, salivating as their tongues drooped from their mouths. The strangers would not evade them for long.

Cononsareth put the ointment from his shell on Rhin's face and it stopped bleeding instantly. Nothing else happened, however.

"Still he does not wake," Cononsareth said, puzzled.

His large eyes searched for the wound on Rhin's face.

Chainæïa grabbed Rhin by the shoulders and shook him, "Come on, master. Get up! You are Rhin Akvius. You must wake up."

"Don't do that," Luu-ka pushed the Vevlea.

"Stay back, girl," he retorted.

A flash of gold beamed from Rhin's backpack. Luu-ka quickly opened the bag and removed the golden hand. There was another flash and Rhin's hands glinted in the light, too.

His eyes opened, shining a violet-blue. He jumped to his feet and spread his wings wide, almost blocking the sun from the others.

The voice that was not his spoke through him, "From death I arise, unscathed."

"Rhin!" Luu-ka exclaimed.

"My lord," said Aroukana, awed.

"No one can deny that he is a God, now," said Chainæïa, reveling.

He had to admit he had experienced some doubts over the past few months. But, when he witnessed Rhin awaken after having nearly every bone in his body break, there could be no more doubts about the boy's destiny.

Rhin looked around the area and realized where he was. His arms felt so heavy they fell to his sides. His head slumped as he tried to hold himself upright.

"Rhin, are you alright?" Chainæïa asked.

"Strange," Cononsareth uttered, "yes, very strange indeed."

Rhin spoke for the first time, "I'm alive, right?"

"As alive as you will ever be," Aroukana affirmed.

"And we're on Orronor Mountain?" he asked.

"That much is certain," Chainæïa answered.

Rhin felt a great joy, the wonder of being alive. He had cheated death, and he promised himself that from then on he would see life in a new light. Lacking the strength to stand, he did the next best thing which was to drop to the ground and lean against a large boulder.

Luu-ka took Aroukana to the side and asked, "What does all this mean?"

"It means he's going to kill Jiaïro, more or less."

She watched Rhin, shy for a moment, then went to him. Aroukana smiled.

"Man wak'en up," Groaer howled.

"That is'en it'enen. We attack'en at moon time'en," another snarled.

They gathered a bastion of Ogres and prepared to take their battle positions. Only a simple strategy was required for the Ogres to destroy their prey. They would circle the helpless victims and with their superior numbers, attack and kill instantly, before the would-be-meals could scream.

The only thing they feared was sunlight. It was like acid to their flesh.

In the morning, their chief resource was the odd, stray irlorn. The Orronor developed quick reflexes, suitable for catching small animals, but this did not satisfy. So, considering the fact that they never had enough to eat, the Ogres were enthusiastic about the idea of a Vevleï stew or a Conkatokæ roast.

They marched across the mountain and slipped into hiding. Finally, when night drew nigh, their victims approached.

Dusk came too fast. Rhin and his companions reached shelter just in time. The fresh twilight air cooled them after a brutal day of climbing and riding. The Uderraad were excellent mountaineers and had followed Rhin's group faithfully, their spoke-like claws piercing the rock.

The stone in the cave mouth stunk of animal blood and some were even stained with gore.

"I do not like this place one bit," Chainæïa told them.

"We do not have the sun's protection. We are as good as dead, if we do not stay quiet," Aroukana hissed.

"Still, it's a fine place to put a temple. I'll wager the priests were all eaten," said Chainæïa with an exasperated puff.

Rhin worried whether or not the fire was a good idea. It was less a source of warmth to him than a beacon for potential predators.

When he brought this to Aroukana's attention the Vevlea answered, "Ogres are afraid of fires. Have no fear, Rhin."

Rhin wondered if Aroukana's bravado was feigned. Perhaps all there was to it was good fortune. Perhaps the old Vevlea was relying on his reputation of walking encyclopedia to bring the others comfort.

Rhin sat by the fire. He took one of the cookies that he had received as a gift on the ferry and warmed it before eating it, to help heat his body. Luu-ka crept next to him.

"We thought we had lost you forever," she said. "You must be very strong to be able to survive a fall like that."

"I saw," he started, "I thought I saw death. But somehow I knew it was a lie."

"How did you know that?"

"Because if I were truly in heaven an image of my friends would be there, waiting for me, reassuring me until we would be reunited," he said and nudged her shoulder, smiling.

"Who did you see?"

"I saw a figure dressed in black. Why is always black? His face was skinless. His eyes were popping out of his head and he kept telling me to come with him."

Luu-ka changed the subject in response to the utter silence that had just surrounded them.

"I had a dream a long time ago," she said, "I was probably about nine or ten years old. I was falling from a gray covered sky. I kept on falling for what seemed like hours. When I was about to hit the water, I saw a blue crystal, like a sapphire. Then a winged creature grabbed me just milliseconds before I hit the cold surface. The crystal became bigger and bigger. The creature set me down on it and flew away. In the crystal I saw my grandmother and a blue sword. Then I woke up."

Rhin did not know whether she was done, so he kept quiet.

"I never found out what it meant." She turned away and said, "I must be boring you to death."

Rhin knew she needed reassurance so he said, "Not at all. Dreams can contain important messages."

They both smiled and said in unison, "Goodnight."

"Go'en," Groaer commanded.

The Ogres charged out with their clubs made from rock, screaming, growling, and smacking their lips.

"What was that noise?" Chainæïa whispered.

"Wake them," said Aroukana in the Vevlehen speech.

Half-asleep, Rhin asked "What's going on?"

"The Orronor come," hissed Chainæïa. "Up. Hurry!"

It was too late. The Ogres had surrounded the cave and there were no other exits. Rhin saw them in all their horrific detail. They were tall, of course. Some had a sort of sharpness to their forms, like their bones were trying to escape their skin in places. Others were fat, looking more like giant sacks with arms and legs and very little neck. But the worst of all was the shortest one. That one exuded a shrewdness not unlike a man, which frightened Rhin to no end. They were all restless and hungry.

Aroukana and Chainæïa each drew a circle in the sand and clasped their hands together.

"May the flowing Spiral of Life be kind to us," Aroukana prayed.

The Vevleï then unsheathed their blades. The raucous Orronor gritted their slimy, moss covered teeth and ran into the cave.

Amidst it all a clear voice—ancient yet energetic—sang in the night.

The Ogres turned and saw ten luminous figures, towering in the darkness. They were dressed in green robes and wore hoods that covered their faces. A flash of lightning revealed their identities to Aroukana.

"The Resurrection Priests!" he said.

They moved and spoke as one, uttering words in the ancient tongue.

A scintillating light surrounded the Ogres, and they were forced to cover their ravenous eyes with their bulky deformed hands.

"Kill'en the green ones," Groaer commanded.

"You shall leave this place," one of the Priests shouted.

A fiery bat shot from his left palm and chased Groaer away. The other Orronor fled, too. Seconds later, accompanied by much yowling, Groaer died at the hands of the bat. The sight of the hulking monster drop left Rhin momentarily stunned.

The robed men approached.

"Are you unharmed?" asked the tallest Priest.

"Yes," Rhin answered.

"My name is Lothgar the Tower," he said, removing his hood. "I am the Head Priest of my order. We will provide shelter for you," he alluded to the other Priests. "We shall answer any questions you might have," he continued, looking at Rhin as if he were reading his mind. "Come with us now."

"Your name becomes you," Aroukana said, admiring Lothgar's stature.

"Yes, lord Vevlea. Yet you will find, though I am the tallest of the Priests, that none of us are given the title 'short'," Lothgar said, amused.

The Resurrection Priests led Rhin and his friends via a deep path into the mountain, and then into another dank cave. The darkness was broken by their magic. Lothgar mumbled a collection of words and the cave lit up, as if a million candles had just been set ablaze.

They came into an alcove with rats crawling along the floor. Luuka stayed close to Rhin, in hopes of gaining some small protection, he assumed. The passage was narrow, but Rhin was unafraid.

"I have good reason to fear the rats," she whispered in Rhin's ear as they walked, "Where I come from full-grown Rattus quiri, or King-rats, are the size of a man's arm. They are vicious critters and are known to devour the baby offspring of the Eramkéras. When I was a child I was attacked by one of them and only lived because my family's house—where the King-rat chased me—caught fire. I escaped, but the rat didn't. That was the day my parents and village were annihilated. Every time I see a rat it's all brought back."

"I'm here for you," said Rhin.

At the end of the alcove, there was a green wall beset with blue gems its crevices.

"Stay close," Lothgar commanded and then he mumbled a few unintelligible words.

Rhin's head spun, when they appeared in a vast hall with torches alit in various bright colors, beaming shafts of light. There was an antique green carpet that stretched from one side of the hall to the other. As they walked across it, they noticed small clusters of priests watching them as they passed. Lothgar opened a door and beckoned them into a room with more priests, cloaked in white and gray. None were as tall as Lothgar. This second room was almost identical to the hall.

"Please take a seat, Rhin," he said in little more than a whisper.

"How did you come by my name?" asked Rhin.

It wasn't all that surprising anymore, knowing that complete strangers had intimate details concerning him.

"I know very much about you. Now, you want to resurrect Daish-rog, do you not?"

"Yes, but how did you find us out there? We could have been anywhere."

"Magic. We are not mere priests. We know how to control the energy flow of the planet. Well, 'tap' is a better term for it. The energy is what we summon, what we use to complete our tasks. There are many restrictions though. We can only use it to defend others and ourselves. We must never attack with this energy or we could become demons. We use it to accomplish the greater good, to make sure historical events do not run astray, to avoid a Paradox."

"A Paradox?" Aroukana repeated.

"A change—a mistake, a glitch. A mar to the flow of the River Time. I cannot explain in detail. It is forbidden."

"How can we resurrect Daish-rog?" Luu-ka asked.

"I must warn you that there are rules. The first rule is that you may only enter the Temple once, for it is such a rare privilege to be able to return a creature from the dead. Secondly, only one of pure heart can enter."

"It's worth it," said Rhin.

"Very well. You must fish his soul from within the Duatre, the Underworld."

"There is no heaven?" yelped Chainæïa.

"There is, surely. But your brother, Daish-rog, died full of turmoil. It seems to me he thought his worldly tasks unfinished, and therefore lost himself," Lothgar said, locking eyes with Chainæïa.

"Rixaï is the one who killed him," Rhin stated.

"Precisely. He wished to avenge his family's death at the hands of Rixaï. He assumed he was the last of his bloodline. This fueled his hate and brought about his downfall. He did not know that some of his brothers survived that foul coup."

Lothgar sipped water from a wooden cup, his face impassive.

Chainæïa gaped at the Priest.

"You mean there are others?" Chainæïa questioned.

"Yes. There is another besides you who still breathes," Lothgar answered.

"Where is he? His name, tell me his name!"

"I am truly sorry. But if I were to tell you then I would create a Paradox, the very thing I toil daily to avoid. You are to find him for yourself, if that is what lies in store for you."

"Tell me!" Chainæïa shouted, waving his clenched fists.

"Calm yourself, Chainæïa," said Cononsareth, placing a firm hand on the Vevlea's shoulder. "It is unwise to meddle in events beyond our understanding. First Daish-rog."

Chainæïa answered, "You're right, Cononsareth. First Daish-rog, of course."

But the rage was still in him.

"Follow me," Lothgar beckoned them, robes billowing about his person.

.

Chapter 15
The Duatre

othgar led Rhin into another chamber, the rest of the group trailing behind. The room was circular and vacant. Every few sections of wall there was a pillar with a lit sconce. The only objects of interest were three cups, set in a line upon the floor.

"There is a test," said Lothgar.

"What sort of test?" Aroukana demanded.

"Rhin Akvius, step forth," Lothgar smiled and pointed at the drinking vessels. "You must choose one of these. Each cup contains a different liquid. One will poison you, another will transport you and your friends to the outer-rim of the mountain, and the proper one will win you entry to the hall of Resurrection. Choose carefully."

Rhin looked like he had just been stabbed in the stomach. He moved closer to the cups and stood a while, his mind refusing to focus.

How am I supposed to choose? he thought.

All three cups were fashioned of redwood. The one on the far left had a skull carved upon it, the one in the center a dagger, and the last had a red blotch painted upon its surface—Rhin assumed it was meant to represent blood. He strongly doubted that the skull cup contained the poison. That would be too dull for these priests.

It must be symbolic, he thought. *The skull could symbolize the world of the dead. Although, the dagger could too... This is hopeless. I'm going to fail.*

Then it came to him. It was no great revelation; an angel of wisdom did not kiss his cheek. It was only an idea, but he felt certain enough.

He grinned and said, "I have chosen."

"Which one?" Lothgar's face presented no hints.

"It's a trick. Alone *all three* cups are wrong," said Rhin, crossing his arms.

"What do you mean, 'alone'?" Aroukana asked.

Rhin stooped and took the dagger and skull cups in his hands. He emptied the contents of the dagger cup into the skull one. He lifted the redwood rim to his lips.

Luu-ka, who had been shaking her head, said, "You know this means your chances are twice as bad, don't you?"

"If he is certain, he will drink," Lothgar stated.

Rhin ignored the girl and drank. Luu-ka gasped. Everyone was silent for a bit.

Rhin looked expectantly at Lothgar.

There were a few more tense moments before Lothgar finally declared, "You have chosen correctly."

Rhin let out an audible sigh. His gaze drifted to Luu-ka, who was rubbing her eyes. He did the best he could think up. When she stared at him he gave her a shrug and a smile.

"How did you know?" said Chainæïa.

"The skull symbolizes mortality and the dagger murder. Daish-rog was taken before his time. It just seemed right, Chainæïa," Rhin answered.

"It is clear that you possess the sight, Rhin Akvius. I will now ask that you follow me once again," said Lothgar.

With a wave of his hand, the Head Priest beckoned them through a door into another room. This one was thirty feet across, square and brown but for the one painfully bright orange wall on the far side, which was guarded by two women in white robes. They were twins and remained motionless, standing well over a foot taller than Rhin. Silken hoods covered most of their slender faces. Only their full, pink lips were visible and even those did not shift in the slightest.

Upon the protected wall was chiseled a pentagon, triangles guarding its five corners. The Head Priest traced the symbol with his pale index finger. He pronounced a few magic words and the wall became an opening leading them into the largest of all the halls. It was circular with an enormous pentagon painted on the blue floor tiles in green. At each of its corners, there was a pillar topped with a five-pointed star. At the heart of the pentagon there was a dull, gray circle—the only part that was not tiled.

"Behold, the Chamber of Resurrection," Lothgar said in his deep voice.

Everyone else was speechless.

When Rhin dared break the silence he asked, "Were you really willing to poison me?"

Lothgar chuckled, "I am not a monster, Rhin. The real test was not to choose the 'right cup' but to choose it for the right reasons. They were all correct in that sense."

The priest walked toward the center of the chamber and called, "Step forth, Rhin Akvius."

Pride resonated in his mighty words. He had been waiting for this moment for many long years, the moment when he would find the true Half-God and guide him into the heart of the abyss. Was this destiny?

Rhin took a few awkward steps. All were watching him. He felt like a child on the first day of school.

"Rhin, step within the circle," Lothgar continued.

He obeyed.

"You are going to have to fish Daish-rog's soul from the Duatre."

"How do I go about doing that?" Rhin asked.

"You have to enter the underworld yourself, alone. Stand in the exact center—good. Concentrate on Daish-rog and your memories of him—concentrate hard, now. Do not think of anything else," Lothgar raised his hand.

Rhin experienced the nauseating sensation of being sucked through the ground. Then he began to feel ice cold. The world turned a dull gray. As he shivered, he realized that he was actually sinking through the floor. He looked up and saw his body, sprawled in a ridiculous position like a child's doll. He heard voices from above but they were muffled as if underwater.

"What happened?" yelled Chainæïa.

"You killed him," Luu-ka cried.

"No, I did not. He merely left his body temporarily. He has about half an hour before the breaking of the spell and his forceful return," Lothgar said, raising his hands.

The Priest addressed Rhin, his words far more discernable, "Find your friend. Go now."

As he sank downward, Rhin saw hundreds, no, thousands of corpses. Skeletons of many creatures laid out in agonized poses. This realm's ceiling was the floor of the above world. Rhin had never imagined purgatory was so near reality.

These desolate caverns stood between Rayïm and Kaïle, and went on forever. A limitless, dry wasteland. A world where lost, proud souls wandered before their ultimate meeting with Rayïmus, the Judge.

In the Pits of Rayïm, the barrier between the realms of the living and the dead, Rayïmus had many names. Adrianotis, the most common one, was used by his servants. He was the absolute unbiased Judge of all the souls that descended. In the end, it was he who decided where the deceased would dwell for eternity. Tales of the underworld always concerned the Judge. Although impressive and frightening, he was incorruptible and fair.

Kaïle, on the other hand, was the hellish sphere where Evil would regroup and ascend to earth to stalk the nights. Tortured souls ran amuck within that never ending nightmare. Evil could not truly die and so Kaïle was the stage for its continuous revival.

Rhin gagged. All about him were the bodies of Conkatokæ.

Are these Cononsareth's friends? Are they all trapped here? Had their sudden deaths imprisoned their souls? Will they ever find peace until they are avenged? he wondered.

He felt ill. The place smelled like a combination of bad eggs, rotten fish and mold.

He saw no souls, just bones, until he walked a little further and came upon the spherical soul of a Daïmaan. It was black as onyx, a horned skull within the ethereal ring. There were other spirits there as well. Those that were not demonic moaned and cried in tormented despair.

To an outsider, all the souls of the realm were represented as circular orbs emitting pale, spectral rays. Within the spiritual energy of each soul the creature's face could be seen—though, in truth, seen as through a dark mirror.

He pressed on, scanning the wasteland. Then he found a soul, wandering at random. Rhin recognized the thin face.

"Daish-rog," Rhin called, certain it was him.

"Rhin!" The voice sounded distant and off key.

He ran to the soul. The light moved in close to him. The face within the eerie glow gave a weak smile. The pathetic grin appeared to hurt him a great deal. It was definitely Daish-rog, but he had changed during his time spent in this pit.

For a split second, Daish-rog thought this was all some new form of torment brought about by the evils around him. But his vision of Rhin changed that feeling. The being that he saw sported angelic wings and was obscured from view by a concentration of intense light. How could this be a trick?

"Come on, no time to explain. Let's get out of here," said Rhin.

He ran ahead, beckoning Daish-rog to follow him.

"Am I truly going to leave this place?" Daish-rog called, the same tinny distortion to his words.

"Just hurry. We don't have much time," Rhin replied.

"Indeed you don't," said a voice as cold as a snow storm.

The frost of those syllables crept up the length of Rhin's spine and made his brain tingle. The Lord of Kaïle appeared in front of them, blocking their progress. The demon overlord wore a sullied white cloak, a chain of onyx linking it around his neck. His inward nose wrinkled, eyes half-shut.

He said, "I may not be able to harm you while that imbecile, Lothgar, protects your soul and the thin thread that binds it to your body, but remember this: you will not live long enough to savor this victory. And when you come to my realm rest assured that you will have your own private, distinguished hell awaiting you."

Rhin brandished his sword and a shaft of spectral light filled the Duatre like a lighthouse piercing a foggy night. The cavernous wasteland shone with the pure glow of the blade.

"This is not your realm. Back to Kaïle with you! I don't fear you," he said.

"That will change," the demon hummed in the deep.

He left the same way he had come, calmly strolling into a crevice that led to the bottomless abyss that every creature on Iora feared.

Rhin returned his sword to its scabbard and faced Daish-rog. They pressed on. The souls of the Daïmaans around them laughed and called to them.

"Run, little Rhin. Run to your mother!"

"She's right near here, too. We've been taking good care of fair Meela!"

Rhin almost ran at the taunting Daïmaans, but he knew even then that they were lying.

He heard repeated crunches beneath his feet, his soles grinding bone to dust. Black darkness turned to gray fog, then white light. Soul and guide entered the circle and ascended, reappearing in the world of the living.

Rhin returned to his body, which felt strange at first, like he was wearing an oversized rubber suit. Daish-rog's soul had reanimated him, a bizarre and rather disgusting sight. A body seemed to sprout out of thin air. A skull, then a brain, veins, heart, lungs, blood, and finally flesh. It expanded until its features were recognizable as Daish-rog.

He was back in his old body. Well, he had 'grown' an entirely new one, identical to the original. The final missing piece of Daish-rog's puzzle, his Orb, dug itself into his forehead.

Once Rhin adjusted to his own return, he realized his friend's new vessel didn't come with a set of clothes, so he took a robe Lothgar had at the ready and handed it to his resuscitated companion.

When he felt decent again, Daish-rog turned his head and what he saw was unimaginable. Chainæïa, his long lost sibling. The brothers remained open-mouthed and silent.

At last Chainæïa said, "Greetings, Daish-rog."

"Greetings, Chainæïa."

"It has been a while."

"Far too long."

They embraced one another, tears of joy streaming down their faces. Rhin smiled and left the gray circle. He shivered as if he had been dipped in arctic water. Lothgar, upon taking notice, passed Rhin a bottle.

"It is called rhumémata. It will warm you," Lothgar whispered.

"Thanks," Rhin said.

He felt better even after just one sip of the stuff.

Luu-ka came up to him and kissed him on the cheek. Her face was beaming.

Rhin looked at Aroukana, who smiled in acknowledgment. Then he saw Cononsareth, hanging upside-down off the ceiling with his eyes closed, and laughed.

Daish-rog and Chainæïa stayed up all night talking about the past, up until their tragic separation.

"Are there any others who survived?" Daish-rog asked.

"I know there are some, but I do not know where or who…"

"It was forty years ago."

"Yes, an eternity. How did you survive, Daish-rog?"

"Our mother spirited me away during the battle," Daish-rog said, twitching as if he were feeling the pain of an old wound again.

"Is she-"

"Vanished without a trace."

"I… that monster," Chainæïa patted Daish-rog on the back and said, "We will find him, together."

"How did you escape, Chainæïa?"

"I saw it, little brother. I saw it happen. I saw Rixaï behead our brother, Garcho. Rixaï then started toward me, but mighty Morcha stood in his way. Rixaï cut him down, too. Rixaï caught me across the stomach and I passed out. I awoke in an inn and stayed there with the servants of a rich nobleman. I ran away as soon as my legs would carry me, only to live a nomad's life. I stayed mostly on the outskirts of Rosh and lived in the forest for a while."

Thus they bonded until the sun rose, reunited at last.

Rhin flew out the window to exercise his wings. They had fully recuperated and felt better than ever before.

He was lost, not knowing where to go next. He reviewed everything the Sword of Purity had told him.

Gliding downward, he landed and unsheathed the weapon, admiring the jewels glittering in the sunlight. It was covered almost entirely with gold and sky-blue gems, but there were hints of silver on the hilt. It was a fine weapon and undeniable in its deadliness.

"You are wondering what you must do next," said the sword.

"That's right," Rhin replied.

"You tread the right path. If 'tis the five Temples you search for, the nearest one—the Holy Eye—is here on this Isle. With precise details, I cannot help you. You must find its location yourself."

Rhin strapped sword and scabbard to his belt and returned to the Temple of Resurrection.

He found his friends eating breakfast on a long rectangular table in one of the many similar halls. The food was plain compared to the feast on Luu-ka's island, but it was fresh and filling. There were stacks of brown bread, some butter, raisins, oat cakes and bowls of milk.

He stood before them and said, "Now that we have resurrected Daish-rog, my next destination is the Temple of the Holy Eye. It's a dangerous journey and I won't force any to join me. So it's up to you."

They all looked at him.

Are they considering? Or do they think I'm crazy? Rhin thought.

"What are you thinking?" Luu-ka asked.

"I'll understand if you don't want to go-" Rhin started, but Cononsareth interrupted him.

"Are you mad? Did that tumble from the skies damage your brain?"

"As ever, I go with you," said Aroukana.

"We all go. With you we would brave the Pits of Rayïm themselves," Chainæïa added.

"I already have," Daish-rog laughed.

Rhin tried in vain to suppress a wide grin. His friend was back.

Chapter 16
The Second Stage

When Daish-rog felt comfortable enough in his body, after a few days rest within the sanctuary, Rhin and the others set out to undertake the second stage of their journey. They bade the priests of Resurrection farewell. Lothgar had advised Rhin to search for information about the Temple of the Holy Eye in a quiet town set against the outer reaches of Ogre Mountain.

The sky was a clear royal blue. The muddy ground and mucky, slimy puddles that blanketed the land made it hard work for the Uderraad, their long legs trudging along. Rhin and his friends decided to dismount and proceed on foot to make it less harsh on the poor creatures. By noon Rhin was exhausted and his boots were full to the brim with mud. It seemed hopeless and, above all, pointless.

"How can this be? Impossible. In all the years I have lived I have never had the misfortune of encountering weather such as this," said Aroukana, scratching at the thin beard that was growing in along his jaw.

"We must keep going. There is no point in quitting," Cononsareth answered.

"I beg to differ. If we wait, perhaps the weather will change for the better," Chainæïa argued.

"I agree with Cononsareth," said Luu-ka.

"As do I," said Daish-rog.

"I do, too. And four is the majority, so we keep going," and with those words Rhin knew he had settled the dispute.

They hoped the strong sunshine would dry some of the muck they had to cross through, but the conditions persisted.

When nightfall cast its glare over the winding grasslands, it was at last time to rest. Posting the tents proved no facile feat, however. And then, when Chainæïa became fussed over it all, he tore off his red bandana and chucked it into the woods. He regretted it later, for he had to slosh out in the dark to retrieve the cloth.

In the end, setting a decent camp proved impossible and the group was forced to post themselves against trees, or sleep in between the broad roots. Although this provided escape from the muck, in the morning they all awoke sore and bruised.

And the next day was much the same. Rhin knew they could not stop, as they would run out of food, so there were no alternatives.

"Ugh," Chainæïa grunted.

"Will this never end?" Daish-rog commented.

"Just keep going and try not to think about it," said Rhin.

"We could try. But it is easier to say things than to do them," Chainæïa said.

"I've never seen so much mud," Luu-ka said.

"Rhin is right, it does not help to obsess over it," Aroukana said.

So they went on. The hot sun beat on Rhin. His back was drenched with sweat. The air was hot enough to sting his lungs as he breathed.

This can't be natural, Rhin told himself.

The wicked man always watched. He sprinkled some purple dust over the Crystal of Sight.

"If the mud defeatshh you, then what, Akviussh?" he laughed. "But you are in doubt Akviussh, are you not?"

"You remember what Ryul told you. You do not undershhtand. Washh he bluffing? That ishh what you are thinking, ishh it not? He told you that it would be her undoing and he did not lie. Oh boo, shhad ishh it? You shhall die and shho will the reshht of thoshhe idiotshh! Agony, you do not know itshh true meaning yet."

He went on talking to himself and cursing Rhin from afar.

The dark room became illuminated for the first time in five hundred years. He hated the light, but a specific kind of spell required its use. It was a rare occurrence that the sorcerer needed to resort to such a powerful incantation. More oft then not, this sort of spell was considered a folly. Wheezing, he began to work.

Aroukana sat atop a hay-stack, observing the animals around him. In the fields it was easy to achieve the peaceful state necessary for meditation. The horses there were magnificent and ever graceful.

He breathed, his eyes closed, distancing himself from the 'real world'. It was at that moment that Luu-ka chose to approach the Vevlea.

"You like horses, don't you?" she asked.

"Yes. They are stunningly majestic creatures. I suppose you could say I have a connection with them."

"I don't know much about horses," she said. "Could you teach me something about them?"

Aroukana opened his eyes and looked at the girl. "Yes, I could." He began his tale, "My people hold a belief that when a great Vevlehen warrior perishes in combat, he or she is reborn as the horse of the next valiant warrior. This is because the warrior spirit is still within him or her and thus the soldier's soul gives aid to the following generation. This is considered an honor to us because horses are pure and wild, and my people have formed a kinship with them over millennia. You see, we do not capture horses and 'train' them to become less independent, we form a spiritual bond with the animals and call them 'friend' or 'brother'," Aroukana looked at the girl and said, "I have most likely bored you now."

"No, no. Not at all. That story was captivating."

The Vevlea was rewarded with one of her smiles, which he found to be soothing and pleasant.

He then glanced across the fields and spotted Chainæïa amidst the young stallions. With a flick of his eyes and a quick jerk of his fingers, he pointed this out to Luu-ka who laughed. Chainæïa waved at the pair and shouted something, grinning all the while. Aroukana nodded and waved back.

Luu-ka could not hear what had said. She stared at the sharp arrow-head-shaped ears of the ancient Vevlea.

It's truly amazing how they can pick up such soft sounds, she thought.

Luu-ka, of the Eramkéras, had her own benefits. She could discern a singular scent from amidst many and could tell exactly what it was and where it originated. Her race had long used this gift to their advantage in such activities as foraging for food, and sniffing out traps or people they wished to avoid. They were quite a clever brood in their prime. That was before Jiaïro's rise, however.

"She is dead," someone said in Rhin's dream.

"Who are you?" Rhin asked.

"She is dead," the voice repeated.

"Who?"

"You know."

"Show yourself," Rhin commanded.

"Wake now, Rhin Akvius."

Rhin sprung upright. Night had come to the valley under the mountain and all were entwined in profound sleep. His paranoia was rewarded by a painful head rush. Rhin took a calming breath.

Then it hit him—where was Luu-ka? He panicked, stumbling and tripping. His boots kept getting stuck in the accursed clay. When he looked ahead and saw Luu-ka walking beneath the shadow of the mountain, he was relieved. But as he watched her, two red eyes appeared in the gloom.

"Luu-ka!" he called.

He ran. The red eyes moved faster. He moved as rapidly as the mire would allow, yet the red eyes got to her first.

Rhin saw the rest of the creature's body, a dim black shape in the shade of night. It was a Daïmaan, a sentinel from Kaïle.

He pumped his legs harder, flapping his wings for support. He realized with horror that they were dragging through the mud, too weak to carry him. He pumped them with fury, but to no end. He could only run and hope. And this he did.

The creature sprinted up to the girl and kicked her over. She landed face first in the mud. When she resurfaced, she was gasping for air.

As he propelled himself toward Luu-ka Rhin wanted to scream: Why is no one else awake?

The answer came to him. Rhin was suspended in time. All noises and movements were only being witnessed by him, Luu-ka and the stalking demon. No other creature stirred during the brief moments that Rhin shot forward.

"No, leave me alone!" Luu-ka screamed.

Why isn't she fighting it? Rhin thought, feeling the fear well in his throat. *She must have left her weapons at the campsite!*

The Daïmaan shoved her into the muck. The goop snagged her on contact.

"Pitiful," it said. "No mercy for the weak."

"No!" Luu-ka screamed again.

"I know you are out there, Akvius. Let this be a warning to you."

The Daïmaan raised its clawed hand and held Luu-ka up by her hair, preparing to carve a scarlet smile across her throat.

Rhin bridged the gap in the desperate race. He willed himself to move faster. He knew that he must.

He continued the dramatic push and came up to the Daïmaan. Rhin smashed the fiend in the small of its back and then hurled himself in front of Luu-ka. The blow the sentinel had prepared for her had struck his shoulder instead and his flesh screamed in protest.

"Leave her be," said Rhin.

The Daïmaan struck another blow. Rhin blocked it with his golden sword and retaliated with a stab at the demon's shin. The horrific beast made an awkward sideways jump, nearly losing its balance.

"Rhin," Luu-ka whispered.

"I'm here," Rhin replied, kneeling beside her. He held her to his chest.

He laid her down and sprung to his feet, facing the demon.

Though Rhin could never explain how, he understood this one was female. She was dark gray, her flesh tainted with random black boils. Her evil eyes were no longer red but black and empty, and the claws she used as weapons were stained with blood. Rhin prayed that none of the blood belonged to Luu-ka. His own trickled down his arm.

The Daïmaan laughed. "If you want the girl, fight for her."

"Suits me just fine," Rhin growled.

"Now, you will know the name of your doom. I am Sutryuse and I challenge you!"

Rhin shone azure in the darkness.

The very air seemed to hum. For a second, Rhin appeared to be made of solid gold. But it was revealed as an illusion caused by the coruscating light around him.

"I don't fear the silence, I don't fear the dark," said Rhin.

The light concentrated into a single beam which pierced the demon, blasting a crater into her chest. Sutryuse's flesh melted like candle wax while she squealed her distress. Finally, she burst into tiny, fiery fragments. Her ashes were reclaimed by the earth.

Rhin drooped as if unused to his own weight.

After he struggled to his feet he asked Luu-ka, "Are you alright?"

"Yes, I think so."

"I'll carry you back. Hold on."

He picked her up and trudged back to the encampment. The wind whistled. The crickets sang. Time had resumed its steady, inexorable course.

Rhin set her upon her blanket and turned away. But Luu-ka caught him by the hand and guided him down to her. Her lips brushed against his. Rhin closed his eyes, captured by her warmth. But scarcely three heartbeats later she pulled away.

She fell asleep moments thereafter. Rhin knew he would not find rest. He knew it the second he wrapped himself in his sleeping bag. For once, though he tossed and turned for hours, evil visions did not plague him. Instead, he was thoroughly confused for entirely novel reasons.

Aware of every little movement in the dark recesses of the night, he tensed each time something twitched out there. Rhin was scared for Luu-ka. His urge to protect her had become more powerful than ever. That night, as his stomach burned, he understood that he cared more for her life than his own.

Rhin took to flight for comfort. With Ryul's words still fresh in his mind, he wondered why the demon that attacked Luu-ka had come alone.

He flew higher, the clouds streaming past, until he pierced the ashen veil.

"There still is a moon," he murmured to himself.

It was freezing up there, turning his blood to ice. He gazed at the limitless heavens and caught sight of an odd star.

Is it a star? he asked himself.

It was larger than the rest and was tinted jade. He looked straight at it and felt a burning in his chest. He dropped a few feet. He soared toward the false star and it twitched. Then it lurched backward and fled.

He realized what it was: a Soræs.

These creatures were used during the Eon of Rebirth as spies. Their scaly hide was green with an underbelly of banana-yellow. Their eyes were tiny and red, speckled with yellow dots. Fast and obedient, when threatened they could emit invisible, but harmful, rays. The Soræs was a breathing being but its genetics were modified using magic.

But these things haven't been used for centuries, Rhin thought, astonished, as he chased after it.

He had studied them while he was in 'school'. Being a scion of the poorest family in the village, a customary education was denied him during his formative years. More often than not, he would 'borrow' books from the library.

One article had caught his eye long ago, on one of his midnight excursions.

"Be the challenge great or small, Soræs is fit for the work."

This title was a scrap from an ancient textbook that had been copied and translated at least half a dozen times.

Among the illustrations of the Soræsi by various artists the only one that even came close to Rhin's sighting was the one made by the legendary alchemist, Valabei-atoria. He was reputed to have invented the Soræsi by restructuring another animal's genetic code. The original specimen that had been modified, rumor had it, was a tangus* bird.

---

* Reptilian fisher-scavenger. These beings of the air voyage in large groups, migrating across the isles every few months. Their scaly flesh is golden-brown with slight gray specks, depending on age and nutrition.

His fellow villagers simply called it 'a whole magical mess' and dismissed the entire genetic code idea as soon as it had started.

When Valabei-atoria at last was questioned concerning his methods and theories an arrow burst through his neck as he explained.

Those who had witnessed the murder saw a shadowy man retreating into the trees. They thought it was all for the best that the madman had been put down. Once again all was peaceful in the community.

Later, Lord Gerloïn III, king of the East Kingdom, Falasbadonéthan, caught wind of this alchemist's deeds and sent a search party to Valabei-atoria's house. There they found manuscripts containing his research and a secret alcove underground housing two dozen Soræsi 'prototypes'.

The king then used these critters to guard his kingdom from unwelcome visitors and during that time, he documented them.

Rhin raced on after the Soræs, but it outmatched him in speed. It was like chasing a stray arrow.

What was it doing here? How did it survive for a thousand years? Rhin asked himself.

He gave up and returned to the campsite. It was already nearing dawn when he touched earth and the sky was clear enough that he could see every remaining star, every constellation.

An hour later, it started to rain, thickening the mud and the humidity. They pressed on through the infernal conditions.

Rhin could tell Luu-ka worried. Angst clouded her eyes as she peered at her old maps.

"It's this mud," Rhin told her, "it's not your fault."

"Still, it's slowing us to below half speed," she replied.

Rhin touched her hand and said, "We'll be fine."

She pulled away from him saying, "Let's just keep moving."

Rhin cursed his stupidity, a black mood enshrouding him.

It was laggard going, as anticipated. The concentrated, brown sludge tore at their soles all day. Though the sun had fled, the damp air caused Rhin's sweat to gush forth in torrents. Around noon he was dehydrated, but then he was the first to see the thing that would lift all their spirits.

"A river," Rhin cheered.

The riverbank was blanketed with moss and wildflowers, a blessed haven from the muck. He dived right in.

They drank and refilled their flasks, swam and lounged. Cononsareth, who had suffered the most from the drought, performed acrobatic feats for the others. As he splashed through the liquid, the spray of droplets formed a hundred miniature rainbows.

When it was time to move on Rhin did so with reluctance. The river was the only source of refreshment they had found since the Temple.

Not long after he and the rest had left the watery vein behind, lethargy set in. None of them desired to keep going, but they did.

They walked on and on until darkness set upon them. Halting at the only patch of grass they had seen in four miles, they relaxed by a flowerbed. Admiring the various baby blue and apricot petals, they waited for sleep to claim them.

"It is lovely," Luu-ka breathed, picking at puffs of pollen swirling in the wind.

The diverse colors soothed Rhin after that trying day.

"Akviussh, Akviussh," the man repeated, slapping his cheeks until they pulsated.

"Why do you shhtill move on? The circumstanceshh that I created did not shhtop you, Akviussh? Why? I want to undershhtand why!"

He tore through the pages of his book until he found what he wanted and began to chant.

This transparent spell would have to do. This boy and his pathetic circle of friends had made him wroth.

"I shhall deal with you myshhelf, Akviussh."

He clucked as he gathered determination to see his plan through to the end.

His apartments shook as lighting struck outside. He spilled a glass of water on his singed right hand and hissed in pain. It never ceased to burn ever since he had fumbled a spell and seared the frail flesh.

He had seen many centuries, witnessed the rise and fall of dynasties. He was quite ancient. And now he was vexed. His wrath he retained for Akvius.

Rhin watched as Aroukana sprinted atop the hill.

When he reached the crest, he spun in place and descended.

As he came to Rhin's side he announced, "There's a village just beyond."

Chainæïa gave off a huge sigh.

"What's wrong?" Rhin asked, catching Aroukana's frown.

"We have a problem," he answered. "See for yourselves."

Passing over the crest, as Aroukana had minutes before, the problem became all too apparent. Steel-clad soldiers, black metal lined with crimson paint, surrounded a palisade wall.

Rhin and his friends crouched as they heard the soldiers below shuffling with unease, the hinges of their armor grating.

"Jiaïro," said Rhin as he hit the earth with his fist.

"One hundred," counted Chainæïa.

"Veteran mercenaries. The finest, faithless footpads money can acquire, and the False God is rich," Aroukana said and scowled.

Rhin overheard a conversation down there. He strained his ears to catch more.

"In the name of Jiaïro move this palisade aside," the general shouted.

"We don't want you scum in here," a voice equaling thunder shouted defiantly.

"You are bold for a rabble of ragged villagers. Let us in or we enter by force."

"May it be so. Come in by force. We dare you."

"You dare us?" the general started to laugh.

"We are not afraid of the afterlife. But you will die before we do."

"Very well," the General roared. "Archers, ignite and fire at will!"

Daish-rog, Aroukana and Chainæïa, whose ears were keener, heard screams and yelps of pain coming from inside the village. Little did they know that it was all an act.

All of a sudden, the wooden palisade burst open and a giant came striding out from the wreckage. Twice Rhin's height at least, his arms were the size of tree trunks. His hair was jet black with patches of wild electric blue. His eyes shone like red gold.

He unsheathed a sword the blade of which was equal to the length of Rhin's entire body. He trampled the first and second ranks of soldiers, leaving the maimed corpses behind.

The rest of the villagers passed through the ruined barricade armed with pitchforks, butcher's knives, lumber axes and torches. Large and small, old and young, men and women—all joined the fray.

The giant rammed his sword into the ground creating a calculated tremor which sent enemy troops flying. He pushed half a dozen, hurling them into those behind. The jangle of steel that ensued resembled the crashing of kitchen pots.

By this time the soldiers had grouped into a circular formation, conceived by Jiaïro, known as the Ciraucles. In this stance they were confident that their three hundred and sixty degree vantage would give them the advantage. But when the giant leapt into the center of the formation they scattered like dropped pearls off a broken necklace.

From the hill it wasn't easy for Rhin to catch much of what was happening. Nonetheless he heard the screams and witnessed yet again the madness of battle. This one lasted but minutes and, perhaps because of the giant's prowess, was one-sided.

It came as no surprise when the general shouted, "Retreat!"

The men fled, trounced, in every direction. The giant's laughter could be heard from the hilltop where Rhin stood with his arms crossed.

Luu-ka and Daish-rog gaped. The Vevleï applauded and cheered.

"Good show. So sad that it had to end," said Chainæïa to Aroukana.

The wind tugged at Rhin's hair as he said, "I'd very much like to meet this champion."

The village itself was plain and conventional, its clustered huts built of wood and straw. The meal served that night was anything but moderate. The town was alight with a roaring fire. The townsfolk feasted to celebrate their victory and drank in honor of their champion. The champion did not stay long.

Pork and rabbit stew with chunks of potatoes boiled in pots over the fire. Mead and wine were served along with whitefish and mint. There was sugared corn and roasted garlic and cabbage aplenty. The giant left suddenly and without a word, shuffling along a path leading into the high hills. Rhin chose to follow.

Leaving his friends behind without much of an explanation, he flew high above the champion. Rhin's curiosity drove him. He soon spotted the place where the giant must have been heading: a lone house resting atop a hill, encircled by trees. The house itself was unremarkable but the surroundings were a different matter. Decking the hills were masses of graves. The giant entered his home and closed the drapes, heavy woolen blankets to ward off prying eyes.

Rhin landed in the yard and examined some of the graves. Most were marked: Middle Rank Soldier, Three-Star, Low Rank Decuri, Two-Star, High Rank Captain, Six-Star, Middle Rank Lieutenant, Three-Star, High Rank Soldier, Five-Star, Low Rank Lieutenant, One-Star.

These are the graves of all those he's slain, Rhin thought.

And there were endless stones.

"I show them the respect they deserve," Rhin froze in response to the voice, "Though they were my enemy in life, in death each one is just another soldier. Soldiers deserve a proper burial." It was the giant who'd spoken. He asked, "What's your name?"

"Rhin."

The giant seemed to consider this a moment as he tugged at his beard. "I've heard of you. You've caused quite a mess for Jiaïro's loyalists to clean up, they say."

"I wouldn't know about that. What's your name, champion?"

"I am Kayre-Ost of the Denzak. Now, why did you follow me?"

"Guess I wanted to see what you were up to."

Kayre-Ost grunted in acknowledgement.

"These graves," Rhin flicked his hand to indicate the cemetery about him, "there are so many."

"An important rule is to respect your opponent, no matter who he is. I've had to kill a lot of men, but I never do it lightly."

Kayre-Ost ducked down and retrieved a large steel spade.

As he swung it over his shoulder he said, "I've got dead to bury. Go back to the village."

"Are you coming too?" Rhin asked.

"I'll be over later. I promised the kids a story."

The giant's mighty voice echoed through the dirt-paved streets. There were throngs of children sitting about him, enthralled with the tale. Once Chainæïa overheard a bit of it he was drawn in as well.

"When I was a young boy, barely older than any of you, I lived in a valley far away. My village had many enemies, but we were all very strong. My sister, when she was only six, could arm-wrestle all the boys twice her age," Kayre-Ost's voice grew fainter towards the end. His eyes glazed over for a moment. Then he resumed with his tale, "One night, my home was attacked by Ogres!" he paused for effect. The children held their breath. "My mother had to pull my little sister away from them—she was so eager to fight. My father had left a long time ago, so I was the only one who could protect my family. It was dark. There were two huge, fat Ogres watching me. They charged, so I just took one of them and threw him away, up into the sky. You see that star, over there? That's where I sent him. I threw him so hard that he is in heaven now and he turned into that star. That's why it's called 'Ogre star', you know," Kayre-Ost said.

"What happened to the other Ogre, lord Kayre-Ost?" a three year old girl squeaked.

"Yeah, your right, I forgot to tell you what happened to the other Ogre. Well, you see that?" He pointed at the village monument which just happened to be a representation of an Ogre.

"Yeah, I see it," the little girl said as she squirmed with excitement.

"That's him," Kayre-Ost said and chuckled.

"That's the Ogre?"

"It is."

The children gasped, exchanging smiles.

"Well, kids, it's late. Off with you," said Kayre-Ost as he got to his feet.

Sighing in disappointment, they did as they were bid. Most of the fires had burnt out and the moon had fled behind a veil of thundercloud, and if they did not return soon their parents would scold them.

When Rhin returned he was approached by Luu-ka.

"Where were you?" she said.

"Out. Why do you ask?" Rhin replied.

"I was—we were worried about you. We wondered where you'd gone."

"There's no need, but I appreciate it, Luu-ka." Rhin placed his hand on her shoulder. She looked deep in his eyes and—

"We have to find an inn or somewhere suitable," said Cononsareth, "unless you all want to sleep under the stars—though we won't be seeing many stars this night."

The party scoped out the heavens. It was obvious that a rainstorm was coming. The idea of getting soaked to the core was not met with much enthusiasm.

So they walked a while, searching for a decent place to spend the night, and met up with a cloaked, blind old man.

Rhin approached him and in sympathy handed the man some money.

Then he said, "Forgive me if I'm being rude. We are travelers and I was wondering why you did not join the feast."

"You're not being rude at all, kind sir. You helped this coot. Now I shall tell you what you need to know," he said as his weak legs wobbled.

"Thank you, sir," said Luu-ka.

"Please call me Talg. Now just what is it that you need?"

"Alright, Talg. Could you tell us about Kayre-Ost?" Rhin asked.

"Yes, indeed I could, kind sir. He arrived in the village a few months back. We were under attack and Jiaïro's men were burning one roof after another. So Kayre-Ost came and smashed them into dust. Of course I did not see this, but I heard the cries of joy and praise. He has been our champion ever since. Yet, we of the village fear as well as respect him. Kayre-Ost is a mighty warrior and is easily offended, I hear. I did not join the celebrations because I'm an outcast. I have never been accepted. But I am used to it. They call me 'Loner'."

The man cringed, as if invoking past pains, and said sharply, "Now, be off with you."

"But sir, we are your friends now." Luu-ka's attempts at comforting him were met with hostility.

"No. Just go. The Loner has no friends, they say."

So they left Talg, full of regret. He was just someone who had been alone for so long that change seemed impossible.

"Well, I wish we could have done something," Luu-ka sighed.

"As do I," Chainæïa said.

Cononsareth said nothing. A few tears of sorrow flowed forth from Aroukana's eyes.

"I know of his torment, I've seen it in a many an eye," he said.

"We have to find shelter. The only thing we can do is talk to Kayre-Ost," Rhin told Luu-ka.

The people were still dancing and singing, keeping some distance from their hero.

The group walked right up to Kayre-Ost and bowed low in turn.

The mighty giant's voice echoed, "You don't have to show such strict respect, Rhin."

"What would you have me do, champion Kayre-Ost?"

"Nothing except grant me one favor."

Rhin and the others remained still in anticipation.

"A duel. You versus me."

All within ear-shot regarded the giant in utter stupefaction. He held out his hand, his face ambiguous.

The biggest shock came when Rhin said, "I accept," and took the hand.

As Rhin marched down the cobblestone roads toward the opening in the palisade Luu-ka hurried after him. Rhin made for the butte where the champion awaited.

"Did you see what he did to those other warriors? And there were lots of them and there's only one of you," she spluttered, stumbling as she tried to keep with his pace.

"Yes, I did see."

"Then, why?"

"I don't back down from challenges."

With his bold answer he soared off into the cool night. Dirt and loose strands of grass were sucked into the vacuum that followed.

"You'd better not get hurt, that's all," Luu-ka whispered with a frown.

The young, winged man heard this in his mind and whispered back, "Don't worry. You won't be rid of me. I'll always be around."

Rhin stopped his flight, turned and gave Luu-ka a mock salute. The girl beamed at that.

"Kayre-Ost," Rhin called.

No answer.

"Champion Kayre-Ost, I await you."

This time there was an answer, though it was confusing, "I've awaited you for years."

The giant sprang from the shadows.

"Ready?" he asked.

Rhin allowed his stance to answer for him.

One hand to his side, sword up, legs planted. He would never be more ready.

The adversaries touched blades.

"Why do you want to fight me?" Rhin asked.

Taken aback, Kayre-Ost said, "I want to see if you're worthy."

"Worthy of what, exactly?"

"You'll find out when you win."

"Well, I'm afraid you've been deceived. I'm not an invincible warrior."

"Maybe you aren't. Maybe I'll be disappointed. Only one way to find out," Kayre-Ost replied.

The duel began.

Daish-rog was the first to notice Rhin's return. He was limping but bore a triumphant smile all the same.

"And?" Daish-rog asked.

"I lost."

Daish-rog raised his eyebrows, asking, "Is there something I should know?"

"I lost with such ridicule, Daish-rog. You should have seen it," Rhin laughed.

Rhin walked off. Aroukana stepped up to Daish-rog's side.

"Am I missing anything?" Daish-rog asked the Vevlea.

"Rhin has learned respect and grace in defeat. Kayre-Ost appears to be a good teacher," he answered.

"I agree," Cononsareth began, then spotting Rhin's limp, he added, "though perhaps a bit rough."

Later that night Rhin rested in a recliner chair in a room made of nothing but wood. He found himself in one of the village's two diminutive inns, the Golden Faerie. A fire sputtered in the hearth in a corner—the logs were wet—and this gave the place a nice temperature. Rhin's foot was propped with pillows upon a brown-green ottoman. With his left hand he held a bag of crushed ice to his pulsating leg.

While Rhin had been off dueling, Aroukana had procured three rooms for them at the inn—which was almost all the space they had. The Vevlea was resourceful, no doubts there. It was a cozy establishment and the elderly woman who owned it, Mrs. Poarry, came in almost every quarter-hour to check on Rhin.

It came as no surprise when Kayre-Ost walked in.

"How's your leg?" he asked.

Rhin snickered "Doing better, I suppose."

"Don't use any more ice. The swelling will have stopped by now and it's best to have the wound be warm at this hour," the Denzak instructed.

"Alright. Thanks."

Rhin removed the ice bag that he had been putting to extensive use.

After a while Kayre-Ost spoke again, "I have a favor to ask."

Rhin looked up at him. The Denzak had to stoop to avoid hitting the ceiling, his hirsute beard wagging.

"I want to join your group," said Kayre-Ost.

"Can I ask why?"

"I have my reasons. I don't like Jiaïro very much, let's leave it at that," a pause, "Anyway, what do you say to that?"

Rhin's five friends chose this time to enter the miniscule room. It was a tight fit.

"Not meaning to sound rude, of course, but are we supposed to blindly trust you, Kayre-Ost? We did just meet you," said Chainæïa.

The Denzak grunted, "Well, you can't be sure."

"I say he's welcome to join," said Aroukana.

"You certainly would be of great help in dangerous situations," Cononsareth added.

"Is it settled then?" Kayre-Ost inquired.

"I'd say so," said Luu-ka.

Kayre-Ost gave a brief smile, and then announced that he had to leave. It was awkward, and some of the others had to step outside to allow him passage. As soon as the giant was gone Daish-rog said, "I think this may be a little rash on your part, Aroukana."

Cononsareth listened to the spirited debate. Rhin looked at him, at how hushed and harmonious he was. Then, as the Conkatokæ flicked a foot up to scratch his scalp, he said, "He is a trustworthy and kind-hearted soul. I have sensed it. We Conkatokæ have a gift for these things. His only noticeable shortcoming is a gruff outer shell. He can do us no harm, and he can do Jiaïro severe harm."

"I trust your judgment, Cononsareth," said Rhin.

As the Conkatokæ left, followed by Chainæïa and Luu-ka, Rhin watched Daish-rog and Aroukana keenly. The two hadn't been getting along well since the Temple of Resurrection. Rhin wondered if this had something to do with jealousy. Maybe they both saw themselves as the mentor of the cast?

He abandoned the thought. He was sure that they would grow to understand one another soon enough.

The six, then turned seven, left the village behind at noon. After a hearty breakfast and a lot of good-byes on Kayre-Ost's part, they set off for the region of Lerkas.

"Are you still sure you want to leave your home, Kayre-Ost?" Rhin asked.

"Not my home. And yes, I do want to leave. It's time the people learned to get on without me. Besides, I carved myself quite a reputation while I was there. None of Jiaïro's men will attack the village now. Not so soon after being crushed again and again each time they stopped over. I'm not worried," he said. "I'll be more useful here than back there."

"Well if you're sure you made the right choice. It must be tough, leaving all those friends behind."

"I never really had any friends, Rhin," the giant said. Then, as he hoisted his sack over his shoulder, "It's time to move on."

At that, the conversation ended and Rhin's thoughts strayed to the kingdom they were about to enter.

Then Aroukana said, "According to folklore, two dominant races inhabit the country of Lerkas: the castle-city folk, and a colony of twisted, scaly demons. They are constantly at war with each other, I hear, and both sides claim the land is theirs by right. This feud has lasted over five decades."

"Another danger. Yet, we must cross this perilous landscape to further Rhin's quest," said Cononsareth.

Rhin knew not where the Temple of the Holy Eye lay but he hoped that the inhabitants would be of a helpful nature. All he knew for sure was its general location on the southern part of the Isle. To get there he would need to cross the treacherous passes of Scietse, the heart of the so-called demons' kingdom.

Ambling through a clearing in the forest, Luu-ka heard the distinct thuds and tears of splitting wood. Curious, she approached the source of the sounds.

It turned out to be Kayre-Ost, slouched over a tree stump. The giant hefted his axe and then brought it down, ripping through another log. Each time the cut was perfect and, from his halving, two superb, symmetrical pieces were formed.

Luu-ka watched a while in silence, so as not to disturb the Denzak at work.

Soon Kayre-Ost paused and rested his weight on the steel hilt of his impressive double-bladed axe. He turned around and upon noticing the girl said, "Oh, didn't see you. How long have you been sitting there?"

"I don't know. A little while, I guess."

"Right," a lengthy silence followed. Then, "Weren't you bored watching me cut wood?"

"No, no. Not at all," she said hurriedly. "Do you like to chop wood?"

"Well, it's a job. Someone needs to get firewood for the group. But I do enjoy it, really. It makes me feel sort of peaceful."

"That's good. It's a form of meditation then," Luu-ka smiled.

"You could say that," the giant sat down in front of her. "What do you like to do in your spare time?"

She gave it some thought. "I suppose I've always liked learning about fish and other animals. I love to read. Back in my college there were many books I enjoyed reading over and over again until I'd sucked up every drop of knowledge inside."

Luu-ka sighed.

Kayre-Ost said, "But you're not at your college anymore. You must miss it."

"Yes, I do. But I wanted and still want to accompany Rhin. And his friends."

Kayre-Ost grinned, "You like him."

"Who?" her face flushed.

"Rhin."

"No I don't. I mean he's a good friend but… you *know*," her cheeks burned red.

"Say no more. Anyway, we should head on back. The others may worry."

Kayre-Ost strode off and Luu-ka had to sprint to keep up with his grueling pace. She stared at his back, pure embarrassment written all over her face.

He'd better not say anything, she thought.

The day they reached the border came at last. Most of the boundary that marked the beginnings of Lerkas consisted of trees and cliffs but there were leagues of man-made walls to fill the gaps. Ahead there was a fort encircled by oaks and jagged heaps of rock. Pavilions were set in the castle's shade and hosts of soldiers were huddled by their fire pits.

Once they spotted Rhin and the rest, one of the men was shoved their way.

With a weary tone he asked, "Who goes there?"

"We are travelers heading for the Castle City of Kranfaraas," said Kayre-Ost.

The soldier scanned Rhin, weighing and judging him. He paid particular attention to the clean, white wings. Furrowing his brow, he said, "Come along."

The warriors gave the Conkatokæ queer, even sullen looks as he had passed them by. And so, to compound the alienation, he did a handstand and 'walked' off.

The party followed him to the castle gate.

"Open it up."

Kayre-Ost entered first followed by Rhin, Luu-ka and Cononsareth, then the two Vevleï and Daish-rog. The gate was only large enough to fit two men abreast, so Kayre-Ost had to walk in by himself. He was not a fat man, but with all his gear and weaponry there was no other option.

"You have a good five days march ahead of you," the soldier said, sounding near death with boredom. "Head west and you will find the village of Varmsŷrul. There you can find supplies and maybe even hear some of the folklore." But his face lit up when he said, "I hear those nasty devils are abroad again, though. Could mean another battle is near. Best be careful."

"Thank you, we will," said Cononsareth with a soft wave.

After they were well away from the fortification Chainæïa asked, "Devils? The ones you mentioned, Aroukana?"

"It would seem so," Aroukana answered. "But in truth I believe it is a superstition. The soldiers of Kranfaraas simply demonize their opponents to aid in their campaign against them. Fear is powerful motivation and panic rallies armies. Besides, it is also very effective crowd control," said Aroukana, ever suspicious of gossip.

"I don't know. They could be right. After what I've seen these past few months, I'll believe almost anything," Rhin stated.

"Anything is possible in this world," Cononsareth added.

"Devils or not, if they try to harm us they won't get very close," Kayre-Ost said, holding his chin up.

"Yes, but don't go killing anyone without reason," Luu-ka said.

"Never," Kayre-Ost snapped, perhaps harsher than he'd intended.

"You think the citizens of the Castle City will tell us what we want to know?" Rhin asked.

"Only time will tell. The question I think is: can they tell us? Most people these days don't know much about anything," said Daish-rog.

"How much trouble do you think we'll have from Jiaïro in this land?" Luu-ka asked.

"Not as much as he'll be having from us," Kayre-Ost's boomed.

Night fell soon thereafter. They fell asleep, with the exceptions of Rhin and Luu-ka who sat by a pool of clear water that reflected the white moonlight.

"I never got a chance to thank you properly for rescuing me, Rhin. So, thank you."

"It's all right," he said, looking at his feet.

"I think I figured out what part of my dream meant."

She edged closer. "You were the angel that saved me. I must have always known that I would meet you."

Rhin's gaze drifted upward and he saw her smiling at him. He stared into her blue eyes again.

How many times have I done this? he wondered.

All he could do was smile back.

"I also knew I would meet you," he said, "I had a vision a few months ago, before I met Aroukana. I heard voices and saw a temple and a grass field. A woman was running. A demon was chasing her. I ran to help but I didn't make it in time."

No words seemed appropriate so Rhin was silent. Luu-ka was too. Rhin watched a fish leap from the pool, then the expanding ripples in the once serene water.

After a bit, he said, "But I'm very glad I did get there in time when the nightmare came true. Very glad."

Luu-ka turned.

"Rhin."

"Yes?"

"I just..."

When he saw her struggling for the right words he laid his hand on hers and they were quiet again.

They fell asleep hand in hand.

In the morning, when the air was fresh, Rhin felt good. It had been a little embarrassing to wake up still holding Luu-ka's hand, what with the others, but he dispelled the sentiment. He liked Luu-ka a lot, but he remained abashed.

The group continued the trip to Varmsŷrul. As the day wore on it became hot and humid and beads of sweat trickled down Rhin's brow.

"What I would not give for a nice lake right here, in front of me," Aroukana said.

"A shame you are not a Conkatokæ. We have a sort of cooling system that keeps us adapted to the weather. So we are never hot or cold, we are always at a perfect, balanced temperature," said Cononsareth.

"Sometimes I envy you, Cononsareth," said Chainæïa, mopping his face with his bandana.

"Of course," Cononsareth added, "it only works if we remain hydrated."

"I've been in worse times than this," said Kayre-Ost.

"Oh, sure," Luu-ka said.

"Hey, Cononsareth, why don't you turn that cooler of yours off and share in the misery?" Kayre-Ost suggested.

"Thousands of years of evolutionary improvement and you want me to 'turn it off'?"

"Yeah."

"Keep dreaming," the Conkatokæ laughed aloud.

"My aching feet," Rhin moaned.

"Quit complaining," Luu-ka said, shooting him a playful smile.

"I'll do as I please," Rhin replied, waving his finger at her.

Luu-ka shoved him into the sand. They both burst out laughing.

"Break time," said Kayre-Ost, clapping his hands.

"Might I converse with you a moment, Chainæïa?" Aroukana asked, pointing to an isolated grassy patch in a sea of sand.

"Of course," Chainæïa replied and they walked off.

"I don't know if you heard about the legend but it clearly stated that Akvius would come and fight with us," said Aroukana.

"I have heard."

"Do you plan to join the Vevleï resistance when the final battle is at hand?"

"Of course. I have wished for little else all my life."

"Excellent, my brother! We shall fight together and, by the Gods, we shall win."

They shook hands.

"And what of Daish-rog?" Aroukana asked. "He is not fully Vevlea, is he?"

"No, we had different fathers. Daish-rog's father was a man," Chainæïa answered, "but I know in my heart that he will fight alongside us as long as there is breath in him."

"Glory and victory," said Aroukana.

Daish-rog gazed at the clouds. He hadn't uttered a word for the past few days, spending most of the time thinking. He had inherited his father's sword and powers and become a lord in service to the spirit of Nature. Yet he felt he could not fulfill this great honor because his murderous desire overwhelmed him. He could not help but think that he would never have his revenge if he stayed with Rhin. He wished to avenge his fallen siblings by destroying Rixaï, but he owed Rhin his life. His heart told him that Rhin was the greatest man he had ever known, so he would have to grant the wish.

Daish-rog felt guilty, full of a wretched rage, but above all he was fearful. He dreaded the dangerous shuffle down that abject path. Because of his everlasting debt to Rhin he could be dishonored if he left. He was torn. It was as if two people had grabbed his heart strings and each yanked in opposite directions.

Rhin approached him and gave him a pat on the shoulder. Within the space of that moment, Daish-rog made up his mind.

"Rhin?"

"What is it?"

"I wish to leave."

"What?" he looked dumbfounded.

"I want to hunt Rixaï down for honor and revenge. I can't allow him to live after what I've suffered. There will be no more failure on my part," Daish-rog said as he watched a falcon in flight. "I won't die again, Rhin."

"I know."

"Rhin, you are wise far beyond your years, so I ask you to understand," Daish-rog's voice faltered.

"I do," he said, "Go then. May the gifts of the Gods go with you and keep you from harm's way. Come back to us safely, Daish-rog."

"This I promise you. Thank you, Rhin Akvius. You are truly the greatest friend anyone could ever have. May the blessing of Cryöd Lumoræ* go with you, and guide you on your way."

"Do you want to say good-bye to them?" Rhin asked as he flicked his head at their companions.

"No. I don't like farewells. Although you must tell my brother, Chainæïa, that if I fail he should head for the ruins of Alkari. There lie the remnants of his race and the Vevleï resistance. Heard that during my... service."

"I will tell him. But don't you think Aroukana-"

Daish-rog cut him off irritably, "You shouldn't put all your faith in that one. He may not be as wise as he tries to make everyone think."

"He's done nothing but help me," said Rhin, straightening.

"I know," the other replied, softer than before. "I just want you to be cautious."

"Don't worry. You watch yourself, too."

Daish-rog shook Rhin's hand and ran off.

"Good luck, my friend," said Rhin as he waved.

When he was but a fleck on the horizon, Rhin thought that he saw him transform into a bird and take flight, but was never sure of it.

---

* Each God or Goddess had a second name that revealed their nature, personality, or destiny. For example, Lumoræ means Lord of Light. Each second name was a word in the Eldest Language that was given by another god or goddess close to them.

Back with his friends, Rhin told them of Daish-rog's departure and of his message to Chainæïa.

"They truly reside there? Alkari! What better place than the remains of the capital of our once glorious kingdom?" Chainæïa said. "But why did he have to leave?"

"He has a responsibility," Aroukana stated. "His duty, in a sense, is to rid the world of a profound Evil. At least part of his desire is pure."

"And the other part—vengeance, I presume?" said Cononsareth.

"He will return and Rixaï will at last be dead," Chainæïa told them. "Although I am saddened by his departure, I know in my heart that my brother and I will meet again. Our family will finally be avenged!"

Before too long, they arrived at the village of Varmsŷrul. Befitting his character, Aroukana vaulted off to digest as much raw knowledge as he could from its denizens.

Rhin decided to take it easy. There was a fountain set upon the cobblestones at the heart of the market place, a winged man standing atop a sphere with incandescent tears flowing from his eyes. Beneath the shade of the bronze fountain Rhin found solitude. He watched the shadows shift as the day wore on. He waved when he saw one of his friends mingling with the townsfolk. The sun faded, passing behind a ceiling of white. It was still bright outside, but the light was masked.

Aroukana returned with Kayre-Ost and Cononsareth. Chainæïa and Luu-ka reappeared soon after, she hugging a stuffed irlorn doll, he holding a silver compass.

"So, Aroukana, what did you learn this day?" asked Cononsareth. He proceeded to lick his forehead with his tongue.

"I have found the treasure at the end of the cavern in terms of lore," Aroukana smiled as he spoke.

"Tell us then," said Chainæïa, pocketing his shiny new compass.

The adventurers rested themselves around the fountain, Luu-ka sitting closest to Rhin. Before Aroukana began his monologue, she positioned the irlorn doll on Rhin's head with care. He turned to face her and simpered.

Aroukana cleared his throat and said, "To the southwest lie the mountains of Scietse, and even further west the titanic volcano, Cortak. A great wall of rock formed by the eruption of that volcano, thousands of years ago, separates south from north. In the past the inhabitants of the kingdom of Lerkas have tried to tunnel through it to simplify sea and land travel but found that the rock was impenetrable. This barrier became known as the Sŷrul Wall.

"At some point in history the flying devils moved in and created large fortresses atop the peaks and spires. These cliffs meet at the prodigious Spekfer Mountain, which is the straightest way of crossing to the other side of the Isle—with the exception of flying—but also the most foolhardy.

"Most nearby villages are ports, fish being the chief resource of nearly the entire realm. This fact gives the region its common name of Verklandsag, or 'Fisherman Crags'. The fishermen pay special heed to a giant tidal wave that crashes through here every year near the end of summer. The wave pours through the villages, covering everything. The water eventually subsides. Before the arrival of the wave, the villagers scale the nearest cliffs and there they remain for a week or two. When they return, their homes are still in good shape with only minor structural damage. This, I hear, is because the houses are incredible in their sturdiness, being made of stone from the shoreline. Even after the seasonal beatings the stuff stays strong. You see, the minerals in the rock excrements possess special properties which, when extracted and mixed with certain oils, form a durable substance. Once straw-meal is added to the concoction the final product is smooth to the touch. Alchemists are revered in these parts, for obvious reasons."

"You were hard at work, I see," said Chainæïa with a cheerful grin.

"It's what I do best," Aroukana said and shrugged, inclining his head.

Daish-rog was no longer a man. He had become a magnificent gray-winged, mauve-beaked hawk. Even he was unable to recognize his new species. All he did was will himself to fly. He could not help but feel pride for all the other avian creatures trembled at his mere passing. Whenever he flapped his great wings he created gusts of air.

He had been scouting, putting his sun disk eyes to full use. He shot straight for the North Isle, Nénamburra, where he and Rhin had begun their journey. His destination was the Old Nature Tower where he hoped to find clues to his early days... or discover the scent of Rixaï's blood.

For twenty hours he made his solitary migration, until he arrived at last. His landing was clumsy. Once on the ground he skidded, hasty as he was, to the ruined gate.

He'd been but a child when he was spirited away. Still, the place was worse off than he recalled in the dim haze of his childhood. His family had been the sworn guardians of a lost relic, a container of vast energies. They were a veritable clan, living in yurts around the base of the structure. It was all gone. The only edifice that remained was the tower.

The wooden door and frame were black from decades of rot. Vines had conquered much of the tower's surface, be it stone or plank.

Daish-rog transmuted into an ash-colored wolf and stood on his hind paws. Using his forepaws he bore down on the moldering enclosure. It felt like soggy leaves to his touch.

Before him lay the stairs. One thousand spiraling steps. As a child, his mother had warned him not to play on the steps. If he did he might fall, and that would break her heart. But it was his mother who had died, and his heart that was broken.

He reached the end of the stairs and entered the room where the Nature Crystal had resided forty years before. Glass from the shattered windows was strewn about the floor. A decaying rug that must once have been red was now a milky brown rag with bugs scuttling underneath. There were moldy books and papers on the floor and a set of plundered chests as well.

This is my legacy.

Most of his family had been butchered at the base of the Tower, but his father had been finished in this room. They all died fighting Rixaï. They died to defend the Nature Crystal. Rixaï delighted in slaughter, however, and while he was preoccupied with Daish-rog's clan, the spirit that slept within the Crystal was able to call upon falcons and escape.

The coward's flight, Daish-rog thought, bitter tears stinging his eyes. As he looked around the ransacked chamber he told himself, *Had I been old enough I would have been dead, too. Why did the spirits not help my family on their darkest day?*

He detected a scent hiding among the rot. No doubt, it belonged to Rixaï himself. Even after forty years such a foul stench could not disappear.

He followed it.

He would not turn into the hawk again, for fear of losing the scent.

It was a good first day. He was getting closer. The anxiety all but overwhelmed him.

Rhin and his friends were lodged at the Lounging Bear Inn in Varmsŷrul. The yellow building was crammed between an ale brewery and a cheese maker's shop, so the smell was unequalable. It was a quaint establishment, with mediocre meals and cheap wines aplenty. But Rhin could not complain because the prices were cheap and Luu-ka needed to be as sparing as circumstances allowed. The sign suspended on hooks outside was by far the best part of the deal. It was a painted cut out of a drunken, black bear reclining on a lavish couch.

They had not entered a moment too soon, for a cloudy night had come, bringing with it rain and thunder. The rhythmic rapping on the malformed windows alleviated the day's stress.

Rhin lay in bed, counting. He concluded that it had been about seven months since he had set out on his journey. Though, he might have been stretching the days a bit.

What would have happened if Brekk and his scum had never found Lynca and killed my parents? Would I have stayed there and never found who I was—who I am supposed to become? he asked himself.

There came a knock on his door and he jumped up.

Aroukana poked his head in and when Rhin gestured him in, walked over to the bed, saying, "Rhin, you know there is a legend about you where I come from."

"You've hinted at it. I'm supposed to be the 'Savior of the Vevleï' and all that," Rhin mocked, throwing his hands up.

"Rhin, listen. This is important. The legend tells us that there is hope no matter what happens. I did not dare hope until I met you, honestly. But I see now that you fit the perfect description of Rhin Akvius. That tattoo you have spells out your destiny. It means that you will do great things," Aroukana explained.

"You think it's true?"

"Yes. You have already done great things. But in the future I will need a favor."

"What would that be?"

"You must fight alongside the Vevleï armies and help us emerge victorious in the struggle against Jiaïro," Aroukana stared straight at him, into his heart. "Can I ask this of you?"

"You had my sword from the start," said Rhin.

To show it, he hefted his sword, unsheathed the weapon and offered it pommel first to the Vevlea.

Aroukana took the sword, and said with a happy smile, "Thank you, Rhin. You are gifted with unmatched skills, and yet you are humble. It is my belief that we could all learn from you."

At the hallowed hour of dawn, Rhin and his friends regrouped at the town square. It was a ghostly morning and immaterial curls of mist screened the stone roads. At random they chose a person to approach. A man, maybe forty years old, dressed in a plain green tunic with his hair oiled back.

Kayre-Ost approached him and said, "Morning. Know a good way to cross Spekfer?"

The man's eyes bulged and his breaths were shallow as he said, "You want to cross that mountain? You're crazy! There are those devils about the whole place. I'll have nothing to do with you."

The green-garbed, agitated man moved away.

"He walks almost as fast as I run when on two legs. He must have a prior engagement," remarked Cononsareth.

"Talkative, aren't they?" said Rhin.

"Quite," answered Aroukana.

Luu-ka said, "I think you were too gruff, Kayre-Ost. You're very intimidating."

"Try it then," the giant suggested.

"I will," said the girl, adjusting her skirt.

"What about that person?" Chainæïa offered.

Another man walked by, balding with only a thinning ring of grey strands arcing the rim of his skull like a weathered crown. He wore a faded blue vest and white leggings.

"Excuse me, sir," Luu-ka asked him, "I am a traveler. Could you explain how to pass over the mountain of Spekfer?"

"You are all lunatics," he declared, and scurried off in a hurry.

"Humph," Luu-ka puffed.

"Will there be anyone who won't think we're a bunch of lunatics?" Rhin massaged his temples one handed, his stress reliever for when things didn't happen as they should.

"We must keep trying," Aroukana sighed.

Two hours later the mists had dissipated and they were sitting around the town square. None of them had found anyone who would provide directions. Most screamed or ran. Rhin felt as if they had spoken to everyone in the village.

"If we continue like this we'll have the militia after us," Chainæïa warned.

"To be true, I'm surprised they haven't come already," said Cononsareth.

The sun was torrid and their faces were shining with perspiration, while sweat tumbled down their soaked scalps.

"If nobody wants to help us then we'll help ourselves," said Rhin.

"What do you suggest?" Chainæïa asked.

"I'll fly ahead and scout for a way over the mountain," Rhin replied.

"Since we don't have a better plan, it is worth a try," said Aroukana.

"I'll be back by sundown," Rhin promised.

With that said, he was off.

When he propelled himself upward he brushed his hands over roof tiles and pretended to run on thin air. These acts caught the attention of several towns' folk. They shouted and pointed but soon returned to their daily routines.

Hard to please, Rhin thought.

Rhin flew over a deserted field, devoid of animals and even flowers. He wondered if this had to do with the war between the devils and the king's men.

Then he set his sights on the great Sŷrul Wall and Spekfer Mountain, which seemed to blend together in the hot air. In his peripheral vision, he glimpsed a shape darting across the sky, a green blur, and chased after it.

Lightning flashed and thunder sounded, but it was in broad daylight with nary a cloud in the sky. And, strangely, the lightning coursed from the ground up.

Something struck him from behind and he dropped a few feet. After regaining his balance he saw what it was, a skeletal green creature with bat-like wings. It palmed its head and growled.

"I'm sorry," Rhin said.

"Move aside, I must help my kin!" the thing said in a penetrating tone.

The creature surged toward the earth. A second later there was an explosion of blue fire and a deluge of scarlet lightning.

Rhin was startled when he heard the beast talk but then another one of the devils burst a rock in mid air giving way to a hail of fire.

Rhin flew after one of them, cupped his mouth and shouted, "What's going on here?"

"Battle! A strike on the men of Lerkas," it answered.

And then it spat a well-aimed fiery projectile down at the men.

Again, Rhin was astonished. Then he saw the sun reflecting off the helmets and the gleaming silvery armor, the flash of swords and spears, the clearing of war horns.

How did I not see them before? Rhin thought as he rubbed his eyes.

More Lerkas men came marching from the north, escorting seven armored siege scorpions. Rhin watched the commander—her rank was obvious because of her gilded plate mail—lift her arm and shout orders. The woman had light brown hair, bound in a ponytail.

"They are going to fire!" Rhin warned.

In response, the devils attacked and obliterated two of the siege weapons. The remaining five shot fiery, man-sized bolts into the sky.

With a rain of green and red, many devils fell like flies onto a bed of flames.

This infuriated Rhin. As far as he could tell, the devils had not shed any blood. They only incapacitated or threatened and not a single Lerkas soldier lay dead. Rhin chose his camp.

He flew over to one of the catapults and cut some ropes. The pieces collapsed, littering the grass. Outraged, the soldiers shot at him. One arrow zipped past his head, tugging at a few strands of his red hair.

Rhin ascended as more fiery shafts blazed through the air and thunderous blasts struck the ground.

Another arrow zoomed past his head.

He looked at the sky. It was nearly sundown. Flying back to the town square now would be cowardly and dishonorable. Although even he had to admit that it was going to take a miracle to save them.

That miracle came.

Lightning struck the remaining siege engines and they burst into flames. Rhin looked up and saw nothing but light. Even when he looked away it was so bright that he had to close his eyes. The light became less bright when he opened them again. He saw the Sword of Purity in the center of the beam. How this had happened was beyond him.

The sword transformed into a woman bathed in the light. She was clothed in silver silk and dotted with gold markings. From her neck and wrists hung sapphires and upon her brow was set a single diamond.

Rhin squinted at her.

"Who are you?"

"I am the Spirit of Purity," the woman said in a voice that resounded with wisdom and nobility.

"How long have you been in there? Why did you not show yourself before?"

"I have resided within your blade since the beginning. But my power had little influence until this moment, when it was fully restored."

"How was it restored? And why now?"

"You will learn everything you need to know in good time, Rhin Akvius."

Her voice was so soft it seemed the world itself strained to listen.

"Can you help me save these creatures?"

"Yes, I can."

"Will you?"

"Nothing would make me happier," and as she said this her eyes sparkled.

The woman reached her arm in up and with that swift movement, all stood on its head. The clashing of swords, the blaring of thunder and sparks of lightning, every intention of fighting ceased. Rhin watched this angel of light promulgate her gift of peace.

It started to rain as storm clouds melded.

"Master," she said, "Master Rhin, do you remember when you forged the Sword of Purity?"

A host of memories jumbled in Rhin's mind. From amid the chaos he found his answer.

He remembered the name Miara and who she was.

"I do, Miara," he said. "Your soul became one with the sword. But I never understood why you did it."

"My love for you was so profound that I was willing to sacrifice everything for you, my Rhin," Miara, the Spirit of Purity, shook her head.

"You didn't need to do so much," Rhin touched her cheek and a silvery tear fell from her eye onto his hand.

It warmed him.

"Truly, it did not come without a price," she whispered, "I was a prisoner of the sword for two thousand years."

"I'm so sorry."

"I am not. Not for helping you, I will never be more proud than I was then. I am free now and shall continue to help you through your quests. My last blessing will be to grant this sword greater power. Let it remind you of me. Let it be your instrument of justice."

She kissed the blade and it shone the brighter for it. Then she returned to Rhin.

"You will know fear and face tremendous peril, Rhin Akvius. But you will overcome," said Miara with a small, white smile. Then she whispered,

"Seek thine Holy Gifts
One from the forest where old things dwell
One from the eye of this world's hell
An aged one from the far marsh lands
Keeps the third for you in his hands
The fourth from the abysmal rock
Where whispered lies and maggots flock
The last from a treacherous rat
Yet he fears you, he'll realize that

On the tip of Jiaïro's throne
Knock him down, on his own cold stone
The pieces have been set in place
As the game begins some will lose face
It falls to you to right the wrong
Or all life will end ere too long"

Rhin was silent. He drank in her every word.

"I will always be with you, my Rhin," Miara uttered, pressing his cheek with a long, pale finger.

She vanished.

As if Rhin was released from a spell, he looked at the sky. It was now well after sundown and scarlet clouds rushed past him. The men made for their homes and the flying demons returned to their mountain.

Chapter 17
The Crossing of Scietse

Daish-rog ran through the woods. With each step a branch cracked under his feet. To make better time, he became an erlmerk* and padded along the paths for days without tiring, his lean body near-unable to contain the fiery fury within. Hot on Rixaï's trail, the scent was sharper than before and unmistakable even to the nose of a non-wolf.

When several miles lay between him and the Tower, he sensed he was being followed. The stench of Jiaïro's bootlicks was pungent, the wind carrying it forth from behind. Later, there was a faint rustling a few yards from him and he came to an abrupt stop.

He saw the clear outlines of a puddle of blood and sniffed the faint odor of murder. Death swayed with the trees. The forest itself moaned in sorrow. The hair on Daish-rog's erlmerk neck stood on end.

He became a wolf, snarling as he inhaled the bloody odor. It was female, and had been shed not half an hour past. His ears pricked when he heard a scream, the sound of steel on flesh and the splash of red water. It was close.

He crept in silence among the broad pines and before long found the scene. A woman lay impaled upon a sword, twitching as she wept.

---

* A species related to the irlorn, with larger ears and hind legs.

In one leap, and without thought or abeyance, he pawed the face of the one responsible and bit into his throat. Blood poured out into Daish-rog's lupine eyes as he turned back into his original self, his jade armor casting a supernatural glow in the dark night. The man he had mauled had short-cropped gray hair and a goatee. Lying there he looked almost innocent. But his garb was colored red and black and that spoke volumes of his character.

Is Jiaïro the cause of all the world's woes? Daish-rog asked himself, shaking his head.

With his sword he wounded the graying man again for his own assurance.

He made for the woman and grabbed her wrist. Her pulse was weakening, almost gone.

"You need help," he gasped. "Let me carry you."

"It is too late... for me."

He looked at her.

Her eyes had wrinkled from old age and were a tear-filled emerald green. Her hair was a bushy gray mass against her black clothing. In his heart he did not doubt that this was his mother.

"Mother?" he whimpered and pulled her closer.

She put a frigid, shaking hand to his cheek.

"I know you. Daish-rog, my baby boy," her eyes closed.

Her hand dropped.

"Mother, no!" he screamed pressing his face into her hair.

He became a wolf and ululated his heartache, the grief echoing across the moonless sky.

Then he returned to the man on the ground. He was suffering, clutching his chest and taking the shallowest of breaths. Daish-rog could not fathom how he remained alive.

"Why did you kill her?" Daish-rog asked as he shook the man.

The dying man staged a pitiful laugh and then said, "She had been in hiding for forty years. I represent the law here. I am..."

But Daish-rog wasn't listening, for on the man's left shoulder was a pad complete with a single straight spike. And as he knew so well, in Jiaïro's accursed army, the number and formation of spikes on an officer's shoulder indicated rank. This one was a sergeant.

"She was just an old woman, you bastard!" Daish-rog yelled and spat in the figure's face.

And, with his sobbing voice, Daish-rog cursed the sergeant until he died. It did not take long.

Then he caught Rixaï's scent once more and resumed the chase, a new sense of loathing driving him onward.

Everything has been taken from me, he thought.

It was more than he could bear. His rage consumed his every judgment.

His sole purpose was to destroy Rixaï. If his bloated sense of vengeance killed him he would at least have tasted revenge and dealt one fraction of the pain contained within his shattered heart.

Among the boulders and veins of trickling water, on the edge of the steep rock wall, Rhin and his friends scaled the immense mountain of Scietse.

The sun must always shine on this Isle, Rhin thought, wiping his brow.

The sky was baby blue and clear. For being so close to the North Isle, Nénamburra, Freeland seemed a different world.

The climb was harsh and, above all, long and strenuous. It was pretty much a steep, straight-arrow climb to the top—though, once in a great while they found a platform or a gentler incline.

Rhin had returned the night before and recounted the details of the battle and his meeting with Miara. The history of the Sword of Purity and his relationship with Miara had all come back to him—though he kept some details to himself.

In that moment all his doubts washed away. He knew now that he was the true Rhin, Master of Swords. He knew without question what he must do: throw Jiaïro off his throne and end his reign of tyranny. Of course, that had been his plan all along, but now he recognized it as inevitable. They would fight to the death. Simple.

His quest was to find the five Temples of the Holy Gifts. And he knew for a certainty that his brothers, the marshals of Jiaïro, would do anything to stop him.

"Tell me, Rhin do you think it possible for you to not get yourself mixed up in a war—just for a day or two?" Aroukana had asked.

"I could try," Rhin had replied with a grin.

The pink sky heralded the coming of night, as the sun descended behind the Cortak volcano to the west. It had been a grueling day, but now Rhin and the others were rewarded with a gentle, cool breeze.

"Almost there," Chainæïa grunted.

"A little farther, indeed." Aroukana added in the same tone.

"A little hike too much for you?" Kayre-Ost mocked. "People will think you're milksop."

"We are not milksop," the Vevleï said indignantly.

At that they tripled their speed.

"Ah, much better," Kayre-Ost shouted after them as they zoomed past him.

By that time Luu-ka and Rhin had reached the top, and were lying flat on the rocky surface.

Breathe, breathe, Rhin thought as his muscles cramped and lurched.

Then Aroukana and Chainæïa flew past them and panted in triumph, "We've won."

"It's strange to feel young again," Aroukana said, as drank air.

"Aroukana," Chainæïa wheezed, "what is a 'milksop'?"

"Well, since I am a lizard, and wise, I shall take my time," Cononsareth told the cliff.

The Conkatokæ did not make use of the rope. He leapt from rock to rock with the aid of his powerful limbs, digging into stone with his claws.

When they had all reached the top there was a loud snap and an unraveling sound.

"The rope, it would seem, has become… unusable," said Cononsareth.

The group scrambled to the edge of the cliff just in time to see the remnants of the line tumble down.

"And now?" Aroukana asked.

"Be thankful we weren't still climbing?" said Luu-ka.

"Well, yes. In fact, let's all make a mental note to find the merchant who sold us that shoddy piece of mountaineering equipment," said Aroukana, removing his gloves finger by finger. "But what do we do for shelter?"

"Maybe if you hadn't expended all your strength on that little tour de force you'd have noticed *this*," said Cononsareth, bowing low as he indicated a cave.

"Good work. Let's set up for the night," said Kayre-Ost.

Rhin sat under the ceiling of stars and, with a flat rock, acuminated the Sword of Purity. He looked up and saw Chainæïa standing before him.

"What do you think we will do when we are done looking for the Temples, master?" he asked Rhin.

"We will head for the ruins of Alkari. There I'll stand with the Vevleï. Your fight is the same as mine, after all. But, Chainæïa, please don't call me 'master' anymore. We aren't all that different," Rhin shrugged, adding, "I just have wings and everyone in the world is trying to kill me."

Chainæïa laughed. "Well said. I shall endeavor to emulate your humility," he paused and took a few deep breaths. "Once our work is done, the Vevleï shall rebuild Alkari, the lost capital, the city that Jiaïro sacked so many centuries ago. I was born into the gray years, ages after my homeland was but dust. Thus it is my purpose to renew it, so that my children should not suffer the same tragedy—the same hopelessness."

"In my heart I know that is my purpose, too. Though for me... let's just say, having children is a long way off for this renegade."

"Thank you very much for your efforts, my friend."

He clapped Rhin on the back.

Early the next morning, in a pool of his own sweat, Rhin stirred to the devils' howling as they shot across the skies in great ranks. He ascended to their level and stopped in front of one of them. He was ignored.

"Good morning," he greeted them.

From the look it gave Rhin, it either did not understand him or was unused to the respect.

"Move," it commanded, finally breaking the tense silence.

"But I was just wondering-"

"Move," it repeated.

Another devil joined the limited discourse, flying over to Rhin, "Célals, that is no way to treat a potential ally. Honestly, the first man we meet who isn't horribly racist toward our kind and you try to antagonize him," the devil chided, shaking its head. Then it turned to Rhin, "Please excuse my friend. He's a little sharp in the morning. Is that not right, Célals?"

The more polite devil nudged the other with its jagged elbow.

"My name is Ferask. Pleased to make your acquaintance, sir. Who might we have the honor of addressing?"

"I am Rhin Akvius," he said somewhat proudly.

"Rhin?" asked Célals.

"The Rhin?" Ferask choked.

"Many a book has been written and many a myth been sewn concerning you," stated Ferask.

"Why are you here?" Célals asked, scratching his bald, scaly head.

"My friends and I are trying to get to the other side of Scietse," Rhin answered.

"Why?" they inquired.

"To find the Temple of the Holy Eye."

"But it is simply impossible to cross the mountain. There is a steep drop on the other side."

"We have to try. It's the quickest way to get there."

"How much cord do you have?" asked Célals.

"None. There was an accident."

"But you can fly. Why do you not use your wings?" Célals pointed at Rhin's extra limbs.

"My friends can't fly. I'll share their fate."

"Quite right you are. It would be utterly rude any other way," said Ferask.

Célals gave a curt nod.

"But can you tell me where the Temple is?" Rhin put his hands together in a pleading gesture.

"Ah, afraid we cannot help you there. But even if we could we would not have the time. You see, we are off to battle the Lerer men," Ferask said and shook his head.

"Lerer men?" Rhin repeated.

"The men from Lerkas. They constantly attack us. We know not why. I think they look at us as devils—absurd," for a brief moment the jest made Célals smile for the first time, but then he was serious again, "We only fight to defend ourselves and our mountain. But because we know the ways of magic they think we are evil or some such."

A horn sounded. And many battle cries ensued. Ferask unclasped a spear from his side and Célals brought forth a mighty axe from its scabbard which was strapped over his shoulder.

"It is time," Célals told Rhin. "Farewell."

They added their shouts to the others and were off. Rhin soared back to the mountain.

"I've actually seen those creatures before," Luu-ka told him when he rejoined the group. "They used to fly around my island and howl at the sky. They are called Scerps. They frighten you at first but can be pretty friendly, if you don't invade their homeland. One took me flying when I was a little girl. His name was Ferask."

"Ferask? You're sure?" Rhin asked.

"Yes. Why?"

"Because there he is," Rhin pointed at the receding dot in the sky.

"I draw closhher, Akviussh. Shho closhhe."

The Sorcerer soared through the air with great speed. He had been flying for a week without pause. His spells and potions were prepared and soon he would come to the peaks of Scietse, where his dark purpose would be fulfilled.

A great storm was brewing in the East. He would have to be wary. The air was full of dust and pollen, for indeed it was spring. The sprouting flowers with their blooming buds gave him an ill feeling in the pit of his stomach.

"Shhpring will not shhave you," he muttered as he hastened in the night.

Every second counted. Rebellion was coming. Soon all the world would tremble as the darkness made way for the light. It was a bleak fate that awaited all Sorcerers should this be the outcome. There was but one way to avoid this calamity and he knew it all too well. Rhin Akvius must perish.

The wind blew something fierce on the spires of Scietse. Dust coated the rock and clouded the air, so that breathing became a chore.

There was but one more peak to brave, but this time around they had no line. It was far more dangerous, maybe even suicidal, to make the last trek without support, but Rhin and his companions were determined. Though they knew not what would be waiting for them on the other side, nor how they would manage to climb down, Aroukana advised them to worry on that issue later and tackle the task at hand.

After another few hours of hiking they reached the tip of the giant. The sun burned Rhin's eyes, making the daring attempt even more ludicrous.

He looked down and saw a city that stretched over the entire valley beneath the mountain.

"The merchant city of Sfersurul," said Aroukana.

But once Rhin noticed the rocks that formed a jagged labyrinth below, his heart nearly stopped.

He had suffered from vertigo ever since his childhood. And now that he thought about it, it was pretty ironic that he could fly. Somehow, though, it was different when he was in the air. When his feet touched earth and there was a drop before him all he could think of was falling.

"What now?" Kayre-Ost asked the world in general.

"If we all had wings like Rhin, we could fly down," Chainæïa said.

"Well, we do not. Are there any other suggestions?" Cononsareth asked and looked at each of the others in turn.

A piece of rock crumbled down and shattered to pieces when it hit the bottom—after a long fall.

"This will just never work without rope, Rhin," Luu-ka answered.

"I could fly and get more," Rhin said, hands on his hips.

"You could," Kayre-Ost tugged at his beard.

"I'll go. I'll be back soon."

"That's what you said last time," Luu-ka commented.

But Rhin was already airborne by then, before Kayre-Ost had time to mention that Rhin always seemed to find trouble whenever he flew off alone.

The sky was dark again the moon casting an eerie glint. It was as if the world watched him, as if every decision he made affected the rest of Iora.

He flew right past the merchant city because their prices were far too high, according to Luu-ka.

"You're paying for the stamp of Sfersurul and the tax goes straight to Lord Gluttony," she had said, her voice full of contempt.

So Rhin traveled further south until he found a small town.

"Welcome to Surulnar," a yellow and red sign read.

Black, iron lampposts cast a dim light over the streets in the growing twilight. Though the hour grew late, for the sun set near midnight during spring in the East, the crowds around him were still bumbling through their self-absorbed business and babbling.

He did not have the time or desire to make conversation. He scanned the signposts in the streets and the printed flyers on the walls of the gray-brick houses until he saw a shop that caught his eye. 'The Travelers Stock', proclaimed the wooden sign. Beside the door was a stone statue of a bucktoothed, grinning dog standing on its hind legs.

A bell chimed as Rhin entered.

Bear pelts, fox furs, brown cloaks, steel pocketknives, brass-buckle belts, provision sacks, and glass bottles were all on display.

The store manager walked over to him and asked, "Can I be doin' anythin' for ya, sir?"

"Do you have any extra thick rope?"

"Oh, we be a havin' that, sir. How long a piece would ya be wantin'?"

"How about one Cut*."

"Sure, we be a havin' that. You be a climbin' mountains, eh sir?"

"Yes."

---

* A measurement equal to a kilometer.

He rolled the rope up in a bundle and tied it with a triple knot and then handed it to Rhin, who then paid him the amount of Vilt coins that he owed and smiled.

"You be havin' a nice night, sir."

"You, too."

Rhin left the shop, the bell chime resonating after him until the door shut, and flew back toward the mountain. Once more, as he took off, he attracted the gaze of peasant and lord alike. He was used to it by now.

Great black clouds circulated in the darkened sky. Rhin felt uneasy, as if waking from a bad dream.

When he arrived, his friends were huddled by a fire, the only source of light in the obscurity. They took the rope, attached it to a sturdy stalagmite and let the rest of it slip over the edge. Their goal was to descend the mountain before the storm hit. At this altitude a shower of rain and lightning would be lethal. Rhin went first and behind him, in order, went the Vevleï, Kayre-Ost, Luu-ka and Cononsareth.

But as they started there was a tremor and boulders tumbled down after them. So they all scrambled back the way they came, rushing to find shelter before the worst of the storm struck. A bent outline of a man waited for them atop the cliff.

"Shho you thought you could avoid me forever, Akviussh?" the figure screamed.

"Who's there?" Rhin shouted.

"It wassh a long flight, sshurely, but I arrived," the figure laughed and spread his arms wide.

"Who are you?" Luu-ka asked.

He was a stark silhouette against the continuous blare of lightning behind.

"My name ishh Liutgart, a name you will not shhoon forget, Rhin Akviussh," he spat. "I, the world'ssh greatessht Sshorcerer, have prepared a teshht for you."

The wind sprayed the spittle of his words.

During a sequence of three bright flashes he beheld Liutgart in detail. He stood tall and ominous, yet had an eerie, bent shape that made him look aged. His ugly, black beard complimented his scabby, brittle, yellow skin. His clothing clung to his slender shape, the suit made of scales and adorned with black jewels. In his clawed, leathery hand he held a long staff, a crystal on its crown.

Liutgart screeched unintelligible words at Rhin and time stood still. The wind stopped and the leaves rustled no longer. The area was quiet, suspended by the force of a wicked will.

"Shhee you in Kaïle!" said Liutgart.

The Sorcerer placed a rough boot on Rhin's shoulder and let the weight dig in. Rhin was shoved over the rim.

As Rhin fell he saw Liutgart's snickering face peering over the edge at him. Rhin tried to flap his wings and soar back up but they ha become lame and useless. His stomach tied itself in a knot, and cold sweat flowed into his nostrils. He collided with branch and leaf, crashing through the canopy. Then he saw nothing as his hands groped in desperation.

"At lashht," Liutgart cried. "No more Akviussh."

In his excitement, he repeated it over and over again in a sickening, piercing squeal.

"No," Luu-ka screamed.

Then the Sorcerer loosened his hold over them, certain they could not yet move.

"Look down at your friend now," said Liutgart.

They could only drag themselves to the edge and stare at the torn branches and shredded growth below. It was unbelievable. Kayre-Ost tried to stand but tripped over his own feet.

"Fool. You are not completely releashhed from the shhpell."

They heard a noise. Leather on gravel.

Liutgart turned around as Rhin climbed over the ledge.

"Akviussh," the Sorcerer bawled. "How can thishh be?"

"For a Sorcerer, you aren't too clever," Rhin said as he made for Liutgart. "My arms and legs still work, see?"

Rhin punched Liutgart in the nose and grabbed him by the collar of his scale-suit.

"Get away from my friends," Rhin warned as he shoved Liutgart down.

Then he took the staff and smashed the crystal on Liutgart's teeth.

The others arose. The magic was dispelled, shattered with the crystal.

"Do not dare think this is over, Akviussh," Liutgart vociferated as shards of his teeth spilled from his mouth.

Then he vanished, leaving only a wisp of smoke behind. The storm relinquished, leaving the moon and deep-set stars to patrol the sky.

"Are you alright?" Luu-ka asked Rhin.

"Fine. Are any of you hurt?"

Rhin looked at each of them.

"Who was that, that," Chainæïa tried to devise an apt word and, finding none that fit, he finished with, "person?"

"I still sense the magician," Aroukana muttered, rubbing his eyes. "He has not gone far, for his spells would not allow it. He is but six hundred yards from here, at the base of the cliff and much of his energy has been consumed."

"If he comes back there won't be a hex in hell that'll spare him my axe," said Kayre-Ost.

"I confess I was not prepared for such incantations. I recognized the energy, however. This one was responsible for Luu-ka's incident," said Cononsareth. "His signature is… familiar."

Luu-ka stayed quiet, but her eyes shifted from side to side.

"The storm seems to have stopped. It must've been part of Liutgart's magic," she observed.

"Let's get off this cursed mountain," said Rhin.

Daish-rog rested in his wolf form, the hovel of his stomach rising and falling with each of his heavy breaths. The forest around him was almost black in the new born night. No sound came from it, not even crickets dared breach the deep silence.

Daish-rog was the only creature that broke the calm. Now and then, he howled his pain at the moon and it would cower behind the blood-red clouds. The sun set itself behind the gorn trees, burning glints of orange here and there between the wooden guardians. Outside it was still light out, but in the woods it was night, both in the world and Daish-rog's heart.

Finding Rixaï was all that concerned him.

He had crossed camps and fortresses owned by Jiaïro's soldiers and left a trail of destruction in his wake. He had used his new powers to annihilate evil in an ever-growing lust for vengeance. He would find his nemesis and purge his soul of its Evil origin. And he saw corruption in all hearts but his own.

It does not matter, I am righteous and pure. He is the Evil being. He deserves to die. Daish-rog convinced himself.

But he knew in the darkest corners of his heart that he himself walked an evil path, one that could lead him to a dead-end. A little voice in his head told him that if he did not take heed he would be destroyed. It should never be so easy to deal the punishment of death.

He ignored the unwanted burst of conscience. All he longed for was vengeance.

He pressed on in his wolf body, exhausted though he was. His mind was set, his will unyielding. He would find Rixaï and shed his heinous blood, and he would rejoice when it stained the fields of the North Isle.

Sfersurul was a large city, covering several massive hills. Its northern side pressed against the cliffs of Scietse, the other end was protected by a long stone wall. Three gates provided checkpoints for merchants and their cargo and set them on their way to the other merchant cities of the Freeland. The gate to the southwest was on Shine Road, which was an almost perfect, straight route to Surulnar and, beyond that, the western coastline.

Aroukana and Chainæïa went off early in the morning, when the last of the spring frost still paved the knolls, to the nearest blacksmith. Their blades needed sharpening and their whetstones had been lost to Scietse.

Once they might have forgone whetstones and renewed the blades' edges by will. But Vevleï magic was not the same used by Lothgar and his circle of priests. It was more a way of life that they had adopted. The Vevleï had developed a mastery of sword craft and what they called "high-smithing". Through meditation, great Vevleï smiths and elders were known to sharpen (and on rare occasions even forge) blades without tools. It should be noted that the creation of every mystical Sword in existence was accredited to either the Gods or the Vevleï. Most believed the Vevleï borrowed the essence of the divines for their craft.

But today's work required a steady hand and heated forge. The forge was on a hill devoid of grass, the heat having stamped the last of it out long ago it seemed. The smithy was open and airy, the roof held up by thin wooden poles that were little more than sticks. The roof itself was made of reeds and whistled when the wind passed through, which it did often. Sun beams wriggled through the frequent gaps in the reeds, breaking the shade.

And so, Aroukana and Chainæïa stepped under into the patchy shadows and waited. Soon thereafter they were greeted by the apprentice smith. He was a young, broad man. His shirt torn and soot covered, he smelled of smoke and his face was flushed from the heat.

"What can I do for you?"

"Could you get to work on these?" Chainæïa asked.

"Let me have a look," said the apprentice.

They handed him the swords and he gasped. His eyes darted from the weapons to the Vevleï and then again to the swords.

"Where did you get these?" He noticed their pointed ears and swallowed a hiccup. "You're Vevleï," he said.

"Yes we are, but you must keep your voice down," Aroukana shushed him.

"Jiaïro and his men could be anywhere," Chainæïa added.

"You are part of the Resistance Army then?"

"Yes. But we must stay hidden. I trust you are on our side," Chainæïa answered.

"Yes, oh yes. I can't stand those soldiers all about the place. Demanding that I forge weapons for Jiaïro, taking my swords and not even paying me for my effort," the smith nodded with vigor.

"Can the work be done?" Aroukana asked.

"Yes. I'll do my best."

"Thank you," said Chainæïa.

As they left the smithy, with a growing sense of unease, they heard a lot of commotion. Ahead the townsfolk were rushing about like squealing hogs,

"What in the blazes is happening?" Aroukana asked.

"I hear chanting. War songs," said Chainæïa.

A command was bellowed from outside the town's walls.

"Shut up already," it echoed.

The clamor had a slow death in response.

The Vevleï pushed their way through the crowds till they came to the southern gate. From behind the portcullis a captain posed in confidence, his armor buried somewhere among all the jewels he wore, with a host at his back.

When even the whispering had stopped, the captain shouted, "Through a tip, I know that you harbor Rhin Akvius."

There was a rustling of voices around square. The legend of the Lord of Swords had been heard here.

"Surrender him and your city and lives shall be spared. Do it not, and the full wrath of the One God, Lord Jiaïro, will be known to you all," he let that soak in. "The one we search for has red hair and wings."

Rhin stood out like a weeping willow in the middle of a desert. The townsfolk grabbed him on sight and dragged him to the gate.

"It is you," one shouted.

"If we hand you over they will leave us be," came the shrill cry of an elderly woman.

Rhin tore himself from there pawing grip and flew up and away. Then some of the angry townsfolk threw tomatoes at him from a nearby cart. A few chucked stones.

"I will go to them," he promised.

He passed over the wall and landed in front of the captain, sword drawn.

"You must be Rhin. So good of you to join us."

Before he knew it, a net was loosed and twisted about him. The more he struggled, the more its grip tightened. He was trapped.

"A caged bird cannot fly away, Rhin," the captain growled.

"And a dead captain has no army to command," Kayre-Ost, who had hopped over the wall as if it was a low picket fence, replied.

Kayre-Ost lifted a nearby siege ram and hurled it at the captain like a ball. With a crunching noise the officer died, and the nearby soldiers shrieked.

"Captain!" one loyal trooper wailed.

"Any takers for the second dance?" Kayre-Ost asked.

"Cavalry," the second in command ordered.

"Ah, the cavalry. About time," Kayre-Ost commented.

Kayre-Ost grabbed the catapult again and used it as a shield. He took out his axe and flung it sidelong at the heavy cavalry. Then using his favorite technique, his earthquake, he unsheathed and dug his sword into the ground, creating a shock wave that sent the horsemen flying. Then the second in command, a Seeker, galloped sword drawn, charging Kayre-Ost. The Denzak swatted him as a man would a bothersome fly. The Seeker crumpled.

"Keep fighting, you fools," were his last words.

But the troopers seemed to have no desire to commit the equivalent of suicide. A lieutenant blew his horn, signaling the instant retreat of the army.

The giant considered the speed at which the soldiers managed to get out of his sight remarkable.

Rhin crawled up to Kayre-Ost and said, "Another victory for the champion. Thanks."

"Don't mention it. There were only a few hundred."

Kayre-Ost dropped the catapult, untangled Rhin from the net and retrieved his axe.

When they went back into the city, the crowds were cheering and waving. They begged for Rhin's forgiveness. Rhin obliged, knowing they had been fear driven.

Children danced around him and men offered their swords to his cause. The women asked if he would break bread with them. Holy men kneeled and prayed in his name.

Cononsareth, the two Vevleï and Luu-ka were waiting for him beyond the masses.

Luu-ka ran over to them and said, "I would have come and helped, but the people would not let me pass."

"No problem. Kayre-Ost handled the soldiers," Rhin smiled.

"I'll say. I could hear them from over here," Chainæïa told them.

"With help it wouldn't have been fun. Over too quickly for me, I mean." said Kayre-Ost.

"We should continue the quest, Rhin, for it would not do to stay here," Cononsareth stated in his serious manner. "I found some old maps here that date back six hundred years or so. They are the only maps I could find of this region."

Rhin looked to Aroukana, who sighed.

"Trust me, they will have to do," the Vevlea said.

As Rhin and his companions made their way to the southeastern gate, the townsfolk sobbed and asked them to stay.

The children pleaded, but Rhin answered with, "There are tasks that need doing."

To himself he thought, *How fickle they can be. One minute they are willing to serve me on a gold dish to their great enemy, but once the danger's past they treat me like their savior, the angel that comes to war with evil.*

Chapter 18
The Temple of the Holy Eye

The solemn, single-file march had gone on for two days. No one spoke. It was boring and slow, but they made it to the dusty fields of Arar, the southernmost region of Freeland. From there on, west and east, was nothing but open sea. This area's only denizens were some nomadic tribesmen and herds of docile Raow—shaggy, round beasts with brown manes. And, of course, the field lions that preyed on both.

Aroukana spotted a gray shape set against the sky. The Temple. He could almost feel its walls.

His eyes had started to burn since he had left Sfersurul behind. The sensation was almost unbearable by now. Sometimes he dropped to the ground as if some illusive weight was pushing him down. But the weight was in his eyes.

By nightfall they had arrived, the cool breeze soothing the pain Rhin had been feeling. They went up to the threshold. A pair of massive double-doors impeded their progress. Upon the wood was carved in the Eldest Tongue: "Seek your higher self through what you desire."

"I don't think we can budge them," said Rhin, though after he did he realized how stupid it sounded—they had a giant with them. "Kayre-Ost, could you fix this?"

"Way ahead of you," said Kayre-Ost, and pushed the huge doors open, grunting with the effort. "They were pretty stuck," he said.

Rhin and the rest laughed.

They stepped inside with care, ever on the lookout for danger.

The hall was empty and unlit but for the tongue of light that now poured in from outside. The dust that had accumulated in there must not have been stirred for centuries. They came to a table that was twice the length and width of Rhin's body.

A voice emanated from the stillness. Rhin had grown accustomed to hearing voices speak to him. It did happen often, more so than he would like.

"Step forth, Half-God."

Rhin said nothing but looked around at his companions. He held his breath for a moment expecting the walls to come falling down on him. The cataclysm he dreaded did not occur, though.

"Step forth, Rhin Akvius," the voice insisted.

Rhin stepped onto the table.

"Lie down."

Again, Rhin obeyed. Then a blue flame and a gold-lit shield fell to his left and right and spun around him, illuminating the hall. When the spinning stopped, the world was bright blue. Rhin realized that it was just the flame in front of his face. Without giving him a second to absorb these happenings, the flame was sucked in through his nose. He felt the heat travel along through his insides until it reached and burned his eyes. He floated from where he had been lying. The pain was phenomenal. Just as he was prepared to tear his eyes from their sockets, the agony ceased, all at once.

He exhaled and felt great relief. His eyesight was much more attuned. He could make out every detail of the hall. He could see every cluster of floating dust in the musty air.

"One fifth of your power has been restored, Rhin, Lord of Swords," said the voice.

The light vanished, as did the golden gleam around Rhin. He fell to the ground with a thud and rolled down a few steps. His wings were now covered in dust and grime.

"Bring fear to your enemies, Rhin Akvius."

He stood, having received the Gift of the Holy Eye. "Piercing darkness with their gaze, thine eyes now harbor holy rays."

His friends looked at him in awe.

The blue flames blazed again and he was transported to a new chamber. He cast a quick glance about him and found his friends weren't there. After a moment's wondering, he understood where he was. The chamber from his dream the day after Lynca had been put to the sword and torch. There were the five symbols, each a unique shape and color and fused with precious gems or metals. Then something Rhin would never have dreamed: the chamber sang. The verse filled Rhin's mind.

"In darkness blaze the silver gaze
The fires of Kaïle bring burning hail
To destroy all that we fought so hard to build
The last of us died in those dark days
We are all that remain, the last of the guild

We, the servants of the Sword
We existed only to protect our Lord
Our lives are gone
But our Spirits live on
To bring justice to this misguided world

Beware the gaze of Rayim,
Take heed of the one with no soul
Our strength is yours
Our Lord of Swords
Power beyond mortal control

We, the world as one
Dark, Light, Nature, Time and Heaven"

Five spirits appeared and the symbols that had been resting on the walls shot forward to insert themselves in the figures' foreheads. They spoke in soft, succinct voices, one after another.

"Rhin-"

"You have done well-"

"-in coming this far."

"We are the guardian-"

"-Spirits of the planet."

Each whisper weaved itself into the others, forming complex syllables of an unearthly language.

"We have been watching you," they said in unison.

"Who are you?" asked Rhin.

"We are without names. I am the Spirit of Nature. I guided your friend Daish-rog to his father's Temple and granted him my power."

"I am the Spirit of Light. I have guided you along your own path."

"I am the Spirit of Time. I guide nothing but the flow of Time."

"I am the Spirit of Heaven. I balance all."

"I am the Spirit of Dark. I drive the forces of Evil."

Rhin took a moment to absorb this.

He looked at the Spirit of Dark and asked, "Are you Evil?"

"No. We help all beings by keeping the Sacred Balance," the Spirit of Dark answered. "But the forces of Evil have become too powerful. Jiaïro's rising has corrupted the Balance. The time has come to defeat his Evil to restore the Balance."

"If you know how to defeat Jiaïro, please help me," Rhin pleaded.

"We can only tell you this," said the Spirit of Light. "Go to Tümraark and find the two Temples there."

"Now off with you, Akvius," the Spirit of Nature said.

"Fear not, for we shall meet again," the Spirit of Nature reassured him.

"May the True Gods be with you," the Spirit of Time added.

The Spirit of Heaven held its arm up high in a motionless wave and Rhin reappeared in the Temple of the Holy Eye.

He opened his eyes to find Luu-ka shaking him.

"Rhin wake up," she said.

Rhin opened his eyes and murmured, "We have to go to Tümraark. The next two Temples are there."

Rhin swiveled his head—he was so tired—so he could look at Cononsareth. The Conkatokæ nodded in awed silence.

Chapter 19
The Journey to
Tumraark

*D*ays had gone by since Rhin and company had left the Temple of the Holy Eye. The small group of valiant Iorians headed for the port town, Fornarce. To get there, they had to cross the perilous quicksand beaches of Sŷrulko and finally the deadly Sŷrul Wall.

The Wall had been created by an eruption of the volcano, Cortak. The lava had covered the entire southern part of the Isle until, breaking up bit by bit, the tide took the debris to the open waters. A great stone wall had remained, barring the former trade routes. The new ridge made it hazardous to attempt sustaining the old alliances.

The group had two choices and both involved crossing the Wall (again). There was the port beyond Ofern, the foothold from which they had first stepped onto eastern soil, or Fornarce, which lay in the easternmost valley of Freeland.

The thought of returning to Ofern was met with reluctance and complaints, thus there was but one route they could take: Sŷrulko.

But Rhin also felt a strange desire to speak with Ferask. He wanted to know of Luu-ka as a child, to consult with someone wise concerning recent events. And to shed some light on his inner emotions. For one reason or another, he was drawn to Ferask.

So when night came and the smell of pine filled the violet shroud, he took off, making for Spekfer.

Rhin glided through the air for the first time without hurrying and found it to be a magnificent experience. He went higher and higher, until he could see most of the East Isle beneath him, its cities were but toy houses aglow with a million fireflies. To the west he saw Cortak, and understood why the locals called it "god's navel".

In the distance he saw the city Kranfaraas, capital of the Isle, and beyond that the wide expanse of Ofern Forest. It had been a month since he and his friends had arrived at the port there.

He pivoted to the left and spiraled, shouting with joy, toward Spekfer Mountain. His thoughts drifted to that beautiful isle. It paid homage to its name, Freeland.

The East Isle had not always been free. Once it had been divided and the fragments of that broken kingdom had been ruled by ruthless warlords. One fateful day, eight hundred years ago, the realm had been united by King Frinnar who made Kranfaraas the capital of his empire. One could not say that he was just. The King was iron-willed and subjugated all peoples around his kingdom, ever expanding his borders during his lifetime.

At the peak of his rule he was murdered by a mysterious assassin. After that, the monarchy fell to the hands of the common people. A senate was elected and its representatives were selected from the people by the people. The island was renamed Freeland. There was still a King of the East, but his seat was more ceremonial than anything else, and he did not descend from Frinnar. This man, Gyles the Greedy, or Lord Gluttony as the peasants called him, had a reputation for siphoning tax revenues to fund his personal projects.

Soon Rhin was soaring over Spekfer. He landed beside one of the twisted bone-pillars that stood as a silent warning to enemies.

A guard shouted something in an alien tongue.

"Rhin Akvius."

Rhin did not speak the language, but it was obvious to him what the guard wanted.

The guard did not speak again until several moments later. This time he asked, in the Common Speech, "What do you want?"

"I wish to see Ferask."

The guard had no intention of questioning Rhin any longer.

He went into a cave and reemerged moments later with Ferask, who gaped at the sight of Rhin.

"You have returned. Why?" Ferask asked.

"I want to speak with you."

"Do come in."

"Thank you."

Rhin was insightful enough to realize that politeness was not frowned upon here.

Ferask sat down on a green plant that looked like a cushion. Rhin did the same. It felt like a cushion too.

"What brings you here, Rhin Akvius?"

"Questions that I think need to be answered."

For the first time Ferask's face looked ancient, a network of creviced wrinkles. But his eyes glittered in the dim torchlight of the cave. The flying creatures that inhabited the mountain didn't have noses in the traditional sense. Instead the winged race had two slits for nostrils. Their skin was as leather and their eyes were beady, but brightly hued. The weatherworn bronze spikes protruding from their backs were merely there to impose fear upon their enemies. When in the heat of battle, little sockets in their knuckles would shoot out claws like a rocking chair would a rusty spring. This gave them a natural weapon when they had no alternative, and a great advantage, if their foes were ever so unlucky as to be unarmed.

Ferask happily explained the anatomy of his race to the Half-God. Rhin was surprised at the being's immense knowledge and scientific expertise. Their discussion drifted to another topic, and another, as the hours rolled by.

"For the past few months I have traveled and met many foes. I have slain two of my brothers and have found the Temple of the Holy Eye. Most consider me a hero or an angel, but I am not sure which path I take," Rhin then finished, "In my eyes I am more of a demon."

"You have indeed tasted the bitter-sweetness of Evil, but you have surpassed it. You are not Evil, Rhin. There are many who require your aid now. The true Evil has grown strong these past six centuries. Many chose the path of the blind and ignored it, but they are the beings who need your help most of all. The first part of your quest is coming to an end."

"The first part of my quest? What do you mean?"

"Know only this: the Sacred Balance cannot be restored until Jiaïro is slain." After a lengthy pause he added, "I sense that you have more questions."

"That's right. There is a girl who journeys with me—you have met her in the past—she has a certain gift."

Ferask nodded, "Luu-ka Mæfæovér. She has the gift of finding the Evil in anyone or anything, and disrupting it with the love in her heart."

"When Evok tempted me with darkness, she cleansed me. I felt a sort of unearthliness rush through me. I feel as if I have known her before, in the distant past. Who is she, really?"

The stern look on Rhin's face made Ferask frown. Did he realize that Rhin would accept no lies?

He was almost reluctant, when he answered, "She is the great-grand daughter of Fae Mæfæovér, the Goddess of Water."

Memories rushed into Rhin's mind. His face had the word 'incredulity' written all over it.

"Fae? So Luu-ka is part divine, like me," said Rhin, bewildered.

"Yes. But where you will go at the end of your quest to defeat Jiaïro none can follow. For you are destined to fight against the legions of Evil alone. I can help you no more."

"Why alone?" Rhin asked, his face sagging into a dejected frown.

"I sense strong feelings for her in you. It will be painful. Nothing I say can change that. I am sorry," Ferask whispered. Then, "Now, off you go. Gods go with you."

Sŷrulko was not so much a beach as a desert. Despite the proximity of the sea and the steady blowing of the ocean breeze, the air was boiling. The group crossed the quicksand beaches in silence. Danger was everywhere and nowhere. The name Sýrulko meant "hidden peril", and it was an apt title. There was heat which distorted the blue skies and besides that nothing but white sands.

As he trailed behind his friends, Rhin could not help but wonder if he should have gone to see Ferask, for it seemed to him that all he said had been bad. Worst of all was the idea of separation.

The ground gave way beneath his feet, and he sank downward. As he cried out, he knew he had fallen into one of the quicksand pits that they had been warned about by many people in the settlement near there.

Luu-ka turned around.

"Rhin," she yelled.

Chainæïa fumbled with a length of rope, tearing it from his pack he tossed it to Rhin. Rhin grabbed it with his right arm, struggling to free his left. After an extended wrestling match in the burning sand Kayre-Ost yanked him out, but something else came out with him. A Quick-slug[*] clung to his leg with its tentacles, its rotating, circular, saw-like teeth ripping through Rhin's pant-leg and into his skin. Its head was as big as a hand with eight piercing eyes. It had slimy white skin and a bulbous forehead, a mock ruby adorning its surface to allure prey. Rhin cut at the creature's tentacles with his sword. At last, it jumped off of him with a screech and slithered back into the sands of Sŷrulko.

Rhin gasped, gazing at the blue heavens above. The temperature was unbearable. He could feel his skin sizzling. His armor, made of leather and bearskin, threatened to cook him alive. His sack had been super-heated in the intense warmth of the sand.

"Are you all right?" Luu-ka asked.

"Fine."

He met her gaze and she looked away.

"We should get going," she said.

Kayre-Ost looked at both of them and scratched his beard. The two Vevleï glanced at each other, passing their thoughts back and forth without words. Cononsareth stared down at his golden knives a moment, and then he continued along the track with the others.

---

* Parasites of the deserts. Also known as 'leeches'.

Daish-rog could sense the presence of Evil closing in all around him. Any second now he would find Rixaï, he could feel it.

The darkness of that black night was broken only by the moon's desultory glare. It had rained most of the day, and now the smell of wet wood and slush permeated Daish-rog's senses.

He had no map and no clue whatsoever where he was, but the hunger for revenge grew stronger by the hour. Strong enough to take away his need for food and sleep. He did not know when it was that he last ate.

Dark dreams were his constant companion, his sole ally. He never shut his eyes, but he dreamed as he traveled and his dreams were unkind.

That monster cannot hide. What does he think I shall do, lie down and die? he thought.

His eager heart got the better of him as he caught the scent of Evil. Rushing around a bend, a blunt object bashed his skull. He lost consciousness.

When he came to, Seekers had surrounded him—with pointed spears and vile grins. He was two-legged again and able to think clearer, but the thoughts came so slow. He felt the back of his head. His scalp was slick. Blood.

One spoke, "What should we do with him?"

The voice that followed was at once recognizable. It was none other than the demon himself, Rixaï.

He said, "Wait. I wish to speak with him."

"Why does the king of vomit wish to speak with me?" Daish-rog said and spat a mouthful of bloody saliva.

"Hah. I wish to inquire why you would die by my hand and be resurrected only to chase me and meet the same end. It seems pointless. Are you mad or just plain moronic?" Rixaï mocked.

"Neither," Daish-rog answered. "You killed my family, and for what? Death should be brought to you. Your life is a cancer upon the world. I hope you rot in Rayïm along with Jiaïro."

Daish-rog's heavy breathing set the beat. Rixaï shook a finger at him.

"You'll have to kill me first. And you seem to be a bit squeamish," he said.

Daish-rog held out his hand to show its steadiness.

"Speak your words," he said and scowled.

"I knew you would aid Rhin and gain God-like powers. And to serve Jiaïro, I had to prevent that at all costs. There was a bonus along with this packaged deal. By killing your family, I prevented them from gaining power and could claim the Crystal of Nature for my Lord Jiaïro," Rixaï sneered.

"I have gained my powers and tracked you down. I will not fail. The Crystal is not in your possession," Daish-rog's face contorted into a grimace, "I feel as sick as a dog at the idea of ever having worked for you or your lord. Even unwillingly."

"Jiaïro is not my lord. My former host, the late Reng, was indebted to the arch-devil since birth, the sixth son of a decaying line. But I shed Reng's body as a snake sheds its flesh. I serve Jiaïro now, but only for power. I may even replace him one day."

The lust was plain in his eyes as he spoke.

Daish-rog, disturbed, stayed silent. The demon wasn't done talking, and there still remained one pressing question that needed answering.

"You don't remember, do you?" Rixaï laughed so hard that several globs of spittle splashed on Daish-rog's face. "Of course you don't! My last chance to stop your ascent was to force you into servitude. I knew you would not come willingly, so I played a little Daïmaan magic game with your brain. You never knew what hit you until that brat Rhin came along."

"I knew I could not bring myself to do your dirty work... you cheated my mind!" Daish-rog shouted.

"I cannot say I don't regret the deed. You were the most pathetic soldier I had ever seen. I had no need of one such as you. Yet my hands were tied. Your presence among our ranks was vital to my plans."

The Seekers laughed.

It was clear to Daish-rog now, when Rhin had struck him with his blade, the dark curse within him had been dispelled.

Rixaï's tone was so revolting, Daish-rog spat in his face.

"Why you insolent... very well. You have chosen your fate, twice. Anything to say before you die?"

"For my mother!" Daish-rog shouted.

He unleashed a surge of energy and the Seekers bodies' split open, revealing beams of light. Their Orbs fell after their bodies burst.

Rixaï fell with them, but chuckled as he regained his footing.

"Is that the extent of your power? Maybe I shouldn't have bothered with you," he said with a shrug.

Rixaï spat fire and made to tackle Daish-rog. Daish-rog caught him in mid-vault and knocked him over, thrusting hard into Rixaï's shoulder. Rixaï unsheathed the Sword of Darkness and made a wild slash at Daish-rog. The stroke took him across the chest, spinning him to the ground. When he stood again, Rixaï was concentrating all his energy. Daish-rog followed suit. The waves mingled, jade with black, sorrow with fury. Soon they were both spent and the energy patterns faded. Both demon and lord dropped to one knee.

"Did I ever tell you that I drank the blood of your brothers? Or that your father begged for mercy right before I split him in two? You are just as weak as the rest of your family," Rixaï panted.

"Then why not finish me now? If I am so small and weak, then finish me now!"

Daish-rog flung himself at Rixaï, aiming his sword tip at the demon's sick heart. With all the strength that he could muster he stabbed again and again, unleashing all his hatred, a lifetime of homelessness, upon the Daïmaan.

Rixaï took shallow, arduous breaths, but soon Daish-rog couldn't hear him breathe at all. Black blood poured from wounds seen and unseen.

Daish-rog then stuck his blade in the earth. When he removed it, all the dark blood had been cleansed.

"It is done," Rixaï said.

His body evaporated, leaving only his Orb.

"No, it is not done. Not yet," Daish-rog took the Orb in his hand and crushed it. "I have peace, at long last."

He lay down on the grass as it whistled with the wind, holding his sword-hilt to his heart. He spent his last moments of consciousness admiring the shining stars.

"Daish-rog, please rest now," said Chainæïa, sensing his brother's energy patterns fade.

Daish-rog's thoughts entered his brother's mind.

Chainæïa smiled and whispered, "There are no stars where we are, brother."

The two Vevleï could sense the turmoil in the heavens. War had been raging on and on for all eternity, yet now it would change. The war's cause would change, and there would be a definite outcome.

As told in Vevleï tales, Rhin would put an end to all this chaos and destruction with his acts. But none could help or prepare him.

The Vevleï kneeled, facing each other. The reason for this was simple. They were attuning their minds to more subtle forms of communication. They practiced by speaking to each other using only their thoughts.

The Vevleï had to establish a link between each other's minds. Once the connection had been created, the minds that shared such a link could converse over great distances.

Aroukana smiled, "It is working, friend. Our minds are in tune."

Chainæïa returned his thoughts and added, "Yes. The mind is a remarkable thing. The Mugé is a most brilliant form of speech."

The elder Vevleï reflected, "Mugé. It means 'whispered words' in the ancient tongue. It is one of the more advanced arts that our people fashioned."

Chainæïa's thoughts turned dark for a moment, "I used the Mugé only a moment before to speak to my brother, Aroukana. He only responded with simple images."

"Perhaps he is sleeping, Chainæïa," Aroukana smiled.

"Perhaps. He has succeeded, however. Rixaï is no more." He saw Aroukana nod and then added, "I do not know whether he will live."

Aroukana relayed his train of thought to his friend, "You must find comfort in the fact that he will always live on as long as you remember his courage. Other deeds of similar or even greater valor are soon to follow and we must prepare. Once a sleeper, the world now transforms into a rebel."

"And what of Rhin?" Chainæïa seemed concerned.

"He must face his destiny soon and he must face it alone," Aroukana thought, ever blunt.

This grieved both Vevleï. However, no more help would be permitted and that was that. The energy of the world is changing. Aroukana stared at Chainæïa.

They both nodded.

It was actually astoundingly easy—compared to the previous attempt, at least—to cross the Sŷrul Wall a second time. Rhin and his friends had done just that. They had found a low cliff face past the Sŷrulko wastes, near the ocean. They landed on the other side without a hitch and headed for the port town of Fornarce. From there they would take a ship to the West Isle, Tümraark.

Arriving at the gates of the town, the group was besieged by officials demanding they identify themselves. Rhin thumbed, indicating his wings, and the guard ordered the gate open. As Rhin walked by, one of the men complemented him on his work. They even removed their shiny, silver helmets out of respect for the lady, Luu-ka.

They walked through the silent roads of the town, never pausing. Lampposts, much like those Rhin had seen in Surulnar, were placed at each intersection, bringing light to the streets even on the darkest of nights. Water rushed through gutters, though it had not rained in a week. But when Rhin saw the waterwheels, he understood. This city's water flow was regulated to keep the streets clean and help douse fires should they spark.

The beaches, the eastern side of Fornarce, were ornamented with brown reed-huts. Even at this late hour citizens walked the sands, the soft, dampness cooling their feet. Beyond the beaches were the docks, and the ships. And it was a ship Rhin needed.

Arriving at the port, Rhin took notice of one particular ship. It had all the required qualities, but somehow seemed more massive and distinct, as if it was something else in disguise. On the bow was an enormous, wooden head that bore the likeness of a demon. Upon its eyes were carved symbols that Rhin had seen before, on Cononsareth's island: the white circle within the black and the lines that speared the center. He felt that this ship was the one he needed take. Some mysterious force, something overwhelming, drew him to it.

He walked over to the ship and shouted, "Is this ship headed for Tümraark?"

"Why, yes. Indeed it is," came the response. "Name's Tith. Would you all like a ride? Free of charge."

"Yes. Thank you, captain."

Free passage, what are the odds? Rhin asked himself.

He felt he should be a bit more suspicious, but the ship was reassuring in its majesty.

"Come on board then, lad."

Luu-ka turned to Aroukana and asked, "Isn't it a little weird that we get free passage at the mere sight of Rhin?"

"Why so? At the sight of Rhin, we were let into this town. At the sight of Rhin, Jiaïro's forces cower and crumble. Besides, this particular ship seems somehow inviting," he answered.

A gangplank was set in place, inviting them in. It had strange twists and angles that no ship should have had. The hull was narrow at the stern and widest at the bow. It was the sturdiest ship Rhin had ever seen. The boards beneath his boots did not creak in the slightest, despite all the gear he carried. The keel seemed to be made of something stronger than wood, and the hull was a V shape, promising speed in the waters of the world.

The night became foggy all of a sudden, the lampposts' glow no longer comforting but estranged. After Rhin had been on deck but a few minutes the captain, concealed in shadow and fog, spoke to him.

"Next stop: the coast of Tümraark. From there you can travel to Vrouk. I hear the second Temple lies within the domain of Tora, not far from that town."

"Excellent," the Vevleï pointed out.

"What did you say?" Chainæïa said with a jump.

"How did you know of the Temple?" Rhin asked, fingers at his sword hilt.

"Ah, come on, lads. Let's drop the charade. I'm good old Tith, captain of this bloody thing, and Rhin here's me master."

That put them all in their place. Kayre-Ost and Rhin made their way to the front of the ship.

The giant scratched his bearded chin and said, "I know what you're thinking, Rhin."

"I know you do. Everyone always does."

"You are one strange man in the end. You come from a small village, from the poorest family, and you are here to save the world."

"You're strange, too. Where do you come from?"

Kayre-Ost paused a moment, then answered, "The South Isle, a land of fierce creatures and harsh storms. I'm a Denzak, a race of giants. We train ourselves for years, channeling hidden strength from the depths of our souls. We are masters of skills that others have forgotten. Everyone has them, but most never awaken them."

"These powers are hidden within me, too?" Rhin asked.

"Of course they are. You already use a huge portion of them. They are what give you your God-like strength."

"This God-like strength is more like a curse. It's as if my whole life has been pre-ordained."

"That can be frustrating," Kayre-Ost said as his eyes caught the light from a distant storm. "But if you keep fighting, it will be worth it one day."

Rhin left at that, following one of the crew to his allotted cabin and lay down. It was not long before he slept.

Rhin awoke, unable to tell if it was night or day. Staying in bed, he looked at the ceiling where he saw his holy symbol again. Wondering how the captain had recognized him at once, Rhin pieced together broken memories of the ship, of his life. He felt the anger welling inside.

"How could I have forgotten all this?" he asked the empty room.

He heard a knock on the door but before he could answer, Luu-ka burst in and exclaimed in excitement, "Rhin, you've got to see this."

She took his hand and pulled him out of the cabin. Together they witnessed the most spectacular sight. The ship sailed, sure enough, but not through water. The vessel sailed through black emptiness aglow with billions of tiny lights.

"What is this?" Rhin asked Luu-ka.

"I asked the captain, Rhin, and we're in space. Do you know what that means?" she asked through grinning teeth. He shook his head, so she continued, "We're outside Iora, higher than the sky. Isn't it amazing out here? Just look."

All around them they saw blazing, gold stars and soaring, jade comets and other worlds. Then they turned around and saw their own planet, Iora, and observed its spectacular beauty from the heavens. They saw it all, great blue seas, rugged mountains, lush fields and vast islands.

"Would you look at that, Iora's round," Rhin said and rubbed his eyes.

"You never read a book before?" Luu-ka teased.

"I have," he said. "Sorry, but I don't live in a college. I come from a little village at the end of nowhere."

Luu-ka laughed, and kissed his cheek. His face flushed as he stood beside her, watching some ominous red clouds float by.

All of this was new to Rhin. Lyncans had no knowledge of space or astronomy. Rhin felt so small, laid bare for the entire universe to see.

And then there was the terrible sight of a black hole, a great void, an abyss that devoured everything.

Rhin thought, *I can think of no better way to describe Evil than this thing. It consumes all in its path.*

Rhin and Luu-ka clung to each other, arms wrapped around one another so tight that they were like one being. Together they witnessed the passing of swirling clouds of rock and the death and birth of stars.

After the two had taken it all in, they realized what they were doing and let go.

Rhin backed off, stuttering, "I'm going to… speak to… captain."

Having left Luu-ka behind, he found Tith.

Rhin asked, "What's going on here?"

"Faster travel, Master Rhin."

"How is this possible?"

"This is how you always used to travel back in the golden days after you had lost your right to enter Ragamandæ. We were your humble servants and friends, taking you anywhere and everywhere. As it happens, we're almost there so I suggest we all wait in our cabins because when we re-enter the atmosphere, we will burn up should we stay on deck."

As the descent to Iora began, Rhin could see through the windows in the cabin that the ship was surrounded by twisting, red flames. Sparks fizzled and flew every which way as the vessel rocked back and forth. The descent lasted only a few minutes, but to those on board it seemed more like hours.

They crashed upon the waves right off the coast of Tümraark, creating a disturbance that must have roused every creature nearby. The sun was hot on their faces when they stepped out of the cabins.

The sun. After viewing it up close it was hard for Rhin to see it in the same light.

Rhin scrutinized the green water, its waves and patterns, the red carp that slipped through it. The water was much clearer than the cold blue of Nénamburra.

The West is more beautiful than the North, as Luu-ka is more beautiful than any girl I've seen, Rhin thought.

This was the perfect avatar of the fertile, free world that Jiaïro was poisoning. This land was boundless and filled with possibilities and opportunities. Rhin was willing to die for it, for this ideal.

Death in return for life, Rhin cerebrated. *A strange idea. One life fades, giving way to the next.*

Then his thoughts dwelled on the dark vacuum of space and his father, Jiaïro. He spat over the deck's edge at that.

"Jiaïro is not my father," he told the West.

He had four more Temples to find. Two on Tümraark and two on the South Isle, if all went well. If.

Rhin and his friends climbed into five rowboats, which would take them to shore.

"At last," Rhin said aloud. "We're a step closer to the end of this." Then he turned and asked, "What is the name of this ship, Tith?"

"The Æbækér. The fastest ship there ever was."

The name conjured up more memories for Rhin, memories of days long since past. Memories of flying on and alongside this ship in times of war and peace alike. He had been but a Half-God and did not own the right to travel like the true Gods. But the Æbækér had been one of his ingenious ways of thwarting these laws.

He could almost taste the air the day that the Gods had taken away his powers and made him Mortal. Two thousand years had passed but he could still feel the energy being siphoned from his veins, his life force being drawn from his blood. He let them do it, too. He remembered that much well.

As they drew closer to the shoreline Rhin reached down into the sea and from the sand he removed an orange shell. But before he could stow his trophy he felt the presence of Evil around him as the rowboats dug into the soft white-yellow sand.

As Rhin stepped off the little boat, the captain took him by the shoulder.

He spoke so only Rhin could hear, "Beware of the Tarkai-han."

With a glint of moonlight in his blue eyes, the captain took a step back and removed his hand from Rhin's shoulder again. Like mist, he recoiled, disappearing with his crew. The next to fade were the rowboats, then the noble ship, Æbækér. Gone.

After those few surreal moments, Rhin stood there, wondering how a man saw moonlight in the morning.

Chapter 20
The Second Temple

The group of six traveled the road that led to Vrouk. The village was reputed to be the most prosperous in all of Tümraark. The road they walked on was well paved and smooth. Trees towered around them. Glinting hummingbirds and dazzling butterflies fluttered in and out of view as toads sang in the soggy mulch. The serenity was disturbed only by falling fruits dropping from their branches.

Rhin's mind was focused on Tith's grim parting message.

Who are these Tarkai-han? he thought.

Such questions tugged at Rhin's mind though he had no way of answering them yet.

Night came swifter in the West. Rhin and his friends were unused to it, but it did not stop them from carrying on, for luminescent specks, ranging from every shade of turquoise to every shade of yellow, floated around to light their way.

"Beautiful," Luu-ka murmured.

The Vevleï gazed in wonder at the colors. Cononsareth took a closer look.

"Night Wisps, tiny pixies that emerge at dusk to illuminate the darkness and dance their traditional dance of radiance," he said.

"Another of nature's miracles," said Aroukana.

Nature. Rhin's thoughts wandered to Daish-rog. *Does he live?*

Aroukana sat down on the prickly grass while Chainæïa went searching for firewood. Kayre-Ost and Rhin sat down, too, and began the process of keening their swords. Luu-ka wandered along the road, back and forth, admiring the Wisps. Cononsareth joined the rest on the grass and crossed his long bony legs.

Rhin observed him as he slipped into blissful serenity. He soothed his body and mind and breathed deep. He started to hum a common Conkatokæ tune that Rhin had heard him hum the day before.

"Baleika," Cononsareth had said. "Every youth learned this happy song. But when I hum it… it brings back old days and saddens me."

Rhin hadn't known what he should say to that. So he made a promise.

"We have a chance to calm the spirits of your loved ones that were sent astray by destroying Jiaïro and his long list of minions."

"Perhaps you are right," Cononsareth had answered, his expression glum.

Rhin knew even then that it hadn't helped, but a promise was the best he had to give.

Now a cool wind touched their faces, refreshing them. Then the first stars appeared in the twilight as the midnight blue blanket was smoothing itself out for the evening.

The Iorians didn't have many names for the stars, nor many stories to tell about them or adventures that had been written about them. Deep down, Rhin and Luu-ka shared a sadness. Once the stars had held many stories, but when Jiaïro rose he abolished the old gods and heroes. Yet another way that Jiaïro had made Iora less than it should have been, yet another reason to end his reign.

"I wonder what lies beyond the stars," said Luu-ka.

Cononsareth answered her, though he kept his eyes closed, "Vast worlds and galaxies and an immeasurable amount of space. It is helpful whilst meditating to think of such calming and quiet atmospheres."

"Tell me, how do you know so much about this 'space'?" Luu-ka looked at him, tilting her head to the right.

The Conkatokæ said, opening his eyes, "Quite frankly, I do not know. The knowledge is just there, in my mind, resting. I cannot explain.

I think there will come a time when the common people of Iora will awaken and realize the beauty of the universe and then my knowledge of it may be of some use. Perhaps it is my destiny."

"You are one of the strangest creatures I have ever met, Cononsareth. I have not yet experienced a dull moment with you."

"I will consider that a compliment," Cononsareth smiled, his beak parting to reveal an array of small, pointy triangular teeth. "Good night, Luu-ka."

"Pleasant dreams, friend."

After a quick breakfast of nuts picked straight off the branches, they journeyed a few more hours before reaching Vrouk. Passing under a welcoming arch, they saw not one man, woman or child outside.

Vrouk had but one road, about a mile long, and the houses and shops were built on either side. The buildings were all square and painted white, the second stories complete with balconies overlooking the road. Behind every corner Rhin expected to see signs of life, but was disappointed each time. The flowers had wilted in the pots hanging from the balconies.

Rhin made to shout, but Aroukana stopped him.

"This town is dead. We should leave," he whispered.

When they had passed the halfway mark a ball rolled into the street, thirty feet ahead.

"A child's toy. The villagers must just have left," Luu-ka sighed.

"That's no child's toy," Rhin swallowed, tasting bile. "It's a child's *head.*"

There had been a trail of blood as the gruesome thing had rolled onto the road. The head was that of a girl, perhaps five years old, with sandy-blonde hair and green eyes.

"Why are we still here?" Cononsareth hissed. "Run!"

The rest of them obeyed. For a few seconds all Rhin heard were the footfalls of his friends but then, from all sides at once, rushed black-clad soldiers from the doorways. They erupted from holes in the earth and leapt down from the second stories of the homes.

"Clever trick," said Kayre-Ost with distaste.

Flaps opened and more soldiers gushed forth. There came an order, "Capture them. Take them alive or I'll skin you all."

Rhin and his companions drew their weapons.

Rhin fought with all his might, even using his wings to distract his foes. The army kept pouring into the streets like a continuum of chaotic black ants. Rhin hovered several feet above the ground, slashing at skull and collar. The air from the wild beating of his wings pinned the soldiers, allowing him to lash out with boot, elbow and blade.

Kayre-Ost took hold of his broad-axe and unleashed his fury. He knocked down the first group to approach him. As he moved to help the others the captain stepped forth and blocked him.

Kayre-Ost gasped, *"Grysen!* Not you."

Captain Grysen, the bald giant, laughed, "What? Surprised to see me, old friend?"

"How could you betray us?" Kayre-Ost shouted.

"What better plan than to side with the winners?" Grysen asked.

Kayre-Ost spat in his face, "You stupid fool. I hope your oily hide burns in the fires of Rayïm!"

Kayre-Ost charged him and they exchanged a fierce series of blows.

Rhin saw the two Vevleï and Cononsareth encircled. In desperation, Rhin soared to their aid but enemies pulled him down by his legs. Then, all Rhin saw was black steel and all he felt was a rain of blows to his chest and stomach. He tried to roll away or stand, but each attempt was met with kicks from steel-toe boots and more hammer strikes. There was no air left in him when the abuse stopped. Gasping he rolled his head to the right, painful explosions tearing through him, and saw Aroukana, Chainæïa and Cononsareth fall captive to the enemy. Rhin got to his knees.

Further down the road, amidst a pile of corpses, Kayre-Ost slashed at Grysen who sidestepped just in time. Nonetheless, the blade caught him on the shoulder.

And Kayre-Ost bawled, "Jiaïro will never win! I'll see to that."

Grysen knocked him down and laughed, "Take the Vevleï and Conkatokæ. Fall back."

Thus, the army began to fight in retreat. Rhin shot up and raced after them, ignoring the pangs of hurt inside, ignoring the bloody drool that bubbled from between his lips. No matter how hard he tried, he could not approach the captives. A shower of arrows from enemy archers kept him at bay.

After the soldiers had disappeared behind a hill, a final few stray shafts flying, Rhin clenched his fists and shouted, "You think this is over?"

That last, desperate call echoed through the fields and the derelict town. It was then that Rhin felt the full effect of the blows he'd received. He dropped, resting on his shins. Blood dribbled from his mouth, but he willed himself to recover and he did. Within moments he was feeling stronger again and soon the blood inside his body dried.

"What now, Rhin?" Luu-ka asked, standing behind him.

"We rescue them," he said through gritted teeth.

Then Kayre-Ost said, his voice clear as rain, "No."

"What?" Rhin and Luu-ka asked at once.

"You two need to find the next Temple. I'll go get them."

"The Temple can wait," Rhin barked.

"No. You have less time than you think."

The stern look that locked Kayre-Ost's features reminded Rhin of his duty. The giant would not budge, that much was obvious. Rhin nodded and looked at Luu-ka.

"We can trust Kayre-Ost."

He turned to the Denzak and said, "Good luck."

Rhin held Luu-ka in his arms and flew west, to the Tora Plains.

Toras Stere was the reputed home of the great bull Tora. Wild flora grew in abundance in that land, untamed, colorful flowers. The great bulls roamed the valleys, grazing the fields. These massive, proud beasts owned the land. Men had made many attempts, centuries before, to subdue the realm but were always unsuccessful. Toras Stere was a feral country. One relic of days of old remained, the Tower of the Bull, the Second Temple.

It was a land of wonder, but also great danger. For in the hills of Toras Stere now roamed a pack of intelligent creatures, besides the bulls, whose ruthlessness knew no bounds.

To the northeast of Vrouk lay Haït Castle, where Chainæïa, Aroukana and Cononsareth were being brought. It was the enemy's most formidable stronghold in all the West and Kayre-Ost heard rumors that Jiaïro himself made his home within its walls.

Kayre-Ost ran, never slackening his pace. But the soldiers that held the captives were relentless, never allowing the gap between them and the Denzak to shrink.

Kayre-Ost became more and more determined, despite the hopelessness of the situation. If the soldiers made it to the castle before he caught them the game would be over. Although he was a fierce Denzak warrior, he was alone and assaulting a castle was insanity.

He heard the chirping of birds as dawn drew near and just as he was growing weary, he spotted stragglers entertaining each other, spittle sprayed around their dead camp.

Kayre-Ost, stepping from the brush, warned, "I'll give you one chance to tell me where you took the Vevleï and the Conkatokæ."

Kayre-Ost's face seemed vacant, but he knew they saw the menacing power behind his eyes. If they incited his fury, it would be their doom.

"Hah, the odds are hardly even, wouldn't you agree? There are ten of us and one of you," the soldier taunted.

"You're right. Would you like to call for reinforcements?" Kayre-Ost said with a sneer.

"Who do you think you are?"

"We'll have to teach you a lesson, you worthless maggot."

They charged and Kayre-Ost grabbed the first two, one in each hand, and bashed their heads together. The others hesitated a second but then ran forward. Kayre-Ost sidestepped and clothes-lined one, then elbowed another. He grabbed the next two, each of his massive hands closing around a leg, and spun them in circles. When he let go, they crashed with much clanking into the trees.

"I'll understand if you want to take a breather," Kayre-Ost said with a pretentious yawn.

The remaining soldiers threw down their weapons and begged for their lives.

"Where are the captives being taken?"

"To Haït castle, a two day march from here," a soldier whined, pointing to the northeast.

"I knew it," said Kayre-Ost to himself.

One of the soldiers overheard and asked, whimpering, "Why did you pound us if you already knew?"

"I was testing you. You must be important to know where the dangerous fugitives are being brought," Kayre-Ost said with a smile as grim as death.

"Is he gone yet?" breathed one of the beaten men.

"Oh, you could hand over any rations you won't be needing," the giant suggested.

"Just give him the food, make him go away," moaned the battered one that had encountered the tree.

The men that could still move scrambled and tossed the giant all their food. Chicken legs, cabbage and onions.

"Now, was that so hard?" Kayre-Ost asked.

Rhin landed on the plain of Tora Stere and set Luu-ka down. It was well into the evening and the sky was once again aglow with the light of the Night Wisps.

They were greeted by a bull which trotted right up to them. It was dark brown all over, with one horn chipped. Luu-ka looked closer and saw two cloaks slung over the bull's back.

The beast beckoned them to follow with a flick of its head and they complied.

They walked for a half hour and another bull bounded toward them. This one was golden with brown patches and a bristly white mane. The animals stepped forward and before Rhin and Luu-ka knew what was happening, they were riding on the backs of two wild animals deep into Tora Stere.

They rode for an hour and a half to a vast cave. By that time it had started raining so they hurried in without speaking. As they entered, it lit up with Night Wisps.

The Great Bull of the fields, Tora, stepped forth from the shadows. He was unmistakable to Rhin, who had heard the stories. He was silver and had blue eyes and his horns were ridged and twisted. He spoke to Rhin and Luu-ka using telepathy, his mouth unmoving.

"Mush, Grayboel, what have you sent me now?"

Tora's voice seemed ancient and had a sort of shaky stuttering to it. It was a singular voice.

"Ah, now I see. Rhin Akvius and Luu-ka Mæfæovér. Step forth Iorians. I know of your need and in the name of all the animals of Iora, I wish to carry you to the Tower of the Bull."

Rhin was shocked, glad and relieved all at the same time, "Thank you, Tora of the Plains. It is with honor that we accept your generous offer."

"Then mount."

They found that Tora was large and strong enough to carry them and still have room for another person. At a brisk pace, his sheer power and grace of movement was breathtaking.

The rain wet Rhin's face and hair but then he remembered the cloaks and found that they were neatly folded over Tora's twined tail. Rhin was grateful and wrapped the cloak about his shoulders. He did the same with Luu-ka, who was sitting in front of him. He noticed that her breathing became clumsy as he touched her neck, and he blushed.

The moon was so low its gleam seemed to mingle with the Wisps. The cool night breeze blew more often. Rhin and Luu-ka watched their surroundings, illuminated with green and blue, as the bull rode onward.

They arrived at the giant Tower of the Bull. The great wooden doors were sealed shut. Tora approached the doors and Rhin and Luu-ka dismounted.

Tora mooed in a strange way. It was half a bark. This was known as the Word of the Wild.

The doors opened.

"God's speed," Tora communicated and galloped off into the darkness.

"Let's go," said Luu-ka, reaching for Rhin's hand.

He took it and gave it a soft squeeze.

As they entered, the eerie darkness of the Tower engulfed them. They came to a flight of stairs and began the ascent. Flight upon flight unveiled itself as they climbed up the spiraling Tower.

They were panting when they reached the top. From the gloom, a small creature approached them. Rhin's heart did a back flip and he almost fell down the stairs

"Greetings, Master Rhin. My name is Hobanataï. Come along now, you mustn't tarry."

Hobanataï stepped in front of a single candle, which was equal to him in height. He was not so much child-like in stature, but more a miniature man.

He shouted, "Master Rhin is here."

As the small creature stood there, distrust crossed Rhin's mind. But as soon as the feeling had breached his thoughts, it left him.

Golden light spread from the candle's flame until it filled the obscure room.

Then Rhin found himself in the familiar chamber. Sky-blue flames lit the ceiling and the five figures stood in silence.

"We must be brief for there is little time," said the Spirit of Nature.

"We have brought you a single warning," the Spirit of Light continued.

"Beware of the Tarkai-han. They are close at hand," the Spirit of Dark finished.

"Who are these Tarkai-han?" Rhin asked.

The vision ended.

"Wait," Rhin yelled

But it was too late.

The final message he had received had been the unspoken description of his new Gift, the Hawk's Claw, "With this you will be able to travel swifter than any man that ever lived."

When that sentence stopped echoing in his head, he repeated to himself, "Beware the Tarkai-han."

Rhin looked around to find that Hobanataï was gone.

He began to think, I have trusted all of the spirits I have met in the Temples until now. I'm not sure about this Hobanataï. He seemed unreliable.

When he and Luu-ka exited the Tower through the huge doors they heard an intense growl like that of an infuriated wolf, followed by three more. A brief flicker in the shadows was all they could see, however.

"What's happening? Rhin, what are these things?" Luu-ka asked in a hushed tone.

"Tarkai-han," Rhin said, taking her by the hand again.

Three beasts leapt at them from the darkness and kicked Rhin over, pinning him while another snatched Luu-ka. Rhin could not see anything but dark silhouettes in the night. The moon was gone. The only source of light was in the glowing green eyes of the veiled shadows.

"Luu-ka," Rhin screamed, struggling, spitting dirt from his mouth.

The creatures that had been restraining him released him and bolted. So fast that Rhin thought for an instant that he would never be able to follow.

But he remembered the Gift he had received from the Tower moments before, the Gift of Hawk Claws, giving him enhanced swiftness.

He used this Gift to catch one of the creatures, and smacked him down.

"Where are they taking her?" Rhin screamed in its face.

"To Haït Castle. You will never win Rhin. Do you hear me?"

"And why is that?" Rhin asked, shaking his captive.

"It is because Jiaïro himself holds your companions."

The beast choked and looked at him with blind eyes.

Rhin held the Sword of Purity in his right hand and said, "I release you to the Judge of Rayïm."

He then lowered the blade. The monster gurgled one last phrase, "T'is fair, m'lord. The Judge is just."

Rhin let go of the corpse.

He felt useless. He had not saved one of his friends from capture.

Rhin's path lay clear before him. He would go to Haït, and may the Gods save whoever stood in his way.

Chapter 21
Castle Haït

Kayre-Ost crouched amid tall grass on a hill that overlooked Haït Castle. It was a cold night in direct defiance of spring. It was dark as well, for the Night Wisps dared not near the foul fortress.

During his hunt, Kayre-Ost had encountered a few more patrols and from their babbling and silly pleas for mercy discerned some valuable information.

Haït rested atop a hill, a deep moat twisting about its base, its many watchtowers giving the garrison the advantage in defense. The castle had a strong outer wall that had never been breached. Each segment of wall was guarded by watch towers and archer outposts. The inner wall linked to the barracks, where most of the soldiers lodged.

The southern wall was where the main gate was positioned. This was where all the 'official' business came through. Jiaïro had placed the soldiers' encampment by the road that led to the gate.

The western wall was where the soldiers entered the castle. This gate was smaller but still heavily guarded.

The eastern wall was overseen by three watch towers and had no gate.

The northern wall was less guarded and thus, at first glance, the ideal means of breaking into the castle. But this stretch was under constant surveillance by patrolmen.

Kayre-Ost had failed his comrades. He had not been able to intercept them before they were brought to Jiaïro's stronghold. Now, he needed to infiltrate the castle and steal them back. He was fearless, but he knew folly when it stared him in the eye. Observing the guards' movements, he discerned no weaknesses in how the patrols were rotated and there were far too many of them for him to slip through unnoticed. There were no discernible weaknesses.

The only being the Denzak feared was Jiaïro. The devil was clever and knew how to defend his fort. If Kayre-Ost should become hasty and be caught, the demon would exert his wrath upon him. And the wrath of a God was to be met with trepidation.

The sentinels always had three men in the same location, so that even when one guard left no stone went unwatched.

With all this security Jiaïro must be here, Kayre-Ost observed.

Within the walls Kayre-Ost could hear loud jesting and toasts being made. Near the front gate there were lines of white pavilions, Jiaïro's unholy standard hanging limp from the poles.

Jiaïro was amassing his armies. Kayre-Ost cursed, watching a brawl erupt between half a dozen soldiers.

Then a fog spread until it covered the fields. Kayre-Ost held a hand out in front of his face and smirked when he found he couldn't see it.

A miracle. Wait... Daish-rog? Kayre-Ost asked himself, feeling the faint presence of the Lord of Nature.

"I am close. You have your chance. Save them," Daish-rog's ethereal voice intoned.

Kayre-Ost knew it had been Daish-rog who gave him this opportunity, and that it was no trick of his mind.

He dashed across the field and pressed his back up against the stones. His eyes trailed upward along the wall as he caught his breath. Scaling it was his only choice.

He would have liked to have a grappling hook but his arms were strong enough to hoist his weight up. Besides, the stones were old and there were gaps between them, providing the all-important handholds.

He took firm hold of one of the smaller stones and squeezed his hand into a slot between two others. He began to climb. It wasn't easy going. More than once he heard iron footfalls above him, forcing him to stop. When he crested the battlement, his arms burning from the effort, he spotted a group of patrolling soldiers coming his way. Flipping over the edge again in what he thought was the nick of time, he breathed a sigh of relief when he didn't hear the dooming call to arms. His alleviation was premature.

"Alek, you see that?" Kayre-Ost heard a soldier say.

He knew he'd been discovered. He did not wait.

"Alar-"

The call to arms came too late. Kayre-Ost was on them. In five quick strikes, he incapacitated them, crunching their bones and armor all at once.

When he was sure no one was aware of his little intrusion he dropped the mounds of mashed iron and flesh over the edge. They landed with a loud splash in the moat.

Kayre-Ost ducked and waited. Several sentinels heard the splash and were shouting back and forth. The Denzak remained patient.

"Nothing. Some stupid slave probably dropped a chamber pot while emptying it," said one of the soldiers.

The giant had wriggled his way through the outer defenses of Jiaïro's fortress.

A great achievement, true, but I'll wait to savor this victory until Jiaïro lies dead at my feet and my friends are free. There's no time to wait for Rhin. The cruel God may be his father, but I have my own claim to his head, Kayre-Ost thought, racing along the battlements.

Once he found a vacant area he hopped down to the cobblestones of the courtyard. A dreary mess. Half the plants were dead and the others were ugly. He caught sight of the entrance to the circular tower, the only obvious means to reach the upper levels. From the empty courtyard he dashed into the inner castle.

The tower's west flank was blocked off by yet another barracks and Kayre-Ost didn't fool himself into believing he could fight three hundred men alone.

Maybe if there were two of me, he smiled despite himself.

The giant opened the large wooden doors he had located at the base of the circular tower, away from the soldiers' housing. His knotted muscles rippled under the strain. He slipped inside, shut the door behind him and bounded up the stairs to the third floor. He met not one soldier on the stairway or the halls beyond, which he thought too convenient to attribute to coincidence.

Kayre-Ost had decided on the top floor because he considered it likely Jiaïro would want no one higher than his throne.

He checked around a corner. He spotted a guard and pounced, breaking the man's frail neck in one stroke. He propped the body in a corner and threw the nearby sconce out the murder hole. Rounding another sharp bend, he saw two soldiers laughing and drinking at a table, a deck of cards split between them. He leapt at them and snapped the table in half with his arm as he knocked them against the marble walls of the tower.

Jiaïro likes his keep to be pretty, Kayre-Ost noted with a scowl.

Afterward a dark voice rang in the giant's mind. It was the voice of the arch-devil himself, Jiaïro. Kayre-Ost was sure of it.

"I know who you are, Kayre-Ost Lacksurel. You think you can infiltrate the stronghold of your God and escape alive?" Jiaïro's vile laughter filled the Denzak's head. "Don't worry about my son for he will be here soon enough. Come along now, little man. Come and meet your maker."

As Kayre-Ost traversed the halls the taunts followed him, "Is that as fast as you can move? Speed along, Kayre-Ost, speed along."

He entered a courtroom with a single door on the other end, sealed by a metal grate. He knew he was close. He barged through the gate and walked down the hall, but at its end he found only anguish.

His friends were in the middle of the room. Some form of translucent energy was keeping them contained and asleep.

As Kayre-Ost entered the large throne room, red tendrils of energy bursting forth from each corner. His screams echoed through the castle. He was burning, melting, unable to feel anything else. He was paralyzed.

Then the pain ceased but the Denzak was defenseless and weak, his will sapped. He surveyed his surroundings using the only light available, white flamed torches that gave off no heat.

"So, here is the great Kayre-Ost, my worthy foe. Hah! Do you really deserve that title? Rhin has been far more irritating than you, little thorn in my foot. Nonetheless, you have served my purpose well. But then, so has your friend Grysen. Ah, Grysen. A fine addition to my noble cause," Jiaïro laughed.

The dark God was cloaked in crepuscule. Only two of his features were visible: rust-colored, sickle-shaped eyes and gritted dagger-teeth.

Kayre-Ost spat at Jiaïro's feet and cursed him.

"You have no chance! One of us will kill you. I just hope it's me. You are no God, only a monster. Nothing more," Kayre-Ost shouted with far less impact than his usual.

"Yet there is no power behind your passionate words, coward."

"I had Rhin go to the Tower of the Bull to increase his powers. He becomes stronger by the minute."

"Yes, perhaps that is true. Of course, that will make the moment when I *tear him in half* all the more enjoyable."

"Kill your own son..."

"He has never been my son, only an obstacle to surmount. I thought I would be rid of him when I cleansed his memory and sent him off to the farthest corner of the Four Isles, as far away as possible. A mistake I will not duplicate."

"He'll come and free me. Then I'll destroy you."

"He will come, but severe emotional distress guides his movements. I'm afraid it has rendered him quite useless."

As the God spoke a gray, veined hand weaved back and forth, but his face was still hidden.

"What are you talking about?" Kayre-Ost snapped.

"A company of warriors, in my service, have captured the girl. I believe they draw near. It was ridiculously easy."

"How did you do it? Your soldiers aren't clever enough to stop Rhin and capture Luu-ka."

"Indeed. The Tarkai-han have been most useful to me these past few days. They have informed me of Rhin's every move and even captured the only descendant of the Mæfæovér line."

"The Tarkai-han?"

"Iora's finest bounty hunters. There is a price on Rhin's head of fifty thousand Vilts. They could not refuse such an offer, the fools. When they arrive they will receive their... *rewards*."

Then the Tarkai-han walked in.

"Lord Jiaïro, we have brought you the water goddess," the leader of the bounty hunters stated and held Luu-ka up by her violet hair, as he would a trophy, so all in the hall could see her sob.

There were three Tarkai-han that accompanied the leader and they stood firm, displaying their proud faces. They had long hair, pointed noses and great claws on their spindly fingers. Their eyes were yellow like those of a cat and their legs were like those of a mountain goat.

"Now, the bounty promised for the delivery of this wench," the boldest of the pack barked.

It must be a custom for the hunters to have the leader speak on important occasions. They must hail from a different world. How thick are they to not know of Jiaïro's treacherous tendencies? Kayre-Ost thought.

"Yes, your reward," Jiaïro growled.

Flames spewed forth just as they had for Kayre-Ost, only the dark fires had new targets this time. And these flames were meant to kill. The Tarkai-han died and left their red and orange Orbs behind as their souls ascended to the Ragamandæ, or descended to Kaïle. Kayre-Ost didn't care where those rats went.

His attention focused on Luu-ka. Jiaïro seemed overjoyed with himself, for he filled the hall with laughter. When he had had enough, he called in his elite cadre, his marshals.

"Thanks to Rhin and Daish-rog, I have but seven marshals left." He called out, "Tydra."

"Yes, lord?" the marshal answered.

"How far away is Rhin from the castle?"

"Close, my lord. With his new Gift, it will take him only moments to arrive."

"Good. I wish to see his face when I slaughter his companions before him. Particularly you," he pointed at Luu-ka, with a pale, yellow-nailed finger.

Kayre-Ost was silent. He was hoping that another miracle would present itself.

A great quake shook the foundation of the castle. Jiaïro and his sons laughed, filling the hall once more with the poisonous sound.

"The wayward brother comes," said one of the marshals (Kayre-Ost didn't care which one).

Then the distinct cries of war and pain rang through the otherwise dead hall. Clashes of steel and the spatter of gore became audible as well. The hall was briefly tranquil. Kayre-Ost held his breath.

An explosion ravaged the room. Out of the fire and clouds of smoke stepped Rhin Akvius, the Lord of Swords. His wings were spread wide across the entrance he had created. His eyes showed power and control as he looked at Jiaïro upon his throne. The God's eyes narrowed.

Rhin spoke, his voice clear and loud, "Greetings, father. At last we meet. What soulless deeds are you committing now? Set my friends free and I will not have to kill you where you sit."

"This is indeed amusing. So confident and secure, when you have no idea of the perilous hole you have dug for yourself," Jiaïro mocked.

"I sense a deeper plot. You could have just tried to kill me, but you passed when the various opportunities arose. Or is it simply the fact that you were too weak for me?" Rhin grinned mirthlessly.

His grin suggested he would never find anything amusing again.

"I suppose I could tell you, now that you are going to die anyway. The Baraïkians are looking for an ancient relic. A sword. They claim it is in this world, my world. I agreed to aid them in their search if they provided me with manpower enough to claim my birthright. But the Baraïkians grew rebellious and slaughtered my army at the funeral of my son and marshal, Joabom. To keep them in line, I retaliated by killing their servants, the Groägs in the Wisp forest. Contrary to belief, the Groägs are not akin to the Béros. They come from the planet Baraïk. They serve the Baraïkians in gratitude for the teachings they received. The Baraïkians made the Groägs into what they are today and in this way subjugated the feral race. There was another goal for my men to accomplish in the forest, however. To find the Crystal of Nature and bring it to me, therefore adding to my growing power. My late son, Reng, was obliterated by the demon Rixaï. But Rixaï was not always at one with my offspring. He had served me in the past. I unleashed him forty years before this day to find the Crystal and kill its guardians, Daish-rog's family. Obviously, he was only successful in the latter. Immaterial now that he in turn has been killed on Nénamburra by your friend Daish-rog, the very man he unwittingly antagonized decades ago."

Rhin was silent.

There was so much to take in at once. But he had to stay focused. This was a matter of life and death.

He wondered which sword Jiaïro was speaking of. It could not be the Sword of Purity.

And he had known Jiaïro did not care about him, but it was now clear that he didn't care about any of his sons, only his ever-growing lust for dominion of all the world and beyond.

"Rhin, my boy, you have more coming to you than you fathom. Do you believe you are going to dwell in Ragamandæ, in the halls of the righteous, after I kill you? No. You will go to Rayïm instead, for you have slain and pillaged, robbed and destroyed."

Rhin cut in, saying, "For the greater good."

"You see things strictly in black and white, just like your divine grandfather, Cryöd the fool," Jiaïro scoffed.

Ignoring that last taunt, Rhin riposted, "And what about the Servant? Does that abomination also belong to you?"

"That fatalistic, fanatical creature one of mine? Don't be such a simpleton."

For the first time Rhin noticed a resemblance between Jiaïro and himself. Neither of them regarded Fate as irrefutable.

"So the disaster that struck Conka Isle-" Rhin began.

"Not my doing, but the end was satisfactory. The Conkatokæ people never respected my rule over them. They would have spread the seed of rebellion quickly. When I kill Cononsareth Onoät, the last of his race, I will rejoice, having ended that civilization of halfwits."

"And the attack on Kayre-Ost's village?" Rhin snarled, clenching his fists.

"Meddlesome Kayre-Ost of the South. That thorn had to be plucked from my noble foot."

"Noble foot," Rhin spat. He had heard enough.

He ran at Jiaïro but was met by the seven marshals, who formed a semi-circle around their master.

"The seven seedlings," Rhin smiled, regarding Jiaïro's progeny. "I remember when there were ten of you."

"You wish to oppose me?" Jiaïro bellowed.

"The storm that was my cradle sealed your demise, Jiaïro," Rhin said. "You just haven't realized it yet."

The seven drew their swords and charged. Rhin slashed from Tydra's eye right down to his leg, in one swift motion, leaving him on the ground.

Jiaïro called out, "Marshals, kill him now! Use any means necessary."

Rhin blocked a blow to his side and returned it, cutting through plate and into flesh. He then danced away from a pair of cross thrusts and brought his weapon down on the entwined blades, snapping the steel. The novel disarm had prevailed but the marshals unsheathed side-arms, straight short swords, and pressed on. Rhin fought with valor, but they outmatched him. They closed him into a corner and pointed their weapons at his face.

"Farewell, Rhin Akvius. I wish you Godspeed," said Jiaïro.

Just as his marshals were about to plunge their swords into Rhin's body, Daish-rog burst into the room and soared at them, decapitating one and gutting another.

"Great timing," said Rhin as he moved to Daish-rog's side.

"Let's finish these worms," said Daish-rog.

One marshal lay dead and two were on the ground clutching their wounds, leaving four able to fight.

"Set my friends free," Rhin commanded.

"No, I do not think I will. You are in no position to be making demands, son," Jiaïro said, rising from his throne.

He was exposed in the dim light now, completely visible. His head was broad and angular. The flaky mauve skin below the corners of his sneering mouth had given way to two little horns, like misplaced teeth. His hair was a chaotic graying mass, as sharp and spiky as the crown he bore. His grand, pointed nose hung beneath two deep-set eyes and he had pierced his cheek with a round shining gem. A gilded broadsword rested at his side.

His mighty three-fingered hand unsheathed the weapon.

"You," he said pointing to Rhin with the blade. "Bow to me."

"No!" Rhin shouted, widening his stance.

Jiaïro flicked his wrist and Rhin flew back, into a wall. The stones broke apart and he was sent whirling into the courtyard. Then Jiaïro grabbed Daish-rog and twisted his arms until they bled and the malevolent God dropped him down onto the hard soil beside his stalwart son. The marshals were able to watch from the throne room and although wounded, added in their deranged snickering.

Rhin flew up through the crack in the wall, but Jiaïro kicked him back down. Rhin crashed into a tree. Daish-rog lay a few feet away, stunned.

Jiaïro shouted, "If you are strong-willed enough, come to Naa-Teria. There we will finish this."

While the fighting distracted everyone, Kayre-Ost had broken the shields around Chainæïa and Aroukana. They awoke in a state of confusion.

Jiaïro turned and expulsed wicked laughter.

"Fine, free your little Vevleï, but Luu-ka and Cononsareth shall come with me."

Then the least wounded of the God's marshals grabbed Luu-ka and the Conkatokæ and vanished with the rest of them.

Rhin stood and called, "Miara!" as blood trickled down his forehead. His left arm was numb.

At last, his call was answered. Miara appeared before him.

"You need not explain. I know all that has happened. You wish to save your friends from the clutches of Naa-Teria. But I would advise you to find the remaining Temples first," she said, touching Rhin's cheek.

"But my friends-" Rhin was cut off by her pure voice.

"Jiaïro cannot kill them. He needs them to be able to destroy you. He knows that you can sense if they are dead and he wants you to come to him. In his unsound mind he avidly anticipates the hour when he can end their lives in front of you. And he does not care if you acquire the Gifts from the remaining Temples, simply because he wishes to absorb your powers. Thus, the more abilities you possess-"

"Fine. I will find the remaining Temples. I will also tell Chainæïa and Aroukana to inform the Vevleï Resistance Army of Jiaïro's location. Maybe we can rally the last of the free armies and defeat the tyrant," Rhin said, his mind clearer than ever before.

He looked at Daish-rog, who now stood, and they nodded in agreement. The Lord of Nature was off balance from the fall but eager to be of service.

"Thank you Miara, you have always helped me in my time of need."

"You need not thank me, my Rhin. I am your servant, now and forever. I will be with you always," she paused, and for a moment Rhin could see the immense sadness in her eyes. Then, "The world needs you. Now go."

Chapter 22
The Fallen King

The Vevleï had awakened confused and flustered. Those endless hours that Jiaïro had them in his snare had dulled their senses, making them blind to the events around them. But Chainæïa rejoiced to see his brother alive. Aroukana returned the group's attention to other urgent matters.

He said, "Friends, the day has come. We either start a battle to end an age old war, or stand aside."

"We need soldiers," Chainæïa stated. "Without an army at our back we will never storm Jiaïro's keep."

"You have an army," Rhin said at length. "Your brothers and sisters, your people, have waited for this moment for hundreds of years. Summon them."

"We require time. It is a long journey, as you know," said Aroukana.

"How long?" Rhin asked.

"Weeks, that's the truth of it."

Rhin glowered. Then he said, "You will find a way to be faster. I know it."

"As fast as Arellian, the Fire Stallion," said Chainæïa, bowing his head. "As quick as we can go. May we not disappoint our lord."

"You could never disappoint me, my Vevlehen brothers." Then Rhin looked to Kayre-Ost, asking, "I'm grateful for your actions, Kayre-Ost. But I need your help again. Do you think you could rally the Denzak? Jiaïro's army is much larger than anyone could have imagined. If all the giants from the South are like you then we may yet live through this."

"I'll do my best, Rhin," Kayre-Ost answered.

"We will meet back at Naa-Teria, for better or worse," Daish-rog said with conviction.

"Deal. If we're not dead by that time, see you then," Chainæïa added, nodding.

"It's time we finished what we began," said Aroukana.

"For Iora," said Rhin.

They then went their separate ways. Kayre-Ost headed northeast to Bevrorenk, the capital city of Tümraark. It was the only city from which ships sailed to the South every other day.

The Vevleï made for the coastal village of Ibbryn where they could find a ship to take them to Nénamburra.

And Rhin and Daish-rog left in search of clues to the whereabouts of the other Temples. They took to the air.

Soon they had left Haït and their companions behind. Daish-rog had heard tales from commoners of an old hermit living in the western wild lands of Tümraark. The place was named Hermit Isle after one who was said to have remarkable magical skill and wisdom beyond compare. Rhin acknowledged that the hermit might shed some light on the location of the Temples.

Using the light of the night Wisps, Rhin and Daish-rog sped along. They kept focused. The few minutes they took to rest, they spoke of their upcoming struggles.

"I will destroy Jiaïro. There won't be a next fight after this one. I won't let him escape again," Rhin told Daish-rog.

"I believe you and if I have to die for this beautiful world, then so be it. I will stand with you wherever you go, my young friend."

"What if the hermit does not help us?"

"He will, for he must," Daish-rog reassured him.

The subject turned to a matter that Rhin had left behind.

"Rhin, why did you depart from the cave of the lion Spætuus? What ailed you?" Daish-rog asked.

"It was Spætuus... he told me to run," Rhin sputtered. "I never meant for those things to happen to you."

Daish-rog seemed to consider this for a long time. At length he said, "It is alright. I have often considered that one choice. After I died I had a lot of time to think while you were heading for the Temple of Resurrection. I thought that if I had never been looking for you, I might never have found the Crystal of Nature and regained my lost legacy. And you might never have found the Temples. In the end it was for the better."

"I guess so."

But Rhin still regretted his actions. He pictured himself once again running from the cave—craven, despairing and alone.

After his mind had sifted the unwanted memories, it struck him. Rhin felt a sense of righteousness that was new to him. After all, it was the very world they were saving.

Rhin knew his own search for self-realization and vengeance had become a noble quest. He knew that the person who killed his foster parents was with Jiaïro at that very moment. It must have been a treacherous marshal for Jiaïro would not have ransacked Lynca, thus rousing Rhin and allowing him to reclaim his identity. One of the God's sons might be trying to claim power for himself, and Rhin, though unpredictable, was the perfect catalyst.

Daish-rog, even after having claimed his revenge, still seemed lost to Rhin. But the young man could understand. Daish-rog's parents were dead and he had only his brother. Rhin had no one at all.

"With my new gifts I should be able to find more survivors," Daish-rog considered aloud. Rhin, dwelling within his own concerns, merely grunted.

"I continuously try, but with each attempt I am met by a barrier to my descrying. Maybe there are some who do not want me to discover the truth. If that is true than Jiaïro must have a hand in it," Daish-rog rambled absentmindedly. "Maybe they are already dead."

It had been a matter of hours when a large hut appeared by the water. Daish-rog and Rhin had taken to the air again. The Lord of Nature had transformed into a great hawk and Rhin flew alongside him.

Hermit Isle was a bog-like patch of land just near the coast of Tümraark. The hermit, the only soul that inhabited the stinking marshes, had built his home of straw on the western extremities of the island. It was said that the old man was not fond of visitors.

Rhin and Daish-rog touched earth in front of the hut. The sky was brown and covered with misshapen maroon clouds. The place was swampy, surrounded by trees that were out of their element and there was a foul stench about the place. Daish-rog returned to his true form and brushed some stray feathers from his armor. Rhin, by accident, landed in a pocket of muck that squelched beneath his feet. He frowned.

Somehow, with a sudden jolt, the hut leapt back hundreds of yards.

"What the devil?" Daish-rog growled, shaking his head in disbelief.

They heard a voice call out, "You seek my power? Be gone! I will have no charity cases."

The voice sounded grumbling, crafty and far more discernable than it should have, despite the expanded distance between the travelers and the straw edifice.

"My name is Rhin Akvius. I have come for your help, hermit."

There was a pause.

"Ah, that changes the matter. Very well, I shall aid thee." Rhin and Daish-rog looked at each other, relieved, until the hermit added, "But only if you can cross my deadly swamp—without the use of flight, mind you."

The two exchanged a stupefied gaze.

"What do you think?" Rhin asked.

"We have no alternative but to brave the treacherous swamp."

Rhin saw that the hut in the distance seemed to be moving farther away.

"Daish-rog, do you see that?"

"This place is ancient, Rhin. It has a life of its own. I sense it is but mere illusion."

They took a few tentative steps and the hut did not recede. It was indeed a trick.

Continuing on, they heard quick bursts of wind. Rhin realized that those were the sounds of darts being fired. He jumped back just in time to see one shoot past his head.

"Flame darts," Daish-rog shouted, as one zipped by his nose.

They spurted along the muddy track. The darts whooshed past them as they jumped, ducked, ran and halted. Jets of flame burst from all sides. The darts' rate of fire increased.

Struck, Rhin felt a stinging pain in his leg and looked down to see the bolt burst into flame. He tore it out of his flesh and rushed on, limping the rest of the way as blood streamed from the wound.

After the darts had stopped flying, Rhin dared hope that the worst was over. He dampened his singed skin with cool mud from the path. That was all he could think to do at that moment.

They came to an abrupt halt, studying strange patterns in the soil, a chain of triangular tiles with holes in between.

"Spikes," Daish-rog sighed, placing a hand over his eyes.

"I may have to kill that hermit," said Rhin, gritting his teeth.

They sprinted through, dodging the holes and the spikes that sprang up. Two shooting spikes clipped Rhin's clothes, each missing his flesh by an inch.

They made it across only to find themselves sinking into the ground. Rhin looked around, a lump in his throat. The revelation was disheartening.

"Quicksand," Daish-rog roared.

He concentrated, reaching for some invisible rope. A sapling sprouted from the opposite bank, its miniscule branches growing outward over the sand.

"It is no use. Only weeds can grow here," said Daish-rog, his eyes bulging from mental exertion.

But he never gave in. Vines shot forth from the roots of the sapling. Rhin and Daish-rog grabbed hold of these as the tree matured before their eyes. They managed to pull themselves out of the sand that had threatened to swallow them alive.

At last, there were no more obstacles between them and the hermit. They ran to the hut and found the elder bowing before them, praying.

His skin was pitch-black and he wore a necklace of shrunken heads. He was bald except for the ring of snowy, white hair around his small head. He wore a makeshift tunic crafted from long since rotten leaves. He had no footwear, thus his feet were calloused and scuffed.

"Any more traps we should know about?" Rhin grunted.

"I needed proof, masters. Forgive me," the hermit said as he stood, leaning on his beast-skull staff.

Rhin said, "You are forgiven. Now, can you tell us how to get to the Temple of the Angel Wings? And another question, could I have some herbs or something for this cut?" Rhin asked, indicating his leg.

"Ah, yes. The next Temple is hidden in mystery, but I have a map for you that will lead to the exact location. And I shall grant you greater power to aid in your struggle against Jiaïro. As for your wound, come with me."

"We will be most grateful for that map and your aid, hermit," said Daish-rog.

"Yes, yes, of course. Now come."

He led them into his hut, leaning on his skull-staff as he moved up to a large bookshelf, which had a thick layer of dust covering its contents. The books were all of the same brownish-green color, with graying pages. He took a book off one of the shelves and from it extracted one of the old moist pages.

"Press this to your wound," the hermit advised.

Rhin obeyed and felt relief the moment the soggy paper touched his skin.

"The power of the written word," the hermit mumbled as he reached for another book from the dozens on the shelves.

He opened it to the brownest page and scratched his nail across the paper. This made an uncommon screeching sound. Directly thereafter, the bookshelf crumbled and dissolved into dust, leaving a massive, untouched brick wall with a single crack in the middle.

He stepped up to the crack and whispered into it.

The wall heaved itself to one side, scraping over stone. A white light shone from the opening.

"Many precautions have been made to protect what lies inside," the hermit said in a hushed tone.

"I see," said Daish-rog.

Rhin leaned through the opening and saw a red room. It was eerie. Everything about it seemed twisted and misshapen, ancient and new all at once. In the center was a pool of hissing, writhing liquid.

The hermit beckoned them inside. The room itself was deceiving. It could barely contain the three of them, and Daish-rog, being taller than Rhin, had to stoop.

The pool started glowing and whirling. It splashed out onto Rhin's arm and ate a hole into his shirt but his tattoo protected him from the acid searing into his flesh as well.

"Step closer to the pool," said the hermit

The acid splashed onto his arm again, but this time his skin welcomed it, absorbing the bubbling fluid. Rhin groaned and shut his eyes. The acid mingled with his blood and a fortitude that had been dormant within him was revived.

He cried a wordless cry. He opened his eyes but saw nothing but a white curtain. His legs burned with the same energy, which then forged on into his arms, then his fingertips, until his whole body was immersed in this new vitality. Each individual strand of hair on his scalp was aflame.

He cried out again. When the pain was extinguished, he looked to the mirror wedged in the corner of the red room. His entire body had been changed. His hair silvered, his eyes were a dark blue and he stood at least a foot taller, having to stoop just as Daish-rog did. Every aspect of his new form seemed more divine.

The hermit spoke from behind, "I have waited six hundred years for this moment. All of the earthly qualities in you are gone."

"What have you done to me?"

"I did nothing except guard this pool. But rest assured: you can shift between your earthly form and your God-like form at will. Your power has tripled. As soon as you find the other Temples, you will stand a very good chance of defeating Jiaïro," the hermit proclaimed, his excitement palpable.

Rhin understood that his tattoo was the key to his transformation. It had been blazed into his flesh millennia past. And it was still there, serving as a reminder of days long gone.

He looked at Daish-rog and as he did, he willed himself to change back. His physical shape reverted. However, Rhin could still feel the strength inside.

"Do not be alarmed. Your face has been wearing a mask all this time. No one has noticed it, not even you. This, what you see before you in the mirror, is the real you," the hermit laughed.

Rhin looked in the mirror and noticed that although he was in his original form once more, he was somehow different. He could see that his hair was no longer a dull red-blond, but it was crimson like the fires of Rayïm. And his eyes were a paler shade of green, almost ethereal.

"Now I will ask you to follow me once more. The map awaits you."

"I hope finding the map will be less painful," Rhin whispered to his friend.

The hermit led them back to the main room and showed them a piece of rock that was on a table in the left corner. Rhin walked up to it and somehow knew what to do. He hunched over the rock, presenting his tattoo, the proof of his identity. The rock, gleaming gold, became a gray piece of paper which stretched across the table. It was scarred with many tears, rips and folds. Rhin took it and rolled it up with care, placing it in his pack.

The hermit led them out of the hut and said, "I would have you stay longer, but time is of the essence."

As they departed, Rhin turned around and asked, "Will you spare us the honor of all those traps as we leave, hermit?"

The hermit laughed and told him, "Even if I didn't, you could brush them off easily. Rhin listen to me a moment. You have two more Temples to find."

"But I thought there were three more."

"This was the third. Well, not really. The Temple was destroyed long ago by the minions of Jiaïro. The pool of sacred acid was spirited away from the ruins of the collapsed structure. But the acid was always the most important part. Those savage idiots never understood that. Thus, you have just gained the power of the Third Temple."

"Thank you, hermit. May we meet again in better days," Daish-rog said as he waved.

"Good luck. You will need it."

The next day, Rhin and Daish-rog were scanning the "map" that the hermit had entrusted to them. It was no true map, for there were no rivers, cities or forests inscribed upon its surface.

The air was stuffy. Like a mid-summer's day, clouds of pollen floated through the light blue sky. The pair sat under the shade of an archway near the western lake bank.

Rhin balanced the map with one hand and the other he moved over the paper with the gentleness of a lamb. The map had a symbol at its top:

It was the ancient character for 'sword'. Underneath it, Rhin found many strange words. He couldn't comprehend a single one of them.

This is a hard map to decipher. No pictures or anything. Maybe the words are names of cities. Or countries? Rhin thought to himself.

"Rhin? What does it say?" Daish-rog asked.

"A bunch of funny words. And see the symbol there? That means 'sword'. Do you have any idea why that's there?"

"These words are familiar, but I cannot place them. Is there anything else inscribed on it?"

"Yes. Wait, of course."

He looked at the map once more and saw another symbol. An "M" that differed from the traditional form of the letter.

"How did I miss that?" Rhin asked himself aloud. He pointed to the symbol inscribed upon the arch above them, then to the one on the hermit's map. They were identical. He said, flailing his free hand in excitement, "This is it. Munca Lake. The next Temple!"

The Vevleï ran through the near-abandoned streets of Ibbryn under the full moon. The reflected light shone brightly off the waters surrounding the dock.

Ibbryn was made of wood and nothing else. The houses were squat with angled roofs and no windows or chimneys. The warmth of a fire was not needed for it never grew too cold there. The place was nicknamed the Calm Coast for a reason.

"I once heard that Ibbryn was settled in an age past by sea-farers wanting to take root," Aroukana told Chainæïa. "Habraheen they were called, pirates and pillagers. But those who founded Ibbryn were done with the nomad's life, always waking to foreign shores."

"Pirates, that's good. They know how to build ships, at least," the other replied.

They had no idea where to start looking for a ship. Longboats, fisherman's vessels, transport galleys, harpoon ships, none were satisfactory.

The villagers had a distinct look to them. The men were copper-skinned and had oily, black hair, their beardless jaws set in grim faces. They wore simple brown and black cloth and some had olive bandanas. Each Habraheen man Aroukana passed shot a suspicious glance his way.

The women were lighter-skinned and fairer to the eye, well-rounded but short. Most of their height was in their legs, which were hidden behind faded, red skirts. Their hair was just as dark, dangling as long braids over their shoulders, but their demeanor was more pleasant. A few maids cast the Vevlea shy glances and one of the taller lasses gave Chainæïa a warm smile so he returned the favor. But when the girl's husband saw this, he stomped over and demanded an apology for the offense. Aroukana tried to explain that his friend didn't know mean to insult anyone but there were other Habraheen around him by then and it proved difficult. In the end Chainæïa begged the pardon of both husband and wife, telling them he was promised to another and that he was wrong to stare.

To their immense surprise and relief he and Aroukana came across the Æbækér, anchored ahead. The captain hailed them and offered them passage to wherever they were headed. From the look in their eyes, he knew what was happening. Haste was needed.

Behind the wheel, the captain shouted, "Prepare the ship."

A sharp cry from the first mate was his answer, "Aye, sir!"

A frantic ballet of scrambling crew and speeding servants and coursing cabin boys spread across deck.

The captain turned to Aroukana and asked, "Where to, master Vevlea?"

"Ancient Alkari on the North Isle. We are going to rouse the Vevleï and march on to the last battle."

"You heard them, lads. We go north. To Nénamburra!" the captain shouted.

Again came the answer, "Aye, sir!"

The ship took on a red glow. They took cover in the cabins as the vessel shifted and shook the area. Habraheen cries could be heard outside. But soon they were gone, along with Iora, as the Æbækér navigated its way through the clouds and then the stars.

The great rebellion had begun. The forces of the world were uniting to pull the dictator, Jiaïro, from his seat of power.

One of the crew shouted, "For Iora," and soon others took up the call. They chanted it as they labored. It motivated them, drove them onward.

"Just one question though," said Chainæïa. "Will this not take far too long? Last time it took a day to get from the East to the West."

"Point taken. But that was leisure time. Ye haven't seen this gal at full speed," the captain exclaimed and pulled a lever.

Emitting a dazzling display of lights and fire, that most spectacular ship made its desperate flight to the island where Rhin had begun his rebirth. It seemed an age ago.

Aroukana's plan was to unite the Monraïkian army and the Vevlea Resistance. He knew it would be difficult since the two nations were not on good terms. Still, try he must.

After the ship had reached the vacant reaches of space, the two stepped out of their cabins to admire the stars, for they both knew this could be the last time they would see their beauty. The planets passed in a splendorous rush as the ship followed its course, circling the planet.

In a few hours they reached the North Isle. The crew and passengers took cover as the Æbækér prepared to re-enter the sphere.

The same way it had departed, it penetrated again. Although, unlike the last time they used the ship, Æbækér landed not off the coast but on the earth amid the ruins of the ancient city of Alkari which lay to the north of the Wall Forest. The air currents created by the landing of the ship caused a torrent of dust and dirt to beat upon the aged trees.

Aroukana disembarked and scanned the grounds. They were at the edge of a small cluster of gorn trees. The place was deserted. Nothing was to be seen besides the battered stones.

Good, they still know how to hide, Aroukana thought with a smile. He cupped his hands around his lips and called, "Akra, Yuyon, Ryïk, Avalïo! Aroukana has returned."

Then, as if a fog had cleared, hundreds of Vevleï revealed themselves from behind crumbling wall, stone and tree.

A stout, muscular Vevlea walked up to Aroukana and, placing a hand on his shoulder, said, "Aroukana of the South, the Wayward Wanderer, the Preyed-on Princeling."

Aroukana turned to Chainæïa. He was staring at the newcomer, engrossed.

It's the hair. Most of us shave it, so it comes as a surprise, Aroukana reminded himself.

The stout Vevlea had long, fiery locks—strands of gold blazing within thickets of scarlet. Green-dyed armor covered most of his body, but amid the battered plate were traces of a weathered tunic.

"Ryïk of Alkari, the Storm Sword, Bænhil's Brute," Aroukana answered, resting his hand on the other's shoulder.

Two more Vevleï came to him and he greeted them in turn.

"Avalïo Never-Sired, the Shadow in the Green. Yuyon, the Mad Minstrel. Where is Akra?" Aroukana asked, done with formalities.

"He was gravely injured. After you left last year an army came nearer than we should have liked. We launched a strike and ended the threat then and there. Although we were victorious, Lord Akra and many others were wounded in the field," Yuyon answered, his face as stony as ever Aroukana remembered.

Avalïo looked at Chainæïa and asked, "Who is your companion, Aroukana?"

"Chainæïa of Adwren. He has been my faithful and stalwart companion. He wishes to join our ranks," he answered, looking back at his friend, who stood motionless a few yards behind. He looked timid.

"But what has brought you here, lad?" Ryïk asked.

"It is a long tale, but I shall make it short." And so Aroukana briefed them without details. "I found Rhin soon after I left. We have journeyed far together. All of the legends have come true. He saved the lives of many. Jiaïro captured Chainæïa and me, along with a Conkatokæ. Rhin came to rescue us and fought Jiaïro. We escaped, yet the False God still holds two of our companions: a girl descended from the Mæfæovér line, and the Conkatokæ. We owe it to our friends to save them. And, since it is Jiaïro who holds them, we can accomplish two deeds with one stroke. We have come to share the location of Jiaïro's latest hole."

"Where might this place be?" Avalïo questioned.

Vigor and lust for vengeance was chiseled into all of their expressions.

"Naa-Teria. His army is extensive. We will need aid. We must go to Monra, to enlist the aid of Pélénor. Another of our companions, a giant, has gone to ask the Denzak villages for assistance. This fight will be to the death." He looked around at the encouraged faces of his people and shouted, "Retribution is at hand!"

Keeping in spirit, they shouted their battle cries.

The captain of Æbækér called from the deck, "I have friends. I can call them here to transport the armies you gather."

Aroukana smiled at that. It all seemed to be working. It would not be long before his people were restored.

During the night, when the harsh northern winds stirred, the three Vevleï commanders took Aroukana and Chainæïa to the wounded leader of the Resistance, the fallen king. Every Vevlea, no matter how poor or ignorant knew of him. Akra descended from the most noble and pure family in Vevlehen history. The city, Alkari, had been named after his grandfather thousands of years before, when it was first built.

Many fires blazed among the tents, swirling as the winds intensified. Vevleï toasted their upcoming victory, cloaks and blankets billowing about them as they drank. They sang of glory, of lost loved ones and of the revival of Alkari. It had been a long time since Aroukana had heard the old songs sung. The tunes were beautiful and soulful to his ears. Nostalgia swept over him. He brushed the feeling off. There would be plenty of time to mourn once Jiaïro was bled.

Aroukana arrived at the infirmary (nothing more than a cave illuminated by torchlight) and saw a cloaked, weak-looking figure lying on the only feather bed.

Akra turned his head and said, his voice frail, "Aroukana, I knew you would return. Tell me, did you find him?"

"Yes, Father," he answered. "He goes now to regain his power and destroy Jiaïro, just as you predicted."

The Vevlea had a silver beard that rested on his stomach. His green eyes glittered in the moonlight that poured in through the cave mouth, revealing his pale skin and thick brows. Upon his bald head was a crown of silver, crested with green gems which bore the holy symbol of the Sword. Under his cloak was a suit of chain mail. The healers had pleaded with him to let them remove the mail, but he would not part with his armor. He knew he would die and when he did, he would die a warrior and a king.

Lying there, he was long, as if stretched by years of toil. He was the oldest Vevlea alive, having lived for one and a half thousand years.

"Good tidings," said the old king at length.

A fit of violent coughing overtook him.

Aroukana looked his father over and shut his eyes.

The king said, knowing his son's thoughts, "Worry not for me. My time draws near, but with me ends an age of turmoil. As a parting gift, my son, I will send Ryïk, Avalïo and Yuyon with you to unite the Monraïkian army with ours. Tell them that the king asks it of them. His dying wish."

"Yes, my king," said Aroukana.

"I always knew you would succeed. If only your sister lived to see this day. If only she still breathed to fight at your side. I have that same wish. If I were not a useless infirm I would stand by you, Prince Aroukana. I witnessed the battle that sundered our kingdom, but I will not see the one that reunites us."

Aroukana's throat burned. This aged king danced upon the edge of forlornness.

"But you will be with us, sire," the son told his father. "You will be the wind that flies the banners. When the war horns blast you shall be the air in the trumpeters' lungs. When the fire arrows are loosed you shall be the arrowheads, piercing the shields and hides of the enemy. It is true, sire, that your body shall not attend. Your soul, however, will be the blade that strikes truest in our final war. And this I promise, news of our victory will come to you ere your days are spent. Rest now, Father."

Aroukana bowed and left the cave. Ryïk approached him, a woeful look upon his face.

But the prince smiled and said, "Tomorrow we ride."

At dawn, the three Vevleï generals went with Aroukana, the Vevlehen Prince, and Chainæïa on their fresh horses to the city Monra. They rode with pride and speed, in their gleaming chain mail that shone in the sun like flames of glory.

The generals' red-blonde hair buffeted about them. Aroukana and Chainæïa had nearly forgotten those colors, having shaved their heads to hide their identity for so long.

Aroukana looked forward to the day when he could let his hair grow out again, when it would no longer be necessary to hide who he was.

The generals' helmets covered most of their faces. Long, turquoise, Maratosca* feathers, tied to their gear, fluttered in the wind.

The journey proceeded with infrequent interruption. On one occasion, they did stumble upon a patrol of Jiaïro's men trotting through a wood. Avalïo spotted them nearing a clearing.

"Ah, good time for an ambush. Now you'll find out why they call me Shadow in the Green," said Avalïo to Chainæïa as he pulled himself up a gorn to rest among the branches and leaves.

---

* A noble creature similar to an eagle and plumed in turquoise or silver—the latter having been more common. The eastern breed fed on irlorn and erlmerk, while the Nénamburran Maratosca were coastal predators that preyed upon flying fish. Its feathers were used to decorate the chain mail and helmets of generals and kings of the Vevlehen race.

"Pay close attention and you may even learn why I'm Baenhil's Brute," Ryïk said and winked.

Chainæïa nodded and followed Aroukana as Yuyon led the horses away.

After they had crouched behind a boulder, Chainæïa said, "The Brute and the Shadow, that's blunt enough. But why do they call Yuyon 'the Mad Minstrel'?"

Aroukana grinned in their shadow shroud, whispering, "Yuyon was my father's bard before the war. He knew hundreds of songs and was quite an accomplished poet. Now, even in a skirmish he can't stop himself from rhyming and singing. The last thing his foes ever hear before they fall is his strong voice. Quite mad."

Chainæïa shook his head.

Aroukana peeked from behind the boulder and said, using the Mugé, "Here they come. A column. Twenty strong, armed with pikes and short swords. Two bowmen at the end. Avalïo will have the archers. You assault the rear. Ryïk and I will take their front."

Then Yuyon's voice gushed forth from the trees, startling the steel-clad soldiers in the clearing,

> "The lass once said she loved me not
> Imagine that, I was so distraught
> Until I remembered—how had I forgot?
> She owed me seven silvers"

Aroukana jumped up and rushed the enemy. Chainæïa flanked the patrol, crashing into the troops at the end of the column, separating them from their brothers-in-arms. Aroukana saw that the two archers had sprouted feathers. Then Ryïk thundered into them, sounding more like an earthquake than a man, bludgeoning the soldiers with his mace-rod. The broad Vevlea overpowered half a dozen, raining down upon them with the fiercest of blows.

The woods rang with shouts and the scream of steel. One man cried, "Mercy," and this infuriated Ryïk.

He answered, "Mercy? When your great, great, great grandfather put *my wife* to the sword and sent *my child* to the gallows, was there mercy then? Rejoin your ancestors in Rayïm!"

He smashed the man's skull with his weapon, crushing it as if it were a clay pot. More soldiers dropped, shafts protruding from their hearts and eyes. Aroukana deflected a couple of sub par thrusts and ended two more lives. Then he met Chainæïa, who had worked his way through the rear of the column, and saluted.

Yuyon plucked his bowstring, pretending it was a harp, and sang another refrain as the skirmish was concluded.

> "The sky gushed red
> Upon lord's head
> And he was silent ever after
> But all the men, at his behest,
> Were drowning in rank laugher"

Aroukana and his guard sheathed their weapons. There were dead all around them. A dented helmet rolled by the prince's feet.

He commented, "The Storm Sword didn't use his blade this time."

Ryïk grunted, "A blade's all well and good, but sometimes a mace is the better to get the 'point' across."

"The seasons have not dulled your vision, Avalïo," said Yuyon.

"Nor your voice, Minstrel," came the answer as the Green Shadow dropped from the canopy.

After that unique interlude, their ride went uninterrupted. Packs of wolves were common, but they showed no sign of aggression.

They rode through the Wall Forest and past the ancient Light Tower. In the distance they could see the ruins of Kremmä. It seemed to Aroukana that the city still blazed with red flame, as it had done when he, along with Rhin, witnessed its destruction.

The riders made a brief stop in Rore village for food and sleep. Aroukana imagined the townsfolk were troubled by five Vevleï riding through the land, unafraid. Such had not happened in almost six centuries.

They continued through Orno village and on past War Mountain, the historical battleground, the very place Jiaïro had begun expanding his influence. At the holy stone there, they prayed.

They arrived at the city of Monra on the fourth night after their departure from Alkari. They had made excellent time. Their mounts, it seemed, shared their vigor.

When the five Vevleï approached Monra, they found it under siege. Jiaïro's army had torn through the walls. The stone was cracked everywhere they could see. And the houses burned bright, tongues of flame licking the moon. Monraïkian archers were lined up along the front wall firing arrows at the troops below. Enemy crossbowmen launched bolts at the archers and many fell from the wall onto the bloody fields. Screams of pain were the only audible sound apart from the clash of steel.

The Vevleï were enraged. They plowed over the black abominations, hacking at them. They fought their way toward the gate in time to witness the charge of the Monraïkian cavalry. The gate burst open and the purple armored horsemen galloped through, followed by the infantry. They crossed the drawbridge and pushed Jiaïro's soldiers back.

The Vevleï rode in wedge formation, digging into the enemy's rear. Spears and arrows showered down on the servants of Evil. Flashes of emerald colored weapons and shields staged a deathly play across the field surrounding the city.

In no time at all, Jiaïro's thrust was shattered and his forces made to retreat. The Monraïkian horsemen mowed them down. None escaped their wrath.

Then the victorious cry was shouted, "Vara!"

The corpses of the enemy were heaped into piles and burned. The Orbs were crushed. The energy crystals of the fallen Monraïkian warriors were taken to a crypt to be memorialized. Under each Orb would be carved the respective soldier's name.

The Monraïkian people believed in Shiria, the Goddess of Fire, Courage and Valor. She was their most adored and revered Goddess. In second place came the Goddess of the earth and trees, Waion. They presented the bodies of the dead as offerings to those deities.

The Vevleï rode across the sloshing grass, bloodied and blackened. So many bodies, their faces shattered by despair.

They rode on to the gates and found the Captain of the Monraïkian Army. It was none other than Pélénor. His face was red and his expression grim. He looked at them and Aroukana saw a tear of sorrow trickle down his scarred face.

The captain, along with his escort, came up to Aroukana.

Pélénor said, "The day has been laid to waste, Vevlehen lords. What seek you in the city of Monra? Come to help us, perhaps? What have you for news from the North? We have heard nothing for years."

Aroukana dismounted and walked up to him, stating, "The king requires your assistance, Pélénor Half-breed."

"Ah, he requires our assistance. We have fought for decades without his aid and now he requires our assistance? You can tell your king that he can forget it," Pélénor seethed.

"We realize we have been unfair, but our wars have kept us in the North. We are deeply sorry that-" Ryïk started.

Pélénor cut into his apology, "Sorry? I will be sure to pass that message on to the thousands of families that have lost an uncle, a father, a brother or a son."

Then Chainæïa said, "We know where Jiaïro makes his home. The isle of Naa-Teria. Leave this rage behind and unite with us."

Pélénor's face took a drastic change. There was not a trace of anger left. His expression was that of a man contemplating the hitherto unachievable.

He said to his escort, his eyes blazing green, "Prepare the legions. We go to war with the demon Jiaïro."

Then he turned to Chainæïa and asked, "How will you transport so many men?"

"We have a fleet that can get us to Naa-Teria in a matter of hours."

"Again, how?" Pélénor asked, eyes wide.

"The how can wait, you have an army to prepare," said Chainæïa.

Ryïk, Avalïo, Yuyon and Aroukana gaped at him. This common Vevlea had commanded more respect than they had.

The assembling began. Soon the armies of Monra and the Vevleï would face the ultimate nemesis of all they valued. However, whether they would fail or succeed would ultimately depend on one.

The spirits of Pélénor's men were lifted with these words, "We will fight Jiaïro soon, lads. Very soon."

Chapter 23
The Gathering of the South

When Kayre-Ost had arrived at Bevrorenk Harbor, he boarded a cargo ship that he thought would move at a good clip. But he had been sailing for a day and worried that he would not be able to gather his people fast enough and therefore not make it in time to Naa-Teria.

Being a stowaway, it was a challenge to find food without being seen. And his size did not help the matter. But he had managed so far, which he owed in part to the blindness of the crew.

He was lost in contemplation when, for some unknown reason, the shipmates screamed in distress. Waves shook the boat. The sun had vanished from sight and the winds pushed the clouds away.

Kayre-Ost heard only a few words, "Rocks-monster-help."

He ran on deck and saw a towering hill. In the middle of the ocean.

The sailors fired arrows at the massive apparition—a noble, but futile, effort.

Its voice was blatant, "I am not trying to harm you. I look for a Denzak by the name of Kayre-Ost. You there, stop squirming. Come on, people. Have you never seen a walking, talking Namka hill before? Stop shooting at me, please."

The voice was loud enough to rattle the merchant vessel. As Kayre-Ost tried not to lose his lunch (stale cheese and stringy fish), he remembered Rhin had once told him of a stone giant that sank into the ocean. This creature fit the description. Kayre-Ost approached the railing.

"Momagé?" he ventured.

The hill's eyes cracked as he looked down.

It said, "Are you the one the wind and seas hail as Kayre-Ost Lacksurel?"

"I am Kayre-Ost."

"You must accompany me to the South Isle, lad. Your path lies there, within a great tower of dark stone, in ancient woods."

"A tower forged of dark stone? Never heard of it."

"Be that as it may, you still wish to make your way to your home of old, correct?"

"Yes, but how am I to trust you?"

The sea-going men of the vessel surrounded the giant, not too intimidated by his stature, and one amongst them said, "You don't belong here. Neither does the demon-stone. Leave and perhaps you shall live. Stay and we'll kill you, stowaway."

"There is no time. Hurry."

Kayre-Ost glanced about the crew and saw them as easy prey. He could have thrown them overboard and commandeered the ship.

Oh, forget it, he thought. Then he said, "Let's go, Momagé, if that's your name."

"T'is."

"Alright."

The giant leapt overboard and the talking-walking monolith caught him with a craggy palm.

Kayre-Ost turned around and beheld the ship. He cupped his hands around his mouth and called, "Sorry for the inconvenience. We'll just be on our way."

The colossal Momagé turned his boulder-shaped head and stated, "Rhin has told you of my fate, no doubt. Before you ask, I shall tell you.

The magic of the sea is responsible for my survival. It saved me from the depths of the abyss. It told me to find a lone Denzak on his way south, and here you are. When the winds shifted, I was directed to you."

"Listen, we don't have much time. The gathering of the Vevleï has already begun. Their ships-" said Kayre-Ost.

Momagé cut him off, chuckling, "The waves have also strengthened me. I am quite fast."

Kayre-Ost said with a grin, "To Kenner Karg, then. To the South Isle."

"As you command."

Momagé overlooked the sea. He spoke a few words and a red light surrounded him—the same light that covered the Æbækér when it had ascended. Momagé dived and followed a winding course through underwater canyons at a stiff speed. Kayre-Ost clutched his throat, foam rising from his lips, but then found that he could breathe, for there were air bubbles encapsulated within the red lights.

They descended further still. The hill man sped through the rock canals. It was a dismal and ugly place. No life existed within those canals. It was home only to the stench of decaying stones.

The cavernous rocks became sharper the further Momagé swam. The journey took only a half hour. Before Kayre-Ost knew it Momagé rose from the waters and he was above sea level again, the sun blazing in his eyes.

Momagé stretched out his arms and climbed onto the rocky beaches of Kenner Karg. Kayre-Ost jumped onto Momagé's hand and the giant set him down on the sands.

Kayre-Ost then waved and said, "See you as soon as I find my fellow villagers. I hope you can take hundreds to Naa-Teria as smoothly as you ferried me."

"Don't fret."

Kayre-Ost plunged into the forest without a backward glance. It was strange to have met such a gargantuan being. The encounter caused him to rethink the word 'giant'.

He felt glad to be back in familiar territory. He pictured what the expressions of his friends would be when he found his hometown again.

A few years ago Kayre-Ost had been banished. He had never told anyone about his sentence: that he could not return until he found the Being of Light, Rhin, and brought him to the village council. Although he had not accomplished the latter, he thought it might suffice to bring the council to Naa-Teria. He knew he couldn't prove he had found Rhin but he would try his best to convince them. He would be examined by the council and judged by the Chief of Lergat, an old 'friend'. Lergat was his home village and the Chief had harbored a grudge against Kayre-Ost.

It took him three hours to cross the woods and he feasted on nuts along the way. Most of the trees were willows, lichen crawling up their base, so the forest was drunk with sunlight. The buttercups were widespread, bees bouncing from flower to flower.

Many brick paths marked the way to the various Denzak communities. On a normal day this would have been the best method of travel, but Kayre-Ost was in a hurry and cut across country to make better time.

When he found the brick path that led straight to Lergat but it was not how he remembered. Most of it had been burnt. Some bricks were missing and more were scattered ahead. He followed the road to its end and found his village in the same state. Lergat was protected by a strong palisade wall and a spiked ditch. The houses were all built on the north side of the village in a semi-circle. At the south end were the armory and the tunnels, in which the Denzak women and children could hide in times of war.

Lergat was ravaged. The straw that insulated the houses had been burnt and all that was left of the palisade wall was ash and dust. He could not see any of his friends anywhere. But he did find weeping children.

Approaching a little boy, no more than a toddler, he asked, "What happened here?"

"Grysen—help," the boy wailed, tugging at Kayre-Ost's sleeve.

"Don't worry. It's going to be alright. Now tell me what happened."

"Grysen came with his... bad men," the boy sobbed.

Kayre-Ost patted the lad on the head and questioned him no more.

He checked the Tharthra*, his former place of learning, but it was wrecked and desolate. Abandoned but for a tall male, about thirteen years old. Kayre-Ost assumed he was one of the students.

The boy had black hair and a thin, stretched, white face. He wore two silver earrings in each ear and Kayre-Ost saw a rapier buckled to his leather belt. Dressed in black rags but in a strange way, the clothing complimented his toned physique.

Kayre-Ost walked up to him and asked once more, "What's going on?"

This boy did not cry. His face was blank, as if he had seen too much.

"Grysen came and took all the adults of the village into that stronghold," the boy said, pointing westward. "I was not taken because he thought me no threat. I am Tye, the youngest student of the Tharthra. He took everyone except for the children."

"Do you know where this stronghold is?"

"Yes. Let me come with you Kayre-Ost. I want to kill that slime," the boy's face twisted in anger as he said this.

Kayre-Ost was not surprised that Tye knew his name. Everybody had heard of the exile. The Chief had seen to that.

"It's too dangerous."

"I have already studied in the Tharthra for three years. I can fight."

Kayre-Ost sighed, knowing he could not convince the boy to do otherwise. "Alright. You'll do as I tell you. Exactly as I tell you."

"I will. This way," said Tye.

The sun was covered by a shield of gray as they walked down the path and past the split palisade. The children from the village were standing there, watching them go. Each held a hand up in silence, as if trapped in a melancholy portrait. Kayre-Ost and the boy named Tye set off to deliver their friends and family from Grysen.

---

* Where children trained to become warriors. Every student practiced the art of fighting for at least ten years. When they graduated, they entered the world with respect and dignity. Warriors were met with high praise amongst the Denzak.

Neither spoke during the gloomy trek to the towering shadow on the horizon. Grysen's large, pike-shaped tower protruded from the black sands beyond the forests in the distance. Cape Obelisk the Denzak called it.

Kayre-Ost was not at all surprised to find Jiaïro's soldiers in their path, cutting trees and burning the sands to make the world appear acceptable to their God. Tye, on the other hand, was appalled.

As limp as a wet cloth, he dropped to the dusty ground, a faint crush of gravel the only warning. Kayre-Ost shook him, slapped him, but he would not wake.

Eyes closed.

A void unfurled itself beneath his soles. Two poles impaled the darkness. One led the way to insanity, while the other held firm in its defense of the fragile opposite state.

The right pillar was gray and battered. Eroded and cracked from thousands of years of resisting an unspoken aggressor. The second road was golden and inviting, offering an invisible hand. But as Tye pulled away, the pillar turned black. Blood soaked and twisted, a force wrenched at the boy. The invisible hand, no longer friendly and quiescent, grabbed him by the hair and tore at his scalp. With sudden clarity, Tye raced toward the graying solemn pillar on the right. As the concealed fury chased him, a barrier of light surrounded him and the entity was exposed. The inviting, insane and deranged creature was nothing other than a part of himself, the hawk to his rodent. Tye had made a wise choice. The frail pillar had protected him from himself.

Having braved the brink of oblivion he drew himself up. He had chosen the righteous path.

A voice that sounded a lot like his told him, "The true path is not always fairest, Tye. Remember that."

Then a sky-blue sword plunged into the blackness. In a split second of total silence, the sword absorbed all of the darkness. Unconscious of his own actions, he reached and claimed the weapon. It was the Sword of the Mind.

The same voice as before spoke to him again, "Remember, Tye, that the Mind exists in a perfect Balance. Only in Balance can it remain untainted. Two sides of the same coin. Hunter and prey. Order and chaos. Justice and cruelty. Fair and fraud. Remember."

Then there was nothing.

Kayre-Ost shook Tye one final time before he would assume him dead. He growled, "Why didn't I leave you in the village? Get up, boy."

Tye opened his eyes at last. He flung his legs forward onto the hard path and jumped to his feet. Kayre-Ost looked at the boy. He noticed Tye rubbing his back.

Tye turned around and his jaw dropped. Kayre-Ost followed Tye's gaze, glancing at where he'd been lying and saw a sword.

Kayre-Ost asked, dumbstruck, "How did that get here?"

But he received no answer.

Kayre-Ost brushed the dirt off Tye's shirt and said, "You're alright. We'd better get going."

While they walked, Kayre-Ost, eager to bombard the boy with questions, had difficulty restraining himself.

Who is this kid? Too many bizarre things have been happening since I met Rhin. This boy could just be another weird happenstance. Though, looks like he's got more to him than meets the eye, he thought.

When Tye next spoke he sounded much older, "I am the protector of the Mind now, Kayre-Ost. My assignment is to find Rhin Akvius and aid him in the last war. I know of your recent friendship with him."

"How do you know about Rhin?" Kayre-Ost asked.

"It came to me in a dream."

"Well, it doesn't matter now. Look," Kayre-Ost pointed, "that's Grysen's tower, Cape Obelisk, the cancer of the South."

"What's the plan?" Tye asked as they crept through the brush on the side of the road.

"Well," Kayre-Ost looked at the boy, "we storm the keep, beat everyone, free our comrades and storm out again."

"Sounds good to me," Tye said, grinning.

Kayre-Ost noticed that they shared some similarities.

The two Denzak unsheathed their swords and charged. They were met by a patrol of five men, two were flung back by a brutal bash from Kayre-Ost. The giant's follow-through finished them.

The tower was now alert. Bells rang and horns were blown. The soldiers were armed sooner than Kayre-Ost expected, as if they had foreseen the attack.

The troops surrounded them but Tye, his destiny exposed, put his hidden powers to use. The soldiers' helmets shone red as mental strain burst their craniums from within. They froze in time while thoughts flooded their brains and they fell, slain by their own hands. All dead.

"What did you do to them?" Kayre-Ost asked.

"I let them see the truth," Tye answered.

"Which is?"

"They were no longer pure. The divine forces granted them the truth and they repented. They had crossed the line. They were welcomed with open arms back into the light. They chose death to redeem themselves. But the Gods forgive all, even Jiaïro's soulless henchmen. Peace bathes them in its calm waters now. Life after death can only contain bliss."

"I'd be lying if I told you I wasn't frightened," said Kayre-Ost.

"We're all afraid," Tye said, his face taking on a troubled air.

Pushing forward, they tripped, knocked down and stampeded the troops that got in their way. Their gritty, brutal fighting style, though barbaric, proved crippling in its effectiveness.

When they arrived at the gate to the Obelisk a tall man stood in their path, ten large brutes at his back.

"I am Zordon, marshal to the great God," said he, seeming pleased. "That's the last name you'll ever hear, you dense Denzak oafs."

His skin was pale and his eyes a rich gold. He bore a single fang, which popped out from between his lips as he talked, and claws, brown from the touch of blood. He was ugly, maybe the ugliest man Kayre-Ost had ever seen. His armor was the same as all the others, red and black, the colors of Jiaïro's standard. He also stood far broader than the other soldiers, though none were runts.

He asked, "Come to stop mean old Grysen, imbeciles?"

"A choice. Free the villagers or taste our blades," Tye shouted, surprising even himself.

Zordon snorted and mocked, "Look here, men, the little novice is getting aggravated."

The soldiers guffawed.

Tye seemed to shrink before Kayre-Ost's eyes.

"Don't let him daunt you," said the older Denzak.

Zordon continued, "Alas, I am defeated. I cast my weapons down at your feet, oh mighty one."

He took a step toward Tye, venting his unceasing laugh.

"Taste steel, pig," Tye yelled.

The chosen one of the Sword of the Mind stepped forth, exposing his deadly weapon so that all could see.

"Your sword is legendary, boy. But I wonder if its power is truly in your grasp," said Zordon, his eyes fixated on the blade. "Very well, I shall murder you both and take that weapon of yours. Soldiers, kill."

Tye clashed his sword against Zordon's scimitar. The blades sparked with each embrace. Tye was relentless. Flash after flash lit the tower walls, accenting the blood and the sword marks that ravaged them. Zordon seemed certain of his imminent victory, putting little effort into his fighting. Because of this, Tye knew he could win and taunted Zordon, "Your overconfidence is your weakness."

"And your puny size is yours," Zordon retorted, sneering.

Near the base of the tower, Kayre-Ost let the soldiers chase him into a corner. He had had some trouble with them, for they were more enduring than the usual footpads. He had wounded three, who seemed to take no notice at all. When he was pressed up against a tree, enemies all around, the Decuri removed his helm to reveal a spotted, gangrenous head. The man's lips were black and oozing and his nose was missing, a rough brown scar in its stead.

"And I thought your master was deformed," Kayre-Ost grinned despite himself.

"Joke all you want, wretch. Your flesh will taste all the sweeter if you die in defiance, blood boiling," the Decuri said and smacked his slimy lips.

"Whatever you say," said Kayre-Ost.

He lunged and thrust his palm into the Decuri's chest. His hand punched through the steel plate and even the chain mail beneath, digging into the officer's chest. The Decuri dribbled brown spittle as he stared at Kayre-Ost. Then he died.

The soldiers did not hesitate to attack despite the giant's display. Kayre-Ost resumed the fight with his double-bladed axe in his right hand and his longsword in his left.

"Top quality meat you got for yourself, Zordon," said Kayre-Ost between clashes.

"My soldiers are the finest in the land," Zordon blurted, turning his head to behold Kayre-Ost, "finer even than Jiaïro's men."

The triumph was plain on Tye's face when he said, "You plan to take Jiaïro's place as ruler? Interesting."

"How did you—stay out of my head!"

Now that the Decuri was dealt with, Kayre-Ost made quick work of the remaining men. He deflected a sloppy blow and retaliated with a head-splitting cut from his axe. Two circled behind as another two pushed at his front. He killed all four, spinning around and around, letting his weapons fall high and low, then high again. The last four rushed his front in unison, in shield-wall formation. But their protection was doing them more harm than good. They were slow and could not see well, Kayre-Ost noted. He brought his steel-tipped boot down and crushed the foot of one and jerked himself out of the way, allowing two to deal death-blows to one another by mistake. The final soldier managed to block one sword strike, but never saw the axe calling for his knees. He buckled, howling, until the Denzak silenced him.

Kayre-Ost looked ahead and saw Zordon and Tye still locked in battle.

"What's taking him so long? Just finish it, boy," he said to himself.

"What are-" Zordon was cut off.

"I can do more than you could ever imagine. I have the Mind Sword now, fool, and I do know how do use it," Tye's voice penetrated Zordon's thoughts, locking him in a state of fear.

"Get out of my head, brat!" he yelled.

Then Tye's influence led Zordon into the world Tye himself had visited that same day. The marshal stood before the abyss, the two pillars on either extremity. The calm, left one invited him, while the other clung to the dark like a child to its mother. Zordon, wasting no time, ran to the one on the left. Then all the forces of the Mind released him as he sprinted down the path of insanity.

The marshal's mind was now in chaotic upheaval. Tye had no choice but to release him.

Zordon's eyes looked ready to erupt from his skull. His mind had cracked. He was lost.

"Jiaïro's seat will be mine," Zordon claimed, the muscles in his face twitching.

After those few crazy seconds he vanished.

The sun started to set, turning the sky gold, the few puffy clouds floated here and there, without urgency. As the sky darkened, the drawbridge creaked, lowering of its own accord.

Kayre-Ost said, "Finally," and made for the wooden bridge.

"Wait," said Tye. "How did I do?"

"Alright."

"Alright?"

"I got ten in the time it took you for one."

"I'm only thirteen," Tye objected.

Kayre-Ost shrugged.

The whole tower aged centuries in a matter of minutes. The walls crumbled and dissolved, while the drawbridge deteriorated as if one hundred years of torrential rain had been inflicted upon it in a mere sixty seconds.

Kayre-Ost and Tye passed into the tower and climbed its many steps. With each step the air grew colder, as the sky was colored jade.

When they reached the top, Grysen was waiting in a room that was empty but for rags hanging off the walls and a wooden gorn tree table. He sat on this table, his head sagged down, his chin touching his chest.

Grysen's beard was jet-black but his head was bald—abnormal for a Denzak. His green eyes had grown darker over the years. One would have to admit he did look similar to Kayre-Ost. His armor was light blue and gray. Even their swords were alike, the standard sword used by Denzak soldiers. Though Kayre-Ost happened to notice Grysen's blade had been tweaked in a few interesting ways. The hilt had spikes on one of its sides and the blade had a slight curve to it, not too noticeable, but it was there nonetheless.

Without moving at all, Grysen said, "It," he took a deep breath, "unfolds."

"You deal with Jiaïro now? I thought you couldn't sink any lower," Kayre-Ost could feel his mounting anger as he spoke.

"Where are the villagers?" Tye asked.

"The spell I have created will keep them hidden from you until Kayre-Ost faces me in single combat," Grysen replied.

Kayre-Ost saw a glint of steel, no doubt a concealed dagger.

"If it's a fight you want, I won't disappoint," Kayre-Ost shouted, as he swept his sword at Grysen's head.

As Kayre-Ost began his onslaught Grysen sprang to his feet, knocking the table over as he did so, and retaliated with similar combinations. They fought using their hatred for one another. Blinded by years of rage, without words, substituting with their weapons. It had the same basic effect.

He could not tell why, but Kayre-Ost recalled the day a bard had come to Lergat. He had recited many poems but one in particular stood out for Kayre-Ost. It didn't rhyme all too well but that didn't matter.

> "Roots and rocks may shatter bones
> And words sure can hurt you
> But a blade blow
> From a mortal foe
> Will split your soul in two"

Kayre-Ost dealt a mighty stroke, just missing his foe's neck. The blow hit the table where Grysen had been moments before. Their blades met again, the force shattering the dull, glass windows. Then the adversaries each performed their version of an earthquake. As the quakes met the floor cracked and the ceiling of the tower exploded and toppled, crashing through the trees far below.

They fought atop the tower under the moon, its light appearing fierce to their eyes at first.

Tye wanted to help but he knew that this was Kayre-Ost's personal vendetta for something that Grysen had done to him long before the boy was ever born. All he could do was wait. And so he did.

Both warriors became exhausted. Then Grysen created one more earthquake, the floor cracked, and Kayre-Ost watched as the support under Tye's feet gave way. He was slipping.

He jumped toward the crumbling rock and shouted, "Tye!"

With tremendous effort he reached out his hand and Tye, still struggling to hold on, grabbed it. Grysen ran at them flailing his sword.

For Kayre-Ost time slowed.

Grysen, in all his fury, lunged at him, penetrating his left arm. With his right, Kayre-Ost still held on to the swinging boy. The wind had turned and gusted. Kayre-Ost summoned all his strength and grabbed his enemy with his wounded arm. Grysen tripped and was hurled over the edge.

In his last desperate moment, he screamed. Then, a look of complete shock upon his face, he hit the branches, a mile below. After the cracking and rustling stopped, he had disappeared from sight.

Kayre-Ost pulled the boy up and set him on his feet.

Tye looked down at the trees, where the terrible Grysen had just fallen. Then he looked at Kayre-Ost.

He said, breaking the silence, "What should we make of this?"

Kayre-Ost answered, giving the boy a simple look, "A story for your grandkids, Tye."

"You all right?" Tye asked.

"Let's go free the others."

"But where are they?"

"Grysen said, 'the spell I have created will keep them hidden from you-"

Tye finished the sentence, "-'Until Kayre-Ost faces me in single combat.'"

"That's easy enough," said Kayre-Ost.

They began the long descent. As they walked they heard the cracking sound that had shaken the tower before. This time it was somehow different. A clamor rose up.

"The whole place is collapsing," Tye yelled over the noise.

They raced down the rest of the stairs and when they reached the gate and had crossed the moat, they saw that all the inhabitants of the village gathered there, freed from Grysen's spell.

"Is he dead?" asked an aged man with a failing, white beard.

"Grysen is gone," answered Kayre-Ost.

They praised Kayre-Ost and Tye, their saviors. But they were silenced when Cape Obelisk crashed into the moat that surrounded it, creating a fierce tremor that almost knocked them off their feet. As fast as they had stopped cheering, they began again.

Reunited, they began the march back to Lergat where a meeting would take place. All of the Denzak would gather in the village's largest hut and decide whether to join the battle to dethrone Jiaïro.

Chapter 24
The Denz ak War - Council

The hike back to Lergat was a short and peaceful one with no stops along the way, as the villagers were eager to find their children. The sun leapt out from its hiding place amidst the clouds as it rose from behind the mountains and shone through the tree-covered road, directing them like a beacon. There were no more encounters with Zordon, who must have taken all of his men with him when he fled.

The sky turned a purple-pink. Kayre-Ost found peace for the first time in years and refused to think of the upcoming trial, as it would bring up memories of his exile.

Five years before he had made a grave mistake and for this they had cast him out.

Tye looked at Kayre-Ost and smiled, "I remember you," he started, "you're the one they sent away."

"That's me," said Kayre-Ost.

"Why?" Tye asked.

"I guess it won't hurt to tell you," he paused, collecting his thoughts. "Five years back I lead an army into battle, a group of the village's finest warriors. We were outnumbered, so I ordered a retreat. The men obeyed, but under protest. The advancing army destroyed a village the next day. Hundreds died all because of my mistake."

Tye was quiet, looking at his feet.

"They were all willing to die that day. I thought it was right, the right thing to do."

The giant kicked a random boulder, cracking it.

"I'm sorry. I didn't know."

"Two days later I was exiled and I never ran from a fight since, no matter how great the odds against me," Kayre-Ost finished.

Tye knew this was the end of the conversation so he walked on.

When they arrived at the village the children ran from the abandoned houses and clung, sobbing, to their parents, older siblings, aunts and uncles.

A heart-warming sight. But there's no one to welcome me, Kayre-Ost thought. He glanced at Tye and said, "Hey, don't you have a family?"

"I'm an orphan," the boy stated. "I was told my parents died while out hunting. I don't remember but the village elders won't tell me what really happened. But, I don't see anyone hugging you."

"Looks like we're both orphans, Tye," said Kayre-Ost.

Early the next day the fires were put out and the chimneys stopped smoking. It was a crisp spring morning, with a lingering hint of winter.

In silence, the Denzak gathered in the Chief's hut. The inside was like a courtroom except circular. The seats were set like an amphitheater. The whole hut was made of gorn wood covered with straw to insulate it. The straw also served as a roof, as well as cushions for the seats.

Kayre-Ost saw that the leaders from the neighboring Denzak settlements had come to the trial. And on such short notice. High Priests, Chieftains, weapon masters. Either they expected a hanging, or they thought the defendant might have something interesting to tell them.

A burly man stepped forward and sat down on the highest chair. The Chief of the Denzak tribe of Lergat. He had a long feather attached to his helmet with two horns protruding from each side. Kayre-Ost had never hesitated to state that he looked ridiculous.

The Chief stood and stretched out his arms as if he was about to give a gigantic hug and spoke in a practiced, deep voice, "Brothers and sisters, hear me."

The noise died down.

"The Council is now in session. Kayre-Ost Lacksurel, step forth."

Kayre-Ost moved to the center, before the Council, where all could see. Each villager had the right to vote, but the Chief stood as judge. It did not bode well for Kayre-Ost.

He spoke, feigning calmness, "Chief."

"Five years ago you made a fatal error, Kayre-Ost," as the Chief said this, his voice was soft. But then he boomed so that everyone could hear, "Because of you an entire village was annihilated."

Kayre-Ost clenched his fists and closed his eyes.

When he opened them again he said, "I don't deny it."

"Because of you, half of our friends and family were killed by Jiaïro's mercenaries. How do you plead?"

Kayre-Ost's eyes never left the Chief's as he said, "Guilty."

All eyes were directed at Kayre-Ost. Tye watched, helpless.

"Was it not you who ordered the retreat?" the Chief shouted.

"Yes. I ordered it."

A tear trickled down Kayre-Ost's face and splashed on the floor.

Tye yelled, "Put up a fight, man."

"Quiet," the Chief roared.

"Leave the boy alone," said Kayre-Ost.

"Such insolent behavior, traitor. Has your prolonged absence taught you nothing?" after a pause to reflect, the Chief's voice was quite different. It had a certain edge to it when he asked, "Do you remember when we charged you and sent you off?"

"Yes."

"Then you might also remember that your only way to return would have been to find Rhin Akvius, God of Light, and thus atone for your horrible crime."

"I remember," Kayre-Ost kept his voice passive.

"You were supposed to bring him here. Did you even find him?"

"I found Rhin Akvius and fought alongside him."

"Liar," the Chief argued. "If you had seen him, you would have brought him here."

Tye rose again, "Did it ever occur to you that Lord Rhin might have more important things to do then to talk to a raging bully?"

"What is this child doing here? Throw him out," the Chief ordered.

Kayre-Ost turned as three Denzak men approached the boy, who drew his sword. The soldiers stepped back and looked to the Chief.

"He has the Sword of the Mind," they gasped.

The villagers had heard much and read more about the Sword of the Mind. It was said to have been created by one of the greatest warriors who ever lived, the first of the Denzak. The weapon served to test the minds of warriors. But that was millennia past. It was an age of war and trial, of destiny and blood.

A woman rose, saying, "He is the one who saved us, along with Kayre-Ost. The boy should have a say in all of this."

"I think Kayre-Ost deserves a second chance. He was only trying to save the lives of the soldiers in his service. He tried to save lives, not destroy them," Tye told the council.

A wave of muttering broke out.

The Chief looked around, his confidence shattering, and said, "All in favor of exiling Kayre-Ost Lacksurel—again—give me a show of hands."

The Chief along with half of the village—those who had despised Kayre-Ost in his youth—raised their hands.

"Those in favor of mercy for this traitor, show us."

All the representatives of the neighboring villages lifted their hands along with the other half of Lergat. The Chief's eyes shot around the room.

Defeated, he shouted, "Mercy."

Only the elderly inhabitants looked the same as the Chief. They still remembered the trouble-making boy. But all of Kayre-Ost's childhood friends hugged him in turn as the eavesdropping children ran in, cheering.

Kayre-Ost looked around with love in his eyes, forming a mental picture that he would always keep with him.

Kayre-Ost faced his Chief and said, "You, old friend, are not fit for this job anymore."

"What did you say?" the Chief asked, glaring at him in incredulity.

"When this is all over I'll challenge you. And the rule of this town will no longer be yours."

Those around had not noticed the daring challenge, anticipating the night's feast in honor of Kayre-Ost's return, but the Chief was put in his place. He did not answer.

Kayre-Ost said, "We came here to warn the Council that we have one chance to destroy Jiaïro. We must rally and make our last stand on the Isle of Naa-Teria. We must face the hordes of enemy soldiers and win. The fate of the Four Isles lies in the outcome of this battle. Who comes with me?"

Tye was first to answer, "I will fight with you."

There was a brief silence, broken by a tall, white-bearded man who stepped forth saying, "The village of Atermin is ready."

Another, wearing dark blue scale-mail armor, said in the same determined voice, "So is Waterlipp."

"Reruk stands prepared to serve," A red-armored, gray-bearded giant stated.

Kayre-Ost looked at the representatives of the surrounding villages and then stared at the Chief.

"Our village will aid you as well, being outnumbered. Though let it be known that I don't trust you," said the Chief, all fury gone.

"Suit yourself," snapped Tye.

"What comes first, Kayre-Ost?" asked the gray-bearded Denzak.

"First we head for the old Temple to await Rhin's arrival. Then, we go to war."

The Denzak roared, the fighters punching the air.

Chapter 25
Completion

Daish-rog and Rhin had investigated Lake Munca for hours. In their exhaustion, they realized they had been traveling non-stop for almost a full year. It all seemed like one grand battle.

Spring had come again as it had that fateful day when Rhin had left Lynca. Now, the season of life seemed too cold. The sun was pale and the wind frigid. Dusk neared. A bleak night lay ahead of them.

As they lit their campfire, the nippy winds gave Rhin a refreshing sensation of clarity. The glowing lights, the Night Wisps, weaved over road and lake. He had been waiting in secret for the end of this hero's quest ever since it began. When he found out he was once a God his life had turned on its head. In the beginning, all he wanted was to put his parents' killer to death. But every time he thought he was starting to understand, something happened to disorient him all over again. Even if he ended the reign of his unholy father he would be lost. He did not know what to do with his life after the war was over.

"Sometimes I can't believe it has been a year since I started my journey," Rhin sighed, appreciating the gentle moonlight for he knew the clouds would soon overtake it.

"Why did you leave home?" Daish-rog asked.

"Vengeance. The village was sacked and burned to the ground. My foster parents were trapped in the house. They never came out. Everyone else died. Except me. It was foggy and raining. I couldn't see but someone told me to find my answers in Kremmä," Rhin recounted. Then he said, almost to himself, "Brekk. Brekk was just the puppet, but I killed him and his demons."

Daish-rog asked, "What do you think you will do after you defeat Jiaïro?"

Rhin was silent.

"It is strange," said Daish-rog, "I am old enough to be your father and yet I respect you as an elder." Then he looked embarrassed as he added, "Ah, but I forget you are not truly so young."

"No," Rhin said with a weary voice, "not truly."

All night long Rhin dreamt of Luu-ka. Daish-rog's question revisited him in his sleep.

After Jiaïro's gone? I just want to be normal again. I want a family of my own. And I already know with whom I want to share that family.

Luu-ka was still a captive of Rhin's demonic father, but he promised the wind and the trees and the birds that it would not be long before she was free again.

I'll throw Jiaïro's head off the wall of his own damned castle, Rhin swore.

Rhin awoke the next morning and searched along the surface of the flat lake, but found nothing. The water swirled. Rhin hovered, scanning the inky liquid. It was a clear, warm day, the sunlight bouncing off the lake. The trees had never seemed more colorful and no less than three rainbows arced over Munca.

Rhin turned to Daish-rog and asked for the map for the twentieth time. Daish-rog handed the rolled-up paper over and raised an eyebrow when he noticed Rhin's smile.

"Daish-rog," Rhin said, his brain working too fast for his mouth, "This map is magical. Whenever we achieve an instruction, it shows us the next. It must have changed when I touched the water!"

Now on the map, in old ink as if it had always been there, Rhin read, "Down in the deep shall the Half God find the door."

Rhin clutched his arm with his free hand as it throbbed. The flesh under the tattoo pulsated. The transformation had been triggered. But had he willed it, or had his body acted of its own volition?

His features became more distinct again, his hair turned to silver and his armor to gold. He held his sword aloft. In the reflection of the blade he saw his eyes, bright sapphires.

Changed, he immersed himself in the lake and swam to the bottom. He used his wings to propel himself. The water was icy cold, but he adapted. As he descended, stringy weeds tangled with his hair.

I wish I could see better, Rhin thought.

At once his eyes emitted light. Wherever he looked white beams illuminated the lakebed.

Convenient, Rhin smiled as he scanned his surroundings with his new night vision.

He resurfaced for breath and told Daish-rog, "I didn't find anything, but I have a feeling that I have to do this alone."

Daish-rog nodded and Rhin submerged himself again. After another moment he came to such murky waters that he had trouble seeing anything at all. His head collided with a solid obstacle, sending a stream of pain along his spine. He looked closer, willing the murk to clear, and saw two massive iron doors marked with the Sword Symbol.

The doors were spotted with sapphires and pearls. The image of a trout was etched upon them, one half on each door. Rhin was reminded of the dagger the fisherman had given him the day he and his friends had arrived on the East Isle. He took it out, examining the wooden handle. The design on the doors was an identical copy of the dagger, only much larger.

He said, "Luu-ka."

Although submerged, that single word was succinct.

The doors opened with a rumbling, a violent crescendo that shook the entire area. He swam through them and, after his passing, they closed. He was still in Munca Lake. Nothing had changed.

Disappointed, he swam to the surface and called out to Daish-rog. His heart sank when there was no reply. With horror, he saw that the forest was gone. The land was covered with fog and the sky with unnatural smoke. The lake water was much filthier than before.

Rhin swam to the bank of Lake Munca and got out of the grimy water. A figure that Rhin knew well enough to recognize sat there on a charred tree stump.

"You again. What is this place?" Rhin asked.

"This is the future of Iora," the figure answered.

"What happened?"

"You failed. This is the world as it will be one hundred years after you fail to defeat Jiaïro and he kills you."

"Aren't you supposed to be in my head? Who are you really?"

"You can call me Self, for I am a version of you."

Then Self changed the subject. "In the few childhood years that the inhabitants of this planet are granted, they are innocent and pure. After they age, they become sadistic and corrupt. They become warriors for Jiaïro or warriors for 'Good', as you call it. The point is that we all fight. We all think we are righteous when, in the end, we all wage war for the same cause: total domination. Behold the result," Self paused to indicate their surroundings. "This is the world you strive to protect. As for that girl of yours, the one you so *deeply* trust… see for yourself. This lake will reveal to you what she is. The water will show you what will happen to her only a few months after you die by the hand of your father."

Rhin looked into the murky waters and saw an image unfold of Luu-ka, a twisted, misshapen Luu-ka. Her hair was no longer violet, but black, with eyes as hollow as a rotting tree. She stood in front of Jiaïro and curtsied. Jiaïro's marshals, with pasted-on sneers, watched her bow down to their Lord, as they huddled around her. She had gained immortality as a reward for her service to Jiaïro and smirked. In that instant she was the same as Jiaïro. She could have been his daughter.

Rhin turned away. He had seen enough.

"You're lying. That pool is lying. She would never join him."

"The forces of Nature do not lie, Rhin. Face the simple truth. Your loved one is Evil at heart. As are we all. We all possess the qualities you so gallantly seek to purge. She will join Jiaïro when you are gone. After she is tortured a bit, of course."

"Why did you bring me here?"

"To show you the truth," Self replied, yawning.

"You want me to believe these lies? Well I won't. You hear me? I won't!" Rhin shouted in defiance.

Self disappeared.

Rhin searched the lake. What little light there was in the area drilled into his body. He felt the stinging sensation of change.

His wings increased in size and strength. He had not even noticed them, for he had become so used to them of late. But as they contracted into his back for the very first time, he knew that they could now be summoned at will.

This was the new Gift.

Well, I can avoid the stares at least, Rhin thought, frowning.

Rhin dove back into the water with the hope that this nightmare would end.

He swam to the doors and muttered, "Luu-ka."

The doors would not open. He tried again and again, yet nothing happened.

Then he knew what to do. Remembering that he had thought of love to part the doors the first time, he summoned hatred to open them once more.

He gritted his teeth and said, "Jiaïro."

He passed through the widening doorway.

And he was in the azure chamber. The five Guardians of Balance floated in front of him.

The Spirit of Light said, "We give your wings greater power."

"Wait! Where was I just then? Was that really Iora's future?"

"We cannot answer that question," Darkness said.

"Why not?" Rhin asked, frustrated and anxious.

"All is clouded. We cannot say. We do not know," said Nature as it waved its arms in an arc.

"Go now. You must head for the Temple of Completion on the South Isle. Then you will be ready for your final combat with Jiaïro," Heaven told him.

"But I have only visited three Temples. And the one on the south island will be the fourth."

"The Gift of Angel Wings, which we now present to you, makes four," Light concluded.

"In truth the Hermit's Temple and the Spirit's Temple were destroyed hundreds of years prior. But their Guardians still remain. We safeguarded the Temple of the Spirits and the Hermit did the same. Your quest has been ages in the making," the Spirit of Time explained.

"You must make haste, Rhin. Time grows short."

Before Rhin could reply he was ejected from the chamber. When his head stopped spinning he was back under the lake.

He resurfaced, rejoicing at the sight of a more familiar setting. It was warm, even inviting. The world was still bright and thriving, abundant in vitality. He swam to the shore and contracted his wings. He transformed back into his red headed, green-eyed self and patted Daish-rog on the back.

"Your wings," exclaimed Daish-rog, "they're gone."

Rhin said, "They're still here. Just not as noticeable. The last Temple awaits, Daish-rog."

"Where?"

"The South Isle."

They made for Yerpator, for some strange force drew Rhin to that area.

The northern peak of Tümraark was covered with trees and the land they formed was named Yerpator. To find their way there, they had to cross the fields and forested glades of Munca.

It was impossible to fly to Yerpator because the trees grew too thick for them to land there. The entire northern area of Tümraark was one gigantic, untamed wood. Thus, the only way to their destination was on foot.

It was completely stupid, to travel to the northernmost reaches when they needed to go south. And all the inconveniences caused Daish-rog to hesitate. Maybe this was some sort of insanity. But his trust in Rhin's judgment quickly overruled his doubts.

The forest air was unmoving, but not stuffy. The birds chirped from all sides on branches in the trees. The wood was dark and noisy and somehow soothing. Rhin would have enjoyed this experience if it were not for the heavy burden that had been placed upon his shoulders.

Daish-rog whistled as they walked along the dirt path. Scattered water drops dripped from the thick branches and brush. For, above the canopy, it was raining.

"Thick trees," said Rhin.

They saw many imprints from horseshoes along the way. This made Rhin wonder if some great army had passed through here not long ago.

After a while the pattering of the rain ceased, replaced by thunder. Rhin felt exhausted. He kept reminding himself that he must keep going. His resolve remained strong.

The journey through the forest was tranquility at its best, but when Daish-rog noticed that the path grew wider up ahead, he brought it to Rhin's attention and they ran for it.

Having entered the more open area they were surprised by a group of horsemen waiting for them.

At first, they looked like Seekers, five of them. Yet they were larger and seemed more complete in their features. With horns like those of a goat and dazzling, white teeth that shone in the dim light. Their blazing red hair covered most of their faces. They wore a leathery armor with the red and black Symbol of Evil sewn over their left breast. And then Rhin noticed something that altogether disqualified them as Seekers: the fact that their lower bodies were not those of horses but of men. They were riders, not rider and steed combined.

The leader spoke, "Parou teha? Parou teha?" Then, with visible effort, he switched to the common language, "Who are you, boy?"

Unimpressed, Rhin answered with the truth, "Rhin Akvius."

The group murmured and the leader spoke once more, "Aeul lata. We have orders to execute you on sight."

"So why don't you?" Daish-rog asked.

"Why does such a worm dare defy Jiaïro? How do you manage to defeat all of our onslaughts and traps?" the captain sneered.

"A single loose stone can bring a mountain down," Rhin told them. "But the real answer would be that your master fears me."

"Insolent pig! Salu, salu," the captain yelled.

Rhin transformed, rose and pointed at the captain who laughed along with the other four. When they stopped, the captain was flung from his horse by a telekinetic blast. He flew backward through the air and hit a large boulder. There came a loud pop and a little fizzing and he was gone from this life.

Rhin then unsheathed his sword.

Daish-rog asked, "Do you require assistance?"

"No, thank you," Rhin replied.

He picked off the next charging soldier, shoving him to the ground. Rhin took special care not to harm the horses. They were innocent of the riders' crimes.

The other three charged all at once, side by side, their steeds foaming at the mouth. Rhin pushed off the dirt and flipped over their heads, cutting at shoulder and jaw. All three riders toppled, falling from their mounts.

As they arose, wounded and covered in dirt, Rhin sheathed his blade and gestured for them to approach with both hands. They made to ram him but he ducked and the horned men crashed into each other instead. Rhin kicked one while he was down and punched another as he tried to stand. The second in command screamed as Rhin broke off the tip of his horn.

Rhin said, "You live only to return to your master. Tell him that Rhin is coming."

The wounded soldiers mounted and galloped off into the forest. Not once did they did look back.

A sudden earthquake made Rhin and Daish-rog jolt and fall over. The ground that separated the two split open. It seemed to Rhin that a huge hill was growing from the fissure. As it increased in sheer magnitude the trees were cast aside like tumbling sticks.

Momagé? Impossible! he thought, alarmed.

Momagé pulled himself up and out. He ripped through the canopy as if he were tearing tissue paper. An entire sea of trees uprooted as the hill stood.

He turned himself to face Rhin and said, with a smile which sent a rolling boulder down from the corner of his mouth, "Tidings, Rhin! Would you mind if I brought you to the South Isle?"

"How did you—when?"

"I shall inform you of my travels on the way to our destination. We must hurry," Momagé told him.

Was this why I came to Yerpator? Am I supposed to have Momagé take me where I need to go?

He knew it to be so. There were no coincidences. Not any more.

Momagé dived into the western ocean and swam down into the lowest depths of its waters. Rhin and Daish-rog clawed at their throats before realizing that they could breathe.

The Namka hill man explained all the details of his escape as he journeyed through the depths of Iora's core.

When they resurfaced he stretched out his hand and placed them on solid ground. With the giant's help they had traveled a dozen times faster than flight would have allowed, and traveling through the crevasses in the depths of the ocean had its advantages. They had been able to avoid torrential winds and hurricanes as they sped along under the world.

Momagé yawned, shaking the earth itself.

He said, "We've arrived. I think I'll sleep awhile."

He lay down between a pair of cliffs and began to snore. Each exhalation sent tremors throughout Kenner Karg.

Rhin trained his eyes on the horizon. There he saw the Gathering of the South, a good five hundred Denzak warriors. Kayre-Ost was amongst them. The Denzak men came to him in turn and bowed. They stood before the Temple, beaming at the Half-God.

Kayre-Ost stepped forth and said to Rhin, "The villages of Atermin, Waterlipp, Reruk and Lergat stand ready to fight the Legions of Jiaïro."

"You succeeded. I'm grateful for that, Kayre-Ost. Once I have the Holy Gift of this Temple, I will have ascended to Completion and we'll do battle with Jiaïro. And we will emerge victorious."

The Denzak raised their swords and spears and shouted, "A-jura!*"

They stepped aside as Rhin strode toward the fifth and final Temple. He stopped in front of the doors and without warning they opened wide. Small and hidden by a shadow, Hobanataï came forth and greeted Rhin and the warriors of the South. He was the little lizard-like creature whom

* The Denzakan battle cry.

Rhin had encountered in the Tower of the Bull. He held a sapphire in his right hand and a gold coin in his left, beckoning Rhin.

As Rhin entered, a great sense of Evil overwhelmed him. Staring at him from the gloom were two pale eyes.

Rhin turned to look behind him but the doors had shut without warning.

The fiendish creature laughed as the sconces were lit. Then he was through cackling. Rhin's eyes burned. He closed them but the pain did not diminish. The feeling spread to his wings and legs and soon his entire body, forcing him to his knees. He fell over and gasped for air. Hobanataï then snapped his fingers and dissipated into curls of blue smoke. The smoke drifted into Rhin's lungs, suffocating him from within.

Soon he stopped struggling and began to fade. He felt his life slipping away. And there was a little voice inside him telling him to let go and give up. He did not, could not. He wanted to live, but the life was being choked out of him.

Then a strong voice inside Rhin's head countered, saying, "This is not the end, Rhin. Get up and show that creature that true Gods don't die."

Rhin coughed and retched. Bending over, he exhaled. The smoke swirled forth from his lungs. The burning sensation that had spread over his body and melted into his skin was gone in an instant. He had absorbed the Evil energy and tamed it.

As he accomplished this he felt Complete. He was now a full-fledged God. His abilities had been regained through the absorption of a minor demon.

"I take in Evil and through cleansing it, in turn I am cleansed."

Hobanataï, back in his original form, let slip a scream and limped over to Rhin.

He screeched and writhed, "This is not possible. You should be dead!"

Rhin stretched his fingers wide on his right hand and lifted it high in the air. Gold light flashed and the hall became dark for a split second, but then Rhin morphed into his God-like body. The hall, now illuminated, seemed to move and shift with his every breath.

Hobanataï then unsheathed a knife and ran at Rhin.

The God, without touching him, lifted Hobanataï with his hands and said, "You have tried to kill me, Hobanataï. You have betrayed all the forces of Good in doing this. Yet I forgive you. So long as you never again show your face in any Holy sanctuary."

With those words ringing throughout the Temple, Rhin opened the doors. Hobanataï sprinted off, screaming. He was never seen again.

Rhin stepped out into daylight. Lifting off, he rose high and shouted, "The day of retribution has come. We shall dethrone Jiaïro and Light shall return."

The Denzakan army hailed him and they unsheathed their weapons, held them over their heads and answered, "Long live the righteous. All hail Rhin Akvius!"

Chapter 26
Faith, Fire and Fate

he Gathering of the South, Rhin, Kayre-Ost and Daish-rog at their head, marched through the Forest of Chirki. The road to the army's destination was a hard one. As they crossed through the wood they chanced upon a river bank. The river itself was broad, swift and deep.

"What now, Kayre-Ost?" Rhin asked.

"We have to cross here. This is the straightest way to Perkweir. We're not going to let a stream best us, are we?"

"No, you're right."

Then Kayre-Ost called to the army, "We cross the river. Carefully boys, the current is swift."

Rhin raised an eyebrow when he heard some of the Denzak actually burst out laughing.

Once the company had crossed, the rest of the journey was less harsh. Before Rhin knew it, a scout reported that Perkweir lay but three miles ahead. The Gathering quickened its pace.

As they neared the town it was far too quiet for a harbor that was famous for its raucous natives. The company entered through the battered, broken gate.

Rhin had seen this kind of desolation far too many times to doubt which hand had wrought it.

Jiaïro's forces had pillaged Perkweir not a week past, from the look of it. All of the houses had crumbled and were charred from days of burning.

The army walked in shocked silence through the dead streets. There were corpses covering the roads and the stench was unbearable. Yet this only deepened their resolve.

Kayre-Ost sent patrols to locate survivors. Upon their return, they reported, "No survivors. We searched every street, alley, house and gutter. Sorry, sir."

"Jiaïro is trying to frighten us," a soldier said.

"It won't stop us from going to Naa-Teria. Why this useless destruction?" Kayre-Ost asked.

"Because he can," said Rhin, shaking his head.

When they reached the dock they found seventeen longboats, empty and untouched. Each had a large, broad and hollow deck with twenty oars and a roomy cabin at the stern just in front of the rudder. They did not rest high above the surface of the water, but appeared watertight all the same. These vessels would have to do as transportation across the sea.

Kayre-Ost stated, "Looks like Momagé won't have to carry us after all."

"Where is Momagé?" Rhin asked.

No one knew.

Rhin suggested, "Maybe he provided the ships."

Maybe not. It didn't matter.

They used sixteen boats for the warriors and one for the few horses (there were but twelve, though they were immense) and their keepers. A perfect fit. Their first stroke of luck.

Rhin was on a boat with the finest Denzakan warriors, including Kayre-Ost and Tye. Daish-rog stood beside him as the keel cut through the sand, the ship sailing slowly away from the wooden docks.

Rhin said to his companions, "Finally, a chance to end this once and for all."

"I will be glad to fight by your side, Rhin," Daish-rog smiled, "even if all the soldiers of Jiaïro surround us."

Rhin clapped Daish-rog's back.

Kayre-Ost came over and asked in a low murmur, seeing the anxious look on Rhin's face, "Are you scared? It's alright."

"No. It's not that," Rhin said, "It's Cononsareth. And her."

Kayre-Ost nodded as Rhin turned away.

The giant said, "We'll be there before dawn. We'll discuss strategy when we arrive," and left Rhin to his worries.

The sun set and the half-moon took its place. Mist rose from the gray water, the surface of the river almost flat. Rhin knew the boats had not reached open sea yet because the water was still too calm. Once the vessels were pushed into the wide ocean, every man would need to be awake and alert for the remainder of the voyage.

On either riverbank spindly, arching trees spread their roots to the edge of the sands. Though spring had come, they bore no leaves. These trees were sinister.

Monster trees? Relax and get some sleep, Rhin, he told himself.

Four Denzak warriors shared the watch, holding lanterns aloft in vigilance. The pale, yellow light served only to make the fog more intrusive. The watchers were replaced by another group every hour.

This appeased Rhin's angst a little, but he could not sleep a wink. As soon as he shut his eyes vivid and abhorrent visions of what might be happening to Luu-ka and Cononsareth filled his mind.

Am I too late? Are they even still alive?

Hundreds of different nightmares plagued him. But listening to the boat slice through water and the faint splashing of flying fish, he became so exhausted that he slipped into slumber at last.

Rhin awoke to the spray of saltwater on his face. The longboat was lurching. It began to rain. The Denzak were shouting orders.

"Get to the oars."

"Lower the sail."

Each oar was manned by a Denzak. Others were occupied with wrestling the ropes into submission. Rhin watched as the oarsmen rowed in unison, grunting with each stroke. Counting, Kayre-Ost kept them in time.

"One, two, one, two. Turn right!" he shouted.

The longboat swerved. Rhin watched a rock zip past.

That was close, he thought.

It was clear to him that the Denzak were not inexperienced sailors. He decided it a good plan to just stay out of their way. The sixteen other ships followed suit, their sails tied down as well. Rhin didn't know if the longboats would hold in these conditions, or if they would all arrive safe at Naa-Teria, but he chose not to worry anymore.

And so the day wore on, Kayre-Ost's voice booming as he called orders, the vessel climbing and falling on the waves and the steady beat of twenty oars crashing into the sea. All the ships had braved the storm, and all had emerged undamaged. Luck was still on their side, it seemed.

Rhin stepped into the cabin and sat down. Before he knew it, he was asleep again.

A messenger came into the single cabin, to inform Rhin of the fleet's arrival at Naa-Teria. It was two hours before sunrise. They had made great time. He sat up and felt a rotten stiffness in his back and neck. He exited the cabin and waited in mute anticipation as the ship neared the shore. He was perhaps not as surprised as he should have been to find that the sands were black. There were no trees, just black dirt.

When they hit the beach, Rhin patted his wings. He waded up to the dry land and stood amongst the generals of the Gathering. Among them were Loden, who was Chieftain of Atermin, Jeho, the Chief of Waterlipp and Tenrek, the High Priest of Reruk.

They saluted Rhin.

"The Commander of the Vevleï Resistance Army asks permission to join us," a pair of scouts on horseback informed.

"Permission granted," Jeho said. "We will need all the help we can get."

"Best news I've heard all year!" Loden boomed.

"Agreed," Tenrek said.

A tall Vevlea, dressed in royal blue, rode up with his escort of four. Each wore an array of shining feathers upon their helms and shoulder pads. The commander dismounted first and Rhin saw he bore an adamantine crown which sparkled despite the faint light.

As the Vevlehen group came forth, Rhin ventured, "Aroukana? You look different!"

"Did you think I wouldn't show?" said the Vevlehen Commander with a smile as he spun around so they could get a better look.

"You're the leader? I didn't know you were royalty," said Kayre-Ost.

"Let us save the pleasantries for some other day," said Chainæïa as he came up to Aroukana's side. He removed his glinting helm and added, "Though it does warm my heart to see you all safe and well."

"We need a sound strategy to fight Jiaïro's legions. Lord Aroukana?" Tenrek said as he turned to face him.

The group sat about a foldable wooden table upon which was placed a hand-drawn map of the isle. All the gathered information of Naa-Teria had been inscribed upon it.

"Our archers are posted atop the hills. They can fire at the enemy from a long distance with deadly accuracy. If we can draw the enemy out, we can thin their numbers," Aroukana explained.

"Our horsemen can perform the task of luring the enemy. We can cut through their lines and circle around to stomp their archers as well," Loden said, a bold look on his face.

"I disagree," said Jeho, "the horsemen would be subject to a danger far too potent. I suggest we have them behind our infantry and then, at the critical moment, they should split and strike at the flanks."

"That would effectively mount the pressure. I think this plan would prove most effective," said Aroukana.

"I will leave the strategizing for the armies to you, my lords. I know where I'm heading," said Rhin.

"Oh?" grunted Kayre-Ost.

"Straight for Jiaïro himself," said Rhin. "He won't make it near the you. Not if I can help it."

The leaders nodded.

"The Monraïkian Army will aid the infantry. They have joined us under the leadership of Captain Pélénor. And the Tarkai-han queen requested a hearing with us. Are there any objections?"

"No, commander. We shall hear of her plight."

"Thank you all. Bear in mind: whether we should trust her or not, I leave the decision in your hands," said Aroukana.

The Queen of the Tarkai-han stepped onto the beach. She was as tall as Kayre-Ost and fit the description of the other Tarkai-han. The only difference was that she stood broader than her subjects.

She said with a dignity that could be born only from nobility, "I am Queen Bilai. I have come here to join my forces with yours."

"Why the change of heart, Your Grace?" Rhin asked.

"Jiaïro deceived us. The death of one of our elite is not easily forgotten. And Jiaïro, the False God, slew three. One of them was my brother," Bilai told them. "Honor dictates that I appease their souls."

"More help won't be unwelcome," said Kayre-Ost.

"But until recently you were our foe," Chainæïa reminded. "How can we trust you?"

"I am yours to command, my lords. I swear it on my bloodline. I swear it by the very life of my people. We are all prepared to die on that field," said the queen, pointing south.

"We accept. But know that these men have no desire to be betrayed. Violate our trust and you will be damned in this life and beyond," Jeho said as he looked into Bilai's eyes.

"May it be so."

Bilai shook each of their hands in turn, thanking them for their trust.

The Commanders positioned their troops for the upcoming battle and prayed for luck and victory.

Rhin shot up and beheld the beach from a bird's eye view. Four different peoples gathered under one banner to fight for the freedom of Iora. What was even more spectacular was that they had all come to this island in about a week.

This is it, Rhin told himself.

Midday had come and gone, unnoticed. Atop the jagged, rocky hills of the island Jiaïro's fortress loomed, threatening all who should dare approach. Picture the sky darkening and a storm brewing. One could almost feel the tension in the air as the world held its breath in anticipation of this moment.

The hellish clouds shone magenta and the first flash of lightning in the gloom signaled the beginning. The boom that followed was all but drowned out by the sudden sound of the deafening footsteps of thousands upon thousands of soldiers clad in black that poured as liquid across the field.

The battalions carried banners bedecked with the symbol of their foul lord. The Vevlehen archers, with their keen eyesight, could clearly make out the weapons of the enemy. Horrible, twisted steel tools used for torture, not war.

Yuyon, who was among those brave enough to populate the frontlines, said to his brothers-in-arms, "I wanted to sing, ever since I was a boy. Now, the bow is my harp and the deathly scream is my accompaniment. Blood is my muse. Doom is my audience."

Trumpets sounded. From behind the infantry, the war calls of the Seekers could be heard by all.

Jiaïro gazed from the window in the crown of his tower and ordered, "Attack. We have no reason to fear them."

He could see the hunger in the eyes of his sons as they sent out the orders to their legions. How beautiful they were, clad in their terrifying armor.

For good measure, Jiaïro added, "Exterminate this vermin."

The Vevleï elite were the first to fire as the murderous tide approached. Soon they were joined by the Monraïkian archers. The first round of quivers having been depleted, the infantry was forced to join in the conflict to buy them time to re-supply. Rows of Jiaïro's finest were leveled, littering the ground. Black blood dripped from their carcasses.

When the opposing force took cover out of range, the Vékéran bowmen had used all their arrows.

The Vékéran unsheathed their swords as the Tarkai-han, along with the Monraïkian infantry and the Denzak ran over the hills. With Rhin and the Commanders at their head, the warriors attacked.

When both sides collided then began the splicing of axes, the clashing of swords, the sound of steel on steel, the screams of pain and death and the gushing of blood.

Rhin fought as never before along with his comrades. He hacked at legs and arms and chests until the ground was covered in the blood of both sides. The Denzak used their earthquakes and various other techniques, inflicting massive damage. Their Spear Dance* knocked down the first rank of the opposing army.

The Seekers began their onslaught, relishing the taste of the free peoples' vital fluid on their horrid lips.

The horsemen galloped into the chaos and rammed the flanks of the God's forces. This split them into several groups. Separated and disoriented, they could not hold their ranks and were slaughtered.

The marshals led the second wave and slew many.

And then Jiaïro, alone, stormed the united army, using his telekinetic energy to smear the Vevleï across the battlefield.

Rhin spotted his demonic father and soared after him. When he caught up, Rhin struck Jiaïro in the chest, but it seemed to have no effect.

Jiaïro yelled, "You dare strike your father? Die, ingrate."

"It's you who will die, tyrant," Rhin retorted.

The two Gods flew higher and they came to blows in a ferocious duel. Rhin moved around to his father's back and plunged his sword into Jiaïro's flesh. Although Rhin was lightning-quick and precise, his father seemed to take no interest in his open wound at all.

"Not immortal after all, father."

"Pain comes with power. And it is pain that you shall receive, my son."

Jiaïro kicked Rhin in the chest.

Rhin flapped his wings and bounced back, cutting Jiaïro from gut to gizzard. Still no reaction.

"Who is Ryul, anyway?" Rhin asked as he dodged a sword swipe.

"Since you are about to die, I might as well tell you," Jiaïro shot a wave of telekinetic energy hurling Rhin across the sky.

---

* A popular technique taught within the confines of the Tharthra. A Denzakan soldier would grasp his weapon and spin in circles, chopping up or wounding any opponent nearby. It was effective when the warrior was surrounded by a horde of enemies. It was this skill that Kayre-Ost had used at the foot of Grysen's tower.

"You are overconfident. This battle is not yet decided," Rhin shouted.

"Ryul is my twelfth son, born directly after you. I kept him hidden from everyone, for he would one day be my second in command. I feared the Gods would send an assassin after I came to dwell in Iora. Thus I kept him safe, and he lived on."

"That slime cannot be my brother," Rhin said, disgusted.

Rhin recalled his other brothers and how terrible they were. Yet Ryul, with all his scheming and trickery, seemed the worst of all.

"Embrace the simple truth, irredeemable son of mine," said Jiaïro as he lunged at Rhin.

The sword entered his stomach.

As Jiaïro removed his weapon from his son, Rhin clutched the gash.

"Look down, boy. Your armies are dying in agony. So are those friends of yours. One by one they will all be killed," Jiaïro whispered in his son's ear.

Rhin saw the bodies of the Vevleï, Monraïkian soldiers, Tarkai-han and the Denzak. He then turned to face Jiaïro. He spat in the God's face.

As his father snickered, Rhin attempted a strike. The arch-devil dodged it with ease and punched his son in the small of the back.

Rhin plummeted and crashed in the blood-covered dirt. He could not move but he could see plenty. All around him the soldiers of Jiaïro's army relished the taste of war as good men and women died. He saw his life flash before his eyes.

All the sound around him faded and he found himself in the blanket of blankness for the third time. Self sat there among the nothingness. He greeted Rhin.

"I told you that you could not win. I told you of the part Fate had portrayed for you," Self told Rhin.

"I don't believe in Fate," Rhin shouted, face red and fists clenched.

"Then how do you explain this? No matter how you try, with all the efforts you have made, you are still lost. Time spins in cycles. Ever does it replay itself. You die, have died and always will die here."

"No... No. I won't believe this. Let me out!"

"Aren't you listening? You can't get out. You can't escape. You are dead."

Rhin unsheathed his sword and assaulted Self. But Self disappeared to reappear in the blank emptiness of Rhin's mind, his arms crossed.

"Kill me and you kill your essence, your life. It's as impossible as catching the wind with a net. See how violent and disturbed you are? You're trying to obliterate your own mind."

"Self, I will kill you. I don't know what will happen but I swear I will kill you if you don't send me back. I know you have the power—I know I have the power to do this."

"Rhin, haven't you understood yet? I am you. We are one and the same. Strike me down and you will vanish. You can't live without me. I put your inner forces in Balance. I am your dark side."

Rhin seethed with rage. He was beyond mortal anger. The only thing he wanted now was to destroy Jiaïro and his alter ego, Self.

Self isn't real. He is an illusion. He has to be! he thought loathingly.

"Embrace your death," Self shouted.

"If I'm already dead, it won't matter if I kill you."

"You're maniacal," Self puffed.

"One last chance is all I'll give you, Self. Free me, or be destroyed."

"You can't escape, Rhin. Frankly, you're beginning to annoy me with your pathetic outbursts."

Rhin lunged at Self.

"You don't have the stomach to kill me," Self stated, crossing his arms and legs as he floated.

For a split second Rhin thought about it all. Doubt gnawed at him as he flew through the emptiness. But in an instant all that was left was his scorching detestation for Self. Rhin flew straight at him and thrust the Sword of Purity into his childish body.

Self gasped in disbelief.

"*No,*" his voice became deeper and deeper—more and more like that of a demon—all the while shouting and repeating that word, until the tone was so deep it shook the entirety of Rhin's body. "Fool. You have annihilated your own mind!"

And, with one last excruciating howl, Self burst into light.

Only his voice remained, "You have defeated your own dark side. This thing no man should have ever been able to accomplish. Know this, I will continue to taunt you, and guide you down the dark path for the rest of your *miserable*, little life."

The menace echoed for a while then faded into the depths. Rhin stood on the blank canvas in the painting of his mind. He reflected on the obvious truth. He could escape from this place. He willed himself to wake up. He felt his head become lighter, his senses dimmed. He was floating in some peaceful world of nothingness, similar to a dreamless sleep. He then wrenched his mind loose and freed his limbs so that he was in complete control of his every muscle.

A voice inside his head spoke to him, proud and uncorrupt, "Stand tall, Rhin."

This voice was new to him. It was kind and noble. This was his positive side, the light and good that was in him. Now that Self was weak and half faded, the good side of his mind had almost full control. Rhin knew that Self would never be gone but it was comforting to know that the kind side was there, and that it was capable of such deeds.

The command he gave himself had its effects. Rhin was slow at first but as he felt more and more revived his speed returned. His head spun. He opened his eyes to the sounds of clashing steel and screams of pain. He lifted his head and looked up into the sky. It took a moment for his eyes to adapt to the dimness but when they did, he saw Jiaïro, gaping at him.

"Impossible," the Evil God screamed.

Rhin leapt into the sky but collided with another man. Red hair, black eyes and great bat-like wings. He wore dull gray armor and was more demon than man. Rhin recognized him in an instant.

"Ryul."

The two of them fought, as if by some unspoken instruction. Jiaïro watched his sons in their gravity-defying struggle. Ryul was quick to lose. He was no match for Rhin.

"Your powers have regenerated, Rhin. It is clear to me that I underestimated you. Go ahead, finish me," Ryul panted, a pointed tongue lolling from his mouth, as Rhin held the Sword of Purity to his throat.

"No," Rhin said, "You're not worth my time."

Ryul stared up at him, and for the first time Rhin saw his true nature. Rhin beheld, in all its unholy glory, Ryul's unmasked contempt for him. He gave it no afterthought. Throwing himself at Jiaïro, father and child resumed their climactic battle.

"You cannot win, son," Jiaïro taunted, "It is only a matter of time before you perish."

Hearing that, Rhin flung his sword at Jiaïro. The blade struck the devil. It penetrated and traversed his body, drenched in dark blood.

The sword fell from the skies and landed blade first, puncturing the earth. It became a beacon of light on the battlefield and all the soldiers of the united forces rallied there to make their final stand against the hordes.

Jiaïro turned and shot off. The son chased the father.

Catching a glimpse of the pillar of light, Aroukana gave the command, "Fight, brothers and sisters. To the light!"

Obeying, the soldiers paved their way to the beacon made by the Sword of Purity, cleaving a path through the enemy.

Their once brightly colored tunics were bloodstained and torn. Their shiny breastplates and armor reduced to a collection of gashes and dents.

Chainæïa was near at hand. The young Vevlea was acting as leader for a battalion of discouraged warriors.

"Stay close. Hold the ranks. Do not let them break you," he cried as he halved a foe's head.

He soon met up with Aroukana and his soldiers. They shared hasty words.

"Do you think we can make it? It's still several hundred feet to the beacon and to get there we must pass the battle below," the elder Vevlea said.

"I can sense the light is of Rhin's make. We must try."

Aroukana nodded, saying, "Have your men form a semi-circle and our archers will fire from behind. We move together."

The Vevlehen fighters did just as Lord Aroukana instructed. Once in position there were perhaps fifty fighters in all. The first of the Seekers to approach them received a volley of such accuracy they could not have felt the impact before dropping, the life stolen from their material shells by metal shafts lodged in their brains and hearts.

The second wave was composed of more resilient enemies than the last. A few succumbed to the arrows but more than half came too close. The largest reared its ghastly head to behold Chainæïa subduing several foes. The Seeker captain pulled its spear-wielding arm back, as if it were working on springs, and just as it was about to hurl its instrument of doom, it was no more.

Aroukana had paid particular interest to the captain and had readied his final arrow, his lucky arrow. The shaft, made of silver, struck the Seeker square in the eye and punctured the tissue of his inner cranium, causing instant death.

Chainæïa caught hold of this, though it would have been too late to save his own life, and called, "Remind me to thank you when this is over, Aroukana."

"If I live that long," he answered.

"You will, you have my personal guarantee," the last word was punctuated with a brutal head-splitting cut, ending the life of the last of the second wave of enemies.

They moved in a spiraling motion until they reached the Sword of Purity.

For a moment the warriors stared in awe, entranced. Then the black tide was upon them.

Zordon was caught in the fray along with his most loyal men. The soldiers fought like demons, but would it be enough? These freedom lovers were tenacious in their resistance.

One of his messengers had informed him of Tye's presence on the island, and the marshal had a score to settle.

Zordon's insanity clouded his judgment but still allowed him to recall whose fault it was that he was in such a state. Tye would meet his fate at the hands of Jiaïro's rightful successor.

"There you are, boy. Come to me. Face me and face death itself."

Tye hacked and slashed his way over to the marshal and answered, "Haven't you heard? Fate is only a tool of Evil used to control the lives of men. It is in Destiny that I place my trust."

"Fate may be our tool, worm, but Destiny merely grants hope to the hopeless—those who have no business living. We, the chosen, are the only true rulers of Iora."

"Return to your masters then."

Aiming for Zordon's neck Tye struck, keeping his feet in constant motion. Zordon in turn deflected the blow and stomped at the boy, who was ready for him. One swift pivot to the left and Tye spun round the marshal to dig the Sword of the Mind into his spine.

Zordon screamed in agony as he was devoured from the inside out, "You horrid, little-"

He then disintegrated. His black Orb was all that remained.

Tye's courage renewed by the defeat of another of Jiaïro's lackeys, he made for the beacon of light.

As for the ex-marshal's energy crystal, it was soon crushed under the weight of iron-clad feet preoccupied with the atrocities of war.

Jiaïro sped along the coastline of Naa-Teria, almost touching the jagged cliffs to the right. Rhin stayed close, Ryul trailing behind.

"Come on then. Keep up, children," the God shouted back at them.

The chase continued. At the center of the isle, they spotted a cliff topped with a massive temple.

Is this where he wants me? I won't disappoint.

Lord Jiaïro halted, landing with heavy feet on the cliff's edge. Ryul rested in front of his father, to protect him.

Jiaïro eyed his two sons and laughed.

Ryul then said, eyes locked with Rhin's, "He won't harm you. I'll end his life."

"No. You will not," said Jiaïro to Rhin's surprise.

The wind whispered. Just as Ryul was about to ask the fateful question: "Why?" the God, with disturbing unpredictability, impaled his son. When the steel had been removed from his innards, Ryul turned and looked at his father. Jiaïro, seeing his son's hopeless and defeated expression, pressed a clawed and disfigured hand to Ryul's forehead and pushed him over.

Ryul lay there, arms and demonic wings spread across the gray rock. Tears poured from his eyes, mingling with his blood.

His body dissolved.

Rhin was convinced he saw his brother's soul regard them both with a sad expression before ascending. The Orb containing Ryul's former strength tinkled as it struck the ground.

"Your powers will serve me well, my son," Jiaïro smiled.

The Orb shone red and burst. The shards were absorbed into the arch-devil's body. Jiaïro's eyes flashed with the new power.

Yet another pointless death, Rhin thought. He faced the God in fury, saying, "I demand an explanation for all this, Jiaïro."

"What do you want me to explain, you idiot?"

"I want to know your diabolical motivations behind this entire plot. What the hell is going through that sick head of yours?"

"Total domination, Rhin. It is as simple as that. I want to rule the universe. Those fools up there," Jiaïro pointed at the sky, "they have had power long enough."

"But they are immortal. How are you going to take control? Gods don't die Jiaïro, I thought you knew that."

"They are not immortal. No one is, for that matter. They all have weaknesses. I have the key to destroying every last one. Then I will rule *all* matter."

"You are truly insane. How can you create an army large enough to kill hundreds of Gods? And how will you transport them anyway? It doesn't make sense."

"Who said anything about planning to bring troops into space? I will lure them all here and destroy them when they are most vulnerable. Neither you, nor anyone else, will be able to stop me. I will commit atrocities of such magnitude that they shall be forced to take notice."

"Despite what you repeat to yourself constantly, you're not invincible. You're not even a real God."

Jiaïro flinched and his eyes focused on the cliff's edge. He then said, "In all my years in heaven and on Iora there has only been one other soul who dared say that to me: *Monos-Khar*. I know you have heard this name before."

The book in Joabom's temple, Rhin realized. "He defeated you and your soldiers. A shame he wasn't thorough enough, that's all. I plan to rectify his mistakes."

Jiaïro laughed, "That will be the day. You have no chance against my ultimate power."

"Back off, Rhin. He's mine."

Rhin spun round and saw Kayre-Ost and a battalion of Vékéran warriors, swords readied.

"He's my father," Rhin growled, "therefore, my responsibility."

"You don't know anything. Jiaïro may be your father but Monos-Khar was my ancestor. The duty of slaying Jiaïro rests on my shoulders and mine alone."

"You're of Monos-Khar's line?" Rhin asked.

It made sense. Kayre-Ost was a formidable warrior.

"I wonder how long it will take you to realize how deluded you are. You shall both die at my hands. Rhin, if you want your captive friends back, you will follow me. And you, giant, will find us there," Jiaïro pointed to the cliff and shot off.

"Where is he heading, Kayre-Ost?" said Rhin.

"The temple," said the Denzak, "Here, you'll need this." The Denzak tossed him a longsword and added, "Don't think this means I won't be the one to kill him. I've waited too long."

"I've waited two thousand years," Rhin responded.

He took flight and sped toward the temple that Monos-Khar had constructed millennia beforehand.

"Vékéran, with me. This day we destroy a God!"

The warriors began the treacherous climb to reach the temple.

Rhin stood in front of the temple gates, glanced up at the stained glass window and did not hear a sound. That did not mean anything in particular. For all his cowardice Jiaïro could be waiting behind any pillar.

The gate rose of its own volition. Rhin entered, careful in his movements.

All around him were frescos. Artistic renderings of the battle between Monos-Khar and Jiaïro. In the final mural Rhin saw the God kneeling on the ground, defeated before taking to the heavens in a beam of light.

"Coward," Rhin cursed.

"I never much cared for this place," Jiaïro revealed himself from among the shadows, "That runt of a giant defeated me by pure chance. Soon, however, I will take revenge on his one and only descendant. The Denzak Kayre-Ost's blood will spill on the altar of his 'great' ancestor."

Rhin answered, "Not if I end it before he gets here."

"You could never defeat me here, in this putrid hall of pathetic worship. Even the 'True Gods' cannot save you now."

"I don't need saving. I can handle my own affairs. Now face me, or are you going to flee as you did with Monos-Khar?"

This appeared to anger the God a great deal. "You will beckon oblivion with open arms long before I am through with you."

Their blades met with a spark. The longsword Kayre-Ost had given him proved to be a durable weapon.

Jiaïro lashed out and, missing Rhin's neck, struck a pillar. His weapon now lodged in the stone, he was left wide open for a kick in the chest from his son.

The God panted, and wiped his brow.

"Mongrel!"

The sparks from their connecting strikes lit the dark halls. To Rhin every pillar, every wall, every wooden artifact was a weapon. Using his wings to support him he bounced off one of the columns and leapt downward, sword first, at Jiaïro. The God dodged and their blades met.

The sun was setting outside as the Vékéran warriors, led by Kayre-Ost, made their way up the cliffs. What they did not know was that a veritable army of Jiaïro's finest and most loyal holy men were coming up the other side.

Garbed in black and white robes they chanted as they ascended to their Lord. Their voices resounded as one as they touched the crown of the mountain upon which lay the sacrilegious temple.

They did not discontinue their dark chanting for one moment, even when they cast themselves alight in a holy pyre in the name of their Lord. In a blazing frenzy they scrambled toward the temple where they would serve their final and most sacred purpose.

"Burn the wood. Set fire to the temple against our God. Stone does not burn. To the beams of wood, brethren, to the roof top," the priests screamed.

It was pitch dark inside the great hall of the temple.
"Submit, my son. There can be no victory for you."

"Your heavy breathing says otherwise, father."

Rhin lay with his back pressed against a broken stone column across from where he believed Jiaïro was, though in the darkness it was hard to be sure. His every limb ached with exertion. His head hurt and his fingers felt numb. Yet, he held on in desperation, keeping himself focused and prepared for whatever dangers should arise.

The hard column he leaned on pained his back, but Rhin did not know how long he could keep himself going like this, so he welcomed the rest.

"You know, from the instant your mother and I first saw you we were disgusted," the God told his son.

"Were you? That's a shame."

"It was not any physical ailment of which you suffered. You had an aura about you, a vile glow that made you appear a saint. But we could see through it—and you."

"Whatever happened to my mother?" Rhin asked as he felt a lump in his throat.

"She died. I had to kill her."

Rhin's eyes widened in the gloom. "Why?"

"Later she regretted what she'd done and tried to find you. She wished to return you home, to us."

"And then you killed her," Rhin's voice quavered.

Though he had known of his real mother or even heard her name spoken by a living soul he felt as if another abyss had opened beneath him.

"Yes... I loved her. Yet, the love I felt was shadowed by a far more powerful emotion. Hatred. Hatred for her *weakness*, hatred for you! Pure, burning hatred for all the creatures of this worthless world," Jiaïro's voice filled the temple, the syllables weighed down by something that sounded a lot like regret. But seconds later, the anger flared again, "Now you will all burn in my holy fire, a blazing flame of retribution that will purge this planet of all rebellion. Rejoice, Rhin Akvius, you will be the first to turn to ash in the name of my new world order!"

Rhin leapt to his feet and cried, *"False God!"*

He then heard a rattling against the windows of the structure.

"My priests, burn it! Tear it asunder with your holy flames," Jiaïro roared.

Rhin cast about him in despair, thinking, *There are so many.*

Then one of the priests clinging to the window closest to him was pinned in place by a shaft.

Kayre-Ost's voice was heard, "Don't let the priests reach the roof. Stop them at all costs!"

The hall was illuminated by the suicidal priests' ignited bodies.

Jiaïro cursed and screamed, "That whelp is proving to be as cumbersome as his ancestor."

The God smashed through the walls, dashing toward the Denzak and the Vékéran.

He was intercepted by Rhin, who held him back with a furious rain of sword blows. In the midst of preparing a deadlier attack, Jiaïro caught Rhin's sword hand. The God took hold of Rhin and held him in place. Despite all his violent efforts to break free Rhin was trapped, suspended in mid-air and at the mercy of his father. Jiaïro gained altitude and then hurled his son, aiming for the temple. Rhin crashed through the roof and down into the hall, taking several pillars with him.

The God commanded the priests to quicken their pace.

"Yes, Lord," they answered.

"You're mine," Kayre-Ost boomed.

The Denzak bent his knees and leapt from the craggy ground up and up until he collided with Jiaïro himself. Furious, the God, grappled with the giant. Kayre-Ost, ever careful to hold on tight—as he could not fly—retaliated with his own blows.

Faced with this onslaught Jiaïro crashed his body into a nearby cliff wall. He had shaken Kayre-Ost. The God hoped he was dead.

Just as he was beginning to savor his long deserved vengeance, a sharp, stinging pain exploded in his upper back and then spread itself all over and inside his body.

Rhin, who had been behind the God, had stabbed his sword into his enemy's flesh.

Jiaïro, blade still in his back, turned and in an instant lunged and grabbed his son by the throat.

"Now, now. No son of mine is going to behave in such... such an unruly manner."

Jiaïro squeezed. Rhin could feel the life drain from him as he struggled in vain, fighting the ultimate inevitability. His head pounded as Jiaïro throttled him. He stayed there a few more moments, suspended a few feet in the air by his father's murderous claws.

This is it, he thought, *this is how it all ends.*

Then a rush of movement and two strong hands clasped the God's neck. Jiaïro let go of Rhin, who collapsed, gasping for oxygen. He couldn't think. He noticed the fighting—the struggle between the two—but then the God had the upper hand once again.

In less than an instant Kayre-Ost was gone, tossed over the edge of the cliff upon which lay the temple of Monos-Khar, his greatest ancestor and first of the Denzak.

"No," Rhin's lips moved, but he couldn't speak.

Jiaïro regarded his still panting son and then with a swift movement removed the blade from his own back and held it up to the moonlight.

"It is made of black steel. A very fine weapon indeed. If you will excuse me, I have a temple to annex."

A force of blazing priests made their way up. They were nearing the wooden high beams of the roof.

"If that temple is gone, then hope will fade as well," one of the Vevleï elite cried in near-despair.

The commander of the Vékéran, deciding to take the fight to a suicidal level of heroics, rallied, "Swords, attack."

The Vevleï warriors drew their weapons in unison and ran into the fray. Steel clashed with flame and frenzy mingled with certain death, yet the Vékéran, the proudest of all, would rather all die on that cliff top than see the last monument in defiance of a false God destroyed.

A single priest had made it to the top. Caught up in the triumph he called to his God of his victory, "In the name of Jiaïro."

"Burn it you cur!"

As the smoldering holy man prepared his 'leap of faith' to annihilate all the unbelievers' hopes and dreams in one strike, he was launched into the skies by a determined projectile.

The priest was impaled by a black steel long sword and hurled off the roof into the courtyard below where his holy fire sizzled into oblivion.

"I have had just about all I can handle from you," Jiaïro said as he turned.

"We have a battle to finish. No more games, no more delays-" said Rhin.

"No more tricks, no more fire-" Jiaïro, pensive, continued.

"Just you and me," ended Rhin.

"Very well, son of mine, we shall complete this circle of death. Fate will decide the victor."

"I don't believe in Fate, and neither do you."

"Fate exists whether you believe in it or not. It is the force that drives us on to our inevitable—and unjust—end."

Jiaïro flung himself at Rhin. His aim was off. Instead he struck the earth. The force of the impact cracked the stone around them.

The God was overjoyed, "Rejoice, Rhin Akvius. Your end is near. You'll die with this temple."

Jiaïro bestrode his son who had been forced to the stone ground by the quake.

"Embrace your death, *hero*, for all ends here. Do not worry. I will have my marshals finish your friends off after you are gone," and then he whispered so Rhin could just hear him, "And I will take the girl."

Rhin looked into Jiaïro's horrible, beady eyes as the demon stood towering in front of the temple gates.

Rhin launched into the God with a fierce uppercut that pushed him into the air right in front of the massive stain glass window depicting his singular defeat thousands of years prior.

With his back to the window, Jiaïro was unaware of the irony but was instead caught up in a whirlwind of punches from Rhin.

Dazed, the demonic God watched with unseeing eyes as the following events unfolded:

Rhin summoned forth his last remaining energy. When he reached the zenith of his power, he sent forth a surge of azure force that shook the world around them and collided with his father, sending him crashing through the stained glass window and into the temple.

The entire structure trembled and for a moment it seemed it would collapse. But the quaking subsided and all was quiet.

Rhin found the silence eerie but still achieved the courage to look down through the window and what he saw was startling, unsettling, amazing and unimaginable all at once.

"He's not breathing."

Jiaïro's lifeless form lay in the center of the altar. Statues of the True Gods peered down at him with blank, stone eyes. The message was clear. The False God was no more and the wrath of the True Gods had been appeased.

Jiaïro's corpse evaporated and made way for his black and red Orb. Rhin picked it up with his right hand. He gave it a disgusted look and crushed it in his fist.

The Vékéran had watched as Rhin slipped into the temple. They did not know what to expect next.

He approached an open book in front of his dead father and as if under the control of a far more powerful being read a passage.

"The False God is slain, his wrath undone. The world is purged of wicked rule and the fields are green, the ocean blue. With the people freed and the tyrant dead, behold the restoration of the Balance Sacred."

The gates of the temple were flung wide open and it was then that Rhin realized how much pain he was in. Fresh blood coursed down the sides of his legs and from his forehead down his nose.

His divine form passed and he became his regular, old self again.

Rhin stepped outside through the archway and was greeted by a cool breeze. The doused corpses of the suicidal priests lay strewn about the temple.

"Jiaïro is dead," Rhin told the Vékéran.

And they cheered.

Below them, fires were lit and songs were sung. The battle had been won. The God's forces lay dead or dying, the seat of their once glorious empire now under the rule of the freed races of the Four Isles.

After an eternity of wars against the forces of Evil that threatened their homes and lives, the Denzak, Vevleï and Monraïkians had at last overcome all the obstacles—despite tremendous odds against them—and slain their oppressor.

Rhin grinned as the moonlight speckled his face.

Epilogue

The names of the mighty commanders and their valiant deeds were forever remembered.

Captain Jeho of the cavalry, Lieutenant Tenrek of the infantry, and General Loden of the archers. And, of course: King Aroukana, Lord Regent and Protector of the Vevlehen race.

Tye was honored with the medal of heroism and was noted to be the youngest warrior to ever receive this award.

Chainæïa took command of the reconstruction of Alkari and later became an Elder of the city. He lived a long, healthy life and had many children.

Tales of the Champion Denzak, Kayre-Ost, did not go untold. In legends it was said that he defeated two hundred men alone. But after the battle he was never seen again. Most refused to believe him dead.

Aroukana kept his promise to his father, bringing him the joyful tidings of Jiaïro's death in person. The old king died with a smile on his lips. The prince became the new king and lived to be several thousand years old. His name was instated as the new word for 'wise one' in the language of the Vevleï. He witnessed the beginning of the prosperous age that came after Jiaïro's death and lived to see it bloom. When he was laid to rest, his first born son, Arauru, ruled the Vevleï Empire.

Captain Pélénor of the Monraïkian army died in the stand. It was said that as the black tide crashed upon the last defense he threw himself in front of Aroukana, saving his life from several Seeker spears. In light of the Captain's valiant self-sacrifice, his Orb was preserved in a tomb fit for a king.

And the legend of Rhin's rebirth was told to all the children and their children and their children's children for the rest of the generations to come. The tale would be remembered until the end of the world.

In the years that followed, all of Jiaïro's loyalists were hunted down and brought to justice. The dark priests, however, refused to be imprisoned. Most committed ritualistic suicide, dedicating themselves to their God even in the afterlife.

Rhin stood there, on the cliff-top. The wind embraced him like a brother.

He was ready to rest, to experience the years of life and joy that he craved. But he remembered that his work was not yet done. The image of Luu-ka and Cononsareth raced through his mind.

Where are they?

He limped back into the temple. Rhin searched until he noticed a barred door off in the distance. As he approached, without warning, the door exploded and from the blue fire a spirit grasping a blade entered the main hall. White light shone from the spirit and the sword. Rhin shaded his eyes.

The phantom spoke, "I have waited for this moment for two thousand years. I am the spirit of the Time Sword, Daïcra."

"What do you want?" Rhin asked, forgetting his manners. There didn't seem to be call for any.

"I am a creation of the Spirit of Time and have come to transport you back in the ripples of the River Time in order to undo the years of Evil this world has suffered."

"No. I can't leave. I-" Rhin's mouth froze.

"You have only won one battle. You have only defeated the puppet. The ones who are pulling the strings have yet to be uncovered."

"Jiaïro was a *puppet?*"

"Yes. There are Evils that rank higher than Jiaïro. You must undo them. Someone seeks to change Time and create a universe of complete Evil. He works independently from the others, yet he has them do his will. You will find that there shall be many that will try to thwart your path. Yet you must continue the struggle. This is your destiny."

"I've had enough of this. My life has been filled with deceit ever since I lost my home. Tell me why I should trust you!" Rhin shouted.

"You must discover the truth yourself. You must travel back in time."

"How many years?"

The phantom did not answer.

"How many, ghost?" said Rhin.

"Six centuries. The legendary sword, Xaniatacz, was stolen by a minion of the Great Disruptor."

"'Great Disruptor'?"

"A creature of malice and destruction. Rhin hear my words. You *must* travel back. I know it is difficult, but you are the only heir of Cryöd's high blood left in the world. You are the only one who is pure of heart. Only you can wield the ultimate sword without succumbing to its will. You have righted the ending of this tale, but the beginning remains untouched."

Rhin's face sunk. He couldn't believe this was happening.

He should have been done, been allowed to start his life, but this spirit was telling him he had only just begun his labor.

"Rhin, do you know the meaning of your name?" the apparition asked.

"No, I can't say that I do," Rhin managed.

"It is a derivative from a language far more ancient than even the so-called Eldest Tongue. It means 'eternal warrior'. You see, your destiny was written even as your name was given to you."

The phantom handed him the blade it carried. But as Rhin reached for it his hand fell limp and the sword dropped. It made a loud clanging noise as it bounced.

After a long pause, Rhin said, "If I must, then..."

His tongue felt heavy as a brick.

"Take the blade."

The curved blade of the River Time, Daïcra, floated in front of him and hovered there. Just as Rhin thought he could not feel any worse, Luu-ka burst into the hall and paused in front of the altar. She smiled, but the expression was brief for she had read Rhin's mind.

Tears trickled down her cheeks and she stretched out her arms toward him. He stared into her sea-blue eyes for but a moment. He wished it could have been an eternity.

"I will see you again," he promised.

Rhin tore away from her gaze, overwhelmed, and grasped the sword. He closed his eyes. The world screamed. From a great distance, he heard the sobs of a broken heart.

He prayed.

3334790

Made in the USA